GW00541594

To the most divine woman alive,

THE MYTH OF Supply and Demand

with endless love,
Michelle xxx

by

Michelle Keill

GHP

Grosvenor House
Publishing Limited

All rights reserved
Copyright © Michelle Keill, 2010

Michelle Keill is hereby identified as author of this work in accordance with Section 77 of the Copyright, Designs and Patents Act 1988

The book cover picture is copyright to Michelle Keill

This book is published by
Grosvenor House Publishing Ltd
28-30 High Street, Guildford, Surrey, GU1 3HY.
www.grosvenorhousepublishing.co.uk

This book is sold subject to the conditions that it shall not, by way of trade or otherwise, be lent, resold, hired out or otherwise circulated without the author's or publisher's prior consent in any form of binding or cover other than that in which it is published and without a similar condition including this condition being imposed on the subsequent purchaser.

A CIP record for this book
is available from the British Library

ISBN 978-1-907652-58-5

Acknowledgements

The book you hold in your hands now would not exist without the friendship and support of Mark Mason – he is a true *professional*. I am eternally grateful to know him, and to count him as a dear friend. I thank him also for the beautiful artwork. Mark: The range really is good.

For Mr Foster and Mr Walsh, who started it all.

1

There's no point mulling it over anymore. I've made up my mind. If I think it through again, I'll only chicken out. And this is not the right environment for contemplating my future. There's no space in here, no privacy to list the pros and cons one final time, to make absolutely sure. So my decision will stand. No more vacillating. Soon, it'll all be over, and I'll look back – and she'll look back – and we'll say it was for the best.

Even though it's early, the noise and activity has already peaked. Voices are raised, people talk over each other, brows are furrowed, facts and figures – some of them even real – are shouted over the tops of monitors. I seem to be the only person not immersed in the flow of the day – even Simon is making a noble attempt at appearing busy. I lean back in my creaky chair to study those that some would describe as my colleagues, but whom I would refer to as 'the people in the office who breathe the same air as me'.

Two of the juniors (they could be Alison and Laura, but then they could just as easily be Alex and Louise – they're pretty much interchangeable in my eyes) meet by the fax machine, of course not by accident. They exchange weary glances, understanding the other's fatigue, exasperation, and general inability to pay their bills each month on the wages the paper pays them. They're working here for the promise, the dream that one day they'll see their names in print. I asked them why they didn't look themselves up in the phonebook instead and save years of hard work and grief, but they thought I was joking. I wasn't.

Laura, or whichever one she is, rams a sheet of paper into the fax machine so roughly that I feel violated and used on its behalf.

"I was so annoyed last night," she says to the other one.

"Why was that?"

"Well, I was out with Rob and we were drinking, yeah?"

"Yeah."

"Yeah, then I said I only wanted orange juice, but I told him he could have whatever he liked, and he just kept on drinking – how rude is that?"

"That is *so* rude."

Clutching the files to their chests and shaking their heads in perfect synchronicity, they depart, leaving me to sit in my precarious chair and blink slowly.

I go back to my screen confused, but probably not as confused as 'Rob'.

I've made a good start on my feature, and by this I mean I've opened Word and am choosing which font to write in. And then Sarah, under the guise of distributing the post (even though she's been told hundreds of times that we pay someone to do this, and that they actually get the post to the right person) decides to saunter over to my desk.

"Hi John," she says brightly but coyly, although I suspect this tone has been adopted with intent of having some kind of effect on me.

"Hey Sarah," I reply, not looking up from my screen. Times New Roman, or Arial Narrow?

She drops a load of A4 envelopes, a pile of briefings, a few journals, and a small rainforest of paper next to my keyboard. "God, I don't know what you do with all these numbers."

I could tell her the truth, but it would only perplex her.

"Hey, did you hear?" Sarah says, oblivious to the fact that I'd clearly prefer to ignore her. She eases herself onto my desk, so that one of her microscopic buttocks is nestling on my mouse mat. "Apparently they're going to make some people *redundant.*" She speaks the word as if it were a Mediterranean herb she's learning to pronounce.

I don't so much as blink at her revelation. "This is a newspaper, Sarah. Rumours like that do the rounds on a daily basis."

"I know, but this time it sounds so…real." Enjoying the drama, Sarah purses her lips, and two parallel frown lines manifest themselves on her forehead, as though someone's playing a game of Hangman on her face. "I'm scared, John. I'm only twenty-four. I can't be made 'redundant'. It would be wrong."

She says this last word so emphatically she could be discussing mass genocide, or some overseas violation of human rights. If you know Sarah like I do, you'd realise that neither of these topics are likely to trickle out of her mouth without the aid of a teleprompter, or her body being possessed by a *Guardian* reading demon.

She lowers her eyes, so that for a second I think she's reading the serial number on the top of my monitor, and then her lashes swish upwards. Without invitation, there's one of those pauses. Oh, okay, I get it. This is her flirting with me.

There's not a guy in the office – the building – who doesn't have a secret thing for Sarah. This is an unforgivable comparison – which never stopped me before, but Sarah is rather like the herpes virus: once you catch it, it lies dormant in your system, plaguing you with outbreaks for the rest of your life. It merely flares up and subsides with unpredictable regularity, depending on crucial factors such as how short her skirt is, whether she's seeing anyone, whether you're seeing anyone, how bored you are, and other highly significant issues.

Although I've worked here for nearly five years, far longer than Sarah, whether or not she is interested in me is still somewhat of a conundrum. More than that, actually. It's a game for us, like 'Battleships'. We both act as though we don't find each other attractive, only I'm better at it than she is, probably because I'm ashamed of myself. Yes, she is relatively pretty, and she does have great legs, but no, I can't hold a conversation with her that doesn't at some point make me want to pull out my eardrums, deep-fry them in batter, and sell them in Glaswegian chip shops.

When Sarah first started working here the only thing she was prepared to talk to me about was her boyfriend. If I recall correctly, his name was Steve. Good old Steve. She told me he had a bike, but I was never able to maintain my attention span long enough to discover whether she meant a Harley or a BMX. But one day, everything changed. A blitzkrieg of her simultaneously being dumped by Steve and finding out that I have a girlfriend, altered the landscape of our relationship irreversibly. She went from a catchall "Morning!" to stopping by my desk to deliver a more personal, "Hi John" seemingly overnight. Oh, how I miss Steve.

And, Jesus, she bombarded me with thousands of questions.

"How long have you been going out with her?"

"Nine years."

"How old were you when you got together?"

"Twenty-six."

"How old is she?"

"Twenty-eight."

"Do you live with her?"

"Yes."

"Do you love her?"

"Yes."

"Are you happy?"

Pause. "Define happy."

It's a fact that the only guys women are interested in are the ones with girlfriends (me), and the gay ones (definitely not me).

Let me tell you, the concept of the sisterhood is a joke. Women, I'm sad to report, like a challenge. They challenge themselves by picking the bad boy, the married man, the onelegged Russian who speaks no English and, more disturbingly, they challenge each other.

At least we men are blatant about our need to compete with each other, and we find ethical outlets for it. We play football, rugby, squash, Playstation, X-Box; we buy a better car than the one our best friend has just bought, we have drinking contests, pulling contests – everything is out in the open. By comparison, women are slippery and clandestine, staging their competitions in a secret arena. Clever really, when you think about it. Women compete in secret, and therefore lose in secret, and so none of their so-called 'sisters' need know that their boyfriend was on the verge of being ambushed and prised away from them.

This is not what I think Sarah is trying to do. She lost any real interest in me back when it became clear that I was not going to cheat on Lola. But every now and then she dips her toe in the water, checking the temperature to see if I am weak enough to succumb. So far I haven't, but I'm intrigued as to what will happen when I become single again. I'm sufficiently curious to pre-empt the truth and break the news to Sarah right now, just to see what happens, but common sense prevails. I'm not too familiar with the concept of right and wrong – it's not something I refer to often – but at a guess, I probably shouldn't tell Sarah I'm single before I tell my girlfriend.

"You know, Sarah, I'm kind of busy at the moment. Could we maybe finish this conversation later?"

As I knew it would, her interest jerks up several notches. The rule, I think, is not 'treat 'em mean to keep 'em keen', but don't treat 'em at all.

"Sure." Her finger traces one of the grooves I ground into the desk with the edge of my stapler during a recent and chronic episode of writer's block. "How about we go for a drink one night after work? That's if Lola – is that her name?"

I nod, even though it's obvious we both know what my girlfriend (I need to keep referring to her as my girlfriend while she still is) is called.

"If 'Lola' doesn't mind."

"Lola doesn't mind what I do," I lie.

Sarah considers this, a wry smile on her face. "Now that's odd. Because if I were her, I wouldn't let you out of my sight for a second." Her face contorts into such a determined expression that I don't doubt the sincerity of her statement.

It's apparent that she wants this remark to be her parting shot. She slides her tiny derriere from my desk, poised to sashay over to the photocopier. I can't let her have the last word. If I don't bat something back at her she'll think I'm interested, which I kind of am in the way that I miss having spots because I liked squeezing them, but I don't want her getting the idea I'm a pushover. Plus, I need to get her ultra-keen so that when I'm newly single, and hence no longer pose a challenge, she still wants me.

"Hey, Sarah."

She swings around, an expectant smile on her face.

"I'll be sure to pass that on to Lola. She'll love it."

The deterioration in the atmosphere is palpable as Sarah's sultry expression evaporates into a sulky one.
She scowls at me, then disappears in search of a female colleague to slag me off to (she won't have to look very far). If only her reaction had been less predictable, if only she'd done something dynamic, like giving me the finger, then she might be potentially appealing, instead of standard visual office fodder.

Why do men who leave their wives for their secretaries always regret it? Because they haven't yet learned that attractive female colleagues are simply women you wouldn't look twice at outside in the real world. Inside the office, any Olive from *On the Buses* can morph into Grace Kelly. It's the routine, the banality of work – it distorts the male mind.

I allow myself a glimmer of a smirk as I type a whole load of gibberish into the computer. The sight of a blank page makes me anxious, reminding me I'm expected to string letters together to form words, which in turn must grow into sentences, paragraphs and pages, and hell, they even have to make sense. These days, the task seems too immense for me, and I'm living by the motto that typing something is better than typing nothing.

I'm supposed to be composing an inspiring feature on the effect of the strong pound on the balance of payments, which is less of a contradiction than it sounds. So far, it's been a struggle. It's hard to convince people that one pound equals two dollars and six cents might be a bad thing when most of them are in America buying Calvin Klein pants and Levi's for less than half-price and, fundamentally, because I Don't Care. Really, I don't – no pretending necessary for this one. Admitting this to anyone would be an act of high treason against myself, but I will be glad if there is a recession – joyful. It might make them appreciate the good times. And it might make them listen to me.

I lean back in my creaky chair and survey my morning's output:

The government doesn't know anything, and neither does anyone else. Economics is a big waste of time. Let's all go down the pub and forget about it.

I'm sure most of my readers would wholeheartedly agree with this, but I doubt my editor, Charlie, will share this sentiment. But deleting this rant means confronting the white screen of doom again. I consider cutting and pasting one of my columns from last year, to see if anyone will notice. Regretfully, Charlie will. He might not understand much of what I write, but he's good at remembering it. He can quote verbatim some of my worst predictions from three quarters ago. So instead, I click the mouse and the 'office assistant' appears. When the inanely cheerful paperclip asks me what I would like help with

I type, 'What will Lola do when I dump her?' The paperclip obviously has no idea either, as it provides me with a wealth of information about how to turn off automatic completion of file names and URLs. Fascinating, but not quite the response I was hoping for. It appears that Microsoft is of the opinion that URLs are easier to explain than women. Well, nobody could accuse Bill Gates of not being insightful.

As a consequence of my desk being strategically placed en route to both the photocopier and the vending machine, I receive a lot of visitors. Not that Simon needs an excuse to come and talk to me, despite the fact that I am clearly very busy. Years ago, Simon perfected the art of appearing to be consulting with me on a feature he's writing, when in reality he's disturbing me by blabbering on about what is universally agreed to be total and utter arse.

"John, you've got to hear this."

I give Simon my standard 'this better be good' expression even though, through some bizarre process of elimination, he's my best friend and I'm sure this is going to be worth listening to.

Simon holds open the magazine and begins to read aloud. "Astrology is a thing of the past. The sure way to tell if you and your man will survive the test of time is to check your argument prototype." He flashes me a grimace of consternation. "Can you believe this crap?"

"And I've only just worked out what my star sign is. Go on."

"Okay." Simon makes himself comfortable on my desk but, unlike Sarah, his buttocks are far from microscopic. "According to this article-"

"Entitled what?"

Simon checks the top of the page. His spherical face reminds me even more of a full moon as he grins. "You'll love this one, John. It's called 'Do You Fight Right?'"

"Fantastic. I'm giving that one a grade four."

"And rightly so. Want to hear the basic premise?"

I wave a hand for him to continue.

"Right, this woman-"

"Name?"

"What the hell does it matter?"

"I'm a journalist, I might meet her one day."

"I'm a journalist too." Simon says, his tone heavy with indignation.

"By definition only."

He frowns, and I see him consider answering back, but he changes his mind. It's never worth it.

"Anyway," he says, "apparently 'Felicity Burrows' thinks that in order for a relationship to work, you both have to argue in the same style. For example, 'to match a sulker with a non-grudge holder is kamikaze dating.'" He rolls his eyes. "This is verging on fascist ideology!"

"Maybe she has a point."

Simon snorts in derision. "She can shove her point up her arse."

"I think that's a separate article altogether."

"Well, she can fuck off then," Simon replies, in case anyone in the next postal district hasn't quite heard him. "When Penny and I have a row, all I have to do is put my foot down and she comes round. That's how we fight. End of."

"End of? Is 'end of' why you had your plasma TV sent back to the shop?"

"It was a little ostentatious."

"And the sculpture she bought for the garden instead wasn't?"

"Marriage is all about making sacrifices."

"Which is why I'm not married."

"You're not married because Lola is out of your league."

"Thank you for pointing that out. I wasn't aware of it in the nine years and eight months we've been together."

Although saying this aloud is like having my testicles acupunctured with knitting needles, I can't allow myself to waver. I have to stick to the plan. But there's no getting away from the fact that nine years and eight months is a long time. There's enough room in there for a boom and a slump and back out again (depending on global conditions of course). Nine years and eight months is a lot of football seasons. Who won the league the year we got together? Man. United – of course. See, the fact I had to think about that one is exactly my point: I've lost touch with what's really important in life. I resolve that when I am a free agent, I will religiously absorb Sky Sports 1 to whatever it goes up to these days. No more will I be forced to concede my viewing pleasure to watching dross. So take that, Ricki Lake, Oprah, Ellen, Maury Povich and all you others who have contributed to my emasculation. Piss off *Extreme Makeover*, *America's Next Top Model*; bollocks to *Glee* and *X-fucking-Factor*. From now on, the TV will show only programmes that I want to watch. Hello History Channel, hello repeats of *Top Gear (*which is not, Lola, a programme for 'idiots'), and goodbye Living TV, anything about looking good naked or how fat you are, and all those reality shows that make me wonder if having a functioning brain is really a necessity in the twenty-first century.

"Want to come over for a beer tonight? Penny's going to aerobics."

I raise my eyebrows. "She still bothers with that?"

"Yeah, even though she's fatter now than when she started all that exercise crap."

Simon has the thickest skin of everyone I know and, being friends with me, it comes in handy.

I think of Lola, her lean frame and soft features, and experience a premature pang of regret. "I can't. I have plans. Tomorrow, maybe?"

He grunts and heaves his corpulent frame from my desk. The wood groans and I make a mental note never to permit him to sit in my precarious chair. "I won't hold my breath."

"I wouldn't – you'll poison yourself." I gesture towards the flashing cursor on my screen. "Sorry, I need to finish this. I'm really busy."

"So am I!" Again, the offence is audible. "I have to finish Botox versus collagen."

"I'm sure the journalistic world is holding its collective breath waiting for that one," I say with a smile as I resume typing libellous comments about the government.

Outraged, Simon turns away to disturb someone else, muttering a good-natured 'fuck you, John' under his breath as he goes. I'm so used to hearing the phrase that 'fuck' and 'you' are almost part of my name. I am Mr. F. Y. J. Black.

Bring it on.

2

Feeling fidgety, I take the Tube home. I need to get home quickly, get the task over with. For the eighty thousandth time today, I wonder how Lola will take it. I can picture it, hear it, right down to the words that spill seamlessly out of my mouth.

They are carefully chosen words.

I explain myself succinctly, telling her sensitively yet passionately about my quest, my need to investigate what's out there (although, let's be clear, I mean 'who's out there', but Lola doesn't need to know this). Because this is my imagination, I then see her taking a second to compose herself before nodding, fighting the lump in her throat, the quiver of her slender shoulders the only outward evidence of her inner turmoil. Then, naturally, she admits she'll always love me, that she'll never find anyone like me, and will never completely get over me. I nod, understanding, stepping up to the pedestal she's about to forever put me on. Then – crucially – she takes hold of my hands and tells me she understands precisely why we should break up and that, although it hurts her, it's probably for the best.

When I come to, the skin on my forearms is prickling. I drift back into my surroundings and pledge to do this right – after nine years, I owe her that much.

A glance around the carriage reveals I'm standing opposite a mismatched couple, whom I judge to be in their early twenties. She is pretty, but not notably so – the Sarah of whichever office she works in. Her boyfriend is average, the human equivalent of beige. He's probably one of those people who says he 'belongs' to a gym because he doesn't belong anywhere else. He probably also subscribes to magazines and journals he never reads just so he can leave them on his coffee table.

The boyfriend is hanging on Pseudo Sarah's every syllable. I can't make out what she's saying, but his rapture is blatant. As she speaks, he gives her the purest look of adoration I have ever seen, and lunges for the hand she's not gesticulating with. He doesn't even flinch when she pulls a handkerchief from her pocket and proceeds to blow her nose laboriously. It strikes me instantly that Lola would never blow her nose in my presence, and she'd rather kill herself with a blunt instrument and an audience than use a handkerchief (never mind using it in full view of a carriage packed with judgmental strangers). Lola has boundaries, and I am grateful for that. The bathroom door should, in my opinion, always remain closed (preferably locked and soundproofed as well) – exceptions to the rule: none.

Lola had boundaries. I must start thinking of her in the past tense.

I begin the short walk from the station to the house and am pleased to find that there are a few random drink cans scattered around for me to kick. What the hell – it's a special occasion, so I spoil myself, booting them up the street and imagining the roar of the crowd and my name being chanted.

As I curl, nutmeg and shoot, I muse that in every couple I see there's a disparity, one party who is keener than the other. The beige boyfriend and his Pseudo Sarah are Exhibit A. She was indifferent to his transparent veneration, and I'd bet good money – any money – that she's the one who eventually ends the relationship X days/weeks/months/years down the line. There seems to be no balance to it at all; the scales must be tipped in favour of one person. I don't know why this is, but I'm sure it's part of the reason why so many people suddenly find themselves alone. There should be no surprise in this to anyone.

Just as every relationship is unevenly weighted, each party involved instinctively knows which end of the see-saw they're sitting on, and whether their feet are dangling in the air or not. Think about it.

I shake the rain from my hair as I step inside, neglecting to take off my shoes before entering the house because that's so bloody tedious. I'm soaked through, probably more than I should be due to all the puddles I leapt into during my game of foot-can.

It's like I've wandered into another dimension by accident. As soon as I'm on mutual territory, I find that my mind instantly clears itself: control, alt., delete, restart, wipe the hard drive. I have no preparatory speech, and no concept of when, where, and how I am going to break the news. If only there were a spin-doctor around to help me out, or some other bad news to bury it under. But what could be worse?

"Lola, the bank is repossessing the house. We have to move out and live on the streets. And by the way, I'm dumping you."

"Sit down, I've got something to tell you. Your father has decided to become a woman, and henceforth would like to be known as Dolores. I'm here for you, darling, whatever you need, but let's talk while you pack 'cos you're chucked."

"Honey, your Mother's had a heart attack. I know – it's terrible news. I'm very sorry. Would you mind dropping me off at Simon's on the way to the hospital? Great. Why? Oh, I'm leaving you."

I draw a line under my daydreams. Fantasising about Lola's mother having a tragic accident is not something to amuse myself with. Not right now, anyway.

Panic nestles within me and takes firm root in my gut. I should probably go and find her, put us both out of our misery. Well, to be more accurate, put me out of my misery and put Lola in hers. That would be the adult thing to do.

Instead, the kid in me, whose will is stronger, heads straight for the kitchen and forages for a beer.

The pristine whiteness of the fridge interior mocks me with a gaping, toothless grin, and the shock of what I find inside is like the unmasked villain coming back from the dead. Of their own volition, my fingers ball into fists, and my irritation level rises to a dangerous altitude. The plan has gone awry, and hence my first words to Lola are:

"Have you drunk all the beer?"

She blinks at me a few times, as though I'm talking utter gibberish. "Are you being sarcastic?"

"No. There's no beer."

"Well, there's only one person to blame for that, isn't there?" she answers calmly and, annoyingly, correctly. "You know I hate beer."

Indeed I do, and I don't even like it that much myself, but she's in the wrong kitchen at the wrong time. She walked in just as I was psyching myself up, and to do this properly requires beer – cold, wisdom-inducing beer. Heading for the spirit cabinet for one of the heavier guys, Jim Beam, or Jack Daniels, will only make her suspicious, so I'll have to do it sober. Shit.

"You're late home today."

"Uh-huh." I fill the kettle, having remembered caffeine is a stimulant. It has to be better than nothing. I then realise that standing here waiting for the kettle to boil with Lola frowning quizzically and me trying to summon the words to end our relationship will be hideous. I glance around the kitchen and spot Lola's food blender, which could suddenly prove useful for the first time ever. I consider the idea of pouring the jar of coffee and a pint of milk into it, and hitting the start button. That would do the trick.

"I thought we could leave in about twenty minutes. To be honest," Lola says wearily, a tone she gets to use often, "I thought you'd be home earlier than this."

I have no idea what she's talking about, but I start an argument anyway. It'll be easier to do this if she hates me already. Brainwave: maybe then she will dump me! Yes, that way I can be the victim and none of our mutual friends will ostracise me. Why didn't I think of that before?

"I had a deadline."

"Yes, but I specifically asked you to be home early tonight." Her voice slips into the higher octaves of the danger zone, but then she thinks better of it, which is typical. When I actively want an argument, Lola never complies.

"Oh, don't worry about it. We can leave a bit later, if you want. I don't suppose it'll matter," she adds in a way that previously would have alerted me to the fact that 'it' probably does matter and I should tread carefully. Thankfully, I am no longer obliged to care about 'it', or anything else.

I edge past her and go into the living room, carrying my lukewarm cup of coffee. There's a newspaper on the table, which is great, even though I read them all at work. I pick it up and use it to obscure my face. That should provoke her.

Lola follows me, adopting that slightly confused expression I used to think was endearing. Now I just want her to hurry up and bloody well join the dots. Her pupils are darting everywhere as she tries to work out what I'm up to. She chews her bottom lip, debating what to say next.

"Can you believe Kay is thirty?"

I put the paper down so quickly I almost tear a hole through 'Today in Parliament'. It dawns on me in a flash, and at once this whole scene makes sense.

"It's Kay's birthday party," I realise out loud.

"Yes," Lola says slowly, as though I should've had nothing else on my mind. "I'm sure it won't take you long to get changed, John."

I flex my muscles, preparing to dive in. Here I go …

"What makes you think I'm coming?"

There is a split second between the disbelief registering and the remonstrations beginning.

"Because, John, you said you would. Ages ago! I even put a reminder in your stupid hand computer!"

"Blackberry." I say this as though she's stupid, which is totally unnecessary, but I'm off the starting blocks and onto the track. "I've changed my mind anyway."

Even though I've gone back to the paper, I can still see I've wounded her, and it makes me wince. But, no pain, no gain, Lola. I'm sure there must be something in this for you too.

"John," she says, as though she's about to scold a small child which, in many ways, she could be. "Why are you being like this?"

"Because I don't like being your 'plus one.'" I blurt it out, losing my grip on my temper – definitely not in the plan. "Why should I go to Kay's party just because you are? She's your sister – you go." Yep, I have emphatically left the diving board for dust and am plunging headfirst into the water. A perfect ten. The judges go wild, except the one from Germany, who by default is a complete-

"John, we're a couple. Everyone will expect you to be there!"

Only to a woman could this be a valid reason for doing something.

Lola laces her fingers together, staring at them as though they are an alien part of her body. "You're more than my 'plus one'. We come as part of a package, two for the price of one. It's never bothered you before."

"Yeah, well, it does now."

There is a terrible moment of silence. Truly, it's horrendous. It falls between us like a twenty-first century Iron Curtain. Our relationship has never, in its entire nine years, experienced a silence as ominous as this one. I bury my head in the paper, my pinched lips worryingly close to a photograph of the Prime Minister, not wanting to watch her face as the inevitable slowly registers. Despite watching *Hollyoaks* religiously, Lola isn't stupid.

I'm notorious amongst my friends, colleagues, and random people unfortunate enough to come into contact with me, for my short fuse. Some days, I'm not sure I even have a fuse at all. Lola, however, knows me. She understands I am inherently a bastard. When I'm in a mood because I'm troubled by US foreign policy, or have just lost to Simon at PlayStation, she knows better than to take it personally. She'll either remind me how infallible I am in every other way (PlayStation), or she'll tell me that the only people who ever see the end of war are the dead (US foreign policy), which makes me glow inside because my girlfriend has read Plato (even though she still finds it funny to call him 'Pluto' or 'Playdoh').

Today, something different happens. She knows the sands have shifted. Is it female intuition, or does she simply know me too well? In a masochistic sense, I'm riveted, waiting with warped curiosity for the guillotine of her response. Her face goes through a number of expressions. I tick off bemusement, annoyance, sadness, outrage, and then we stop at something I don't recognise, something I am unable to classify. Whatever it is, it's deeply disconcerting. Oh no…Please God, don't let her cry. I can deal with anything but crying.

She stands up, teetering on the unfeasibly high heels that make her feet blister, and starts to speak. Except the words get caught in her throat and her mouth flaps open and closed, so that for a few seconds she resembles a particularly elegant koi carp. Words are my trade, so my mind is already racing, filling in the blanks for her:

"John, you are a complete shit, and I'm better off without you."

"John, maybe we should just see other people."

"John, you're the best lover I've ever had, but I hate you."

"John, thank fuck, you've saved me the trouble of breaking up with you, you utterly spineless bastard."

If this were a film, we'd be hugging each other by now, laughing and reliving the memories we've shared. There'd be a montage of happy moments we've enjoyed over the years, in chronological order, so that our clothes and hair become progressively less ludicrous as the footage rolls. But we're closer to Holloway than Hollywood. Instead of warm nostalgia, Lola is cold, putting a hand to her throat, her piano fingers rubbing her collarbone.

"John?"

"Yeah?"

"Are we breaking up?"

I stand up, welding my hands into my pockets. This is it – this is really fucking it. Sound the bells; roll out the red carpet, let rip with the twenty-one gun salute.

"Yes."

Never has a solitary word granted one man his freedom back with such alacrity.

Her hand cups her mouth, and she sinks into the chair she deliberated over for sixty-four minutes in Ikea. I remember it so precisely because I was standing beside her, counting every resentment-filled second. Who goes out to buy furniture on the last day of the football season? Lola. And, being her 'plus one', I had to tag along. Two for the price of one. And she's surprised we've reached this point?

She's not saying anything, and it's disturbing. She's just sitting there, her hair sweeping over her shoulders as she stares at the polished floorboards she made me spend a whole weekend and eight hundred pounds installing. I told her we could've had a brand new carpet for three hundred, but she wouldn't listen.

She looks so feeble, hugging her knees to hold herself together. It seems incongruous that she's all dressed up, wearing the black dress she absurdly calls her 'thin outfit'. Everything is out of place. She's out of place in her make-up and cocktail dress, and I'm out of place just by inhaling and exhaling.

I stand there like an idiot, waiting for the onslaught. I want this to be over with. I want her to yell at me, break a few ornaments I never liked anyway, and then help me divide up the CD collection. I feel no sadness or loss, or end-of-an-era wistfulness. I'm aware only of the clock ticking on the mantelpiece, and the overwhelming urge to start tapping my foot impatiently, which I manage to control. Just about.

Words are my trade, and I'm pretty smug about my dexterity with the English language, but with one lone word, she manages to bring my entire nervous system to a grinding halt.

"Why?"

Jesus. Ask me something else – anything else. Ask me my views on human cloning, civil partnerships, petrol or diesel, Third World debt, why the Mini Clubman is so ridiculous – anything but "Why?" To emphasise her point, she rises unsteadily to her feet and says it again. Several times. Each one is like a bullet fired from a submachine gun, hitting me squarely in the solar plexus.

"Why, John? Why are you breaking up with me? Why?" Her eyes are wide and full of hurt, and she looks so fragile I worry she might snap.

Frantically, I start thinking. I do the kind of thinking I used to do in exams, when every grain of knowledge I accumulated over the term whizzed through my brain at breakneck speed, advertising itself in bright neon lettering. I see my thoughts on global politics, the legalisation of cannabis, pants versus boxers, the sweeper system, big breasts or little ones, and so on and so on, but nothing substantial about why I've reached my current predicament.

I'm a prosecutor with only circumstantial evidence. Whatever my rationale, I do know that I can't be with Lola anymore. I just can't do it. She doesn't feel right now. You know how some people kind of feel like home? Well, Lola's the childhood house that I've outgrown. I've been living in her for too long, I need my space. I need to find out who I am without her, because it's been so long that I've forgotten. I need to ride my horse off into the sunset, to be a man. But I certainly can't tell her that (especially the horse bit, she'll only point out that I don't have one, nor can I ride one), so I'll have to make something up. Not usually a problem for me.

"It's just not working anymore, Lols," I say, surprised and proud at how talk-show smooth my voice sounds.

I never call her 'Lols', and picked a staggeringly bad time to start.

"Don't bloody call me that! I am not some kind of chocolate!"

"Yeah, right, because we wouldn't want you to be a food with any calorific content, would we?"

Now she starts throwing ornaments I never liked anyway. A crystal vase is plucked from the mantelpiece and whistles past my left ear, smashing on the eight hundred quid floor. I can't help but think that the vase might have survived if she'd agreed to the carpet instead.

The vase was monstrous, and I definitely won't miss it, but I have to drum up some kind of obligatory righteous anger.

"Hey, I bought you that!"

She picks up a picture frame I also bought her – in which she tellingly chose to place a photograph of our late cat – and that is flung at me as well.

"Great aim. Maybe you should try throwing something your mother bought us instead."

Her hands ball into fists and then her fingers splay outwards and inwards several times. I'm transfixed by this wordless yet effectual display of how she's really feeling. Her fingers coil tightly, and I brace myself.

"I knew this day was coming. I knew it! You've been acting even more of a prick than usual these past …" she searches her mind, "… for a while, anyway. I tried to pretend everything would be all right in the end, but I knew we were finished. I knew!"

Her apparent psychic abilities grate on my last nerve. "Congratulations. Would you like to see the star prize?"

I soon shut my smart mouth when the TV remote connects with my right shoulder.

"Hey, that hurt!"

"Yeah, well, too bad you're still conscious!" she yells.

Lola takes a step towards me, perhaps to strangle me, and it seems almost cruel that I can smell her perfume. The vanilla fragrance has the power to teleport me to days when I couldn't wait to get home and get her into bed or any other available surface. Now I just want to finish breaking up with her so I can go down the pub to see the effect my newly single status has on the women of N19.

She thrusts her face close to mine, her lips forming a perfect shiny pout. "Look me in the eyes and tell me you don't love me," she demands.

Whoa, back that horse up.

I know this one. This is a cheap trick. When women ask you to look them in the eyes and tell them something, usually you're supposed to either be unable to go through with it, or say the complete converse. Employ this tactic in any other arena, and you get yelled at for saying things you don't mean. What Lola is actually asking me, is to tell her I still love her, or not to tell her that I don't love her. According to the female psyche, they both equate to the same thing. I wonder how I'm going to get out of this one.

I look her in the eyes.

"Lola, I do love you." Her body heaves a visible sigh and she relaxes. "But I don't want to be with you anymore. I can't explain it any better than that."

I'm watching in slow motion. Her body tenses from the feet upwards, an undulation of rage. Her hands become dainty fists again, and her chest swells. For a second, I fear she might tip her head back and roar.

"Get." A definite gap here - she is taking a breath to release the, "OUT!"

I let her finish telling the entire street precisely where she wants me to go, and how much she hates me, and then I just nod.

I'm taking my shirts from hangers and stuffing them into a bag. Lola can stay here if she wants to. I'm a guy and I have real friends like Simon, who'll be cool about me dossing at his (although Penny, undoubtedly, will not) because I won't turn the bathroom into a science lab, and won't have to lock myself in there for two hours every morning as a prerequisite to leaving the house. Lola only has her sister, who has her own problems, and Valerie Perkins.

I hate Valerie Perkins. If I were on the verge of death, I wouldn't accept a millilitre of blood from her. She is a pus-filled boil, a verruca, a mouth ulcer, and a haemorrhoid. The reason I know this, is because Valerie Perkins works in my office.

Simon is a real friend, one who doesn't require such high maintenance. Although he can be a self-righteous twat sometimes, and cheats at 'Cluedo', he's loyal, and I can rely on him to be there for me. Women think they have a monopoly on hearts, flowers and true friendship, but when we men make friends, we keep them. We have no time for unsubstantiated gossip. We want the complete picture, the truth, not something a friend of a friend who met a distant cousin at the launderette told someone else.

Thanks to the technique of rolling up clothes that Simon and I read about in *Company*, I have pretty much managed to jam all my belongings into one holdall. Funny, I thought I had more than this pathetic sum total of stuff. Lola fooled me into thinking we had one side of the wardrobe each, but really her things annexed my half years ago. If my clothes are Kuwait, hers are Iraq. Never again will I share bedroom furniture with a woman. Ever. I smile to myself. I should have done this years ago.

"You got over me quickly."

"Huh?" Lola's sudden appearance in the doorway startles me.

"What are you smiling about?"

"Nothing." I don't think she'd be very impressed with the real answer, which would be, "Honey, this is the smile of a free man."

I ease my forehead into a troubled frown, which is far more fitting for this occasion.

"I'll be out of your way in a few minutes."

I hunt around for my trainers. I'm going to need those, as first thing Sunday morning I'm playing football. Did you hear that everyone? John Black is making a shock comeback into the masculine world. I consider taking up darts as well, just to hammer home the point, so to speak. And pies – I'm going to eat a lot of pies. I'll eat them straight from the packaging, in front of the television – in my pants, if I so desire. And I'm going to leave my muddy shoes by the door for as long as I damn well want.

Lola pads into the room and perches herself delicately on the bed. "Your hair's different."

I run a hand through it. "What?"

"It looks different."

"It's the same, Lola." I tug at a clump, to demonstrate. "See?"

She nods. "I know. But I never really looked at it before. I mean, I looked, but I never really saw." She fixes me with a cat-like stare. "You have very nice hair, John. It's almost jet black, isn't it?"

She's stalling me. I urge my heart rate to remain normal. Something ominous is coming.

"Aren't you going to be late for the party?" I ask.

Without even so much as a blink, she unfolds her arms and says, "John, I want you to fuck me." She says this so serenely, she may as well have asked me to turn off the light, or make her a cup of Earl Grey.

The shock causes me to drop my trainer onto my toe. "Pardon me?"

"I will not. You heard me."

This is coming from a woman who can list a swear jar amongst her possessions. "You want to have sex?"

She rolls her eyes. "Yes, John, I want to have sex. Do you want me to draw you a diagram?"

"What … we did just break up, right?"

"According to you, yes."

"So, we broke up, and now you want to have sex?"

She averts her gaze. "Please, John. One last time."

Never before has a woman begged me for sex. Traditionally, it's been the other way around. And I know where she's coming from because, now that I think about it, it would actually be rather nice to have sexual closure. Plus, I'm sure the last time we did it, I possibly wasn't quite Don Juan and I don't want to leave her with a bad account of myself. You never know who she might tell. (Not that I care or worry particularly about Lola fucking and telling, you understand.) And while I'm thinking about doing it, my body is telling me that maybe it wouldn't be such a terrible idea.

But the rational side of my brain is screaming that this is the worst idea ever, and that I should flee the scene of the crime without leaving any DNA evidence. There is nothing more despicable than having sex with someone you've just dumped, especially if the dumping occurred only a few minutes previously. The whole scenario smacks of both exploitation and desperation, and usually results in someone bursting into tears.

In this instance, it's Lola.

We have sex, fuck, make love – whatever – on the bed, and it's good. Not as mind-blowing as I'd hoped, but good. It takes far less time than I would've liked, but I'm attributing that to the profound weirdness of the situation. I feel as though I am on the verge of being caught doing something I shouldn't be. I have the same kind of red flush on my neck as I did when I was eight and my aunt caught me stealing a ten pence piece from her purse. In terms of goodbyes, it's more like a cheery wave than a profound parting. That's until Lola starts crying. Then all hell breaks loose.

I don't know what to say in response to her sobs and recriminations, because the charges are true. I am a shit, I have hurt her, it probably will take her ages to recover, although I don't understand why she's telling me that men are all the same as that's a sweeping generalisation and how would I know anyway? The only thing I can do is hold her, taking in that vanilla scent while we lie together and she cries in my arms.

It's a quarter-past eight when she finally stops quivering, and the sniffling stops. She adjusts the straps of her dress, propping herself up on one elbow, studying me intently.

"Will you come to Kay's party with me?"

I suck in a gulp of air. "I'd like to," I lie, "but we can't very well go to your sister's party together and then tell everyone we're no longer a couple."

She gives me a look that says I'm a complete dunce. "We're not telling people at Kay's birthday. We can't upstage her."

Women. Everything is like Sky News, arranged into the most headline grabbing order. Apparently, our break up is more of a 'top story' than Kay's thirtieth birthday.

"We'll tell them tomorrow, or the day after," Lola says. "Anyway, no one will even notice we've broken up. It's not like we ever held hands or anything."

"We held hands all the time, I seem to recall."

"No, John. I held your hand. There's a difference."

She's right, of course. She held my hand; I looked in the opposite direction and tried to pretend it wasn't attached to my body. Why did I do that?

"Come with me." She swallows hard, smoothing a strand of hair from my forehead. "As a friend."

Against my better judgement, and because I feel the need to pay some kind of penance, I agree.

3

The Silent Treatment – usually something I quite enjoy. It's like a mini-holiday, a break from the constant chatter and requests to pick up something from Waitrose 'while I'm out'. But for the first time ever, I want her to start speaking to me.

In principle, I can understand why she's not talking to me. It's her reasoning, or lack thereof, that has me baffled. We broke up – okay, I broke up with her. She yelled, cried, asked me to have sex with her, cried some more, and then said we should go to the party together. This isn't a display of gallantry on my part; she wanted me to come. And now she's behaving as though she'd rather be in the car beside anyone but me.

When Lola came downstairs after the, well, let's just call it the 'incident', she was different. The vulnerability, the hurt, had been replaced by something else – I know it as the need to inflict pain on me. While I don't expect her to be doing cartwheels, humming Kool and the Gang or, preferably, begging me for another roll in the hay (I'm not that much of a utopian), she'd made her point – she made it succinctly when she gave me the first of many dirty looks as we pulled out of our road. I thought we had enough history between us to circumvent her obligation to turn monosyllabic on me. Apparently not.

Since leaving the house, we've exchanged the following words:

ME: Is that dress new?

HER: Drop dead. (Looks pointedly out of car window.)

Seven minutes later:

ME: (Peers through windscreen.) I don't know where all this rain is coming from.

HER: The sky.

Twelve minutes later:

ME: Can you believe this traffic?

No audible reply from her, just a really, really, scary glower in my direction that tells me in no uncertain terms that she'd like to put on a pair of steel-toe boots and kick me in the groin.

A minute and a half later, I mistakenly asked:

ME: Are you okay?

HER: Fine.

And there it was, fired like a ballistic missile, the dreaded 'fine'. One solitary mushroom cloud of a word, small, yet powerful enough to strike a paroxysm of fear into the heart of the toughest of men, second only to 'Don't worry about it', which as we know means, 'Oh you'd better bloody well start worrying, mister'. It's genius – every woman I've ever known has used this otherwise innocuous word to convey that an explosion of rage is about to occur.

So, I understand Lola being upset and angry, but it was her idea for me to drive us both here, and for us to pretend we're still a couple. This uncomfortable situation is occurring due to her sadistic need to maintain a semblance of normality in front of Kay and her guests. Well, she's overlooking the fact that most of those invited have never liked me anyway. It would probably put more fizz into their champagne if they knew we've broken up. They'd be thrilled to discover they now have a tangible reason to hate me. They've been searching for one for years.

It's all part of my punishment, making me sweat while I await the inevitable eruption, which is bound to occur some time soon. But my conscience is pretty clear. I'll be able to sleep tonight, although admittedly I'm not one hundred percent sure exactly where I'll be sleeping tonight. This break-up is, I'm certain, the best thing for both of us.

Okay, at this point I'm certain it's the best thing for me. But everything will work out eventually for Lola too. It has to. And she's the one who's so fond of telling me everything happens for a reason, so I'm sure she can find a way to rationalise it. If not, Valerie Perkins will be only too happy to help her, probably with the aid of pins and a recent photograph of me.

I ease the car into Kay's quaint little cul-de-sac, the scene of many a gruesome afternoon spent gathered around the dinner table with the 'family'. God, how I despised every word of the predictable small talk and recurring inquisition about when we were going to get married and have children. The sight of the row of ridiculously overpriced houses in Kay's street usually fills me with utter dread, but tonight, I'm calm. None of this matters anymore. I don't have to waste any more time trying to think of suitable things to discuss with Todd, Kay's dullard of a husband who suffers not just from penis envy, but also bicep, gluteus, and cerebrum envy. I don't have to pretend to be interested in their irritating-to-the-point-of-self-mutilation children, who will never call me 'Uncle Johnny', no matter how badly Todd wants them to. All these social niceties, the domestic politics, are a part of my former life. I'm done with it; I'm not going to feel bad about who I am anymore. I'm now seeking bliss minus the domestic part.

I bring the car to a halt next to an obscenely stunning Jaguar XK-R, trying to ignore the fact it belongs to Lola's mother (actually, just generally trying to forget Lola's mother). It's not right for such a beautiful car to be driven by such an ugly woman, and it's plain old unfair that the Wicked Witch of SW3 drives a better car than I do.

I switch off the engine, and wonder how long Lola is planning to stay at this party. I'll be ready to leave after – well, I'm ready to leave now. But it's plain that Lola wants to drag this out for as long as she can. No wonder she wanted me to drive – I'm the chauffeur, which rules out both feigning illness and leaving early, or getting blind drunk on Todd's cheap beer. Well done, Lola. She's really bringing out the old-school torture methods. All I need now is an orange jumpsuit.

I unclasp my seatbelt and look over at her. She's staring straight ahead, seemingly mesmerised by the balloons on Kay's fence. I watch them struggle to bob up and down in the wind, their efforts thwarted even before they've gained a modicum of altitude. That, I can empathise with.

"You okay?" As soon as the sentence leaves my mouth I realise it's completely redundant, the most pointless question I've put to her since I asked how she could possibly entertain herself in Harvey Nichols for five whole hours.

"I'm fine."

No surprises there then.

"Right." I fiddle with the car keys, thinking that Kay has appalling timing. She could've turned thirty on any day out of three hundred and sixty-five, but she had to pick this one.

I almost jump when Lola finally moves, manoeuvring herself to confront me, her eyes blazing.

"Who is she?"

I blink rapidly a few times to get my conversational bearings, paraphrasing her cautiously. "Who is who?"

"Is there someone else?"

"Why should there be someone else?"

"There's always someone else."

"Not in this case."

She flashes me an expression of sheer incredulity. "So you're breaking up with me for no reason? Oh, that's just priceless!"

"I told you the reason."

"Oh yes, 'it's not working anymore'," she retorts, in a wildly inaccurate impersonation of me, waving her arms around like one of the Muppets. "Listen, John, you and I have never worked. We've always been completely wrong for each other. You are selfish, and abrasive, and moody, and conceited, and uncaring, and unreliable, and irritating, slightly pretentious at times, and-"

"I am not moody."

"I am not finished."

"I don't need to hear the rest of my alleged faults, if it's all the same to you."

She unclasps her seatbelt so that she can twist her whole body around, maybe to slap me, or maybe just to make it easier to shout at me, so her voice can come out louder. "Oh, but I think you do need to hear them. Because you have no idea how impossible you are."

"Really? Do enlighten me then," I reply, watching Kay's fence and wishing I was a balloon. But then, if I were, Lola would only pop me with the sharpest pin she could find.

"Oh, get lost, John." She slumps back into the seat, her expression illustrating that it's beneath her to explain all this to me.

"No, I want to hear this. Please, Lola, tell me your great theory."

"I forgot that you're also patronising," she snaps, her eyes narrowed.

"I'll add that one to the list."

She sits upright again, her hair trailing across her shoulders. "You know what? I am so tired of this. Being with you is like trying to tread water in quicksand."

I'm about to point out the obvious impossibility of this, but think better of it. Wise, as her tirade is not over yet.

"I'm exhausted, John. And I'm not going to argue with you anymore. You're right, it's over. It was over ages ago, I just couldn't see it. Let's go to the party, smile politely, and then we go our separate ways. It's for the best."

I'm nodding, but inside I'm wondering if that speech now qualifies her as the dumper, and me as the dumpee. I hope not, after all the hard work I've put into this. And what did she mean, "It was over ages ago?" What is that supposed to mean? It was over today, when I said it was.

This is just typical of her. Now I'll be vexed by that statement all night. Oh well, fuck it. After this little ordeal, it'll be nothing more than academic.

We get out of the car and Lola makes a run for the door, holding her coat over her head to shield her hair from the rain. God forbid it should get wet and go slightly wavy, that would be a travesty. It's a shame Lola is unaware how striking she looks when the rain gets to her, when she relaxes, when she's natural. That's when she's at her best.

I follow her, my footsteps matter-of-fact, not caring that I'm getting soaked. In fact, the entire Atlantic Ocean could pour right on top of me this very second and I wouldn't give a shit. I wouldn't. I am the emboldened model of my former self.

I suddenly realise I'm not carrying anything – Lola has both the present, and the customary bottle of wine. This disconcerts me. Tradition dictates that the woman carries the present, and the guy carries the bottle, and that makes sense to me. Women should brandish a carefully chosen, carefully wrapped, soon-to-be-carefully-unwrapped, gift for the host. The male role is to traipse a few paces behind and nonchalantly hand over the most functional offering: the alcohol. Alcohol is necessary for the event (particularly if Todd is invited); a present is a superfluous afterthought. That, to me, says it all about male and female thinking. Now it appears Lola is taking responsibility for both sides of our ex-relationship, and I am already surplus to requirements.

I watch her embrace Kay, and conclude that it's a miracle of genetics how two babies born of the same (probably ratinfested) womb could turn out so differently. Lola and Kay are a perfect example of parental pre-determination. I firmly believe, and have done since I first met both sisters, that as soon as Kay was born Mr. and Mrs. Martinez decided that she was going to be the practical, rational, plain-looking, straight-talking one. So, when Lola arrived a couple of years later, they nurtured her to be at the other end of the extreme: ditzy, flighty, prone to histrionics, and neck-achingly beautiful.

I mean, take their names for example. 'Kay' – can you get more simple and functional than that? You can abbreviate it to just one letter, for God's sake. Juxtapose that to 'Lola' – sexy, exotic, dramatic, and let's be honest here, who wouldn't want a girlfriend called Lola? Simon and I concluded years ago that Kay and Lola are the Ronseal of women – they both do exactly what it says on the tin.

Kay inherited the surname Flint from the delightful Todd, and it suits her. She is like Flint – blunt, hard and, well, useful. I love Kay, really, I do. She's a rare breed. Clear-thinking, articulate, and unspoilt by the mess the media has made of the female consciousness. The only but significant trouble is, she can see right through me.

Today, Kay gives me the special wary glare known as her 'John look', before kissing me on the cheek.

"Hello, John." She eyes me up and down. "What's different about you?"

"I got a tattoo."

"Oh good, you're being facetious already – how unlike you. Come on, what have you done? Oh, never mind, I'll find out eventually." She folds her arms. "Now listen, this party wasn't my idea," she says.

"I know. If I were Elvis and I wanted to surprise the world with the news that I was still alive, Todd wouldn't be the guy I'd come to for help."

Kay rolls her eyes at the mention of her husband's name, an action I fully endorse and understand. "Well, at least this way I'm not surprised as I'm walking in with the kids and a load of shopping. That's not a surprise party, it's a surprise nightmare."

Lola returns from hanging up her coat. "Does Todd know you're not thirty?"

"Have you gone mad?"

"Have I missed something?" I say, before they lose me completely.

"Kay is actually thirty-two," Lola informs me.

"Right." I nod as though I get it. "So why are we having a thirtieth birthday party for her?"

"Why, do you want your present back?" Kay says.

"Huh!" Lola says. "He didn't even buy it."

"I took that as read," Kay snorts. "Is it a colander?"

Lola shakes her head, handing over the irrefutably non colander-shaped box to her sister. "Perfume."

Kay surveys her gift with contempt. "What the hell am I going to do with perfume? I need a colander. Perfume is for women who still want to have sex occasionally. I'm more concerned with draining my vegetables."

"We'll get you a colander next year." I reassure her. "For your thirty-third birthday."

Lola lets out a reluctant giggle, and then gives me a shitty look, as though she hates me all the more for making her laugh against her will. Kay studies us both. I try to calculate the odds of Kay not putting two and two together.

"All right, Mr Journalist," Kay finally explains, "when I met Todd I told him I was sixteen."

"But she was actually eighteen," Lola adds.

"Thanks for that, little sister."

"You're welcome," Lola replies, smirking.

"Oh, right." I'm confused. "And Todd had no idea?"

"Nope," Kay says proudly.

"Hasn't he seen your passport?"

"Hah! Where did you two go on your last holiday?" Kay demands.

"St Lucia," Lola says, looking at her shoes. "But it was a long time ago."

"That makes no difference. We went to Margate. Do you need a passport to go there? Exactly."

"So all this time you've been married to someone you pledged to be with for better or worse, and he doesn't even know how old you really are?"

Kay frowns at me. "And?"

"It's the rule of two," Lola chimes in. "Never tell a guy how old you really are. Always deduct two years. It makes life a lot more enjoyable for everyone."

"Okay, so how come you told me your real age?" I ask Lola.

Lola answers without looking at me. "Just, because."

Kay glances from her sister, then to me, and then back again. "You two haven't had a row, have you? You have. Great, that's all I need."

"Of course we haven't," Lola says quickly, as though the very suggestion is ludicrous. "Well, no more than usual." She avoids my gaze.

I am staring right at her.

"I see." Kay's unconvinced, glancing from me to her sister. "Lola, why don't you come and help me out in the kitchen?"

I'm not the smartest guy in the world, but I know this means they're going to drink wine and slag me off. Apparently, that's what helping out in the kitchen means if you're a female.

"John, go and get yourself a beer or something. Everyone else is in the lounge," Kay says, dragging her sister away to slander my good name.

My only saving grace is that Lola isn't going to tell her we broke up. Knowing Kay, she'd love it. She's never understood what Lola sees in me, and it would present her with the opportunity to say what she really thinks of me – and in front of their mother, no less. Great. Even better than a colander.

I drape my jacket over the banister, indifferent to the fact that it's going to drip all over child number one's trainers. I steel myself, and edge into the lounge.

Thankfully, there are at least twenty guests already huddled around the cheese on sticks and bags of Twiglets, and none of them seem to have noticed my discreet entrance. I scan the room, raising an internal eyebrow as I note that I don't recognise most of them. Either Kay has expanded her circle of friends to include a large number of people who enjoy standing in small groups discussing double glazing, or Todd has invited all his friends instead. I suspect the latter.

Child number one and two are yelling at each other about which banal pop tune to put on the stereo next, and I remember that Todd always plays fucking awful music at these kinds of events. The man has such bad taste it's on the Kelvin scale of decency. Unfortunately I've now spotted him and, even more unfortunately, he is standing next to – guarding – the beer, which means there's no escape. I'll have to go and talk to him. Getting through this completely sober is not an option, so dull conversation over warm, low-alcohol beer with Todd it will have to be.

I say a few brusque 'hellos', just about the right side of polite, to the people who tap me on the arm in recognition as I push past, and make my way over to Todd. He doesn't hide his delight at seeing me. I hope I can hide my dismay at seeing him more effectively.

Christ, I need a cigarette.

"John! How are you? Have a beer, mate." Todd thrusts a bottle into my hand. It's cold – a first for one of Todd's parties – so I count my blessings and refrain from checking if it's remotely decent. Todd is infamous for buying shit beer, the kind adolescent boys would baulk at spending their pooled paper-round money on. He once came to our house proudly brandishing a bottle of Lambrini and four cans of Tesco Value lager, which I then gave to Lola's mother the following Christmas. I hear it went down a storm in Chelsea.

"Hey, Todd, great to see you," I lie, and wait for the inevitable.

"How's the job?" he asks, right on cue. "I haven't read your, erm, column in a while, I have to say."

I'm tempted to point out that Todd's idea of a 'while' roughly equates to 'never', as there are no pictures of topless women in my paper, because I use words of more than two syllables, and because he can't actually read. But that would be rude. So instead I say, "Well, it's kind of a funny time at the moment, what with the economy as it is. I'm placing a lot of focus on the US, and what the effects of the slowdown and the weak dollar could have on us."

Todd is nodding as I'm saying this, even though we're both conscious that he has no idea what I'm talking about.

"And then there's the housing market," I throw in, as I'm out of practise at being cruel.

Of course, he'll never wave the white flag and admit he hasn't got the first idea about economics. Even when I give him advice on his mortgage, shares and various investments, he still won't concede to being clueless.

He fiddles with his bottle. "Lola looks well. Has she put on a bit of weight?"

Instinctively, I check she's not within earshot. "No, but you'd better not speculate on that particular subject. Okay?"

"I'm sorry, John. I just thought she looked well, that's all. I didn't mean any offence." Todd is genuinely horrified at his own faux pas, which is surprising for a man whose very existence on the planet is one big faux pas.

"None taken. But Lola would've taken plenty, so watch what you say."

Todd nods furiously. "Sorry, yes."

Oh God. Now for the small talk. If there was a razor nearby, slitting my wrists would be preferable to having to make the obligatory, "How are things in windows?" enquiry.

"Not too good," Todd replies when I do ask (it's required of me), adding a solemn shake of his head. I then notice that although Todd generally walks the earth amid a cloud of uncertainty, tonight the sense of impending doom seems to have intensified. “We’ve only had one order this week, and that was for a flat. I’m going to have to start thinking about laying people off. If it carries on like this …” he trails off, but we both know what he’s referring to. The unthinkable: losing your job. Being relegated to the scrap heap, having to live with the knowledge that you have no purpose, you’re a piece of slack – that eliminating you from the workforce will help the business to run more smoothly. The spectre of the Dole lies alongside premature ejaculation and impotency in the catacombs of the male psyche – well, in the South-East of England, anyway. Todd almost has me onside.

“Things will pick up,” I lie again, remembering that Todd couldn’t sell shoes to Imelda Marcos, or buy-one-get-two-free arms to Iran. If Todd discovered a lucrative supply of oil in his back garden, he wouldn’t even be able to persuade either of the George Bushes to invade it.

The resultant hope in Todd’s eyes nearly makes me feel bad for lying. Nearly.

“Do you think so? I mean, I’m considering retraining, getting into something safe like IT.”

“Au contraire,” I say quickly, and then wish I hadn’t, as Todd has enough trouble with English. “The IT industry is contracting. There’s been too much expansion, over-estimation of demand. People will be losing their jobs like you wouldn’t believe.”

Other people’s misery cheers Todd up somewhat. “Really?”

“Uh-huh.”

He regards me as though I’m some kind of biblical prophet. “How come you know all this stuff?”

At least he admits he hasn’t read my column in a ‘while’.

Our discussion is then interrupted by child number two, who marches over to express her disquiet in a tone that would erode Mount Rushmore.

"Dad," she whines, "Jeremy won't let me play my new Girls Aloud CD."

I want to run over and hand Jeremy a beer for the great he's done on behalf of civilisation. Todd crouches down to ruffle her hair.

"Susie, what have I told you about listening to your brother? He is older than you," Todd reminds her.

I believe children shouldn't be seen (they should all live in underground caves until the age of twenty), let alone heard, but that sounds unfair even to me. From the puckered look of contempt Susie gives her father, she clearly thinks so too.

"But Daaaaad…" I hate the way children stretch words out like that. "Jeremy is a complete prick."

I suppress the first laugh I've had under this roof in ages. Todd flashes me a glance to express both his apology, and his horror.

"Susannah Lillian Caroline Flint, where did you learn that vulgar expression?"

And I hate the way parents stretch out their kid's names. It's as though they give them middle names solely to use as ammunition when they scold them. The more names their kids have, the more rounds the parents can fire off. If I ever, through some heinous biological accident, have children, I'm naming them X for a girl, and Y for a boy.

Susie sticks out her tongue. "No one," she answers in a singsong voice. She shuffles up to me, and I immediately wish I had something to spray on myself to repel her – VX gas would be good.

One of the (many) reasons I despise kids is that I never know what to say to them. I can't connect with them. Children seem capable only of babbling on about crap. When I was her age I'm sure I had intelligent things to say to adults, and was indeed frustrated by people asking me if I liked *Metal Mickey*, *Action Man*, and the *A-Team* when I wanted sharp discourse about supply-side Reganomics and spiralling unemployment. I'm sure of it. And these days they have iPods, and MP3s, and know things about technology I'd rather die before asking them.

"Joohhhnn," Susie begins, "do you want to go upstairs and see my new Barbie? She's got hair you can really curl."

I would rather drive hot drawing pins under my fingernails with a hammer. Or ask her how a wireless router works.

"Susie, how many times have I told you? It's Uncle Johnny," Todd scolds.

Thankfully, Susie ignores him. "Pleeeeease Johhhhnn, she's got fingers you can really move as well."

I've got fingers you can really move, too. You should see my middle finger flick upwards. Incredible dexterity.

I manage to squeeze an ounce of regret into my voice. "You know, Susie, I'd really like to, but I have to go and talk to your Aunty Lola. Perhaps later." When the Pope has an orgy with a T-Rex and several unicorns kind of later.

"Okay." Susie seems content enough with that brush-off, so I don't have to think of a better one, and she skips off to resume her dispute with child number one, aka Jeremy.

The flipside to getting rid of her by saying I need to talk to Lola, is that I am now required to go and talk to Lola, which was not high on my agenda of things to do in this particular arena. Actually, I was planning to hide in a dark corner until Lola allows me to drive her home. But how bad can it be? My question is answered when, giving Todd a suitably apologetic smile, I head for the kitchen and bump straight into the Queen of Darkness herself, Lola's mother.

"Cynthia. Hi."

She's as pleased to see me as I am her, giving me the kind of look anyone else would save for the discovery of a cold sore on their top lip.

"John. How are you keeping?"

This, folks, is how Cynthia Martinez speaks to people.

"Good. You look… brown."

Actually, she looks more orange, perhaps mahogany at best. She's either been away somewhere, or she's set her tanning machine on the 'human coffee table' setting.

"Maldives," she replies, as though it's her local corner shop. "How about you? You two haven't been away for a while."

What she really means is, "You haven't taken my daughter on holiday for ages, you cheap bastard. Oh, my mistake, you can't afford it because you're the limescale on the toilet bowl of life – a journalist."

"Lola doesn't want to go anywhere at the moment."

This is true – Lola's terrified of flying and has resolved that in future she'll only travel by train to somewhere with lots of shops and rude people, which limits our options to France and Manchester, but Cynthia would think I made that up.

Her eyebrows edge closer together – well, they try to, but the Botox does a pretty good job of stopping them.

"I've just seen Lola, actually. She looks very thin."

The implication here is that it's my fault – oh, wait, everything from terrorism to global warming is my fault in her eyes.

"She's been very busy at work."

"I thought you were going to keep an eye on her, John. Look after her."

I'm about to point out that Lola's a grown woman and makes her own choices, and apologise for being a failure, but then it occurs to me that I don't have to put up with this anymore. Cynthia can't make me feel as though I'm not good enough for her daughter, because I'm no longer trying to please her, or anyone. I'm my own man – free from her opinion, from everyone's.

"I have looked after Lola. I've done my best. The rest, she'll have to do herself. Excuse me."

And I walk off, leaving her standing there dazed. Fuck her. I'm out of here, I don't need to take her "When are you going to get a real job?" "When are you going to move to Chelsea to be nearer to us?" crap anymore. I've had it. The End. Roll credits. Fuck it all. I want to get back in the car, dent her Jag as I reverse out, play 'Rebel Rebel' as loud as it will go, and drive home much faster than I should, showing my arse to every speed camera en route.

I march through the hall and barge into the kitchen, which I know is a bad move as soon as I've made it. Kay gives me a glare so fierce, her eyes seem to flicker red. I have time to notice Lola curled up on a stool by the breakfast bar, before Kay shrieks at me:

"John, you are a complete prick!"

I turn to Lola. Her face is puffy and tearstained. "You upstaged her," I say to her, my voice flat.

"I couldn't help it," she says, her words broken and gurgled. "I'll never get over you."

She's said it out loud, but it doesn't sound as good as I'd imagined.

4

So far, I think it's going pretty well. The world hasn't stopped spinning on its axis, the sky hasn't turned purple, and I haven't woken up to find aliens have landed in Putney. Everything, on the face of it, is normal. Except that I'm here, and Lola is – well, I don't actually know. For the first time in nine years, I have no idea where she is. For the first time in nine years, whole days have elapsed without hearing her voice. Four whole days, to be precise. Four whole days, and one half day. Four days and twenty hours, if I were keeping count.

"This is it, mate," Simon says as he enters the lounge with a supermarket aisle's worth of junk food under his arms. "The night can truly begin. Again. Here," he tosses me a tube of Pringles. "Get your laughing gear around those. They're the beef ones."

On the couch beside me, Penny throws him a portentous look, but he's too busy chewing to notice. So she turns to me instead.

"Would you like one?" I offer her the tube, which she glares at as though it's full of toenail clippings.

"No." She casts Simon a glance of, well, how can I describe it diplomatically?

I've seen her pull that face at him quite a few times since I moved in here. She gives him shitty looks over breakfast and dinner; when he's reading, when he's talking to me, when he's watching football, and when he's unpacking the shopping – there's no real pattern to what provokes her. As long as Simon has the audacity to breathe, he's rewarded with the same expression. At first I thought it might just be her face, that she was doing it unconsciously, but she actually builds up to it. First, her lips purse, then she squints, her over-plucked eyebrows desperately trying to meet in the centre of her forehead, and then the disgust settles on her face like Andrex spreading over a turd in the toilet bowl.

I don't like the way she looks at him. Actually, I don't like her. I never have. Right from, "John, this is Penny," to the present day, there's been something about her that makes my skin hurt. But that's okay, because the feeling's mutual.

I shrug and pop open the tube, putting a couple into my mouth and pretending I actually like this flavour. Penny, I note out of the corner of my eye, is now giving Simon the full-on Face. I have no idea how long it's been since Penny started giving him these looks – weeks, months – but he hasn't noticed. I should say something. He needs to know. Sooner or later, Mount Penelope will start spewing lava, and it'll be better for him if he isn't taken by surprise, if he's got time to prepare. To rehearse.

Simon picks up the remote control and flicks on the television, hoisting his feet up onto the coffee table and sighing contentedly.

"This is the life, eh mate?" He prises the tops from our beers, handing me one.

I smile and take it from him, inwardly cursing Penny for tainting the beer with The Face.

"I'm going out," she announces, standing up rather too forcefully for the size of the sofa. I just about hold in the swear word as a dribble of beer spills onto my jeans. "If you two are going to sit there all night watching football, you don't want me here."

I dissolve into the cushions and desperately signal to Simon, glancing rapidly from him to the screen to the remote, throwing him a lifeline.

But Simon, being Simon, just floats right on past it.

"Huh?"

"You've sat there in front of the TV," Penny says, folding her arms and blocking our view of it, getting our attention very successfully, credit where credit's due, "and I haven't said a word. But if you're planning to loaf around and watch this, then I'm going out."

I nudge Simon.

"Pen, it's Champion's League tonight," he says.

I don't know why I bother, I really don't.

Penny screws her face up, as though she's doing origami with her cheeks and mouth. "And what was it last night?"

"Classic Worthington Cup," Simon answers, as though he's on *The Weakest Link* rather than being asked a purely rhetorical question by a wife – his own – who's testing him to see if he has the sense to flick the channel onto something less sporting and pay her a bit of attention.

He doesn't.

"I'll be back late," she says. "Don't wait up."

Simon says something that sounds like, "Weeeerrewurgnhhhht," but that actually means, "We won't." Penny, however, is unable to translate this. Which is probably just as well. She slams the door, the frame rattling. Simon turns up the volume and relaxes into his chair.

"Chelsea are going to get tanked."

"I think you are as well, Simon."

"What? I've only had half a bottle."

"Penny. She's not happy."

"Oh, she's never happy." Simon dismisses my concern, shovelling some peanuts into his mouth. "It's just her way."

"Her way of what?"

"Of keeping me on my toes."

I glance at Simon, who's slouched so far down in his chair that his chin and stomach are almost fused, a fistful of peanuts cupped in one hand, a beer in the other, and the remote control nestling usefully on his gut. "Yeah, you're almost a fully-fledged ballerina."

"What? John, I'm trying to watch this, mate."

"Sorry."

I pick up the TV guide which, in a thoughtful kind of way, we've wedged in between the cushions for ease and fairness. It's as well-thumbed as a Penguin Classic (much more so because we've actually read it), and flicking through it brings to mind that Bruce Springsteen track, '57 Channels (and nothin' on)'. Bruce obviously has Sky Digital.

"Hey, there's a profile of Himmler on the History channel."

Simon slowly peels his eyes from the screen. I'm sure I hear the suction noise as his eyeballs pop back into their sockets. "Himmler? What about Chelsea?"

"It's not a huge leap in subject matter. And you hate Chelsea."

"Yeah, that's the point," Simon explains, as though I might have learning difficulties. "To watch them lose." Yet another handful of peanuts vanish down his gullet.

In lieu of smoke (banned, along with fun, under Penny's roof), I suck in a breath of relatively clean air. "To be honest, Simon, I'm a little tired of watching football."

For a second, I think Simon's head might be about to rotate three hundred and sixty degrees and spew out pea soup. "You're winding me up."

I'm just as disturbed as he is, but it's the truth, and must be confronted.

There's a rule in economics called the 'Law of Diminishing Returns'. This law states, basically, that the first time you do something, you get a lot of enjoyment out of it. The next time you do it it's still good, but not as good as the first time. The next time it's merely okay, and so on until you get bored and don't want to do that thing anymore. It's brilliant, and can be applied to everything – breasts, crosswords, driving a scooter and, horrifyingly, football.

It started three days ago, when I moved in with Simon and Penny – strictly as a temporary measure. We thought it was some sort of sign that there was a big match on that very evening, a sign that at last we were about to live our lives as they should be lived, and we settled ourselves in front of the TV with something akin to religious fervour. Since then we've seen Fulham beat Man United, Portsmouth hammer Everton, and endless late-night chatter involving retired ex-footballers. We've amused ourselves with the player-cam (who knew Steven Gerrard spat so much), and now we find ourselves stationary in front of Chelsea versus Barcelona. I'm torn between what I should be feeling, i.e. liberation and euphoric contentment, and reality, which is that I think I'm bored.

Simon regards me with suspicion. He does suspicion so well – it's his party piece. Probably because he's friends with me. "You miss her, don't you?"

"Who?"

He rests his chin in his hand, which makes him look really camp, a secret I keep to myself, along with the fact I once owned a Level 42 t-shirt. "I thought so," he says sagely. Again, more peanuts march down into his digestive tract to join those that have boldly gone before. "I can't say I blame you. She is a complete fox."

"Excuse me?"

"Lola. Complete fox."

I pretend not to hear him. Ignoring people is my party piece.

"Sorry, John, but she is. Would you rather I told you she was a complete dog?"

"I would rather we watched the programme about Himmler and you shut your mouth."

"All right then, I will," he says, popping open another tube of Pringles in a much less flatulence-inducing flavour, and pointedly not offering me any.

There's a long pause and all of a sudden I'm fidgeting, a wave of loquaciousness sweeping over me. I pick up one of Penny's embroidered cushions and nestle it in my lap.

Simon tips an obscene amount of Pringles down his throat, swallowing them with an audible gulp. I'm reminded of a pelican downing a raw fish.

"Has she phoned you?" he asks, wiping his hands on his jeans.

"No."

"I'm not surprised." He considers it, staring at me intently for a few seconds. "My God – you are though, aren't you?"

"No. Actually, I'd rather she didn't call."

"Liar."

"I'm not lying," I lie again.

"You dumped her for no reason. What the fuck do you expect? An OBE?"

"It's not like her. That's all."

"How would you know? You've only dumped her once." He makes himself comfortable, adjusting his position in the chair. "You should've just cheated on her. It would've been easier."

"For who?"

"For you, and for her. That way, you'd know for sure she's never going to call."

"I don't want her to call."

"Yes, you do, and you're pissed off that Lola has more pride than you thought," he says sanctimoniously.

"No, I'm not."

"You are."

"I'm not."

Stamford Bridge disappears – if only – as Simon flicks off the TV, a magnanimous gesture, the significance of which I register, despite my irritated state.

"What is it then? See, because if you dumped her, and told her in front of her sister and her mother that you're not sure she's quite what you want, then I don't see why she would possibly want to phone you. What is there to say? In fact, if I were Lola, I'd be pissing on little wooden dollies carved in your likeness right about now."

"What a charming image."

Simon replies via his middle finger.

I think back to the party, and the terrible things I said. The thing is, I meant them, especially the ones about not being ready to settle down, even though I should have substituted 'ready' for 'willing', and added, 'with you.' However, perhaps I shouldn't have said them in front of all of those people. And I shouldn't have yelled at her. And, after nine years, I should've phrased it better. And I definitely shouldn't have called her mother an interfering, perfectionist bitch, never mind the fact that she's exactly that and I could see some of the guests nodding surreptitiously in agreement. I doubt Kay will ever speak to me again. This depresses me further.

What torments me most of all though, is the sliver of undiluted pain I saw in Lola's eyes as she told me precisely what she thought of me. She meant it, too. I did that to her, and I don't feel good about it. It's horrible, the knowledge you can hurt someone so much, and to know that yes, human emotions really are that fragile.

I wonder how she is. An image of her, curled into a little ball and sobbing her heart out in our ex-bed flashes onto the projector I seem to have switched on inside my skull.

"Simon?"

"Yes?"

"How many women have you slept with?"

"Fuck off."

"Come on, Simon. How many? And tell me the truth, not the *FHM* figure."

"The *GQ* one?"

"The truth."

Simon lets out a huge sigh, as though talking to me is suddenly a massive inconvenience to him. "I don't see what this has got to do with anything but, okay. Six."

"Including Penny?"

"Penny's my wife."

"Yes," I say, trying not to roll my eyes, "but presumably you've had sexual intercourse with her?"

"Many wonderful times."

I fight the urge to gag. "Right then, so is she number six or seven?"

He hesitates. "Seven." He stares at me through slightly narrowed eyes. "Why?"

I throw the cushion to one side. "No reason."

"No, come on. How many women have you shagged then?"

"Do people still use that word?"

"I do. Come on."

I sigh. "All right. Five."

"Jesus!"

"No, not Jesus. Just Lola, and some others."

"What about Carrie Marshall's sister?"

"She was her sister-in-law," I remind him.

"Whatever." A beat while Simon does a few calculations. "So you've had Lola," he counts on his chipolata fingers, "Carrie Marshall's sister-in-law, Carrie Marshall...who else?"

"It's not important."

Simon chews his bottom lip while he muses. "What about Emily Abbott?"

"I didn't sleep with her."

"Why?"

"Didn't want to."

"Don't blame her."

"No, I didn't want to."

He gives me an incredulous look. "What? You could've told me! I would've slept with her!"

"Simon, she hated you."

"Oh." His face drops a little. "Yes, you're right. Louisa Garcia?"

"Australian."

"I like Australian women. And she had great thighs." He stares off into the distance for a few moments. "What about-"

"Simon, who they were is not important."

"Not sure I agree, but whatever…"

He gazes at the blank TV screen and we're both quiet while we think our own thoughts.

"Jesus!" Simon says out of nowhere.

"Him again?"

"Does this mean you haven't had sex with anyone that isn't Lola for eight years?" he says.

"Nine."

"So the last time you slept with a woman who wasn't Lola, it was a whole different century!"

"Thank you for radiocarbon dating my sex life."

Simon considers this, and then the light bulb appears over his melon-shaped head, his face widening yet further as he smiles in recognition.

"Oh, I know what this is about. You're worried you're missing out on something." He talks faster, warming to his theme. "You think that instead of being with Lola, you should be out screwing as many women as you can."

"Simon, sometimes I think you should've pursued a career in public speaking."

"Fuck off." His intense scrutiny is making me uncomfortable. "I'm right aren't I?"

I regret that I can't use one of Penny's cushions to smother him.

"Do you ever wonder if being with Penny is stopping you from meeting the woman of your dreams?"

Simon blinks at me. "Penny is the woman of my dreams. I married her."

"Come on, Simon. Surely you must think about being with other women."

He mulls it over. I can hear the rust grind as the cogs in his brain turn.

"Maybe in passing I do. Not seriously. But I wouldn't do anything about it, because I've got her. Penny. And let me tell you something, if you've dumped Lola for the thrill of the chase, then you've made the biggest fuck up of your entire shambolic life."

"The thrill of the chase? Did you make that up all by yourself?"

He's enjoying himself now. "A.k.a. 'the grass is always greener syndrome.'" He drums his fingers on the Pringle tube, for dramatic effect. "The point of chasing something is that you're supposed to stop chasing when you catch it. You caught Lola, and you should've kept her. And as for the grass being greener – mate, you'll soon discover that one lawn is pretty much the same as another. And so are the bushes."

"Is it suddenly 'talking in clichés hour' and no one told me? And what do you know about bushes?"

"Stop being clever for once, and call Lola. Tell her you were having some kind of mid-thirties crisis, and make it up with her. She'll take you back, the soft cow. All that's wrong with you is you're panicking you haven't sown enough oats - that somebody better is out there for you. But that somebody better doesn't exist. I bet it'll only take a week of being single for you to realise that."

"This isn't about 'sowing my oats'. This is about finding someone I can be with."

"You managed eight years with Lola. She could be your soul mate."

"Nine," I correct. "And I don't even know what a soul mate is. I don't want to manage – I want to be happy, to enjoy a relationship, not endure it. Maybe I don't even want a relationship at all. Some people aren't designed for them."

"You were happy. It was as good as it gets."

"Maybe I want better."

Simon snorts. "You do what you want mate, but you're looking for the pot of gold at the end of the rainbow, Lord Lucan, and the fucking Wizard of Oz as far as I'm concerned. And, for your information, I know a lot about bushes. I've had two more than you." He reaches for the remote and switches on the TV, making it clear that the conversation is now over.

I'm looking at twenty-two guys (minus the twats that got sent off) booting a ball from one end of the pitch to the other, apparently with no real tactical conception. I can watch football whenever I like now. I couldn't before, because Lola was always watching 'America's Next Top Prostitute' or some such rubbish on Living TV. But it turns out that I might've liked football better when it was a rare treat. Now, I see it differently. Footballers are stupid people who do stupid things, and get nicked for speeding in cars I want but can't afford. If I'd watched one match it might be okay, but since I've been here I've seen about 3,293, and I'm starting to question my sanity.

I did the right thing – I always do the right thing. It's my trademark, my infallible judgement and unquestionable powers of reasoning. I take hold of myself. It's the shock, that's all – the change. Nine years is a long time. Fuck, nine years is a long time… No, come on, get a grip. I just need to dive right in, fulfil my destiny. Okay, so, from tomorrow, I'm back out there; I'm in the race again. If I want to sleep with a woman on the first date, I'm not going to feel bad about it, even if she does. If I don't want to call, I won't call. I won't buy flowers, strain to remember anniversaries, or put up with mood swings and doing the chocolate run once a fucking month. And if yes, that dress does indeed make her behind look big, I'll say so. Hell, I'll even confirm it in writing.
I refuse to conform any longer.

It begins now – right now. I'm declaring my own War on Terror. Today, I'm reclaiming my right to be a man. From this moment onwards, I will become the essence of maleness. I will allow the tide of testosterone to surge through me and override years of female brainwashing.

Ladies and gentleman - ladies especially: John Black is back in the saddle again.

Chelsea score. Simon gets up without saying a word, and slams the bathroom door.

I pick up the remote control, and flick over to Living TV.

5

I smoke, therefore I am. I don't know if I ever cared that it's allegedly bad for me, or if I like it for that very reason. It's not the recklessness, the cavalier attitude to the nasty, premature death I could be storing up for myself, it's the luxury of it. I smoke because I can, in spite of and in the face of the fact that smoking is now up there with plastic bags and Land Rovers on the public hit-list. I'm told it's unhealthy, a pollutant – anti-social. Well, if that isn't a reason to keep at it, I don't know what is.

I sit back in a cloud of glorious smoke, cigarette between my fingers, and think about everything, and nothing. I should've left for work an hour ago. And I shouldn't be smoking in here – Penny will go mental if she smells it. I peer into the mirror. I should've had a shave, or at the very least a facelift, to make myself more presentable. I shouldn't drink so much coffee so early. And, technically, I shouldn't be alone.

I'm not thinking about Lola – I'm thinking around Lola. I'm merely making little observations to myself now that I have time to breathe, time to be. Nine years – it's been over nine years since I've had this much time to myself, since I had all this space. I've been so used to sharing it with someone else that now I'm like an astronaut, floating around the galaxy, my spaceship having lifted off and left me behind. And it's the little things, the tiny details that catch me unawares. My toothbrush looks lost by itself. I only have to make tea for one person. There's no one to call during the day, and no one to phone me. My clothes are bundled by themselves at the bottom of the bed, a boring blend of navy, grey, white, and black. The smells in the room are all my own, there's nothing sweet, nothing floral. And who knew there was so much room in a double bed? I have to keep a map and a compass nearby just to find my way out of it in the mornings.

But the worst thing, the one that bites the most, is I that have nothing to do with my hands other than pick at my nails, make pathetic little fists and, yeah, smoke. If I was sad enough to smoke in bed, I would.

Penny knocks on my door. I know it's her – Simon would just barge in. "John?"

"Yeah?"

"I can smell smoke."

"Really?" I open the window as quietly as I can.

"I think I mentioned my asthma, John."

Yeah, Penny, you did. Everyone has fucking asthma now.

"So I'd prefer it if you didn't smoke."

"Got ya," I say, even though I haven't, and even if I did I wouldn't tell her.

"There's some coffee in the pot if you want it."

I check my watch. I don't, and I'm late. Oh, what the hell.

When I get downstairs, I realised I've been tricked. There is indeed coffee in the pot, but Penny failed to mention that she would be drinking it with me.

"Morning, John."

"Hi." I scratch the back of my head while she pours, wondering if it would be rude to ask her I could have it to go.

"Sit," she says. "Come on, I won't bite."

I want to tell her it's not the bite I'm frightened of, but the subsequent rabies. I let it go.

"Good coffee," I say.

"You got us that coffeemaker for our anniversary."

"I did?"

"Well, not 'you' – you and Lola."

"Oh." I nod – that 'you'. It's a singular 'you' from now on.

Lola bought the coffeemaker. She did all the couple stuff on my behalf.

"Simon left ages ago," Penny says, although it sounds suspiciously like she's saying this for her own benefit rather than mine.

"Yeah. He shouted me a couple of times, but I was-"

"Smoking?"

"Sleeping."

Penny rolls her eyes. "Don't lie to me, John."

I decide to respect her wishes, so I say nothing.

She pats her hair, pushing it back down onto her head. It's been doused in so much spray that it actually looks more like Astro Turf than hair. If all else fails, Luton Town could play their home games on her head.

Penny stares at the fridge, as though she's reading an imaginary note, or trying to compose a poem from the magnetic letters. I take advantage of the lull in what I'd describe as conversation in the loosest possible sense, and help myself to some cereal.

"John?"

"Yeah?"

Okay, I'll admit it. I have selective hearing. But you know what, if I listened to every single word a woman said to me, I'd never get anything done. There's so much blah, so much flotsam and jetsam. Usually it takes them at least five sentences to get anywhere near the point – if, indeed, there even is a point. Sometimes they just talk to check their larynx is still working. I've got it down to an art – I know exactly when to tune right back in, when to pick up the thread without missing anything important.
So I'm squinting at the Rice Krispie box, wondering if the little plastic toy is still inside and how I can check without Penny noticing, when my senses instinctively kick back in and filter through one of the most horrifying words in the English dictionary.

"...gynaecologist. Are you okay, John?"

I drop my spoon into the bowl. "Yeah. Went down the wrong way."

"So could you tell him, please?"

"Sure."

Tell who? Her gynaecologist? What the hell am I supposed to tell him?

"Just so I'm clear-"

Penny rolls her eyes. "For God's sake, John," she says, to emphasise my dimness. "No wonder Lola was at her wits' end."

Huh?

"Can you tell Simon," Penny continues without elaborating, which is typical, "that I won't be at home this afternoon as I'm going to the gynaecologist."

And down goes the spoon again.

She starts talking again, and there's nothing to stuff in my ears, nothing to block out the sound, not even the snap, crackle and fucking pop. I nod, and sip my coffee, trying not to vomit into the cup. I have no choice other than to listen because my brain, useless cluster of cells that it is, won't let me tune out 'gynaecologist.'. I grit my teeth, say, "Uh-huh," a lot, and make my excuses at the earliest opportunity. Jesus Christ. Getting to the office is almost a relief.

By the time I arrive, the wrong side of late, the morning has well and truly started, and seems to be coping just fine in my absence. There are people running around everywhere carrying bits of paper and files, phones ringing as soon as they're put back into their cradles, juniors carrying more sandwiches than anyone can realistically eat (apart from Simon), and there is a work experience kid crying by the photocopier. I keep my head down like a criminal arriving at court (if only I had a police escort and a blanket over my head) as I make my way to my desk, hoping I'm not spotted by anyone that matters. I'm aiming to keep as low a profile as anyone in a busy office can possibly muster, a technique

I myself have been pioneering throughout my working career. I ought to patent it.

I reach my desk, horrified to find that my monitor, most of the keyboard, and various parts of the mouse are covered in yellow Post-It notes, each of which demands in varying degrees of legibility that I call someone, or do something. My spirits nose-dive and come to rest somewhere below the earth's mantle. I swear under my breath, loosening my tie as I sit down to sort through them. In this instance, 'sort' means read, disregard, and throw into the bin. If it's important enough, they'll call back.

I wade through four days worth of missed calls, and it strikes me that the vast majority of these people are eager to speak to me because they want something. An old acquaintance of mine has written a book about Keynesian economics (like no-one's ever done that before) and undoubtedly wants a plug or seven, some woman named Tanya wants me to speak at a conference (fat chance), a mysterious 'Helen' whom I have no recollection of whatsoever wants something I can't quite read, and someone called Zelita wants to know what my dietary requirements are for the office away day. These are all 'sorted' into the bin, bar two.

The first, I call immediately.

She answers the phone herself, after an impressive two rings.

"Hey. Got your message," I say.

A slight pause, and her voice drops in volume. "Oh, hello." I can hear activity around her. She's not alone

"Do you have something you want to tell me?"

"God, yes. Can I meet you in the usual place? Today?" I can hear the urgency in her voice and the adrenaline surges.

"Yeah, I can do that. Is about five pm good for you?" I'm writing it into my diary as I speak. It's always okay – it's okay without fail. This whole routine is for appearances sake – hers, not mine.

"Yes, fantastic. I'll see you then."

"See you then." I don't replace the receiver just yet, I wait for the-

"John, you won't…"

"Not a word."

I put the phone down and reach for my pen. I chew on the end of it, gathering my thoughts. This is going to be good, I can feel it. And I need it to be good – my standards are slipping. My colleagues don't understand or show much interest in what I do. Simon gets much more of the glory, particularly when he gets one of those massive brown boxes containing the latest cosmetics samples – yeah, he's everyone's friend then. Me, I'm on my own. Just me, my interest rates, my GDP, and my Consumer Price Index. And you know what? I like it that way.

The office is jam-packed with people, a few typing up their interesting and pithy analyses, and a few just sitting there desperately trying to think up some. The number of staff working for this newspaper seems, despite Sarah's constant stories about impending redundancies, to increase every time I look up. Two boys – and I'm calling them boys because their combined age cannot be more than twenty-seven – walk past, complaining about how unfair it is that they have to work. I'm gripped by the urge to remind them about the starving people in Africa, but the thought just makes my stomach rumble, and I pine for the breakfast I was unable to finish.

Fuck it. I take the Post-It and start dialling.

"What in the name of fuck happened to you this morning?"

I disconnect the call I was about to make. "Simon. Hi. I wasn't aware we had to come to work together as well."

He sits down on my desk, seemingly ambivalent to the foul mood I'm wearing on my sleeve, collar, and lapels. "Are you on tranquilisers?"

"Not yet. Any day now though."

"I called you about eight times and you didn't hear me."

"I heard you. I simply chose to ignore you."

"You lazy git. I've been here since eight." Simon says this as though it's something to be proud of.

"Well done Si, Boy Scout's badge for you. I kind of need to make a phone call. Do you mind?"

"Penny was in a funny mood this morning."

For the second time, I regretfully put the phone back in its cradle. "She knows I'm smoking in the spare room."

Simon's moon face reddens. "John! For fuck's sake! What was the one condition of you moving in?"

"That I wouldn't breathe?"

"Yeah, and you bloody broke that agreement too, didn't you?"

I shrug. "You know, Penny mentioned Lola was at her wits' end. What did she mean by that?"

"She meant you're a twat. Anyway, what else did Penny say? I don't suppose you saw her before she left for work?"

"She didn't go to work," I say, without thinking. "She went to the gynaecologist." Oh look, the can is open, and the worms are free.

"What? How do you know?"

"She told me. Over Rice Krispies. It really added the snap, crackle and pop, I have to say. She crackled, I nearly snapped, and my eardrums almost popped." I watch Simon carefully. "I'm guessing you knew nothing about this?"

He shakes his head. "Why does my wife tell you and not me that she's going to the gynaecologist?"

I lean back in my chair. This is a damn good point. I genuinely thought Simon knew. In fact, Penny gave me the impression the whole street was fully conversant with the nature of her gynaecological condition. She went on and on about it until the milk in my bowl began to curdle and I was faced with the choice of either abandoning my cereal, or vomiting in it.

"Simon, can we talk about this later?"

"No we fucking can't. I want to know what she's going for. Is she pregnant or something?" He recoils as he thinks it through. "Please, not a baby." Now I recoil on his behalf, and the imaginary baby's.

I glance left and right. People are pretending they aren't looking at us. If we say anymore, it'll be all over the office in seconds. This is, after all, a room full of journalists.

"I have to go and meet with somebody at five. Meet me in the City at six."

"No. Tell me now."

"Six o' clock or never. Your call."

Sometimes there's no choice but to play hardball, even if people can't see it's for their own good. Simon will thank me for this later.

For now he opens his mouth to protest, but knows me well enough to realise I don't make idle threats. "Six o' clock."

He stomps off towards his desk, swearing not quite under his breath, and I know it's going to be an even longer day for him than it is for me.

When I'm finally left as much to my own devices as one can possibly be in a room containing about a hundred people they mostly don't like, I dial again.

She answers the phone in her work voice, the one that makes her sound as though the ringing has woken her up and she's wondering where she is, or that she had no idea there was a phone on her desk in the first place.

"Lola Martinez, can I help you?"

"That all depends," I say, unable to halt the smile trickling across my face.

"John?" She says this in a tone bordering on disbelief.

"Hi."

"Hello."

There is a considerable, but strangely comforting silence. I am reluctant to break the pleasant tension, but curiosity gets the better of me. It keeps doing that, and I must work on it. "I got a message to call you."

"What? Oh yes, yes. I rang you yesterday, but Sarah – I think her name was Sarah, or Susan – told me you were off sick." She hesitates. "Are you okay?"

She still cares – I note this. "Yeah," I say noncommittally. I took a few days off. You know how it is."

"Yes." She doesn't know how it is. "I need to speak to you about something. Can we meet up tonight?"

My stomach flips over. I attribute this to some kind of panic reflex. "I can't. I'm meeting Andrea."

"Who's Andrea?"

"You know Andrea."

"No, obviously I don't, or I wouldn't have asked," she says crisply.

I'm tempted to smile again. Not only has she called me, she's also jealous. Better than that, she's jealous of a middleaged senior civil servant whom we've had round for dinner on several occasions for no other reason than because we should, and whose number I keep in my Rolodex under 'L' for 'Leak'.

"Andrea is nobody," I say, being purposefully dismissive, a skill I picked up in the womb. "I can meet you tomorrow?"

She sighs. "Okay. Six o'clock?"

"I'm going to be working really late tomorrow. How about we meet at lunchtime?"

"Are you sure you can fit me in?" Now she's being caustic. It's a shame there's not a caustic tournament in the Olympics – Lola would get this country its first gold.

"Don't be like that. One o' clock, you pick where."

She comes back immediately with, "The park."

"I'll see you there. Bye."

"John?"

"What?"

A silence, two beats long. I'm counting.

"Nothing. See you tomorrow."

A click, and my connection with her is severed.

It's going to be a day of Guinness World Record length.

'Nothing'. 'Nothing' is bad. 'Nothing' is the double-syllable equivalent of 'fine'. 'Nothing' bothers me. I turn 'nothing' over in my mind all day and end up doing exactly that.

She called me. She wants to meet up. She wants to talk about 'something', but then there's also that "nothing." I scroll through the options of what they could be. Maybe she's not angry anymore. Maybe she's over the anger part, and now just wants revenge. Or perhaps she's over the rage, and has sunk into a deep depression – maybe she wants to show me the marks on her arms where she's been self-harming. No, not Lola. Knowing her, it could very well be just nothing. It could be, "Can you put some money on my mobile for me?" or "What's the password for my Yahoo mail?" Or… Oh God, I know what it is. Enough time has passed for her to stop hating me, and she's realised she misses me – she misses me, misses talking to me, telling me about her day, snuggling up to me in bed at night, and she's lost without someone to undo jars and unscrew the top from the Tropicana carton. So now she wants us to get back together. That's what she's going to say, isn't it? That's her bombshell, only she's trying to lead me off the scent by tacking it on almost as though it's – ha! – nothing. Shit.

My brain starts to spin with endless park scenarios that involve Lola crying again, and me praying no one I know walks past. By the end of my reverie she's clinging onto my calves, wailing, and I've got my hands in my pockets as I try to shake her off, whistling to mask the noise. I hate scenes, especially public ones. We've been through the crying thing once, and by God I will not go through it again. I have to be vigilant. I must stick to the plan. So she misses me – let her miss me. I might even tell her I miss her. Just a bit. An infinitesimal amount. Yeah, I might throw her that bone, just to make her feel better.

Okay, if I don't regain control of myself I'll end up spending the whole day drinking cup after cup of synthetic coffee. I check my watch. The day is still salvageable.

I click the mouse and find out what the markets are up to, and soon my desk is covered in textbooks, web pages, and briefing documents. I make a few phone calls, turning on the charm, relieved to find it's still there and still appears to work. I plough through my feature, pretending I can't feel Simon's eyes boring a hole into the back of my skull. I'm grateful for small mercies when he slopes off to a launch by some cosmetics company or other for the remainder of the afternoon. If only Valerie Perkins had found somewhere suitable to disappear to, my day might even have been enjoyable in the sense that at least I'm not dead.

When I see her coming, I decide a visit from the Grim Reaper may in fact be preferable.

Valerie Perkins has worked here, by all accounts, since the beginning of time. Allegedly, she's thirty-six, but from the look of her that clearly must mean in dog years. Yes, I know, I'm harsh. But Valerie Perkins can give as good as she gets, which is one of the many, many reasons – oh I could blog myself into a stupor writing about her – why I hate her so much.

She's supposed to be our 'lifestyle editor', which immediately puts she and I into direct conflict, as I find this a source of both hilarity and ridicule. 'Lifestyle'? Who has a 'lifestyle'? For most of us, it's a happy accident rather than a style. Valerie, for her part, maintains that economics is dull and pointless, and on many occasions I've agreed with her, saying that techniques for de-junking your wardrobe are indeed much more worthy of the nation's attention than the fact that the price of petrol is currently eighty-five thousand pounds a gallon.

It sickens me that Lola and Valerie are best friends, and it sickens me even more that it's all my fault. They met at the first Christmas party I went to when I joined the paper, which I only bothered with because Simon told me it would be a laugh. And it was a laugh. It was such a laugh that I left Lola to her own devices pretty much all night, and who knew her devices included the ability to befriend the barnacle-faced raptor that is Valerie Perkins.

"John."

"Val."

She screws her face up. She hates it when I call her that.

I wonder what she and Lola talk about. They are polar extremes; they have nothing in common and it should not be possible for them to be friends. Valerie Perkins is like a Christmas tree weighed down with too much tinsel, whilst Lola is like freshly fallen snow, unblemished by anything not attributed to nature. If Lola is a clear blue sky, then Valerie is grey, overcast and threatening rain. Or perhaps even hail.

"Someone looks busy," she says, curling her lips as she surveys the contents of my desk.

Now I guess Lola and Valerie have something in common at last – me, and what a bastard I am. Lola will have told her about the break-up, and the party, and Valerie's probably been dying to come over here and stick the boot in. And maybe not just the boot, perhaps a fist or two and some fingernails as well.

"Looks can be deceiving."

"Can't they just," she says, her arms folded, towering over me like the Statue of Liberty, but with a stonier face. Here it comes. I wait for her to say something derogatory, or simply deploy a good old-fashioned insult. I imagine the hours Lola has spent on the phone to her, crying on her shoulder – Jesus, she might even be staying with her. Valerie – Lola would kill me for calling it this, but it's factually correct – has a spinster-pad in Chiswick. Lola could well be kipping in the poky box room next to Valerie's, listening to her snoring as she tries to go to sleep every night, and dodging Valerie's knickers drying on the shower rail while she brushes her teeth in the mornings. That thought is a video nasty.

Valerie licks her lips, flicking out her tongue like a gecko. She makes me wish I kept garlic, holy water, a crucifix, a wooden stake, a silver bullet and a tetanus vaccine in my desk drawer. I'd use them all at the same time, just to be sure.

"I see they're still finding some barely plausible reason to continue employing you." She picks up one of the many papers scattered on my desk. "I mean, really, John...."

"Really what?" Go on Val, I dare you.

"What's this – the 'balance of payments'?" She says this scornfully, and all of sudden I'm so defensive of the balance of payments, it's as though I've invented it myself. "Does anyone really care? I mean, honestly?"

"The government does. The Bank of England does. The private sector does. Need I go on?"

"Oh God, don't. What about the man on the street though? Does he care?"

Please don't ask me if I care. Then I really might be lost for words.

"Probably more than he does about the Vitamin A diet. Really, Val, that was genius. Best work you've done in ages. The nation can sleep easily in their beds at night and not worry about a thing. Is there a Vitamin B diet too? Vitamin Q?"

Valerie scowls, screwing up her face. "You know, John, you're not as clever as you think you are. You'll get your comeuppance one day."

"I wasn't aware I'd asked for it."

"Oh don't worry, I have. On your behalf." I believe her. She drops the balance of payments back down onto my desk. "I hope you are as devoted to Lola as you are to your pointless economic endeavours."

My ears prick up. She said "are." Present tense. Did I hear that right?

This could be a trap. If I tell her I am as, or more devoted to Lola, she'll erupt and demand to know why I finished with her then. If I say that I pay more attention to my work, she'll launch into a torrent of abuse about how I let my relationship erode into disrepair and didn't do anything to stop it. It's like playing a casual game of chess with Garry Kasparov – I cannot win, whatever move I make. Women turned professional at this sport many hundreds of years ago. Realising this is very important. Rule number one: admit defeat early, while you can. Leave it too late and it's a slow and painful death.

So, I deliver a curt "Valerie, I really don't think it would be appropriate to compare Lola to a set of economic data," and get my head down, pretending to be overly interested in the 'Monthly Review of Trade Statistics', which suddenly, I am. Compared to Valerie Perkins, it's riveting.

It works on one level as Valerie doesn't say anything else, but she's still standing over me. My muscles clench of their own accord. Please, whatever she's going to say, let it be under two hundred decibels. I hate being embroiled in enforced histrionics. I have my reputation to think of.

"Tell Lola to give me a call. I can't seem to reach her."

Valerie walks away to grate somebody else's nerves, and I put my head down on top of the balance of payments, marvelling at what a superb cushion they make.

So, Lola hasn't told her. I don't know whether to be ecstatic, or insulted. Either Lola deigns our break-up too trivial to bother her best friend with, or there is some other reason. I scrap the first option as ludicrous. Surely, it's ludicrous? She was upset - I saw it for myself. And women love analysing things – they fucking live for it, they organise whole evenings out around it. So why hasn't she told her? But, you know, God himself is probably at a loss when it comes to feminine logic, and he created them. Boy, did they outsmart him.

I shrug, for effect only as everyone is far too busy to waste time watching me, even Sarah, so I get back to work. Rule number one: know when to admit defeat.

The afternoon whizzes by in a slow sort of way, and I managed to avoid any further encounters with Valerie, Sarah, or, well, anyone really. In fact, I'm almost having a nice time surfing Ebay until…

"Johnny! How's it going, old boy?"

The slap of a fat hand on my shoulder blade can only, unfortunately, mean one thing.

"Hey, Charlie."

Charlie folds his arms high on his chest, his fingers tucked into his armpits. "How's my favourite economics editor?" Charlie has a habit of saying the opposite of what he really means. "We keeping you busy?" He really does mean that bit.

"Well, you know how it is, Charlie, there's always something going on."

"Ah yes – balance of payments for me today, right?"

"Right."

"I take it we're all good to go?"

I click off Ebay and switch back to Word, hitting print. I point over at the machine where paper is slowly churning out of it. Charlie snatches it and scans the first few lines.

"Good, excellent." He looks at me. "So what're we saying?"

"Inflation's going down. Interest rate cut."

"We're saying that for sure?"

"Yes," I say.

Charlie goes back to my feature. "Are we saying when?"

I hate all this 'we' business. Yes, this is a newspaper, yes, we're a collective, but the only inflation Charlie knows about is the kind that happens when he uses his penis pump. He thinks the balance of payments is something to do with his wife's numerous credit cards, and as for interest rates, well, they only enter the black hole he orbits when he realises he has less money to spend on lap dancers and Viagra.

"Next month. MPC meets on the first."

Charlie smiles. "Excellent, you're sticking your neck out."

"Yes," I say. "We are."

His smile fades. "Well, let's hope you get it right this time. You looked like a prize prat last month, and that reflects badly on the paper, and then on me."

I notice Valerie's head pop up from behind her computer like a meerkat, a big smug grin on her reptilian face. At least, that's what I think it's supposed to be.

"I'm sure. They'll cut by a quarter of a percent. Trust me."

"Trust you?" Charlie snorts. "You've got to be fucking joking. Give me something snappy to read about the US housing market by close tomorrow."

I open my mouth.

"No buts, Johnny boy," he says, walking back to the glass box at the far end of the floor that he calls his office. "It's what you're paid for."

Apparently, it is.

I mull it over as I wander through the City. When I first decided I was going to be a journalist, it was all about making a difference, empowering people. Now it seems to be about typing enough words to fill my space on the page, logging off, and getting paid. When did I become so jaded? Round about when I realised no one really cared about what I have to say, and shortly after I realised I am constantly justifying my own existence. I thought of myself as an idealist, a romantic, when the words I was actually looking for were 'deluded' and 'pillock'. I thought I could create a world where people had more of an understanding about what our dear old government is up to, and more control over their finances, but it seems no one really wants that. They just want to get drunk, have sex, and buy houses they can't afford so they can get drunk and have sex in them.

I walk up Bishopsgate, and head into our usual haunt. Andrea likes this place because it's right near the station, which means she can jump on the train and get home in time for her basket-making class or whatever it is she does on a Thursday evening. I weave through the throng of people, wishing we weren't meeting on the busiest night of the week, and order a Scotch and Coke for myself, and a Cosmopolitan for her. The barman has trouble understanding what I'm saying, both because it's so loud in here, and also because I'm speaking English. Eventually he hands me something that definitely has enough Scotch in it for my purposes, and something pink in a cocktail glass. Given that she hardly ever drinks alcohol and that Cosmopolitans taste like WD-40 anyway, Andrea will be none the wiser.

I find a free table in the corner through luck rather than skill, and sit down gratefully. I take a generous sip of my Scotch – I've earned it today, and enjoy the satisfying burn. I could quite happily settle in here for the night to watch the circus unfold: women flirting with men, women ignoring men, women deciding whether to flirt with men or ignore men. The game's the same, but the rules have changed. And, I admit, somewhat reluctantly, I'm going to need someone to teach me. And that person, I think as I stand up to greet her, is most definitely not Andrea.

"John!"

She waves at me, the skin on her upper arm waving as well, and she comes over, wearing – God, what is she wearing?

"John…" she says again, totally unnecessarily. "So nice to see you."

She insists on kissing me on both cheeks, possibly because reading 'Heat' is her guilty pleasure and she secretly longs to be something called a WAG rather than an ageing mother of three who works for the Treasury. She looks me up and down unashamedly. "You look so…"

"Tall?"

"No, so good!" She beams at me. "I swear you look better every time I see you." She waits for me to reciprocate.

"Thanks. Shall we?"

"Oh, of course." She folds herself into the chair – it's the only way she can fit in it – and her jewellery, which looks as though it originated from Zimbabwe or somewhere like that, knocks together, making her sound like a human snooker table.

"Is that for me?" She reaches for her drink. "Ooh, my favourite." I hope it still is after she's tasted it. "So, how's Lola? Gorgeous thing that she is."

"She's fine." I don't explain. Probably because I can't explain. Especially when she puts it like that.

I hate that we have to go through this rigmarole, but I suppose her bi-monthly flirtation with me is about as exciting as her life gets. I know this because I met her husband once. It was like talking to a stuffed deer-head. And I should know. Simon and I tried it at some posh function we were forced to attend and, happily, were never invited back to.

"How's life treating you?" I ask, although I have no interest in her life whatsoever and hope she doesn't go into details.

She takes an overly ambitious sip of her drink, which causes some of it to trickle down her chin. "I – ooh, sorry!"

I smile weakly, remembering how she did the very same thing with a cup of espresso I made after we'd eaten dinner at the house. Lola gave me a glance of pure revulsion as Andrea had dribbled coffee from her mouth, and onto the tablecloth. We had laughed about it in bed later that night (Lola was only able to laugh once the stain had completely washed out. Before then, it was almost tears). I resent Andrea for dredging up the memory.

"Well, the kids are away at school now, so the house is really quiet. It's just Dan and me, but most of the time he's working. It's terrible. I feel cut off from everyone."

I nod again, concentrating really hard to stop my eyes from rolling, and to stop myself from reminding Andrea that she lives in Ruislip, not Rwanda.

"I guess he has to do his job," I reply, which is euphemism of the decade as thanks to a combination of her husband's hard work, her parents, and some shrewd investments, Andrea has more money than the Bank of England and takes more holidays than the CEO of Thomas Cook. Her house is worth more than the GDP of Luxembourg.

"Yes," she concedes with a sigh. "But it's hard. I get so lonely." She gazes into the bottom of her glass of pink-coloured piss, for a second or two, swirling the stick with what I think is supposed to be an olive on the end of it. "Anyway, you don't want to hear about my problems." I cannot dispute this, so I don't bother. Her smile falters ever so slightly. "I suppose you want to hear the latest," she says.

"That's why we're here." I dilute my impatience with a smile.

"I suppose we are. You and Lola must come round for dinner one night. We haven't had you round ours ages – the kids would love to see you. Shall I email you with some dates?"

"That would be great." It wouldn't be great at all, not to mention impossible, but I can worry about that when I need to. Plus, there's always the delete button. "So, what news do you have for me?"

Andrea glances around nervously. "Okay, but remember-"

"You'll be a 'source'. I promise."

"I mean it, John. They're really tightening up in there. If they find out, I'm for it. I'm doing this because no one's expecting it. I thought if you put the idea out there that interest rates are going up, it might help to-"

"What?"

"What's what?"

I resist the urge to bounce the olive off her forehead. "Interest rates."

"Oh, yes. That's what I was going to tell you. Revised inflation figures. It's up, way above target. Three point five percent. So it's looking certain that interest rates are going up next month."

Jesus fuck bollocks shit.

"Pardon?"

"Nothing." I drain my Scotch. "No one's called that one."

"I know," Andrea says, her eyes wide. "That's why I thought it would be good to tell you, so you can call it. It won't be such a shock for the markets then, eh? And," she smiles, "you'll look terribly clever. Which of course you are, but you know what I mean."

My glass is now empty. My stomach is somewhere around my shoes, and my head is beginning to hurt. All in all, an average night for me. "Can I get you another?" Naturally what I mean is, "Isn't it time you went home?"

"What? Oh, no. I should probably go, really. I have to catch my train, and it's cross-stitching tonight."

I smile, even though I have absolutely no idea what that is. Andrea tips her glass back and downs the whole thing, some of it even going in her mouth.

"Mmm, that was yum." Her pupils are already dilating. I pity poor Dan tonight, I really do. "So," she gets up, wobbling on her feet. "I'll email you about dinner, and – ooh, I can't see properly! – we'll get together soon, yes?"

I do something that could be construed as a nod, but not enough to be counted as evidence against me. "Bye, Andrea. And thanks."

"Oh no, thank you, John. You'll be doing everyone a big favour, not to mention your career. See you!"

Yeah, in hell.

Andrea's departure gives me time to think, or, as it's more commonly known in melancholic circles, brood. I stare into my drink – the ice has melted already – and see the ghost of John Black past, the one who swaggered around London like he, yes, owned it, the one who was determined, confident, the one who broke his balls and countless other pairs not belonging to him along the way to get his column in a national. An economics column, with his name at the top, in big, bold 'here I am world' letters. Trouble is, the ghost of John Black present now wonders if it was worth it. But that column, and economics, is what I'm infamous for, it's part of my identity. Take that away, and I'm not sure there'd be anything left.

God, that's depressing.

"Excuse me… Hey… Hey!"

It takes me a few seconds to realise it's my attention she wants.

"Hey, hi. Um, do you have a light? Oh, you just seem the type," she explains, when I look at her quizzically. "I just need to-" she gestures her hands in the general direction of outside, the smoker's version of *Give Us a Clue*. Four words, fourth word sounds like 'shag'. I pass her my lighter – usually, I would never do this, but then, usually, I am not approached by attractive women. It's the night for exceptions.

"Thanks – oh, cool, one of those snappy ones."

"A Zippo."

"Uh-huh," she says, as though it was on the tip of her tongue the whole time. "See," she grins, rather cheekily, "I'm never wrong."

"You should play the lottery."

"Huh? No, not with like, everything, just about smokers. I knew you'd smoke. You have the look about you."

I have to ask. "And what look's that?"

"Twitchy." She demonstrates. "Like this, see?"

"I look like I have Parkinson's?"

She laughs. "No! Not at all. Why do you? Of course you don't. No, you look like you don't know what to do with your hands. Like you're used to doing something with them that you can no longer do."

Annoyingly, Lola pops into my head. Lola's fingers, her hands. I did like holding her hand, despite what she claims.

I liked touching her. I liked reaching for her. I shake it off. I press pause.

"See," the woman says, tapping the side of her nose, "I'm never wrong about it."

"Well, that's a very useful talent you have there. You should probably go smoke while the lighter's hot."

She considers me for a few seconds. "You're funny, in a sarcastic, acquired taste kind of way."

I shrug. "It's the only way to be funny."

"I'll bring this back," she says, holding my lighter up in front of me, as though she's about to do a magic trick with it. I hope she isn't. I hate magic. It sucks the fun out of meaningless happenstance.

"Take as much time as you need."

"Thanks, you're an angel." If only she knew. "Hey," she turns back. "You look familiar – do I know you from somewhere? Who cuts your hair?"

"Are those questions related?"

"Sorry. Bad habit. I'll be back," she says, and it's more of a pledge than a parting shot.

I watch her go, deliberately not eyeing up her curves, as she doesn't have any. She's tall, possibly a little taller than Lola, and she has a more boyish figure. Her hair is a little longer. Lola doesn't have a fringe, but she has better cheekbones. It's heaving in here now, and the woman has to squeeze herself and my lighter between several groups of drunk men, none of whom utters a word of protest, although the one with the bald head who calls her "darlin'" does look slightly deflated when she tells him to "fuck right off." I allow myself a little smile. God, where've I been? I was busy growing old and senile while all of this, all of this cavorting and animal behaviour and borrowing of lighters was taking place in bars like this all over the country.

I stretch my legs out and decide to indulge myself in one of my many intricate and detailed flights of fantasy.

This one, which could be up there with my personal favourites, involves me owning a bar like this, except it's my imagination so of course it's bigger, more exclusive, has a higher turnover than Apple, and not only does everybody know my name and is always glad I came, they also admire and fawn over me. And yes, it does enable me to pull a vast quantity of women. Here's how it goes.

"So, John, what do you do?" one of these women says as she reclines on a velvet couch next to me.

"Actually," John takes a sip of his champagne, and leans in a little closer, so she can smell a hint of it on his breath, "you see this place?" He gestures to the lavish surroundings.

"Yes…" She's hanging on his every word, unable to believe he's here with her, looking into her eyes.

"I own it," he says – coolly, and calmly. Perfect delivery.

She gasps, although now it's out there, she realises she expected nothing less. He's so cool and sophisticated – of course he owns this bar. Now, if only he would take her into one of the rooms upstairs and-

"Oi!"

Simon's standing in front of me, clicking his fingers in front of my face. It's a cruel comedown, a bitter reality check.

"Didn't you see me waving?"

"No."

He rolls his eyes dramatically. He learned from the master. "Budge up, fatty." He plonks himself down next to me – Simon will not sit opposite anyone, he hates it, for reasons he has yet to explain satisfactorily. One of his many weird quirks. He puts two glasses down onto the table.

"Can I ask why?"

"The beer's for good news," he says, "the whisky's for bad. You can have whichever one I don't need. Now talk."

"All right." I rub my chin. "Pen-"

"Don't rub your chin! You always do it when you're about to say something unpleasant!"

"Shall I rub my eye instead and lie to you?"

"Rub your arse for all I care," he says.

"Okay then." I rub my chin. I can't help it. Simon scowls at me. "Penny told me she's been getting back pains, and blood in her urine."

"Blood in her piss?"

I wince. "In a medical context, and coming out of your wife, it's urine."

"Piss, urine, who gives a shit? So to speak. Go on."

"Right. So naturally, after I'd thrown up several thousand times and cleaned out my ears with bleach, I asked her if it could be a kidney infection-"

"Woah, hang on." Simon holds his palms up. "How do you know that?"

"I lived with a woman for over eight years."

"I live with a woman!"

"Can I finish?"

"Go fucking on!"

"So, Penny says she thinks it might be a kidney infection, but she's never been in this much pain before, so her GP sent her to the hospital for tests."

"What kind of tests?"

"Simon, it was breakfast time, and she's your wife. There's a limit to my polite curiosity. Also, my vomit was feeling nauseous by that point and I couldn't listen any more."

"Fuck." Simon pours the whisky down the back of his throat, wincing as it burns a path towards his stomach. "Why did she confide in you?"

I do have a theory about this, and decide to share it with my friend. "Maybe it was easier. Maybe she didn't know how to tell you, so she figured she'd tell me instead, as I'd inevitably pass it on. For want of a better phrase."

"But why can't she tell me? It's just weird."

"I don't know. She's your wife." I want to add "thankfully", but don't.

Simon's moon face sags. "What you were saying the other say, about Penny not being happy…"

Shit. "Hey, that was nothing. I could've been imagining things. I do it all the time."

He gives me a 'fuck off' look. I would only take a look like that from him, and under these circumstances. "She's not happy, is she?"

I shrug. Generally, Penny's never seemed particularly happy. The day I met her she had a face like her team had been relegated four divisions and stripped of the FA Cup. Even on their wedding day I recall the photographer saying to her, "Cheer up love, it might never happen," failing to understand that it just did.

"What can I do?"

I remove his hand from my wrist. "I might not be the best person to come to for advice." Simon nods sagely as he realises that's probably true. "But, you know, talking about it never hurt anyone."

"That's not what you said to me before."

"Okay, I'll rephrase: talking about it never hurt a woman. They love it. You'll get a pasting, but just take it. Agree that you're a total shit and it'll all blow over by the morning."

Simon's staring at me, utterly unconvinced, but then I'd be the same if I was getting relationship advice from me. "You know what, mate, you could be vaguely right. I'll talk to her. Let her vent. Whatever it is, we can sort it out."

"That's the spirit."

"Yeah." Simon drains his glass, wiping his mouth on the back of his hand. "I'm offski then. Give us a while, eh?"

"Sure. And Si?"

"Mate?"

"Here." I toss him a packet of gum. "You know she hates it when you 'smell like a brewery.'"

"Oh. Yeah. Cheers mate."

"No problem. No problem at all."

I don't really want another drink, especially not in here. It's now full of people who are old enough to know better, but are busy pretending they're still young enough not to care. It's a meat market, and while it's interesting on an anthropological level, after the conversation I've just had with Simon, I'm not in the mood. I could find a café somewhere, get a coffee or a chocomochalatte or whatever it is they serve these days, get the laptop out and make a start on this piece Charlie wants me to write, even though I know it's purely for his own entertainment and he won't use it. It'd do me good to focus, to knuckle down and concentrate on what I allegedly do best, give it one hundred percent, like the old days, instead of inevitably leaving it until the last minute. Yeah, that's what I should do. I pick up my stuff and head for the exit. Ah, but fuck it. I do a u-turn, and go back to the bar.

"Bottle of Bud, please."

The barman leans in closer and cups a hand behind his ear, an indication that he either wants me to speak louder, or he's going to insert a Babelfish in his ear to translate for him.

"Budweiser."

I stand there for a bit, picking at the label on the bottle. It's weird being here by myself. Usually Lola would be with me or, at the very least, waiting for me at home, or out herself, thinking about me. Still, she might be thinking about me now. It's a possibility. She's probably wondering what I'm doing, who I'm doing it with. I wonder what she'd say if she could see me now. Probably, "that tie doesn't go with that shirt." I glance down at it. Actually, Lola, it does. It's edgy. It's modern. And you bought it for me.

"First sign of madness."

"Huh?"

"Talking to yourself. Here, your lighter. It's very cool, by the way."

It's her. All fringe, height, big eyes, and everything that isn't Lola.

"Thanks."

"You buying?"

"Leaving."

She eyes me suspiciously. As well she should. "Looks like it." She licks her lips. "Rebecca Speller." She holds out her hand. Her nails are short and clean. Lola's are – oh, for fuck's sake.

"John Black."

Her eyes widen, and I wonder if she's seen me on Youtube doing something dubious. "As in 'In the Black'?"

"Uh-huh."

"Oh my God, I love your column!"

I try not to look flattered, or pleased, but can't manage to bypass surprised. "Thanks."

"Actually, everyone I know reads it."

"That says a lot about your choice of friends."

"What? Oh…" She nudges me, like we've known each other for however long it takes to be acerbic, amusing and, yeah, flirtatious. "Don't be so modest."

"Who says I was being modest?"

Rebecca turns and looks at me – I mean really scrutinising, as though she's about to sweat a confession out of me. If she keeps it up, it might just work.

"I think, under that arrogant exterior, you are quite modest. I think, John Black, this is all a front."

"Oh really?"

"Yes," she says, titling her chin upwards, defying me to disagree. "And you know what," she starts rummaging around in her bag, and I'm hoping she's not searching for a pair of pliers and some cheese wire. "I know you'll never call me, but… Here." She emerges not with an instrument of torture, but a business card. She tucks it into the top pocket of my jacket. I don't flinch when she moves in close to me, but I want to.

"You'll never call, but otherwise I'll never know. Now this is my opportunity to be really cool for once, so…" she picks up my beer and takes a long swig. "Goodbye. John Black."

She turns on her heel and leaves me with a wry smile on my face. I take her card out of my pocket, where it's already burning a hole. Rebecca Speller – artist. That figures.

"Hey. Rebecca."

She hears me – just – and spins around slowly. "You've ruined my exit."

"You'll never know what?"

Rebecca goes to fire back a reply instantly, and then changes her mind. Her face breaks into a grin. "If you why but she's an artist and we all know they're a bit weird, salutes, and slips off into the crowd. She's right, I won't call. I leave her card on the bar, along with my beer. I head out into the City to do what I do best. To be alone.

I take the long route back to Simon's, to give them time to argue and me time to think. It was easy with Lola – she made it easy. When I first saw her she was standing by herself, back against the wall, a glass in her hand, a straw pressed between her lips. Going over and talking to her seemed like the most logical thing in the world. I didn't think about what might happen next, whether she might reject me, slap me around the face, or give me a polite "thanks but no thanks" – none of that stuff. She was the most beautiful girl at the party – that I had ever seen, and I was compelled to go and introduce myself by an urge I still don't really understand. Even after I'd made some crummy opening gambit and she'd looked at me like I was the dumbest man alive, it still didn't matter, because she was looking at me. The most beautiful girl at the party, in the world, was giving me her attention. And I swore I'd work hard for more of it, I'd fight for it, I would do anything, everything, it took it to keep her attention, and then I promised, I would never, ever, let her go.

And then I woke up one day, and everything she did began to get on my nerves. The clothes strewn all over the floor, the pots and potions in the bathroom that I'm not sure even she knew what to do with, borrowing my fucking razor and leaving it so blunt I ended up severing an artery the next time I used it, and those stupid bloody magazines all over the coffee table. That morning, I woke up and I couldn't breathe. I resented all of it, everything that was 'ours'. What about me? Who am I? I loved Lola – I love Lola, but she was suffocating me. Every word she said irritated me, and I just wanted out, sweet, glorious out. And so, here I am. As usual, I got exactly what I wanted.

The bus comes to another stop and a woman with a young child gets on. I smile at her and she clutches her kid's hand tightly, giving me a glare conveying her disgust. Ah, well, you can't win them all. I pull myself to my feet, let her have my seat, and I still don't go up in her estimation. She scowls at me, her arm protectively around the child's shoulders as I go down the stairs. I feel her eyes boring into the back of my neck, and it's fine, I know how it is. Protect what's yours. I'd be the same, I'm sure I would, if I was that way inclined, and if I had anything to protect. I get off the bus, and as soon as my feet hit the pavement I reach for my cigarettes. When my hand touches the packet, I almost smile.

I walk up the street, just me and my cigarette, and come within sight of the house. There's a light on downstairs, which means Simon and Penny are probably both in the lounge. The plan is that I slink in, and then sneak upstairs to the room they have so kindly lent to me, without them noticing, and hope I don't get hit by any flying objects en route. I've still got a bruise on my shoulder from the last round.

I take great care to flick my cigarette butt into Penny's hanging basket, although there's a little pile of them in there now, and discovery is surely only a day or so away. As I step inside, I'm slightly puzzled to find the house in complete silence. Either there's been a temporary lull in negotiations, or they've reached a stalemate. Or – please God no – they're upstairs making up for lost time. Whichever way, I have to find out. I hang my jacket over the banister, and tentatively poke my head around the lounge door.

"Si?"

He doesn't answer. He's slumped in an armchair, shoulders hunched over, his fingers loosely cradling a tumbler of whisky, his other hand covering his eyes, as though it's shielding him from some imaginary sun. At first, I think his body is shuddering spasmodically because he's laughing. When he looks up as I enter the room and I see his face, it slowly registers that he's not laughing. He's not laughing at all.

I've never seen Simon cry. It's disturbing. It's unnerving. I want him to stop, immediately, right this second. I want rewind this whole scene, to erase it from my memory so I can pretend I was never here and I didn't see it, and that my best friend isn't crying his heart out over something I might not be able to fix.

I'm not even sure he's knows I'm here. I stand there like a prize plum, trying to think of something to say other than, "What the fuck happened to you?" I thought I was good with words, but recent events seem to have proved otherwise. Well, like my old Dad used to say, it's better to say something than nothing.

"What the fuck happened to you?"

Well, at least he stops crying. Kind of. It's hard to tell as when he looks at me his fat face is still sort of scrunched up, and there's this weird snot stuff on it.

"You're back then," he says.

"Yeah."

He wipes his face, which is a relief. It's like cleaning up the blood at a murder scene – disposing of evidence, if you like. He bites his lip, but the tears spill down his face regardless. "I did what you said."

My heart sinks. That is never a good thing to hear, especially when someone's crying.

"I talked to her," he says. "To Penny. Well, she talked mainly. I listened. Well, I tried to, then she-"

Fuck. I sit down beside him. He leans on me, his body racked with sobs.

"Take your time, mate. It's okay."

That works. His body stops shaking then. He looks at me, narrowing his eyes a little, as though I'm completely mad.

"It's not fucking okay, 'mate.'" He takes a big swig of his drink. "She's fucking pregnant."

I'm not quick enough. He sees my look of horror before I can do anything about it, before I can force my unwilling face into something approaching a smile. And, as it happens, I'm glad he does.

"Yeah, and that's not the best bit, John."

No, please – not twins.

"What?"

Simon juts out his jaw, biting his top lip. His eyes go the mantelpiece, to the photograph from their wedding day in which Penny looks depressed and he looks drunk. Yes, it's true – the camera really can't tell a lie.

"It's not mine, John. She's up the duff, and it's not mine." He turns to me, holds my gaze for a few seconds. And I'm embarrassed – I feel guilty, like I'm the one pregnant with someone else's kid. Then he starts laughing, a horrible, maniacal sound, and suddenly crying and tears are old friends I miss dearly and want back.

"Si… Simon."

"What? I'll fucking kill him, John. I'll find him, and I will kill him." He drains his glass.

Simon has watched 'Taken' too many times.

"No, you won't."

"Pour me another one."

"I think you've had enough."

"Too fucking right I've had enough! I've had more than enough – how is this fair, John? How? Did I not do everything for that woman? And then she does this to me, she-"

He can't finish. The tears have returned. I've got no answers for him, nothing to say, no words of wisdom to take the sting out. I can only put my arm around his shoulder, and just be there. It's the least I can do. Or, maybe, the most I can do.

6

It's now apparent why Lola wanted to meet me here instead of a café, a pub, a good-for-all-purposes Pizza Express, or any other venue a normal person would choose to hold an uncomfortable conversation in. Lola though, isn't normal. She's far too smart, much too quick for me. So we're meeting here, in the park – yes, not 'a' park, but 'the' park, the very one where we had our first kiss. Oh well done, Lola, spectacular. You get a perfect ten for imagination, and off the fucking scale for genius.

I'm sitting on the bench that's tattooed with the least amount of pigeon shit, my arms stretched along the back of the seat, as though I'm about to be crucified. And I might very well be – who knows? To my left a couple of fat kids, possibly French, are feeding the ducks, hopefully British, although they seem to be lobbing more of the stale bread into each other's mouths than at the lake. In front of them, next to me, a few tourists are taking turns to photograph themselves in various choreographed formations beside a bored-looking pelican. After each click they cluster around the camera screen to ooh and aah at their own faces. Why anyone wants enough megapixels to see life in such crystal clear detail is beyond me. It's better viewed from a distance, a little blurry, the edges not quite in focus.

And then, to my right, is the spot, the section of London where it first happened. It should be cordoned off – someone should stick one of those blue plaques there, just so everyone knows. Nine years ago, Lola and I stood on that very bit of gravel, and I took her unconvinced face in my shaky hands and I told her I loved her. She'd frowned and said, "You only met me twelve hours ago, you moron. And you're drunk." Naturally, slurring my words, I told her I wasn't drunk at all. Not in the way she implied, anyway. I knew what I was saying, and what I was doing. The alcohol simply served to speed everything up for me, giving me that unique clarity. I knew I would love that woman – I knew it without a flicker of hesitation. It was there, right in front of me, in her brown eyes: The 'big L,' the be-all-and-end-all, the one thing I never, ever expected to find. Especially not at a party in Archway.

So this is outstanding, a real masterstroke. Coming back to this place for a post break-up post-mortem feels almost like a pilgrimage. It even seems rude and disrespectful to smoke here. It'd be like lighting up a fat one next to the Shroud of Turin, or the Mona Lisa. This place is just as precious. From here I can see us both with our arms around each other, flushed with the excitement of something new beginning. It's so clear, it's as though it's happening all over again.

If it were, what would I change?

I'm gnawing my thumbnail when I hear the familiar sound of Lola's heels clicking on the ground. I'd know those steps anywhere – confident, but uncertain. A perfect summation of Lola Martinez. I hold my breath.

She spots me, and lifts her hand to wave, but not terribly enthusiastically. I stand up, hands in pockets, willing to bite the head off a nearby pigeon for a solitary puff on a cigarette – I don't even care whose cigarette it is.

I want this meeting to go as well as can be expected. I want to say the right things, to be tactful and understanding – for us to part on good terms. To be adult about it, whatever that means. Oh fuck it, what I really want is to go back to the office with a clear conscience. And if she wants to give me her blessing to meet other women, then that would be good too. And no tears. Please, no tears. The last thing I need is guilt.

"I am so sorry I'm late," she says. "I've got a pitch to do this afternoon and I haven't done half the stuff for it and I'm going to look like a right idiot. I should've prepared it ages ago but…" The pause is to let me know that I am to blame for this. Naturally. "Anyway, I was so busy trying to cram I lost track of time. I'm sorry."

"It's okay." I'm the one who should be apologising – who probably will be apologising, at some point soon.

I allow myself a few seconds to appreciate the sight of her. I have to admit, it's a little bit disappointing that she's turned up looking like a Bond girl. It means she's not distraught enough to let her appearance slip, to have stopped wearing make-up and started wearing smocks and Birkenstocks. Or, perhaps, she's done it to spite me. To show me what I'm missing.

"Do you want to grab a coffee or something?" I ask, putting the feelers out to gauge her mood.

"I can't stay long. I have to get back to try and salvage my career. I'm probably going to be getting my P45 by five o' clock. So you're the last person to see me while I'm still in employment. Actually, I had a quick look in the *Guardian* this morning, and I saw this job in… What are you smiling at?"

I didn't realise I was.

Lola is brilliant at her job, brilliant. Her salary is substantially higher than mine is – a fact I am very comfortable with, thank you very much – and yet she's on constant tenterhooks, waiting for someone to discover she's incompetent and sack her, although the reality is she's brought in more clients than anyone else in the firm for the five years she's been there. People like Lola. She's warm, personable, and makes people feel good about themselves. Which, yes, does indeed beg the question of what she was doing slumming it with me for so long.

"Your pitch will be fantastic. They always are."

"There's a first time for everything. This might be the one I mess up."

"But you won't."

"But what if I do?"

There's no telling Lola, nothing I can say to convince her. Even Paul McKenna would end up punching himself in the face in frustration after five minutes of trying to work on her confidence. I wish she believed in herself as much as she believes in other people.

"You won't mess up, Lola."

She rolls her eyes dismissively. "Yeah, right. I'm starting to think I'm in the wrong line of work. I hate the public, and I hate relations – so what am I doing?"

"Being the best PR woman I know."

"The only one you know."

"Maybe because the others aren't worth knowing."

She gives me a long frown, takes the hidden agenda from my words, and then chooses to ignore it. "You look tired."

"I'm not sleeping well," I admit. She's looking at me expectantly, her arms folded across her chest, and I feel obliged to add, "Penny left Simon."

Her eyes widen. "No! When?"

"Last night. She's pregnant."

"But that's…" She decodes my head shake. "Oh. I see. Who is he?"

"Her aerobics teacher."

"Penny goes to aerobics?" Lola is more shocked by the idea of that than Penny's illegitimate child.

"I know, you'd never guess. Chris evidently gave her a very thorough workout."

"Chris?"

"Yes. Men called Chris can, apparently, impregnate women too."

"But I know him. Well, I know of him. Valerie went to one of his classes." I try not to puke at the thought of Valerie in a leotard. "She said he was uncoordinated."

"Well, he can clearly string some moves together."

Lola pulls a face at me – the 'oh John, must you?' one. She uses that one a lot.

"God, that's awful. How's Simon doing?"

"He's devastated. She never wanted kids. She always said she didn't want to ruin her figure." Lola opens her mouth to state the obvious, then changes her mind, as it's not a nice thing to say. So I say it instead. "Yeah, even though she could be about to give birth to a Volvo T5 and no one would notice."

"John…"

"What?"

"So, what's Simon going to do?"

"Not much he can do. He keeps talking about going round and smacking this Chris, even though he couldn't smack his own arse. He's in shock. It's come right out of the blue for him."

"Yeah, well, there's a lot of that going round at the moment," Lola says, staring over my shoulder as she does so.

After a while, you get used to the taste of your own foot.

We begin to walk around the lake in a languid, leisurely pace, probably because Lola can't walk any faster in those heels. I remember when she bought them. She was so pleased with herself, and insisted on modelling them for me when she got home.

"What do you think, John?

"They're lovely."

"Could you look at me when you say that?"

Well, *Soccer Saturday* was on.

She'd said the shoes made her feel like Gwen Stefani, and she wasn't happy when I eventually took my eyes from the television (I had a fiver on Chelsea to lose, and they bloody didn't) and let slip that they made her walk like Albert Steptoe. She's wearing them today out of principle, probably.

"So, how are you?"

"I'm okay," she answers. I can't decipher whether she means it or not.

"You look great."

Her face creases into a frown which, annoyingly, amplifies her beauty. "John, I don't have much time. Can we just cut to the chase?"

Here it comes. I fold my arms, braced, ready to be empathic and sensitive.

"Sure. It's your chase, go ahead."

"We should put the house up for sale."

It feels like someone's plunged my foot into a bucket of freezing water.

I blink myopically at her. "Excuse me?"

"The house. If no one's living in it, we might as well sell up and split the money. If you want it, then you can buy my share from me – I'm not bothered really. Whatever." She tips her head to one side. "I mean, I don't know if now is good time to sell or anything, but you're the economist, you'll know what to do for the best."

I stop in my tracks, feet crunching on the gravel. "You want to sell the house? Our house?"

"Our ex-house," she corrects. "It doesn't make sense to pay the mortgage on a house neither of us is living in. You don't need a degree in economics to know that." She stops, glancing back at me. "Oh, what's that face for? It's only a house, bricks and mortar. That's what you told Sally when she lost her house."

"I was just saying that, Lola."

Lola considers it, then shrugs. "Well, I happen to think you were right. It's not the house that makes a home, but the people in it. And there's no one in ours, which just about says it all."

I wince. "I see your point," I say slowly, in the way I do when I think she's talking total arse, "but it's a bit, well, final, don't you think?"

"But this is final, John. It's over. You said that yourself."

"But-"

"No, don't you do this. You finished it – it's not you, it's me."

"I didn't say that."

"You didn't have to. And anyway," she continues, clearly on a roll, and I hate it when she's on one of those, "it is you. I've been expecting this to happen, you know. And now that it has, it's a relief. Do you know why?"

She's about to tell me.

"Because I don't have to worry about it happening anymore. You always had itchy feet, John. You were always looking over your shoulder. You were never fully in the room, you were never fully with me. Your head was always somewhere else."

"I was with you for nine years." I feel I have to point that out. Then realise immediately it's a mistake, as I've given her a free pass to mention…

"But you didn't want to get married."

"And you were fine with that."

"I was fine with it because I either accepted it, or I lost you. And here's the funny thing, John. I've lost you anyway. So now I don't have to worry about losing you anymore. The worst thing that could possibly happen to me has happened, and it turns out it wasn't as bad as I thought it would be."

I'm sure the tyre prints are visible on my chest from where she's just driven a tank over me. Of all the scenarios I was prepared for, of all the potential things I imagined she'd say to me, this particular conversation never entered even the fringes of my most flamboyant visualisations. She's so cool, so together – worse than that, she's making sense. I'm easier to get over than I imagined. When she puts it like that, I should be.

"Wait a minute." I get back on clock. "If you're not in the house, where are you staying?"

"With Kay. She has a spare room, remember? You helped to decorate it."

I do remember. I hated every second and very nearly bludgeoned Todd with a roller and welded the kids' mouths closed with wallpaper paste. This news, however, explains a lot.

"I thought maybe you were staying with Valerie."

"I was going to, but I didn't think it would be fair. After all, you do work with her, and it wouldn't be right that she has to hear in graphic detail what an absolute bastard you are."

Ah! A reaction! She's not as over me as she's trying to make out.

"Valerie owns the patent on 'John is a bastard.'" I say, and then pause for air. "I am sorry, Lola."

And I am, honestly. Probably sorry more for myself than for her, but at least I've said it, even if it is for my own benefit.

"John, I think you've had library fines you were sorrier about. But, whatever."

That smarts. Is that how she sees me?

She checks her watch. "Right, fun though this is, I don't have time for any more verbal tennis. Okay, how about we start sorting out our stuff? On Saturday morning, I'll go back to the house and start packing my things, and then you can come round and do yours about, say, one o' clock? I should be finished by then."

"Why can't we do it together?"

Lola prods the gravel with the tip of her shoe. "Because." She flicks her gaze into mine and, for some reason, I feel small, unimportant, as though I should have the good grace to look away. "Because I don't want to see you any more than I absolutely have to. It's not healthy."

"French Fries and ice cream aren't healthy."

"And I've given those up too."

A sharp stab of something lances my insides. "I thought you wanted to be friends?"

"I did – I do. But we don't live in an ideal world. In reality, ex-lovers only stay friends on television."

Ordinarily, I would've smiled at that – it's typical Lola – but suddenly I don't feel like smiling at all.

"Right. So what was that whole 'let's have sex' thing about then?"

Her expression hardens and I regret saying it because I'm being 'typical John', and making it easier for her.

"Shut up, John. I was trying to feel close to you because most of the time you kept me at arms length, and you have very long arms. Very. Like Mr Tickle. It was a mistake, and one I'm not going to repeat. You wanted us to be over? Fine, we're over." She checks her watch again. "I have to go. I have a job to be fired from."

"You're going?"

"Yes."

"Just like that?"

"Watch me."

"I will. Oh, this was clever, by the way."

She frowns. "What was?"

"Meeting here. The park."

She keeps looking at me, searching my face. There's a tiny crease between her perfectly groomed eyebrows. "What do you mean? It's over the road from the office. It's the easiest place for us to meet."

"Right."

"Why did you think I wanted to meet here?"

"No reason."

She's still frowning, as though I'm weird. Which I suppose I might be. "I have to go. Remember – Saturday. You get the afternoon slot. See you. Or not."

She tosses her hair over her shoulder, and clicks her way out of my life, although, really, I told her to go.

I arrive back at the office smelling like a Marlboro factory. If they let me smoke in here I'd still be at it, chain-smoking, one after the other, sweet, glorious nicotine, hoping with each inhale that something about what just happened in the park would begin to make sense. I've established that I don't want to be with Lola – I don't – and yet the thought of sitting in what she so coldly calls our ex-house, by myself and filtering through what's mine and what's hers makes me want to slit my throat with a rusty razor.

By the time I'm back at my desk, I'm wired. I am so full of nervous energy that the second my jacket is slung over the back of my ramshackle chair, I roll up my sleeves and begin to type. I write and write, the sentences oozing out of me with an ease I've never experienced before. The office, the world, just slides away, like rain on glass, so that by the time I raise my head to stretch out my weary neck muscles, I find two hours have ticked by. I can't remember a second of time passing in this place without me counting it. It's a first.

Sarah's over at the photocopier, probably copying something (I bet it's a diet) out of a magazine. She waves at me. I throw her a half-smile in return, which she seems content enough with. She takes the sheets from the machine and her, yes, 'Now' magazine, and goes back to her desk to waste some more time. That reminds me.

I reach for my phone. A groggy voice answers. "Penny?"

"No."

"Oh. John." His disappointment reigns supreme. "Did you tell Charlie I've got Bird Flu?"

"Blue Tongue Disease. He said, and I quote "So fucking what?" How are you?"

I can hear Simon shrugging. "Fat. Old. Washed up."

"I asked how you are, not what you are."

"Fuck off. She hasn't phoned."

"Do you want her to?"

"Yes." A long pause. "No." Another pause. "Maybe. What do you think?"

"Well," I choose my words carefully. "It depends if you think there's anything to say. She's with this Chris guy now. Maybe you should leave her to it."

Simon doesn't say anything. Shit. I back pedal. I'm good at that.

"Tell you what, how about I pick up some beers on my way back and we can talk this over with the support of a takeaway?"

"No food. I don't think I can stomach it. Just beer."

"Whatever you want. I have something I need to do for Charlie. It shouldn't take too long."

"How long?" I can hear the panic in Simon's voice, and I hate Penny for it. I mean, more than I already did.

"Two hours. Tops."

"All right. Two hours, John. I know what you're like with deadlines."

"Yeah, yeah…"

I say my goodbyes to Simon and flex my limbs, resting my hands behind my head as I read through what I've written. I scroll down the screen, then up, and then I read it all over again. I feel justified in telling myself that this is the best thing I've ever put down in black and white. It's just a shame it's totally unusable, and I still have Charlie's feature to write. I save my musings onto disk, and switch my computer off.

I'll get nothing done if I stay here, so I get the laptop from the drawer and decide to find some place to write where I can't smoke which, thanks to the totalitarian state we live in these days, is everywhere. I give a passing nod to the remaining people in the office I consider it worth my while to acknowledge, and wander out of the building. Surprise, surprise, it's raining. Pissing down, to use the vernacular, reminding me that Lola, without fail, always carried an umbrella. Sadly, I'm not that practical, so all

I can do is pull my collar up and brave the soaked streets of Holborn.

Despite the weather, the pavement is standing room only. This is what gets to me about London – it breeds people, mainly annoying ones. They multiply, like germ spores, spreading out of control. And most of them are, like Lola, practically minded enough to carry an umbrella, and I'm in constant danger of getting my eyes poked out by errant spokes. I get halfway down the Kingsway, and give up. It will have to be Starbucks.

I step inside, shaking some of the water out of my hair. There's a woman behind me, who appears to be carrying her own body weight in shopping bags. I smile and hold the door open for her, which is most unlike me.

"No, you first," she says, smiling back at me. "Equality, and all that," she laughs.

Dear God – one of those. Still, if it means I get my coffee and first dibs at a seat, then hurrah for feminism.

I can hear her behind me as I ask for the closest thing to a regular cup of coffee you can get in here without being ridiculed and chucked out on the street. Her bags rustle as she requests a skinny latte – I fucking hate them as much as I hate iPods – and I imagine her traipsing round the shops, accumulating more purchases as she goes.

Unlike most women, when I walk into a shop I know exactly what I want to buy, so the transaction takes me a minimal amount of time from start to finish. There are rare occasions when I allow myself to be sidetracked, for example in a music store, where browsing is almost mandatory. But certainly, if I go out to buy a tie, or a pair of trousers, I do not come home with three pairs of shoes, half of Boots the chemist, and a completely new wardrobe minus the items I actually went out to purchase in the first place.

The last spare table is right over in the corner, which is disappointing as it means I won't be able to stare out of the window when I'm supposed to be writing. I take off my jacket, which by now is nothing more than a sodden sponge with a Levi's tag on it. I open the laptop, my heart sinking as the Microsoft logo comes up and it's apparent that the machine is actually working and I'll have to use it. Okay, let's do this. A sip of coffee. A crack of the knuckles so I look important in case anyone's watching. I flick the switch in my head and become John Black, Chief Economics Editor. US housing market? Not a problem, Charlie. I'll be emailing it to you in about ninety minutes.

I've typed eight words, three of which are 'by' and 'John Black,' when the woman with the bags appears in front of me.

"Um, excuse me. Is there anyone sitting there?"

I think about lying, my default setting. I could easily say that I'm meeting a friend, or my girlfriend, or my imaginary friend, but frivolous mendacity will take up too much valuable time, so it's easier to simply say, "No, go ahead," and get my head down and press enter a few times to make me look busy and important.

I try to ignore her squeezing herself into the space opposite me, which admittedly would be a lot bigger if she wasn't carrying enough shopping to inflate the Consumer Price Index all by herself. And she's pretty, in a blonde kind of way. Nice nose – one of those perky ones that turns up at the end. Cute. I type another few words, only one of which, I'm pleased to note, is 'the', and scratch my cheek. And then I make a fatal mistake. I look up again, and catch her eye. Great. Now it looks like I want to strike up a conversation.

She smiles over her coffee. "This rain is awful," she says.

"Yeah." I feel like adding "but nice breasts," but don't. I go back to my screen but it's useless, the moment's gone. I drum my fingers over the keys, hoping for divine inspiration, a Eureka moment, or someone to email me the news that Charlie has just died, so I don't have to finish this.

Instead, I get a coffee tsunami.

"Oh! Oh my gosh, I'm so sorry!"

Who knew there was that much liquid in a skinny latte? It goes everywhere, all over the table, much of the floor, on some of her shopping bags, but most importantly, not on me. But I let her say sorry anyway – other people's profuse apologies are very satisfying, and make a refreshing change from hearing my own.

"I'll get some napkins."

And I do. I rush over and dig out some of those horrible paper things from the counter, and help her mop up the mess. She smiles gratefully at me, and suddenly I'm helpful, a knight in shining armour, and not a procrastinating journalist who needs more sleep and somewhere to live. She looks at me, her blue eyes framed by slightly too much mascara, and I decide I like being the hero. I feel appreciated. If wiping up spillages that weren't even my fault is all it takes, then sign me up for full membership.

"I am so sorry," she says again. "I hope none of it went on your computer." She motions over at the laptop, which I've flung on the chair behind me with no regard for opportunist thieves. In fact, I'm hoping for an opportunist thief to be 'just passing', as it's the paper's machine and not mine. Now that I think about it, I should buy her another coffee and get her to spill that one more strategically.

"It's fine. No harm done," I say, hiding my dismay at this.

"Oh, that's a relief." She has a bright, open face. She's the kind of woman I should be pursuing. "Can I get you another?"

I don't know why she's asking me this, as my coffee is still relatively full.

"That's kind, but I'm just leaving."

"Oh. Good idea. I think I'll do the same." She laughs nervously, and I smile back at her, just to make her feel better. About what, I don't know.

We leave Starbucks slightly more soiled than we found it. Instinctively, I step back and hold the door open for her. She smiles appreciatively, and she and her barrage of bags stride gracefully out onto the street. I admire her ability to remain sophisticated whilst her balance is hampered by the entire contents of Selfridges. I wonder what she originally went out to buy. Probably a jar of oregano.

The rain has eased off a little. I step out into the street, and automatically light up a cigarette, savouring the release as the smoke fills my lungs, and no doubt lines them with tar. You can't beat the feeling. It amuses me that the warning on the packet tells me smoking can result in premature death. I thought they were trying to give me a reason to stop?

Starbucks lady is watching me suck on my cigarette. I shrug to defend and explain my behaviour. She tucks a strand of hair behind her ear and studies her shoes, her mouth twitching at the corners.

Fuck it, I think, I'll get a cab. I'll get home, go upstairs for a couple of hours, and get this bloody thing finished. Then I'll deal with Simon. I stand on the kerb, gazing out into the traffic, and she appears to be doing the same. She notices me noticing her, and looks a little embarrassed.

"Can't get one for love nor money at this time of day," she says.

"I find money is usually the most successful medium."

"Sorry?"

"I tried offering a cab driver love once. Didn't go down well."

"Oh. Oh, aha aha ha ha!" Her laugh sounds like a car alarm. Maybe I can overlook it, providing it doesn't go off again.

"Would you like some help carrying those?" I ask, not because I want to help, but because I like playing the hero now. And I believe in equality too. Women should carry their own damn shopping. It might make them think about how much they can comfortably lift, and afford, before they start buying it.

She peeks down at her bags, as though she's only just noticed them dangling from the ends of her fingers. "Well … if you wouldn't mind. They are quite heavy."

I concur as I take them from her. "Are they making clothes from bricks these days?"

She laughs. "You have to keep up with fashion."

"Not easy, when it weighs this much."

She doesn't seem to mind me belittling her obviously favourite pastime, and this is a huge point in her favour. I like anyone I can make fun of, which is surely why I've been friends with Simon for so long. Regretfully, I part company with my cigarette as I cannot carry this many bags and smoke at the same time. Not with any real dignity anyway, and I don't want to show this woman and, more importantly, myself up by looking like her butler.

Now I notice her appraising me. Yeah, women do it too. And you know what, I hate it, because I never know what they're looking for. Okay, so we guys might ogle women from time to time, but at least there's something on show, to an extent, for us to pass judgement on. Now this woman, I can tell from the swell of her sweater, has got nice round breasts. Her legs aren't bad, calves are a bit fat, but you can't have everything. But what can she tell from looking at me? Yeah, I'm tall, my hair's my own, but what does she get from checking out my crotch and arse? And, you know what else, my hands won't tell you anything. If you want to know how well endowed I am, just ask.

Suddenly, she turns to me, and I think she might be about to. "Hey, would you like to share a cab?"

Relief floods through me, but it's short-lived. On the face of it, this is a simple enough question. But the way she poses it is loaded with suggestion. Does she mean actually share a cab for the purposes of getting home more quickly, or does she mean something else? I evaluate my options. As it's raining and I need to get home, there aren't that many to choose from.

"Where do you live?"

"Finchley."

"Highgate."

"Perfect! I'm Sheila." She sticks out her hand.

"Martin."

She beams at me. "Hi, Martin. I'll get us a cab."

And she does. She stands close to the kerb, fluttering her eyelashes and flicking her blonde hair. On a day of less inclement weather, she's the kind of woman who would've driven me nuts with her contradictory interpretation of equality. But it's raining, and I'm fucking freezing. So as far as I'm concerned she can chain herself to railings and reclaim the night some other time. Today she can use whatever it takes – cleavage, a bit of leg, a hand job – to get us home.

I hold open the cab door, and try not to stare too blatantly at her arse when she gets inside.

"Frognall Road first, please."

The cabbie nods, and pulls off.

She wriggles into her seat, shifting her hips from side to side, so that one of her knees is nestling alarmingly close to mine.

"I've seen you somewhere before," she says.

"I have that kind of face."

"No, I definitely know you from somewhere." She nestles into the corner between the seat and the door. "You don't look like a Martin."

"Apparently I did when I weighed nine pounds and nine ounces."

"You were quite a big boy then? Oh, I didn't mean it like that, aha aha ha ha!"

There's the car alarm again.

Trying to steer the conversation onto something more anodyne, and less funny, I adopt the kind of conversational tack Todd would be proud of, and ask the unforgivable.

"So, Sheila, what do you do?"

"Lots of things. Oh! I mean, I-"

"For a living," I ask, before the car alarm goes off again.

"I own a restaurant. Oh, hey, you should stop by sometime. It's called 'A Prima Vera'. That means the spring. Here." She hands me a business card. Another fucking one.

"In Portuguese, I know. Very nice." I stuff the card into my pocket, and peer out of the window. Technically, we'll get to Highgate first. I should point this out. I want to point this out. But isn't this what I promised myself – close encounters of the female kind? So I let the taxi head north. And pretend I do this all the time.

"How about you?" she asks.

"I'm a plumber."

"Really? You don't look like a plumber. Do you always wear a suit to work?"

"Actually, it's my day off."

She raises her eyebrows. Her eyes are green. Lola's are brown. Lola. Not now Lola, please.

"A plumber, eh? Does that mean you're good with your hands? Aha aha ha ha! Sorry Martin, you must think I'm a little, well, peculiar, it's just that, well, I don't get out much since the divorce. But I did get a plumber in last week, actually. For the sink. There was a bit of Lego stuffed down there – not mine, aha aha ha ha ha ha!"

"Excuse me?"

"Oh, it wasn't my Lego. It's my nie-"

"You mentioned you're divorced."

Sheila's face drops a little. "Yes," she says, picking an imaginary bit of fluff from her skirt. "He left last June. For her. Her name was June." She practically spits the word out. "June in June. Isn't that horrible?"

I nod, as though I empathise, when really I'm regretting not stopping the cab in Highgate and running out into the street screaming for help. Divorcee. Nothing about that word is good, especially when you're trapped in a moving vehicle with one, albeit one with a cute nose and round breasts.

"Oh, just here, please."

The cab comes to a slow and ominous halt. The driver turns around, and grins at me in an "Oi, oi!" way. I scowl at him in a "Fuck off" way, and resent the fact that I now have to give him money.

I reach for my wallet, and Sheila the Divorcee pats me on the arm. "I insist. I owe you. For the coffee."

Again I want to point out it was her own coffee she spilled, but I think if I did I'd be missing the point she's trying to make, despite the undeniable fact that I am actively afraid of the point she's trying to make.

"Honestly," I say, "I've got it."

I hand the driver the cash, which he gobbles up in delight. Sheila, I note, looks a little put out.

Oh right, I remember now. This is another area where we can't do anything right. If I pay for the cab, I'm a chauvinist bastard who doesn't believe a woman is capable of paying her own way. But if I say, yeah, okay, we can go halves if you want, then I'm a tight bastard. Give me the choice of either bastard and I'll take the latter – at least it means I'm a tenner up.

"Oh, now I feel really guilty," Sheila says. "Why don't you come in for a coffee? It's the least I can do."

"That's very kind, but I really have to get back to my friend. He's-"

"Just one drink. I won't keep you long. Come on, it'll be fun!"

That's like the Boston Strangler telling me this isn't going to hurt, or Ted Bundy asking for a job on a university campus. But this is what I wanted. I wanted freedom, I wanted women and, well, here's a real live one. Shelia's already out of the taxi, and I follow her with the bags, up the path to her house, hoping the bad feeling festering in my gut is merely indigestion.

Sheila fumbles for the key. After much fiddling with the lock (which she tells me she's just changed to stop her exhusband coming in), she opens the door.

"Ta-da!" she says.

Ta-da indeed.

It's a house straight from the pages of one of Sarah's magazines. Everything is white, black, and chrome. It's sleek, sophisticated, and luxurious. It's pretty much how Lola wanted our house – our ex-house – to look, only when it came to home improvements, my laziness was a more formidable force than her creativity.

"Please, excuse the mess." Sheila picks up a coaster from the coffee table and repositions it back in exactly the same place. If this constitutes her idea of a mess she'd better stay far away from Simon's kitchen.

"Please, Martin, have a seat."

I stand there for a few seconds until I realise she means me.

"Now, what would you like? I have Darjeeling, English Breakfast, Earl Grey, Green Tea, Jasmine tea, Chamo-"

"Coffee's fine, thanks."

"Filter, espresso..?"

"Nescafe."

"Oh. Sure." She smiles brightly. "I'll be two ticks."

I settle back as far as I can into Sheila's couch without being sucked into it, and enviously eye up the plasma television. I bet her ex-husband is gutted about losing custody of that. Poor sod. He's probably living in a bed-sit in Bermondsey eating Cup-a-Soup while she's lording it up in Finchley watching *Desperate Housewives* on his fifty inch state-of-art Sony.

"There you go. Hope it's how you like it."

"It's wet and black, so it's fine."

She laughs, and I close my ears.

She puts the tray onto the coffee table (which I think is big enough to play pool on), and perches on the edge of one of the armchairs.

"Well…" She sips from her cup. I notice it rattle as she puts it back on the saucer. "Oh, I never drink coffee," she feels the need to explain when she sees me looking. "It's bad for the old, you know." She pats her chest, and I'm tempted, oh God it's right there on the end of my tongue, to say, "Breasts?" But I don't.

"I disagree," I say instead. "I think caffeine is good for the heart. Gives it a good old workout."

"Oh. Oh! Aha ha ha ha ha!"

"That wasn't a joke."

"Aha aha ha ha ah- what?"

"I'm kidding." Although I'm really not. I just want her to stop making that horrific noise. "Anyway," I say, putting my cup down on the table, next to the coaster instead of on it (it's the least I can do for her ex-husband), "this has been fun, but-"

"Martin…"

Huh? Oh, right, that's me. "Yeah?"

"I need to ask you something. Something, well," she peers into her cup, like the words are printed inside the rim, "a little… difficult."

"No, I won't lend you a fiver."

"What? Oh, no, aha aha ha!"

Jesus.

"No," Sheila continues, thankfully composing herself before I'm forced to go over there and smother her with a cushion. "It's something more personal than that. I… Well, you see, I, um… Oh dear."

I just sit there and blink back at her.

"Okay…" She takes a huge breath – really, it's so immense I expect the rug and several of the ornaments to be sucked into her mouth. "I mentioned the divorce, didn't I?"

"Yes."

"Oh, right. Well, the thing is, Martin, since Gavin left, there's been no one. My friends have been great, and my sister's been taking me out to bingo and stuff, but the problem is that…"

My eyes are open, but inside I'm sleeping. I don't know why women do this, and why they always seem to do it to me. Yes, I know women want to be listened to, and most men

– even Simon – have pretty much grasped that basic tenet now, but why abuse the privilege? We do what you want, we listen to you, and then you just abuse our patience and go on, and on, and on, and –

"Pardon me?"

Sheila gives me a coquettish look. If I've heard her right, it's a bit late for that.

"I know it's a bit, well, unorthodox, it's just that since Gavin went it's been so difficult, and I've felt so…unwomanly. I just want someone to touch me, Martin, to feel like a woman again."

I take a gigantic sip of my coffee. She's watching me, waiting for me to say something profound and deep, something intense, or maybe just, "Okay."

I'm thinking about it. Sheila is, clearly, a little bit mad, but there's no denying both that she's gorgeous, and that this is a clear God-given opportunity for me to get back in the saddle again, to break my post-Lola duck. And I should, shouldn't I? Okay, let's weigh this up… Free sex (well, the price of a cab ride home), or inexplicably turn down sex and go home and get drunk with Simon. I don't want to go home and get drunk with Simon, but if I'm honest I don't really want to do this either. But I should. It would be wrong not to, and if I do, well, I get to be the hero again, the Alpha Male coming to Sheila's aid and rescuing her from a life of stale knickers and frigidity.

"I just want sex, Martin. Is that too much to ask?"

I put down my cup. "No, Sheila. I don't think it is."

Yes, I know what this makes me. It makes me one of those guys who take advantage of vulnerable women, and blah, blah. Let me tell you something though, there's nothing vulnerable about Sheila. I'm the one who's weak and defenceless. She's preying on me, cat and mouse style, and I'm lying there dwelling on what Lola said in the park about me having itchy feet. I nearly laugh out loud – I guess

I'm really scratching them now, and you know what? I don't know if it's entirely what I expected.

I've never been one to kiss and tell, but what I will say about what took place on the floor of Sheila's lounge is this: she nearly killed me. She bit, she scratched, she tore my clothes, which may sound great on paper, but in real life it was terrifying. I felt like I'd fallen into the tiger enclosure at London Zoo. You know, I'm lucky she really did have nice breasts and that it's possible for my penis to act independently of my brain, otherwise my reputation, and my confidence, would've been ruined irreparably. The only other detail I'm prepared to reveal is that it was over shamefully quickly.

I pull my trousers up so rapidly I nearly give myself a friction burn. Sheila lies there, still on her back, breathing heavily, a thin sheen of perspiration covering her skin, which seems a bit extravagant given the amount of time the sex lasted. She props herself up on her elbows, looking at me like I've just farted on her fruit bowl.

"Where are you going?" she says, sitting up and covering herself with a cushion. She wasn't so modest about ninety seconds ago, I will say that much.

"I told you, I have to go home and see my friend." Where did she throw my jacket?

"So… You're leaving?"

I find it behind the sofa and have to refrain from singing the first few bars of the Hallelujah Chorus.

"Yes. I said before I have this thing I have to do. With my friend. He's kind of having a bad time. And you said you didn't want anything more…"

"Oh, I know, I did! Aha aha aha ha aha, but, you know, I thought we could, you know…"

I run a hand through my hair and try not to scream.

"No, I don't know."

"I thought we could, you know, talk or something. It's just that, since Gavin left…"

Now you see, this is where the whole equality movement breaks down. Women think they want equality, and I have no problem with that. They should have equal pay, equal rights under the law, and all those kinds of things. What they fail to understand though, is that they cannot, and will never be able to, have sex like men. They can enjoy sex, sure, and they should, but they are not programmed to go around having sex with anyone they like the look of and then get up and leave without so much as a second thought. It's not part of their genetics, and no amount of watching *Sex and the City* will change that. The thing they fail to comprehend is that it's nothing to be ashamed of, and definitely not something they should try to change. It's part of the very structure of the female being, and one of the reasons women are so fascinating. I wish they would concentrate on developing their femininity instead of trying to be like men. I mean, who wants to have sex like men anyway? After this debacle, certainly not me.

"You know, Sheila, this has been fun," I lie, "but I really have to go. I'll see you around." That seems a bit harsh, even for me, so I try to crack a joke. "And if you ever need any help with your shopping…"

It's a miscalculation. She turns her head and gives me a look of utter loathing.

"Just get out, Martin. Get out and never come round here again."

Oh well, every cloud and all that.

I slip out the door with a few less layers of skin than I walked in with, and fade into the distance like the Man With No Name. Oh yeah, except for Martin.

When I get home, Simon greets me like the wife I've never had and never want.

"Where have you been? Two fucking hours you said!"

I put down my bag and fling my jacket over the banister to drip rainwater onto the floor, one of the many perks of Penny not being here. "I got waylaid on the way back."

"Waylaid?" Simon looks me up and down with a mixture of curiosity and derision, and notices my hands are empty about the same time as I do. "Don't tell me you forgot the beer."

"Okay, I won't. You must have some in the fridge, surely?" How could I forget the beer? As easily as I could forget to write Charlie's feature.

"I'm depressed, remember? I drank it all."

"By yourself?"

"No. I invited Burt Reynolds and Mahatma Ghandi round to share it."

"I'm pretty sure Ghandi didn't drink, Simon."

"Well that makes two of us because you forgot the beer."

We stand in the hall, both of us staring absently into mid-air. I'm not really in the mood for another melancholy evening in with Simon, but he's my best friend and I owe it to him to be there when he needs me. I search my brain for a suitable plan to distract him from asking me another thirteen thousand questions about Penny and Chris the sperm-laden aerobics instructor. I have no answers. There's nothing I can say, no script for this. I go into the lounge, glad that Simon at least had the presence of mind to leave the television on.

"Anything good on tonight?" I ask, hope springing eternal.

"*Extreme Makeover's* on in ten minutes," he replies. "Some bird from Texas is getting a nose job, a tit-lift, and new teeth."

"I hope she has a Clubcard. Is it me, or is there always a programme about plastic surgery on some channel or other?"

Simon takes a swig from the mug on the table in front of him. It smells as though it's full of whisky. "It's a sign of the times, mate. No one wants to look like a real person anymore."

"And what does a real person look like?"

Simon pats the extra pounds that have been lurking around his stomach area since the late eighties. "Like this. It's the media's fault, you know. All the talk about dieting and ageing just makes people fatter and older." He's slumped so far down the chair he's almost folded over. "But we can't talk, we work for the bloody media."

"I think you'll find I can talk – I'm the economics guy. You're the beauty editor, and hence are partly responsible for the proclivity for face lifts and anal bleaching."

I instantly regret my last two words as a flash of inspiration registers on Simon's face. His melon-head snaps upwards.

"You know, maybe that's my problem. I should start working out. I bet Chris has got pecs and a six-pack, and all that other stuff."

And we're off. Simon's reached the introspective phase.

"Probably. But I bet he waxes his eyebrows."

"And?"

"And, well, that's just wrong."

"No, John, maybe it isn't. Maybe we're the ones doing it wrong. Maybe," he sits fully upright, more alert than I've seen him in days, "that's what women want – men who are like women."

"Men who are like women?"

"Exactly."

"Do you want to become a woman?"

"Of course fucking not," he says. "I want my wife back."

When he puts it like that, in those uncertain terms, I run out of clichés. There it is, the reality. She's gone, and she's not coming back. I sit down opposite him, scratching the back of my neck as though I'm thinking of some profound nugget of wisdom to impart instead of, "Oh Jesus fuck, what do I say now?"

"You know what gets to me the most?"

I shake my head. I wouldn't know where to begin to guess.

"Penny said she didn't want kids. She said it was too scary, too much responsibility, and it'd ruin her figure. But they all want kids, deep down. They all do."

"Lola didn't," I say without thinking.

"Lola was different."

I bite my lip.

"But you know what it is? Penny didn't want kids with me. That's the truth of it." Simon pulls a face I know so well, one that says, 'I know I'm right.'

I rake my fingers through my hair, wishing I'd paid more attention when Lola read out selected quotes from her endless self-help books. I could do with one now.

"You can't make that assumption. It was probably an accident."

"Oh, right," Simon says. "And that makes it better?"

"You know what, Si? No way of looking at this is going to make it better. All there is, is what it is."

He goes to say something in retort, but changes his mind. It's his way of agreeing. "Can you think of anything more emasculating than your wife getting up the duff by her aerobics instructor?"

"Not at such short notice."

"Bitch." He throws a peanut at their wedding photo.

Ah, the angry phase. He won't be needing me for a little while then.

"I've had a strange kind of day. I think I might go to bed, if you don't mind."

"I do mind," he says, giving me a dirty look. "'Cosmetic Surgery Clinic' is on Discovery Health in half an hour."

I sigh. "Facelifts? Rhinoplasty? Liposuction?"

Simon retrieves the TV guide to check. "Vaginal rejuvenation."

My insides recoil. I've had enough vaginal rejuvenation for one day, but it's best if I don't share that with Simon. "I think that's your domain. I'll see you in the morning."

"Oi, John?"

"Simon?"

"Do you want to come in early with me tomorrow? We can talk on the way."

"Sure. Give me a knock. Enjoy the vaginas."

"I will. It's been a long time since I've seen one."

I say nothing.

Atonement is a good word – now I know why the Catholics like it so much. My penance for the sins I've committed so far on this earth (which we shall call Legion, for there are many) is denial of sleep. I'm so tired I can feel each muscle, and my bones are leaden, but every time my eyelids close it's as though they're made of sandpaper. It hurts. I hurt – everywhere, in places I didn't know existed. I'm feeling pain in a holistic way. It's a thousand times more excruciating in the darkness. There are ghosts: Penny, Sheila, Rebecca Speller, and Lola, who thinks it's a relief that I've finally left her and wants to sell our house.

Our ex-house.

It's so final.

She thinks I have itchy feet.

I do.

I've proved her right.

Jesus! What the fuck is this?

I give up. I turn the lamp on, and find my cigarettes. I should put this nervous energy to good use and finish Charlie's feature – no, start Charlie's feature. I don't suppose Lola is lying awake in bed thinking about me.

Is she?

I should find my laptop. I'll have the thing written in an hour or two.

I get out of bed and cross the landing into Simon's room. I shake him, and the entire bed wobbles.

"Jesus! John, what the..?"

I've seen how Simon looks when he first wakes up. And I never want to again. He actually looks like the girl in *The*

Exorcist, but fatter. He rolls over, with half of the pillowcase stuck to his face, and checks the clock.

"John, it's quarter to three!"

I hover at the end of the bed, needing only a bible and a vial of Holy Water to complete the pastiche. I wait for him to fully come to terms with the fact that he is no longer asleep.

"Lola said I kept her at arms length."

"What?" He groans. "Okay, sit down."

I do. I perch on the end of the bed, the hairs on my arms prickling at the cold. I expect to see my breath in front of me in a frosty cloud.

"Do you think she's right?" I ask.

Simon flops back onto the mattress, rubbing his eyes. "I don't know, mate … I … yes. Yes, you did, sort of."

"Sort of? Either I did, or I didn't."

"Well, you weren't exactly Mr. Up Close and Personal. Remember the time you made her cry at Miranda's party?"

"I told you, that wasn't me. Lola was in a dodgy mood before we left anyway. I had to go and talk to the woman, she's an old friend."

"An old ex is what she is. Lola was really upset."

I rub a hand over my chin. "That was one time. I made her cry once in nine years, if you don't count what happened when I broke up with her. That isn't bad going."

Simon reaches for the lamp but misses. "Twice. What about when she booked that surprise weekend in Paris, and you told her you already had plans."

"I did already have plans."

"Yes, and they consisted of going to the opening night of some jazz bar with me. You could've cancelled."

"I promised you I'd go."

"And I told you, big fucking deal. You should've gone to Paris. She was trying to be romantic. You couldn't have been harsher if you'd slapped her across the face with the tickets, handed her some Vaseline, and told her to insert them up her arse."

I have no idea why I went to The Parlour with Simon instead of Paris with Lola. I've always wanted to go to Paris – the Eiffel Tower, the Champs Elysees, the Sacre Coeur... And now that I think about it, I don't particularly like jazz.

I flop down onto the bed.

"I'm a bastard."

"And you needed to wake me up to find that out? It's probably on the Internet. Anyway, it doesn't matter now. You've set the girl free, she can get on with her life."

"Yeah." I consider this for a few moments. "You're right. You're absolutely right."

"Of course I am. Now go back to fucking sleep before I knock you out. I'm the neurotic one at the moment, okay? Don't steal my thunder like the selfish cunt you are."

"Right. Thanks."

"Don't mention it," Simon replies, rolling onto his side, already snoring and muttering before I've even left the room. I'm envious that he can find peace in the middle of the hell he's going through.

Two hours go by before my eyes finally close, and they stay shut for a grand total of seven minutes.

"John. She's left me."

My turn to flick on the light.

Simon's standing at the side of the bed, looking pale and drawn, his eyes puffy – shit in human form.

I sigh, and sit up. "Come on. I'll make some coffee."

Simon pulls a face. "Nah. Bollocks to coffee. Let's stay here and smoke. May as well make the most of my freedom."

We light up, and pretend that's exactly what we're doing, pretend we don't care. We're good at that.

7

It's always impossible to resist doing something you've been told not to do. It's like when someone tells you, "Don't look now, but…" or the doctor says, "Now try not to scratch, Mr Black…" I'm definitely scratching this one, and even though I know it's a bad idea, and that the consequences are highly unlikely to be favourable, here I am, doing it anyway, regardless. This is vintage me, complete with bells and a tickertape parade. Yes, I'm truly scraping the barrel of common sense with this one.

The street looks different seen through my new eyes. All I noticed when I lived here was the lack of parking spaces, the disappearance of the corner shops and the all-conquering growth of Waitrose. I failed to appreciate how close we were to the Tube, and what a nice walk it was. I moaned about the Northern line being on the blink (it always is – I'm not taking that one back). I told people we were just down the road from the park, but I never went there. Okay, once or twice, under duress, and usually when I was hungover. When I think back, I can remember being happy here, and I can remember feeling stifled. Only, I can't separate the two feelings from each other.

My keys burn in my pocket as I get closer to the door. I half-think that maybe I ought to knock – it would be polite to knock, especially as, technically, I'm gate-crashing. But if I do that, I lose the element of surprise, and that's really what I'm going for here.

I let myself in, quietly, and cleanly. The house is silent except for the sound of Sellotape and paper rustling. The lounge door is shut, and with Lola behind it wrapping stuff up, it's almost like Christmas. Except she's gift-wrapping her own possessions, and all I'm likely to receive is a slap round the face and some colourful language. I go into the kitchen, and stop still.

There are two cups by the sink, one of which has a bright pink lip print around the rim, indicating a large mouth, or a fellatio demonstration. I should've seen this coming. I should've prepared for this. I should've known that when the going gets tough, women call for back-up.

I steel myself, and push open the lounge door, crossing my fingers and hoping she doesn't mistake me for a burglar and whack me over the head with the baseball bat we keep behind it. But then, she might know it's me, and whack me over the head anyway.

Lola has her back to me, perched amidst a heap of boxes and sheets of newspaper. There is the occasional sniffle and sigh as she selects an item, and wraps it. The sight of her sitting there hits me hard. But probably not as hard as Valerie wants to hit me. Naturally, because God hates me, Valerie sees me first. Her mouth, complete with garish pink lipstick (I can only assume that after this she's going to an eighties party dressed as Boy George), opens as wide as it will go, which is pretty much Grand Canyon dimensions.

"Oh my God!"

"No. Just me."

"Oh my God!" Valerie says again with more gusto, when none was necessary in the first place.

Lola looks up, and simply stares at me with a kind of disappointed expression on her face. She doesn't say anything, perhaps because Valerie's saying it all. Lola and I continue looking at each other, so Valerie nudges her sharply and says, "It's John!" as though my ex-girlfriend may have developed amnesia.

"John," Lola says eventually.

"Hey."

"Oh, this is just so typical of you," Valerie says, jumping to her feet, knees clicking in the process. "Didn't I say he'd do this, Lola? Didn't I say it?" She looks down at Lola for some kind of confirmation, but Lola merely sighs and reaches for another CD to wrap.

"You," Valerie says, as she doesn't require confirmation of anything to keep on talking, "are something else."

I lean against the doorframe and fold my arms. "Oh really? And what would that be?"

"Oh, where to begin!" she replies with a little laugh. "First of all-" she starts counting on her fingers, and I suspect she won't be limited by the fact that she only has ten.

"I don't recall this being any of your business. Val."

Valerie's eyes widen. "It becomes my business when Lola phones me up, crying, saying she mi-"

"Please, you two. Don't," Lola says, stepping in between us, which is a shame as for the first time in the history of our acquaintance, Valerie might have been about to say something I wanted to hear. "This isn't helping anyone."

Valerie glares at me. I wink at her.

"Valerie, I think it might be better if you take some of the boxes out to the car."

"What?" Valerie is incredulous. "And leave you alone with him?"

I'm grinning now. It's a hollow victory, but I take them where I can these days.

"Please, Valerie," Lola says. "I lived with him for nearly nine years – I'm sure I can handle being on my own with him for five minutes."

Valerie makes a face at me, to illustrate how unconvinced she is by this. She picks up a box. "I'll be in the car if you need me."

"Bye, Val." I wave as she goes past. She scowls venomously. It's most satisfying.

The door clicks shut and Lola and I look at each other, listening to Valerie's angry footsteps on the pavement, and the car door shutting. Her hair is tied back into a ponytail, and a few strands are falling around her face in rebellious wisps. She's stunning, and I feel stupid.

"Hey. How're you doing?"

"How am I doing?" Lola blinks at me as though I'm missing something glaringly obvious. "John, you're not supposed to be here until one o' clock. Have you forgotten how to tell the time?"

"I wanted to see you."

She stands up, and I think I hear a CD case crack. I can only hope it's one of hers. "That's very nice, but what part of 'I don't want to see you' did you find confusing? Don't you have any respect left for my feelings?"

I notice the CD in her hand. "I hope you're not going to wrap that one."

She glances down at it and grimaces. "No, I wasn't going to wrap your precious 'Bob Dylan'. I never liked him."

I try not to smile. "No, you never got past the fact that he – and I quote – 'wears so many scarves.'"

"He does though. It's like every time I see him – scarf, scarf, scarf. I'm all for keeping warm, but no wonder he's so miserable about everything."

"He wears a scarf on the cover of one album, Lola. One."

"Oh no, it's more than that," she says.

"It isn't."

"Is." She puts a hand to her forehead and closes her eyes. "Why are we arguing about this?"

Because I, John Black, cannot let anything go, even when it's this trivial (well, trivial to her – it is one album).

She pauses, pressing her lips together. "I'm almost done anyway. And thank God Valerie's here to help me. Packing is so boring."

"Your choice," I shrug.

"No," she says, "your choice." She thrusts Bob Dylan into my solar plexus. "Valerie was right. She said you'd turn up like this."

"Valerie Perkins – the all-seeing eye."

"Shut up, John. She's been a rock."

"Yes – a face of pure granite, covered in barnacles."

"This is what I hate about you."

"What?"

"This. You're so…"

"Irascible?"

"What does that mean?"

"Irritable."

"No, you're irritating."

"I didn't bring Simon round to help me."

"That's because you're a man."

"You noticed."

"Shut up." She folds her arms, her face softening. "How is Simon?"

"Not good. He's at the self-torture stage now, wondering what this 'Chris' looks like, all that kind of stuff."

"I'm sure that must be a laugh a minute for you."

I shrug. "He's my best mate. He'd be there for me."

She searches my face. "If nothing else, you're a good friend."

"If nothing else?"

She breaks the gaze and goes to pick up her possessions. "Anyway, I'll leave you to it. I'll come back and start on the rest when I know you're not going to be here."

"What about if I keep showing up?"

Lola rolls her eyes. "Then you can have all my stuff and donate it to Arseholes Anonymous when you're at the next meeting." She struggles to lift the box. I go to help her but she shoos me away.

"John, what do you want? You break up with me, seemingly out of nowhere, and I've come to terms with that. But don't torment me. It's very cruel."

"I'm not tormenting you."

"Then what's this? You turn up here when I specifically told you not to – what would you call it? A coffee morning?"

There's no answer to that. I have no idea what I'm doing here either and I can't think of anything – at all – to explain myself.

"Leave me alone, John. I don't want to see you."

"Lola, just listen …"

"What for? You've already said it all. Or do you need me to remind you, because I can still remember your exact words."

"Lola-"

She barges past me. I hear her outside, with Valerie. The engine of Val's Renault Clio starts up, and the car pulls out. I rest my head against the wall and I look at the room, at all the gaps in the bookcase, in the CD rack, at the missing cushions and ornaments from the mantelpiece and shelves. The room isn't empty yet, but it might as well be.

If paying Lola a surprise visit was amongst my dumbest ideas ever, then this is Simon's equivalent. You want torment, Lola? This is torment. And the hilarious thing is, I volunteered for it.

My legs are aching from being cooped up in the car, and my boredom levels are hurtling rapidly towards critical. Simon sits beside me, his eyes focussed straight ahead, munching absently on a packet of peanuts, licking the salt off his fingers every so often. I'm anxious about this whole endeavour. It's not going to end well. These things never do.

Simon's gaze does not move from the windscreen. "Pass me the binoculars."

Against my better judgement I do so, scrolling through a list of horrible scenarios; Chinese Water Torture, a swim in a shark-infested ocean, death by skinning, Valerie Perkins – all are preferable to sitting here. It's like watching that car crash in slow motion, except I'm in it and I can't get out, because he's my best mate, and I'm driving.

"She might not go to this class anymore. I mean, why would she need aerobics now she's schnooking her instructor?" When I'm bored and anxious, tact is the first sense to go.

Simon gives me an evil glare. "Will you stop talking like that? This is part of my therapy."

"Who's your doctor? I'll be sure to pass their name to Valerie."

"Valerie needs more than a doctor."

"A shaman? A priest? A vet?"

"Keep your voice down!" He scoops out another handful of peanuts. After this, the interior of my car will contain enough salt to kill the slug population of the entire world. "I really think this is going to help," he says with his mouth full.

"Great. I still think this is a really bad idea."

"I know. You've said it about eight thousand times."

"And still you don't get the hint."

Simon peers through the binoculars again. "Okay, people are starting to leave. What time is it?"

"Half-past bad idea."

"John…"

"Three o' clock."

"Yes! Schools out. All we have to do now is wait for them to come out."

I shift position and hope the feeling will return to my buttocks sometime before Christmas. "What about if Penny doesn't show up? How will we know which one is him?"

"Patience, Johnny. He does a class six days a week. I've got time enough to wait to see his ugly mug."

Knowing Simon means this, I start praying, hoping God recovers quickly enough from the shock of hearing from me to make Chris materialise. I appreciate that Simon's at the stage of wanting to know but not wanting to know, but I can't go through this vigil again tomorrow.

We've been sitting in the car park for over an hour, keeping the leisure centre under surveillance in the vain hope that Penny will emerge with Chris so Simon can – well, that's the bit I'm anxious about. What is Simon hoping to achieve? He thinks being able to picture Chris will help him to get over it, and, to a point, I do understand his reasoning. He has to see this guy in the flesh, to visualise the man Penny has chosen over him, but he's only going to intensify his pain. However this scene turns out, it won't be to his advantage. But, I suppose, that never stopped me.

Simon elbows me sharply in the ribs, bringing me to attention. "There she is!"

"Is he with her?"

He thrusts the binoculars at me. "You look."

I take the poisoned chalice, and peer through it.

"Can you see anything?"

"Only your fat head." Simon shifts over, so that he's no longer obscuring my view. "Okay."

"What?" He's stopped chewing peanuts and has started on his nails. On balance, I'd rather have salt all over the seats. "Tell me. Is he big? Is he taller than me?"

"Well …" I take a second. "He probably only seems tall because she's so short."

"She's the same fucking height as me!"

"Did I say short? I meant petite, diminutive. Elfin, at a push."

"Gimme those."

"You know what, let's just go."

"Go? What are you on about? Let me see."

"Simon-"

We engage in a minor tussle as he tries to snatch the binoculars from me. I'm reluctant to let him see that his estranged wife is hanging from the arm of this Himbo as though her life depends on it. Unfortunately, Simon can be quite strong when he puts his mind to it. It's all the fat.

"Jesus! His legs are the size of fucking tree trunks! Look at his arms!"

"Maybe the binoculars are broken." I adjust the button between the lenses.

"I get it now. Look at him, John. He looks like one of those blokes out of *Men's Health*. No wonder she wants him and not me."

I run a hand through my hair. "You know what? There's more to relationships than that, and if she's shallow enough to go for a guy who probably oils himself every night, then you're better off without her."

Simon curls his lip. "You dumped your girlfriend so you can shag other women – don't talk to me about shallow." He has a point. "I'm going to speak to her, make her see sense. Wait here."

I offer a perfunctory protest as he steps out of the car – something along the lines of making things worse and what does he think is going to happen, but he keeps going, smoothing his hair back with his palms. I roll my eyes. Of course, I can't wait here for him to come back, no doubt bruised and flat-packed. Simon's inevitably going to make a twat of himself, and my role is to go out there and perform some kind of damage limitation. I spit out my gum, and catch him up.

"You know, Simon, this is absolutely the wrong thing for you to do," I say, walking double-time to keep up with the purposeful stride he apparently has only learned today.

"Someone has to tell her." Simon stares at his wife and her lover, who are canoodling on the bonnet of what I assume is Chris's love-mobile. It's probably the first time a Honda Jazz has ever been such a thing.

"Tell her what?"

"That she's making the biggest mistake of her life. She's obviously in lust with this … man, and everyone knows that doesn't last."

"But she doesn't think she's making a big mistake. If she's going to come back to you, she has to make the decision for herself. You can't tell her not to want him. If you do, you'll only push her further away from you. You'll give them something to bond over, and that something is you acting like a prat."

As I'm saying all this we're still striding across the car park, and I know I'm wasting my breath. But, he's my mate. I've wasted more for him.

"If you don't like it, you can always go home, John."

As if.

"Oi!" Simon's yobbish greeting breaks the euphoric trance of the woman who pledged to be with him for better or worse. This is clearly the 'better' part. She spins round, and I watch the surprise slowly register. Simon is clearly the last person she expected to see. In fact, so shocked is she, that it's quite possible she forgot who he was for a second or two. Beside her, the Herculean Chris simply frowns, the expression sitting incongruously on his square face. His chin is so impressively angular that if I had a protractor, I'd measure it. He reminds me of Buzz Lightyear, which is bad because it makes Simon Mr. Potato Head in comparison.

"Simon? What are you doing here?" Penny looks from her husband to her lover with an expression revealing that this is her worst nightmare come true.

"I've come to take you home," Simon says firmly and quite, for him, authoritatively.

This is all very gallant, but inside I'm cringing. I hover behind my friend, ready to step in if and when I am needed. My money is on this shaping into more of a 'when' situation.

Chris's steel jaw locks. I hear the click. Penny again switches glances between her husband and her lover, and I wonder what the world has come to – two guys are fighting over Penny and there is still more than one woman left on the planet. I really should point this out to them, remind them that Penny has little hairs sprouting from her chin that she bleaches every couple of weeks (I chart their change in colour with interest).

"But I've left you," she wails in protest.

"So? You can change your mind, can't you? Women do that all the time." Simon's voice is erring dangerously close to pleading now. I will him to maintain the last millimetre of dignity remaining on his scratch-card of pride.

I pop some more gum into my mouth, purely to stop me from screaming, "make it stop!" I study Chris, wondering when he's going to contribute something to the debate. He has yet to prove he can actually speak and stand upright at the same time. This man is going to be a father. I glance at Penny's stomach – she's not showing yet. Mind you, who could tell if she were?

Penny softens her voice in the way women do when they're about to say something harsh. "Simon, I don't love you anymore. I don't think I ever loved you. Marrying you was… I need someone more …exciting." She gazes up at Chris – a fair way up, he's almost as tall as me. "We're happy. And we're going to have a baby."

And women have the front to say men are bastards?

Simon takes this on the chin, which is unfortunately not as wide as Chris's. "I can be exciting if that's what you really want," he says. "All you had to do was ask."

"Asking isn't very exciting," Penny snaps. "I need someone who instinctively knows what I want." She peers up at the towering form of Chris to affirm this, as though he is excitement in human form.

And then, Simon finally sees the red that's been dangling in front of his eyes since Penny left. "Oh really? How do you know it's his?" He turns to Chris. "Really, mate, how do you know it's yours?"

I nod, to no one in particular. Good one Simon. More of this and less of the whining, please.

Then, it speaks. "I don't know what you're trying to insinuate," Chris says in a perfect cut-glass accent, "but I advise you to watch your tone."

My guess is this guy's coming out of the closet in the next three to five years, max.

"Oh piss off. Who asked you?" Simon says, even though he did.

"Now, listen…"

Chris takes a step towards Simon, so I take one towards him. I shake my head and Chris steps back. And then, Penny loses her already poor penchant for diplomacy, and we're off.

"Oh, please just get lost, Simon," she says. "You're wasting your time. We're together, and that's that." She nudges Chris, and they move to get into the car. Simon turns round and gives me a look of despair. This was not the sort of closure he was hoping for. All I can offer is a shrug.

"Penny, wait," Simon calls out.

She has no intention of doing that, crossing over to her side of the car as though he weren't there. Then, as he walks around to get into the driver's seat, Chris sneers at Simon and says, "Hard luck, boy." This might not seem like a big deal, but to us, in that very moment, it represents everything that's wrong with our lives. To Simon, that sneer says, "Fuck you," "You are inadequate", "I'm screwing your wife," and "My other car is a Ferrari F50" all in one single facial gesture. Every grievance we've ever had, every injustice we've ever felt, rises to the surface of our minds. Simon is paralysed, standing there with his mouth agape, and is clearly going to spend the next few weeks thinking up quips he would've uttered at this particular juncture if only he'd thought of them. And me? Well, I just thump the guy.

It happens in a synchronised blur. First comes the sneer, then the tiny second of Simon and his open-mouthed astonishment. Then I step forward and knock Chris out with my left fist. My hand feels like every bone in it is broken, but Chris teeters and topples to the ground like a skittle, his mouth open in surprise, and a warm glow of satisfaction swells from inside my chest and spreads throughout my entire body. It takes Penny a couple of seconds to comprehend that her pillar of excitement has been felled.

"Oh my God!" She rushes to Chris's aid, crouching down on the tarmac beside him, patting his forehead, which is weird because I thought I punched him in the eye. "John, you stupid bloody idiot! How could you do this?"

Then Simon starts laughing, which doesn't help matters at all.

"There!" he yells down at Penny. "Was that exciting enough for you?" Clutching his sides he wheels around, pulling me with him.

I manage to blurt out, "Hey, I'm sorry about that, Penny, but you know how these things are." From the obscenities she yells at the back of my head, she blatantly doesn't. No one ever does.

Simon and I sprint back to the car. My hand is killing me, but not enough to let Simon drive. We get in without a word. I fasten my seatbelt, reasoning that the sooner we get out of here the better, before Penny calls the police, the army, the Taliban, or all three.

I push the start button.

"So, it was true then?"

I turn to my friend, who's beaming at me as though I've told him none of the Beatles are dead, and that Pamela Anderson (who Simon remains stubbornly in love with) fancies him, and so do all her friends.

"About what?"

"About the one punch thing - remember when we went to Berlin, and you told that bloke in the airport bar that you could knock him out with one punch? You meant it."

"Of course I meant it." I put the car into reverse, aware that Simon is still gazing admiringly at me.

"John?"

"Yeah?"

"Thanks."

"Don't be stupid."

"No, I mean it, John. You're a good friend."

I nod. "Yes, I am. If nothing else."

The macho display I carried out on Simon's behalf does wonders to restore his bruised self-esteem. He spends the next few days strutting around the house and starting sentences with variations on, "Did you see the way he fell, John? Right on his arse." He's pleased with himself, and even more pleased with me. Punching Chris himself would've been one thing, but having me step out from the shadows and do it for him is a different ballgame entirely. He has a henchman. For guys like Simon, that's worth at least twenty sessions on the shrink's couch.

I wish I had such a stylised salvation. My head is congested with thoughts and words. They bump into each other, whirling around, searching for the correct place to slot into my brain. I want to decapitate myself just so I can have a bit of quiet, a respite from the incessant pros, cons, and 'what ifs'.

I'm not a big believer in that 'problem shared' maxim. I actually think sharing a problem makes it grow, gives it power, and that somehow saying the words aloud is like admitting it's getting the better of you. But, even if I wanted to, I can't talk to Simon. He'd just make it simple, break it down into something like, "You miss Lola. You fucked up," and I can't, and won't, listen to that. But I have to do something, before my crowded head closes in on me.

So I'm here, of all places. Who knew that the road to Damascus leads to Tesco?

I hate supermarkets. I hate the aisles, I hate the products, I hate the people who use them (yes that includes me, when I absolutely have to), and I hate the inflated prices and huge profit margins. I don't bother to hide the fact I'm merely passing through. I don't pick up a basket, I refuse a trolley with glee, and I certainly am not browsing through the special offers. My hands welded firmly in the pockets of my jacket, my eyes never veering left or right, I begin my search.

I explore almost every aisle, and eventually find Kay at the delicatessen counter, grimacing as she reads the number on her ticket. I approach with caution.

"Hey, Kay."

She takes something out of her trolley. It has a picture of a grinning teenager on the front of it. "Do you have any idea how much crap they put in these things?"

"Actually, yes. That's why I never eat them."

"You'd have no choice if you had kids." She stuffs the tin behind a mountain of bread.

"Which is why I have none."

"You have none because who in their right mind would want to have kids with you."

"People in their wrong mind?"

She narrows her eyes at me. "You're lucky I'm speaking to you. No, you're not lucky – I'm only giving you the time of day because Lola told me not to shut you out. What kind of person is that unselfish?"

"Lola."

"Exactly." Kay folds her arms. "And yet, you still dumped her. Odd."

"I didn't dump her," I say, glancing over my shoulder and wishing that Kay wouldn't talk quite so loudly. "We broke up."

"Is that how you sleep at night?'

"Actually, I don't sleep much at night. Not since…you know. Not since I broke up with your sister."

Kay rolls her eyes and checks the monitor, disgusted that there are still seven numbers in the queue ahead of her. "I get it. You wanted to meet me so I can tell my sister exactly how terrible you're feeling about the whole thing. This is all about easing your conscience."

"No, Kay, that's not it at all." Of course, that's it precisely. "Can I just say though, that I am very grateful to you for agreeing to meet with me. Even if it did have to be here."

"I'm a very busy woman. I have a husband, children, and a house to maintain. I don't expect you to understand that I can't simply drop everything and swan off for coffee whenever the mood takes me, so here will have to do."

"And you know what? Here is perfect, because you get to do your shopping, and I can help you."

She slaps my hand away from a multi-pack of baked beans, as though I might contaminate it. "What do you want?"

A beat – a very short one. "Does she talk about me?"

"No. You only crop up in conversation occasionally, usually when she sees something that reminds her of you."

My ears prick up. "Really? Like what?"

"Like an advert for haemorrhoid cream."

"Come on, Kay. If they sell humble pie in this store I'll buy every single one, and I'll eat every last crumb. Please. I need to know."

She sighs, putting a hand on one of her child-bearing hips. "Well, she used to go on about you all the time. That was during the crying and playing miserable songs phase. I told her you meet somebody new when you least expect it, and all that stuff about fish and the sea. I felt bad for saying it because it's so lazy and clichéd. I never for one second thought I'd be right. God knows if it weren't for Josh I'd still be sitting at home passing her Kleenex while my ironing piles up."

"Right."

And then, with a flash of blinding light, my brain rewinds her last sentence.

This is a bad time for Kay to be served, as I now need and insist upon her full attention. I grab her arm whilst she's watching her kilogram of mature cheddar being sliced and wrapped in that reassuringly white paper.

"Kay, who, or what, is Josh?"

"And a dozen slices of smoky bacon, please. And cut the fat off. All of it." The assistant is clearly terrified – her lip-ring quivers. Kay turns to me. "Josh is … oh no. She didn't tell you about Josh. Forget it, I shouldn't have mentioned him. He's no one." She goes back to the assistant, who is so nervous she can't remember where she picked the bacon up from. "Have you got any Brie?" I tap Kay on the arm again. "Will you quit doing that? You're worse than Susie and Jeremy."

"Just give me details. Who is he, where did she meet him, that kind of stuff. Then I promise I will go away and leave you to your sausages and Scotch eggs."

Kay throws the wedge of Brie into her trolley. "I don't buy Scotch eggs." She thanks the assistant behind the counter who, 'emo' or not, is wearing far too much eyeliner.

"John, I really don't know all that much about him."

"You're lying."

"And you would know."

"I run workshops. Tell me, Kay." When God was handing out the gift of wearing people down, I stole the lot whilst his back was turned.

Kay waves a hand. "All right, all right." We walk down towards the breakfast cereals and she throws things into her trolley without really looking, a testament to the fact that women really can do more than one thing at a time. "She met him at that pub-"

"Which pub?"

"How would I know? The one you took her to. The one with the big windows out the front."

A sinking feeling fills my stomach. "Go on."

"He's called Josh-"

"Josh. Yes, I know." And I hate him already.

"Will you let me finish?" A packet of Ricicles takes the brunt of Kay's frustration, rattling against her towering pile of Super Noodles. "He's called Josh, I've forgotten what he does for a job, but he definitely has one. He's twenty-five and, by accounts, is a nice bloke, so that's a step up for her."

I ignore that, and focus on the important detail. "He's younger than her."

"And?"

"I don't know. I'm just … surprised."

"Why, because you thought it'd take a year or two of mourning before she got over you?" Her eyes widen. "Oh my God, you did. Well, too bad." Kay snorts in disapproval and forces the trolley over to the crisp section.

I watch her perform the quickest smash and grab involving potato snacks in the history of retail outlets, and try to picture Lola with someone else. My Lola. I clench my fists, a twinge of pain from yesterday's vigil giving me an idea.

I need therapy of my own.

8

Josh. Josh. Josh.

His name wails repeatedly in my brain, the syllable on a constant loop, an inner jukebox of white noise. And I can't shut it off. I find myself wishing the Bank of England would declare itself bankrupt, for sterling to drop to twenty-three pence against the dollar, for interest rates to hit minus four percent, a recession of seismic proportions, whatever, so long as it's catastrophic and all-consuming. Anything has to be better than this, my own private Black Wednesday (and Thursday, Friday, etc.). I've even compiled an imaginary photofit of him, and the face I've created is haunting me.

He's suave and slick, with Clooney-like charm. He does karate and can kill people with a copy of 'Q' magazine, Jason Bourne style. He can, probably, fly like Superman, and has a Tardis, and a Sonic Screwdriver. No doubt he lives in a loft apartment in Hoxton, Shoreditch, or somewhere equally bile-inducing. He eats organic food, drives a Prius, separates his rubbish into piles for recycling, and every other thing that makes me want to vomit into my own trousers. He cares passionately about Third World debt and all the other causes I consider only when it's convenient, i.e. not when I need to make a plane journey, or when I'm asked, "Do you need a bag?" Young – let's not forget young – trendy, and charismatic, Josh. I hate him - I really hate him. I want him to go back from whence he came, to be conscripted to fight in the war – any war, I don't even mind if it's not one of ours. We can start one especially for him, it's fine by me. I want to rewind back to when I was unaware of his existence. Most of all, I want him away from my girlfriend.

"Ex-girlfriend," Simon corrects, when I regurgitate this rant to him in the stationery room.

"Hey, I didn't get hung up on semantics when you made me sit in a car for over an hour waiting for Chris."

"Don't say his name out loud!" Simon glances over his shoulders, his eyes bulging.

"Simon, he's an aerobics instructor, not the fucking Candyman. Get a grip." I'm being flippant, but I understand exactly where Simon is coming from. I'm there too, checking out the view. And it's not pretty.

Josh. What kind of a name is that? Seriously, it's okay until the age of about eight, or if you're a *Blue Peter* presenter.

Simon composes himself. "Okay, intelligence gathering time: what do you know about him?"

"Nothing, that's the problem. Kay told me he's called Josh, he's a 'nice bloke', and he's twenty-five. That's the sum total of my intelligence gathering."

Simon purses his lips. "Mm, he's younger than her. And you," he adds, totally unnecessarily.

"Well done. Would you like to try Pythagoras's theorem now?"

"'Nice bloke'. So he's gay then. Where did she meet him?"

I loosen my tie. "This is the killer. She met him in The Parlour."

"You're kidding me." He takes a step back in an attempt at drama. He sometimes does really camp things like that.

"Do I look like I'm fucking joking?"

And then, because it had to happen, Simon starts laughing. He begins slowly, then builds up to a more staccato tempo. The sound, coupled with the image of his melon-head jigging along rhythmically, reminds me of an egg boiling. It's my turn to glance around to see if anyone is watching us.

I fold my arms and glare at him, and he stops.

"Okay, but if it's not funny then it's at least ironic. Lola meets her new man in the very bar you turned down a weekend in Paris for. I bet you're super-pissed we went to the opening now." He starts laughing again and I wonder why, in all our years of friendship, I've haven't punched him. There's still time.

"That's right, laugh it up. And he's not her 'new man.'"

"What?" Simon dabs his eyes. "What is he then? Her accountant?"

"Simon…"

"You have to face it, John."

"Shall we go through all the things you need to face?"

"Dear God, no. Okay…" He tries to look serious which, for him, is a lot more difficult than it is for most people. "So, um, how do you feel about it and stuff?"

"It's right up there with the time my car got clamped round the back of Oxford Street."

"I told you not to drive into town. I said to get the bus."

"I'd rather kill myself."

"Please do." He shrugs. "But you're not jealous, right? I mean, you don't want her back or anything?"

"Of course I don't want her back." I run a hand through my hair. "It's just very sudden. She's obviously not thinking rationally."

Simon pulls a face that is intended to convey his scepticism. Either that, or he's about to burp. "Obviously." He clears his throat. "So, what are we going to do about it then?"

I prod the base of the stationery cabinet with my toe, briefly entertaining the hope that the entire thing will topple over and crush me. I wonder if Lola would cry at my funeral. What would she wear – black? Are we talking proper black, or that cop-out charcoal colour? How much black though? Would she faint and try to fling herself on top of my coffin? Oh God, what about if she brought fucking Josh with her?

Right…

"There's no other choice."

Simon nods solemnly, understanding what action is required. "After work?"

"You're on."

I go back to my desk with the *A-Team* theme playing inside my head. I let it stay there – it's comforting, and at least I feel slightly more in control of myself now. That is, until Sarah swans past to deliver some pamphlets informing us about changes to our pensions – I'm guessing these changes aren't for our benefit – and takes it upon herself to strike up a conversation. For her, striking a match is easier.

"Hi, John," she says, flashing a set of shiny teeth at me. "How are you?"

"Now that you ask, I'm actually really busy," I mutter, typing out a stream of words about the stock market I hope will make sense once I read them back.

"Yes, it's that time of year, isn't it?"

I have to stop typing and look up – this is bound to be good. I notice she's sitting on my copy of the Bank of England quarterly inflation report. It's a fact that if I put anything official looking on my desk, Sarah's arse cheeks will locate it, and land on it. It's a shame her buttocks can't absorb and understand information – she'd learn so much.

"Spring?"

"No," she rolls her eyes, as though I'm the dunce and she's just split the Atom for the seventy-first time. "The time of year when all the tax does stuff," she replies, reminding me all at once why she's a junior at her age. "Hey," she whispers, "did you hear that Tony is losing his job?"

"Who's Tony?" I ask, wishing yet again that I could smoke in here.

"Come on, you must know Tony! How can you work here and not know Tony?" When I fail to display any semblance of recognition, and she very slowly realises I'm capable of working anywhere and not knowing anyfuckingone, she elaborates. "You know, the guy who got thrown out of the restaurant at the Christmas lunch for sticking mistletoe on his fly and propositioning the waitress?"

"I didn't go to the Christmas lunch," I say, her description reinforcing exactly why.

"You never go to any of our social events."

"I like to keep work and play separate."

Her cheeks bulge as her tongue probes her mouth. "You shouldn't rule anything out."

"Except getting a perm and voting Conservative."

"Come on, John." She leans in closer. "You should try it. It can be fun."

"I'll bear that in mind." If I'm at a total loose end and the canteen at Guantanamo Bay is closed.

She pulls back into her own personal space and mercifully out of mine.

"Anyway, Tony's losing his job."

"You said."

She hops off the desk and smoothes out her skirt. "God, you're frosty today, even by your grouchy standards." She carries on smoothing. There are no creases to be seen, and I want to pin her arms to her side with my stapler. "Don't you care? I told you people are being made redundant." She repeat this word in the way other people would refer to gonorrhoea, or syphilis. I get the impression Tony probably has both.

"I'm sure this Tony is a great guy, absolutely top notch, salt of the earth, but I still have a job and really need to get on with it."

Sarah wrinkles her nose. She gathers up her pile of pamphlets, tosses her hair, and sets off to disturb someone else. I watch her non-existent arse saunter over to the woman with the loud blouse whose sole purpose in life seems to be buying coffee from the Pret across the road. What is it about

Sarah that men find so alluring? She's like a Tiffany box with an Argos ring inside.

From across the room, Simon gives me a thumbs-up. I nod at him, and get back to the stock markets.

I'm immersed in my flow, and starting to feel a teeny bit like the old me, whoever he was, when my phone emits a shrill ring. I answer it only when it's clear that it's not going to stop until I do.

"Yeah?"

"Is this John?"

"Yeah."

"John Black?"

"Who is this?"

"Um, it's Rebecca."

"Hi." A beat. Like Vienna, it means nothing to me. "Sorry, who?"

"Oh God, I knew this would happen… Rebecca Speller, from the other night, in the Pitcher and Piano? With the lighter, or lack thereof?"

"Oh, right, Rebecca. Hi. I was going to call, but…"

"No, you weren't. I said you wouldn't call."

"You also said you were never wrong."

"You do remember."

"I remember that bit."

"Well…" She goes quiet for a few seconds, and I imagine her on the other end of the line, fiddling with her hair or examining her nails. "Look, John, here's the thing. I thought there was something – a spark, chemistry, or – oh God, I can't believe I'm saying this…"

Neither can I, really.

"Thing is, John Black, would you like to meet up for a drink one night?"

I open my mouth to come out with a stunning reason, like cancer treatment or religious principles, why a drink with her is impossible, then wonder why I'm engineering fictitious obstacles. I wanted to the play the field, and guess what, here's the field. And unless Rebecca's had facial surgery in the weeks since I met her, she's an attractive field – no weeds or hidden dog turds. And Lola's having a lovely time swanning around town with Josh, so…

"Sure."

"Really? Great!"

I'd be flattered by her enthusiasm, were she not clearly desperate.

"Tomorrow, same place, seven?"

"Um, yeah, that's good for me," Rebecca says. "You should know that I give it ten minutes, then I go."

"I take it you drink shots then."

"No, I mean, if you're late. I never wait longer than ten minutes. For a man. But you don't seem like the kind of guy who'd be late."

"And you're never wrong, are you?"

"I hope not."

I allow myself a little smile. I've earned it. "See you, Rebecca."

"Yeah, see you."

I stare at the phone for a long moment after I replace the receiver. That little exchange has taught me something. If you don't call women, they call you anyway. They just can't let it go. They like a challenge. They don't trust us to do the chasing anymore. Next she'll be wanting to 'tame' me, to change me. Women love trying to change men, like we're something they bought at Topshop that doesn't quite fit. They still have the receipt, so they go for an exchange. But a man will only change if he wants to. If a man isn't perfect for a woman the way he is now, he never will be. So that beer gut, the hatred of shopping, habit of belching aloud after meals, farting under the duvet, and leaving the toilet seat up? Not gonna change. No, not even for you, sweetheart. And no, he's not different. In this respect, we are all the same. And so are you.

Lola never wanted me to be anything more than I am, even though for her, I probably wasn't good enough. Maybe that was where I should've tried to change her. She could've done a lot better. Perhaps she has now.

Sometimes I wonder if a guy's best friend is a merely mirror of his own insecurities. It certainly feels that way tonight, as Simon is currently spouting all the things I'm feeling, but daren't vocalise.

"What about if he works for like, some big investment bank or something, and makes loads in bonuses?"

"Well, he won't this year. Did you not read my piece on City bonuses?"

Simon looks at me. "No. Why would I?"

He has a point.

We keep walking. His legs are going like miniature pistons to keep pace. "Okay…What about if he's got a better car than you?"

"No chance. Just because you drive the most boring car on the planet."

"Oi, there's nothing wrong with my car."

"If you like Fords."

"And I do. This isn't about me."

"Don't get defensive."

"Don't be evasive," he answers back quickly. Too quickly. I don't know where he learned that. "I bet he has an iPhone."

"Then he really is a twat."

"He might earn more money than you do. He might be richer."

"Lola earns more than I do."

"Oh. Yeah." He chews the inside of his mouth. "I'm doing this for your own good, you know. To prepare you."

I flash him a look. "What? Okay, what about if he has a house somewhere like… I dunno… Fitzrovia."

"Good for him."

"What about if Lola goes there? What about if Lola likes going there – what about," Simon is rambling now, "if Lola likes being with him more than she did with you?"

He's come within an inch of hitting the nail on the head, and I come within an inch of hitting him on the head. "Then good for her."

"You don't mean that." Simon almost sings it. "Either that, or you're kidding yourself."

I don't answer. He might be fat, but he's not stupid. I zip up my jacket, and wedge my hands into my pockets. Simon senses exactly what's going through my head. I hate it when he does that.

"Don't sweat it, John. Odds are he won't even be there tonight. And I'm sure Lola's just on the rebound. Either that, or she and Kay planned to tell you about this Josh bloke, just to see how you'd react. Yeah, this whole thing is probably a set-up. There probably is no Josh. He's like Keyser Soze. Women make up stuff like this all the time."

"Only because we believe it."

Simon is about to argue, but changes his mind. "You're right, we do. God, that's disturbing."

"You know what, I hope he is there tonight. Otherwise I'm going to have to keep going back until I see him for myself."

Simon, aware he's complicit in all of this, grunts his assent. There's little point in him saying that he understands precisely what I'm going through.

We walk the rest of the way in silence. Nothing can expel the haze swirling around my brain. I'm at the mercy of fate, my sanity hanging in the balance, pending the result of tonight's escapade.

I haven't been to The Parlour for about six weeks, which is something of an achievement for me as I used to drink here all the time. It was so conveniently located at an equidistant point between my house and Simon's that it became like our village hall, our after-school club, our tree-house refuge from the world. We didn't care about the shit jazz music or the trendy patrons – no, we tolerated both because we could relax in there. It was kind of like finding a UN safe haven in the midst of a war zone (often applicable literally, in Simon's case). We knew that no matter what happened, we would be safe in here. Not any more.

Now I'm seeing The Parlour in a new light. Or not: when we step inside, I notice for the first time how dark the place is. I notice, and not just because Josh allegedly drinks in here, how small it is. Dingy. And yeah, because Josh drinks here I decide it smells of excrement and the beer tastes like piss. I'm never coming here again, and I've lost nothing. The place is an overrated craphole.

But this place was my second home. Josh has violated sacred territory. In many ways. We might have even seen him in here, nodded at him over the pool table. I could've taken a piss next to him in the Gents. I shudder involuntarily.

"How do you want to play this?" Simon mutters to me. He's scanning the place discreetly, although neither of us knows what this so-called Josh looks like, and it's so dark I can barely make Simon out, and sadly I'm all too well acquainted with his face.

I peer over at the bar, thinking I can make out the shape of someone I know.

"I think Maxine is in. I'm going to ask her."

Simon nods. "Good call." He claps me on the back. "You can get me a drink while you're at it."

We wander over to the bar, still trying to look casual, but my insides are churning as though I'm going to order root canal without anaesthesia rather than two bottles of Stella. I feel so out of control of the situation and I hate it. It's unnatural.

Maxine catches my eye and smiles at me. I wait for her to finish serving the customer who's staring steadfastly down her top.

"Jesus." Simon is nearly drooling. "Has Maxine always looked like that?"

I study her more intently, working out what's different. "I think she's cut her hair."

Simon is glassy-eyed and slack-jawed. "That must be it."

Maxine beams. I like that she's so pleased to see us. "Hi, John. Hello, Simon. Long time no see. How've you been?"

I go to exchange glances with my friend, but he's still spellbound, and apparently dumbstruck. "Good, thanks. How're you? You look … healthy."

She laughs. "You noticed!"

"It's kind of difficult not to, as I think Simon's muteness will testify."

"Well," she shrugs, "I decided life's too short. I've always wanted bigger tits so I thought – why not?"

The word 'tits' brings Simon back to life. "What do they feel like?"

I slap his advancing hand away. "You'll never know. Excuse him Maxine, he doesn't get to see real live women very often. Unless he's paid them, of course."

"Fuck off, John."

I raise my eyebrows at Maxine, who over the years has been consistently amused by our unwitting double act. We've always been popular with barmaids. The alcohol fumes impair their judgement.

"See what I have to put up with?"

"Saint John of North London." She winks at Simon. "Usual?"

"Yes please," Simon says in a flash.

Maxine turns to get our drinks. I decide to seize the moment before Simon seizes her newly enlarged moments.

"Maxine…?" I let it hang in the air.

"Yes?" She looks up from prising the tops from our beers. Simon doesn't look up from fantasising about prising her top off.

"Do you know a guy called Josh? He drinks here, apparently."

She blinks at me a few times. "Is this a trick question?" Simon and I exchange cautious glances. I wonder if she's about to say, "He's dead." Then I wonder if I'm going to hell for hoping she's going to say, "Yes, he's dead. He died after his penis enlargement surgery went catastrophically wrong."

Maxine puts our beers on the bar. "Of course I know him. He's my boss."

My stomach plummets like an out of control lift. "Boss?"

"Sure," Maxine chirps. "He bought the place a few months ago. He's out the back – do you want me to get him for you?"

I fumble in my pocket for some cash, and fling a handful onto the bar. "No." It comes out too quickly. I take a breath. "No, it's fine." I turn to Simon. "You know what? I don't feel like drinking tonight. Why don't you have mine? See you, Maxine."

"Oh. See you, John." She looks at Simon for an explanation. He's still staring at her boobs. "Don't leave it so long next time!"

I can't tell her I'd rather donate my money to a terrorist organisation than waste any more of it lining Josh's pockets. I turn to go.

Simon catches up with me as I am about to exit the bar, which is now up there with Baghdad, Beirut, and the Lebanon on my list of places to visit.

"John, mate, are you sure about this? You could have it out with this Josh here and now, get it over with. You know, give him the old one-punch treatment. You'll feel better if you do."

I look at him. "You know, Simon, I don't think that would make me feel better at all."

Roles are reversed: Simon doesn't get back until after four in the morning, and I'm lying awake not quite waiting for him, but almost. But it turns out that when his taxi pulls up outside and he stumbles into the house, bumping into furniture and knocking things – everything – over, I can't face going down to talk to him. I can't face the words sitting on my tongue, the ones banging around as clumsily in my head as Simon is in the house. I don't want to hear them out loud; I don't want to speak them, those four little words.

Where is she now?

9

Having learned the hard way that it's best to keep your options open, I choose a seat with a good view of the door. This gives me the chance to slip out the back way if I see her and decide I can't face it. If I'm honest though, which I am occasionally, it might not be me who makes a run for the exit.

It's not the best time for me to be having my first 'date' with Rebecca – with anyone. This is me, back in the saddle I so badly craved, on a day when I'm such lousy company that she'd probably have a wilder time having drinks with Cliff Richard.

I think, for once, Simon may have been sincere when he told me to fuck off this morning. And I might possibly have even deserved it. He was regaling me with details of his exploits at Maxine's flat, and how silicone breasts actually don't feel that much different to real ones. He was happy, ebullient and, well, it got on my nerves. Yeah, yeah, I know I should've been happy for him – he deserves a decent break, but the effort would've cracked my face in two, or even three. He made the mistake of informing me that getting a shag would solve all my problems. I asked him which particular problem he was referring to, since I wasn't aware I had any, and he replied, "The one concerning you still being in love with your ex-girlfriend."

I should have known better, but I say this to myself so often that maybe the truth is I really don't know any better. It was easier – preferable, perhaps, to pull the pin on the grenade and tell him I'd already got a 'shag', thank you very much, and off went a little explosion in N6.

Simon was instantly enraged that, first of all, I'd had sex and not told him about it, and secondly because I'd had sex with someone before he did, and lastly, that I'd had sex. It didn't help that I made it sound like something I was proud of as opposed to a memory that makes me want to dip my cock in a bucket of bleach whenever it crosses my mind.

"Oh yes, because you're so fucking irresistible," he'd yelled at me. "I go back to Maxine's flat for a fumble, but you have to have women dragging you off the street and demanding sex. Of course, because that just soooo you."

"What, are we in playschool again?"

"We never left." Simon turned away, put his hands on his hips, and then looked back at me. His other really camp gesture. "Do you know what your trouble is?"

Why do people always ask me this and then tell me anyway?

"You don't know a good thing when you've got it. For some sick reason, women adore you, John. To them, you're some kind of dark and brooding type – they want to tame you. And this has turned you into an arrogant, selfish bastard. Instead of thanking God that a bird like Lola would choose to give you the time of day, you got shot of her so you could be a 'man.'" He made quotation marks with his fingers and I wanted to stab him with a fork. "What does that mean, John? How did Lola stop you from being a man? No one can stop you doing anything – you always put yourself first, don't you? Here's some advice – why don't you try growing up."

I sat there for a few seconds until I realised my mouth was hanging open. Then I issued one of my stock cold responses, refuting everything he'd said, telling him I don't have to explain myself to anyone.

"Good," he answered. "Because no one cares anymore." Then he stormed out of the house without finishing his bacon sandwich, a first for him. We avoided each other all day, and

I've been stewing ever since. I'm tired, frazzled, and my mouth feels like someone's tipped an ashtray in it. Yeah, Rebecca will surely be delighted she's spending an evening with me.

I spot her as soon as she walks in. She looks good, just as I remembered – long legs, good figure. I try to straighten my tie, but it feels like I'm strangling myself, so I loosen it again.

"Well, well." She folds her arms. "John Black. And you're early. I knew you would be."

"The woman who's never wrong." I try to smile. "Hi." Just in time I remember this is supposed to be a date, so I pull out a chair for her. "You look great."

"Yeah, well, don't flatter yourself," she says, sitting down. "I've come straight from an appointment."

"Flattery is not something I know how to do. Drink?"

"Whatever you're having."

"Right."

I oblige and come back with a triple Scotch on the rocks. She peers warily into the glass.

"Cheers." I clink my glass against hers. She takes a sip and immediately starts coughing.

"Oh my God! What is this, petrol?"

"Don't worry, it's unleaded."

"It's vile! When it's my round, I'm getting something pink with umbrellas and an olive." She coughs again.

I smile and take another sip, enjoying the burn as the Scotch works its way down my gullet.

We sit there in silence for a few seconds. For Rebecca, the lull in conversation is awkward. She fidgets, fiddling with the ends of her hair and glancing around the bar. For me, the silence is golden. If all that's required of me is sitting here and getting slowly drunk, then I'm happy to date anyone.

"So, how's the world of economics? I read your column today."

I raise my eyebrows.

"Well… Okay, yeah. I mean, I do read it anyway, but I made sure I read it today. Just in case."

"In case there was a test at the end?"

"It's better to be prepared than look stupid," she says. She looks into her glass. The ice knocks together. "This truly is horrible."

"Then stop drinking it."

"I kind of like the horribleness now though. I could get used to it."

"That's great," I say. "By nine o'clock you'll be sitting in a shop doorway with a bottle in a brown paper bag."

"No," Rebecca says, turning her head to one side, exposing her neck. "I won't. You might though."

"I'm practically there already." I'm not joking but, thankfully, she doesn't know that, so she laughs. "How's your work?" I say. "What's new in art?"

"Ah!" She sits up, waving a finger at me. "So you did look at my card!"

"Of course I did. I just didn't keep it."

"Bastard. Why do men never call when they say they will?"

"I never said I would. Even you said I wouldn't. You'd have been disappointed if I had."

"No, I wouldn't."

"Come on. No challenge for you otherwise."

She pulls a face like she's just tasted stale eggs. "I'm not like that, John. But why don't men phone? Tell me."

I take another sip of Scotch – it makes me so much wiser. "Honestly?"

"Yes!" She leans forward, closer to me, our noses almost touching.

"The reason is," I whisper, "because either they don't want to, or they can't be bothered."

Rebecca pulls away. Her nose wrinkles. "What?"

"They don't phone because they don't want to. Or they're lazy."

"But that's mean! And weird."

I shrug. "That's men. Just don't give out your number."

"I don't," she says, folding her arms.

"You gave it to me," I remind her.

"Yes… But I knew you wouldn't call."

"So why give it to me?"

"Because otherwise I'd never know."

"And do you know now?"

She gives me a long look, her eyes twinkling. "I'm getting the picture."

We hold each other's gaze for few seconds. It feels like a long time.

"Wow…"

"More Scotch?"

"No. Maybe later."

She's staring at me again. It's a little disconcerting.

"I'd love you to sit for me one day," she says.

"I'm sitting."

"No, silly, 'sit' sit. Like, as in for a portrait."

"Is that what you do?"

She nods and flaps her hands around. "Yes! I love it – I do portraits and abstracts. For rich people."

"Are there any left?"

"Just about enough to pay the rent. Although," her expression turns wistful, "I'd like to get a mortgage one day. It's hard, when you're by yourself. Do you live locally?"

"The perennial London question. I'm in Highgate. But I'm staying with a friend at the moment."

Her eyebrows rise a little. "Oh? You're a bit old for flat-mates."

"Thank you." And I mean that. I shift in my chair. "I broke up with my girlfriend. My house, our house – our ex-house, is in Tufnell Park."

"Oh…" Rebecca presses her lips together. "How long were-"

"Nine years."

"Ouch." Her eyes are on me, but I'm concentrating on my now empty glass. "Poor you. You must be really hurting."

When I glance at her, I find a generous pity in her eyes. She lays her hand over mine. It's warm, soft. I sigh inside at the relief of being touched, being comforted. And then suddenly it's easier to let her go on, to allow the snowball to keep rolling. She's happy to assume, and I'm happy to oblige her.

"Did it come out of the blue?"

"Yeah, right out of the blue. She's seeing someone else already."

Rebecca draws a breath. "No! Really? Was she – I mean, were they...?"

"No, they just met recently. He owns a bar near where we live. Lived."

"Oh John, that's awful." She strokes her thumb across my hand. I don't think she knows she's doing it. "I must say though, you're doing well to hold it together. I'd be in pieces. You're very brave."

Sympathy is not an emotion that comes my way very often, so I make the most of it. "What else can I do?"

She considers me carefully. "This is probably too soon for you, isn't it?" She gazes out across the bar. "The one time you meet a decent guy… I should've known it was too good to be true. Look, John, I still think we have something here, you know?"

I nod, but I have no idea what I know, and what is a trick of the Scotch.

"So, when you're feeling less raw, when you're healing, you can call me."

"Okay," I say.

"And if you don't call, I'll know it's because you don't want to."

"Yes."

"Or you can't be bothered."

"Sure."

"Good. Well…" She takes her hand away and gets up to put her jacket on. My skin cools, and I am alone again.

"Rebecca." She turns back. "You don't have to go."

"No, I do. I'm not the rebound girl. Call me. If you want to." She kisses me on the cheek. "You will get over her, John. This feeling never lasts. It feels like it will, but it won't."

It's just easier not to tell her it's self-inflicted. It keeps things simple.

I've never cared much about the change in the seasons. I don't suffer from S.A.D., and the cyclical nature of the nights shortening and lengthening doesn't bother me. But tonight, I wish it were brighter. I wish it weren't so cold. There's a chill, right down in my bones, in my blood, but I keep on walking, not because I'm brave, but because I simply have to.

I remember hearing somewhere that the eyes are supposedly the windows to the soul, so I fix my gaze on the pavement, keeping my windows closed, my soul obscured. I don't want anyone seeing inside me tonight.

When I finally stop, my feet are so cold I can hardly feel them. I lean against the wall, watching contended customers trickle slowly out of The Parlour as closing time approaches. I breathe on my hands to get the blood flowing. It doesn't work.

My heart beats hard in my chest. My stomach feels light. But I do it anyway. I cross the road, and go right up to the glass.

Some things in life are painfully simple, and need no explanation. This is one of them. I peer into The Parlour, and there she is.

She's ensconced in a booth, her hair spread out over her shoulders, her feet tucked up beneath her. She has a drink in one hand and gesticulates with the other as she speaks. She loves to talk. She can gossip, discuss, debate, and chatter about anything. She talks with passion and, okay, some of it is irrelevant and tangential, but she says everything with energy and fire. Only this time, she's not talking to me. She's talking to him.

He's sitting beside her, his arm draped over the back of her seat, casually but deliberately boxing her in. He tilts his ear towards her mouth when he can't make out what she's saying, and she gladly slides even closer to him, so that their knees are touching. He raises his eyebrows, nodding in all the right places. He stares into her eyes as she speaks. To him, everything she says is a revelation. She captivates him. He loves to listen to her as much as she loves to talk. He listens to her not just with his ears, but with his entire body, inwardly unable to believe his luck that she's with him. He knows Lola is a one-off, a limited edition.

I knew that once too, but I forgot it, I let it go. But now, I remember.

I stare at Josh so hard my eyebrows hurt Through my green-eyed haze I convince myself that he's too thin, that his teeth are too square – almost unnaturally white, that his cheekbones are too chiselled, his Mother cuts his hair, and that he's just too damn young. In truth though, there's nothing offensive about Josh at all. He seems relaxed, as though he's at ease with himself, the world and everyone in it. His hair is an agreeable enough shade of brown, his clothes trendy, but not flashy. I continue to stare, flexing my fist in preparation.

He'd be pretty easy to knock out. His wiry frame would buckle and drop to the floor with greater ease than Chris's. And it'd feel so good to break up their cosy little scene. I picture myself marching purposefully inside, Lola looking shocked but pleased and relieved to see me, Josh tentatively standing up to defend himself. Then, before he knows what's happening, I knock him to the ground, hopefully chipping a few of those square teeth while I'm at it. Yes, it would feel good – really good. So good, that I put my hands back in my pockets, turn around, and begin the walk home.

One of the many, many great things about being a man is that I can have disagreements with my best friend where we say distasteful things we do mean, ignore each other for the rest of the day, and then just pick up like nothing happened. We don't need analysis, Hallmark cards, chocolate, Bette Midler movies, hugging, or ACAS to restore the equilibrium. We just, well, forget about it.

When I get back to the house I find Simon in his usual position, sprawled on the couch, his eyes glued to the television. He greets me as though we never exchanged a cross word, i.e. he doesn't look up and just grunts. The only anomalous thing about the scene is that Maxine – Maxine! – is curled up next to him.

"Hey."

"John!" Maxine sits bolt upright. I feel like Dad coming back early and disturbing the babysitters.

"Nnnugh." Simon's contribution. "How was..?"

"Rebecca." Maxine is already finishing his sentences for him.

I sink down into the armchair. My feet and legs are throbbing. Simon's feeding peanuts into his mouth, and occasionally into Maxine's, which is unusually generous of him. Before I so rudely disturbed them, Maxine's head was tucked comfortably on Simon's shoulder. Now she's clearly feeling awkward, desperately pulling her skirt down to cover up more of her thighs. I wonder why she didn't simply wear a longer skirt.

"She was nice."

"Baked beans are nice," Simon says, as though he's become a man of the world since I left the house this morning. "Women don't like being called nice."

I look questioningly at Maxine, putting her in a tricky position, but if she's been with Simon all evening it may not be an entirely new sensation.

"Well, I don't really mind it," she concedes. "It's better than being called an old slag or something."

"As if anyone could ever call you that," Simon says, kissing the back of her hand.

Oh God.

"So, come on mate, how was she?"

"I told you," I say. "Nice. What's on?"

"*Top Gear*," Simon replies. "Maxine wanted to watch it."

"Well, I…" Maxine clearly didn't.

"He watches it nearly every day," I explain for her benefit.

"So do you!" Simon says.

"No I do not."

"Yes you do."

"Don't."

"Do."

"Um, Si? I think I'm going to make a move now," Maxine says, and who can blame her? She retrieves her jacket from the back of the couch and tugs at her skirt with the other hand.

"What? No, you don't have to go," Simon insists. "John doesn't mind you hearing about his date, do you?"

I flick through one of Simon's *Marie Claire's*, pretending I can't hear him.

"It's all right," Maxine says. "It's late anyway."

"Want me to drive you?"

"No, it's fine, I brought my car."

"Clio," Simon says, before I ask. I nod. I guessed right.

Maxine turns to me. "Bye, John. I hope it all works out for you." She gives me a smile and an uncertain thumbs-up.

"Cheers, Max. You too," I add as an afterthought.

I try my best not to hear the murmurings and sucking noises filtering through from the direction of the doorstep as they say their farewells. It gets to the point where I am considering tearing out pages of the magazine to ram into my ears when Simon reappears, a huge grin plastered on his circular head.

"There's an article in here about reuniting with your childhood crush." I show him the page. "Have you read it? It's pretty funny. I'm giving it a grade two."

"Who was your childhood crush?"

"Charlotte Lieberman. Though I can't even remember what she looked like now."

"Do you know what happened to her?"

"Sentenced to marriage with four kids. What about yours?"

"She's dead."

I look up. "Pardon me?"

"Yeah, I know. Lucky escape for me, eh? I'd rather be separated than a widower."

"Quite."

There is silence. I know what's coming.

"Come on, aren't you going to ask me about Maxine?"

"No."

"What?"

"Huh?"

"Fuck off."

Smiling, I put the *Marie Claire* back where I found it, on the floor next to the empty Pringles tubes. "I'm listening."

"It's so weird," he says, sinking down into the cushions and staring up at the ceiling. "We've just ... You know, we..."

"Clicked?" I offer, otherwise we'll be here all night.

"Yes! That's it – we've clicked. Loudly. I mean, how long have we known Maxine?"

"Ages."

"Yes, ages – who'd have thought she and I would end up together?"

"Is that what you are, 'together'?"

Simon grins. "I think so. I mean, I've only been seeing her properly since last night, but I'm really into her."

"Right. And this would have nothing to do with her recent surgical enhancement?"

His face folds into a scowl. "Oi, don't talk about her like that."

"It must be love."

"She's a lovely girl. Woman."

"So what does she see in you?"

"Brains, good looks, charm…"

"You sure it was a boob job and not a lobotomy?"

"Shut it, John."

I take off my jacket and reach for the magazine again, while Simon stares at me, still waiting.

"Aren't you going to tell me what happened with this Rebecca woman?"

"Do I have to?"

"Fair's fair. I told you about Maxine."

"Simon, you made me ask you about Maxine."

"Come on, don't be an arse. I want to know."

"All right," I say, sighing not just for effect. "There's nothing to tell. She's nice. She's attractive."

"But she's not Lola."

I wince. "Technically, no. She isn't." I rub my chin. "Do you want coffee? I'm going to make some."

"Nah, I've still got some beer left." Simon reaches down and holds the bottle aloft for me to see that it is still a third full. "Do you want to watch the rest of this with me?"

I look over at the screen. Jeremy Clarkson is taking the piss out of Richard Hammond. They bicker. Hammond pretends to be annoyed, but everyone knows they love each other really. They remind me of two people I know.

"I think I'll catch up on some reading, thanks all the same," I say.

Simon waves a hand. "Whatever. Oh, let me know when you want to go and belt that Josh. I'm well up for it. We should teach him a lesson."

I frown, wondering why Simon is talking like this when, in truth, he couldn't hit a traffic jam on the M25, let alone another human being. The bravado of the newly-enamoured, I guess. "No, we shouldn't."

"What?" Simon says, twisting his head around in an almost owl-like manner. "Why not?"

I fiddle with the door handle. "Because he makes Lola happy."

"How do you know?" he says slowly, as though I've lost my mind.

"Because I saw them together. And I don't know if we ever looked like that – that comfortable. She was glowing." I swallow the lump that's suddenly blocking my windpipe. "I need coffee."

10

Back when she was alive and coherent, my mother used to say to me, "Things must get worse before they get better." If that's true then, thankfully, this surely has to be the lower echelons of worse. If my circumstances deteriorate further than they have in this one mortifying moment, then I might have to shave my head and become a Buddhist monk (if they'll have me – I'm not sure what you have to do to qualify these days). My karma must be fucked anyway: this is probably the most humiliating experience of my entire career.

"This is fucking pickled shite!" Charlie yells.

I wince. Although the door is closed, every person behind it has heard him as clearly as though he were standing next to them. His spittle has probably penetrated the glass and spattered them.

I put a finger to my temple. It's either that, or a gun.

"So you're not running it?"

"Don't play the funny man with me." Charlie's fluffy eyebrows merge to form a forehead scarf. "You're not paid to be funny. And you're not paid to write this crap. Writing this kind of drivel isn't going to get you anywhere, except flat on your arse on the street outside."

Charlie points to the window behind him, just in case I'm clueless as to where both the street and outside are. "I'm doing you a favour by nipping this … 'experiment' in the bud." He holds the pages I carefully emailed to him between his thumb and forefinger, as though they are contaminated with something. This is hard to accept coming from a man who wears novelty cartoon socks and has hair trailing out of his nostrils like ivy.

"With all due respect, this isn't an experiment. I can write about other things, Charlie. I have observations to make. I want to diversify."

He makes a noise that comes out somewhere between a snort and a grunt – the world's first and only snunt.

"This," he spits, waving my own words at me, "is not diversification. This is thinking you know everything when you should be sticking to doing what you're getting paid far too much for. When people see your name at the top of a piece, they expect economics. They expect information, analysis – not this kind of crap. This, I can ask anyone to write. What would they think if they went to read 'In the Black' and found this piece of pasteurised dog shit?"

"I'm sure you're about to tell me," I say under my breath.

"They'd say," Charlie adopts a ridiculous falsetto voice. "'John Black has gone off his fucking rocker! What the hell is this fucking boiled horse crap?'"

The whole building can hear him now. I sit there chewing gum, trying not to dislocate my own jaw.

"I just thought-"

"Don't think. Write. You're losing it, Black. One day you're saying interest rates are going up, then they're going down, then inflation is rising, it's falling – you don't seem to know what you're talking about anymore."

"Maybe I never did. Nobody really does. We're all playing guessing games."

"Ah, but the thing is, you used to be better at it than everyone else, didn't you?"

I'm chewing super-hard now.

"Didn't you?"

"Yes."

"Wrong answer!" Charlie yells, throwing a box of rubber bands into the air. "What you're supposed to say is, 'I still am.'"

What I do say, is nothing.

"And," Charlie adds, as though he's only just remembered, "that feature on the housing market was late."

"By two hours."

Charlie might be about to explode. "Two hours!" He slams his palm down on his desk. I suspect it hurts the desk more. "Let me paint you a little picture." He pulls himself away from the desk, and stands up. "If your train is supposed to arrive at, let's say, Liverpool Street, at nine am and it eventually turns up at eleven, are you going to say, 'Oh, it's only two hours late! Never mind!' Are you?"

I blink at him.

"Are you?"

"No."

"No! You're going to say, 'Where's my fucking train? What use is this train to me, I needed to be there two hours ago!'" Another stupid voice. I'm confident Alistair McGowan isn't about to sue just yet.

Charlie comes around and sits on the corner of his desk, giving me a long look. I scratch my chin, and realise I haven't shaved today. Or yesterday.

"You might think you're invincible, Johnny boy, but no one's special round here. Not even you. Especially not you. Got it?"

"Got it. No one's special. Can I get back to work now?"

"If that's what you call it. And don't waste any more of the paper's time writing this poached turd. Do what you're paid to do. Nothing more, nothing less."

I vow to hold him to the 'nothing more' part.

"And take this bog roll with you."

I leave the feature on his desk. As a souvenir.

I loosen my tie and go over to the vending machine, where I proceed to down two plastic cups of free water. I consider getting a third and pouring it over my head. Or, better still, Charlie's head. I can feel eyes on the back of my neck. I can see subtle nudges, and nods in my direction. I know Valerie's standing there watching, enjoying this. I don't blame her. I've practically gifted this spectacle to her – to the whole office. They'll all be whispering about me soon, sending furtive emails asking each other what the hell I was thinking. If any of them work it out, I hope they forward the answer to me.

"All right…" Simon shuffles over to provide some moral support and sympathy, shaking his melon-head. He gives Valerie a 'what are you looking at?' glare of such magnitude it sends her scuttling into the toilets. For that, I almost kiss him.

"Well, how did it go?"

"You heard him offering advice on various colourful ways to cook faeces."

"I liked poached. You?"

"Was anything pickled?"

"Shite, if I recall correctly."

"I'll take that one then."

"John, you know how good you are. Charlie is one bollock short of being a woman."

I give Simon a grateful smile. "Thanks for that insight. I shouldn't have shown him the bloody feature."

"You did your best, mate. It was worth a try. But it's not like you don't already have a job or anything. You surely didn't expect Charlie to give you another column?"

"Of course I didn't. But I can't write about monetary union forever, Simon. I'll go fucking mad."

"But it's what you do."

"Which doesn't mean I always have to do it."

Simon frowns. "Are you having a mid-life crisis? Don't be silly, mate. You're good at this."

"What about if I'm good at other things too?"

Simon looks at me concernedly, as though he's about to ask me how many fingers he's holding up. "Mate, like he said – do what you're paid to do." He claps me on the back. "Whatever you do, don't fuck this up as well."

His words sound ominously portentous.

When I sit down to try and do what I'm paid – apparently far too much – to do, I realise I'm not entirely sure what exactly it is that I'm paid to do. To spill my thoughts about the world economy? Oh, okay. As of today, it seems I don't have any.

I go through the motions for a while, starting one feature after another, searching for inspiration, until I have about nine windows open and my PC starts groaning under the strain. As am I. I think about calling Andrea – she might have something I can use. Yeah, I'm that desperate. I put down my pen and lean back in my chair. I discovered early on in my career that when I adopt this pose it looks like I'm meditating on some important thought. Actually, I'm watching two pigeons on the windowsill. One of them, which I presume to be the male, is trying to get the other one, hopefully the female, in the mood. He's puffed up his feathers and is circling round her making cooing noises. Then, without warning, she turns round and pecks him so hard he nearly falls off the ledge. He flies away in shame. That, my friends, says it all.

Okay… The screen is still blank, if you don't count the cursor, which I always do. I decide to get up and have a walk, give my legs, and my brain, some exercise. Although quite why I think I'll need to use brain cells over at Sarah's desk, I don't know.

"Hey, Sarah."

She looks up from the magazine she's flicking through. It's *Hello*, or *OK!*, or *Whatever*, and I really should take that as a sign from God and walk away. Her eyes widen in surprise. As well they should.

"John Black. This is a turn up for the books, you coming over to my desk for a change." She's right. Usually I never come over to her side of the office without a visa, several inoculations, and a sick bag. "Um, I'm sorry about before," she says apologetically, as though she'd been shouting at me instead of Charlie. "It sounded very scary. What did you do?"

"Free thinking," I say, wanting to reassure Sarah that it's not something she'll ever be asked to do. I notice another magazine in her in-tray, and given that we've only been talking for about a minute and she already looks confused, I change the subject. "*Newsweek*?" I don't hide the surprise in my voice.

She nods sadly. "It's not mine," she says, in case for one second I thought it was. "I have to brief Molly on the piece about the thing that happened in Mogadishu. We're running a kind of flashback article because everyone's forgotten it happened. I never knew it happened at all. I'd much rather read this. Can you believe they've got engaged?" She holds up a glossy page bearing a photograph of a blonde woman draped over a man whose face appears to have been constructed from orange plastic.

"No. I can't."

"It's a shocker! I thought she was happy with that footballer."

And just like that, I stop listening. "So, Mogadishu."

Her face falls. "Oh. That."

"The failed US mission of '93?"

"Yes! The same one! How did you guess?"

"There was only one."

"Oh. I didn't even know Mogadishu was a country until half an hour ago," she says, as though she's immensely proud of this fact. Her mouth opens so wide as she yawns that I discover how many fillings she has. "Politics is so Dullsville, Arizona. So, how's your girlfriend? What's her name again?"

I long to scream at her until my eyeballs burst.

"We broke up."

"Oh! What a terrible shame!" She says with as much as disappointment as someone who's found an envelope of money on an otherwise empty Tube carriage.

"Yeah, it is."

"Who broke up with whom?"

"It was a kind of mutual thing."

"Hmm… Oh, you'll never guess!"

I can guarantee I won't.

"Steve phoned me the other day." She lowers her voice, as though someone might be bored enough to eavesdrop. "Steve – you know Steve," she explains, when she sees my face is as blank as her Mensa application. "My ex? He texted and asked if I still had the keys to the bicycle clamp. I'm not sure what he meant by that. What do you reckon?"

I pinch the bridge of my nose. "I've got to get back."

"Oh yeah," Sarah says. "Economics. Groovy. Well," she flicks the page of her magazine to reveal the blonde woman and the orange man in swimwear. "If you ever need a shoulder to cry on, or someone to talk to…" she says, lowering her eyes.

I'll look in the Yellow Pages, I think to myself as I walk away.

And so this is the story of how I fail to write another word for the rest of the day. That is, if you don't count signing the visitor's book at the PR firm where Lola works.

The receptionist runs a cursory eye over my signature, and a suspicious one over me. I smile my most insipid smile. My only smile.

Her expression doesn't change as she hands me a pass. "You need to go up to the eighth floor. Have a good day, Mr Friedman."

"And you," I say, not meaning it either.

It's only the second time I've set foot inside this building. It's sleek, all chrome and art deco. When you enter the building I work in it feels like World War Two could still be going on outside. In here, it's like something out of *Minority Report*. I'm almost intimidated.

I'm proud of Lola for coming so far. I can still remember the day she went for the interview. Naturally she thought they'd read her CV wrong, and sent out the wrong letter. She was convinced she was going to turn up and they'd say there'd been a mistake and politely send her home. Instead, they offered her an extra five grand and her own office. She couldn't believe it. I very much could.

I press the button for the lift. The door opens, and a woman carrying a small child gets in behind me.

"Which floor?"

"Ten," she replies.

I hit eight, then ten, and then just happen to glance at her child, merely because it was staring at me, and the woman's face erupts into a 'isn't my child cute?' grin. No, it isn't. They all look the same.

"Harry, say hello to the nice man."

Harry is still watching me in abject fascination or, perhaps, morbid curiosity – you never can tell with the under fours. His head is almost as disproportionately large as Simon's, and his eyes are round and rheumy. I give him a look that tells him that Santa doesn't exist, that there is indeed a monster under his bed, and that yes, the Bogeyman will get him when Mummy turns the lights out at night. Harry begins to cry.

"Ah, he's tired," his mother explains.

Who isn't?

I get to the eighth floor without throwing something at Harry and/or his mother, which I take to be a good omen. The lift doors open, and deposit me into a scene of utter chaos. I thought my office was busy, but this is practically a jamboree by comparison.

The entire workforce, with an apparent average age of about twenty-three, are on their Conversed feet, striding briskly from one end of the office to the other with cardboard tubes and flipcharts tucked under their skinny arms. They're on the phone with pained and anguished expressions, and they're walking around with pained and anguished expressions. They're pained and anguished, slightly unkempt, and yet smart at the same time, wearing bright colours and lots of eyeliner – and not just the girls. In fact, this place resembles Camden Market more than a public relations firm.

"Can I help you?"

A girl – she's about seven years away from being a woman – with dyed black hair cut into an asymmetrical wedge approaches me. She asks the question artificially brightly, as though what she really wants to know is whether I can help her.

"Uh, yeah. I'm looking for Lola Martinez."

She smiles knowingly, as though I've just asked to go through the back of the wardrobe and speak to Aslan. "I'll see if she's in her office. Is she expecting you?"

Dear God no. "Yes."

She glances at the name on my pass. "I won't keep you a sec, Mr Friedman."

"Milton, please."

The girl sashays off down the office, clearly thinking I'm someone important. I stand and wait, conspicuous in my suit amongst so much denim, receiving a string of looks ranging from antipathy to indifference from a boy of about fifteen. He's wearing his jeans so low that by the time the asymmetrical girl returns I feel we're almost intimately acquainted.

"You can go through. It's the blue door at the end."

"Thanks." I lean over to jeans boy. "Your label's sticking out."

"Huh?" He twists round. Yeah, yeah, I know, I'm going to hell for my wickedness. But if I'm evil enough, maybe I'll get my own office down there.

Her name is on the door. I resist the urge to trace my fingers along the letters, and knock gently.

"Come in."

Lola says this as though she means the exact reverse, and she doesn't even know it's me yet. I open the door, and there she is. She glances up from her laptop and does a double take. Her expression flickers from surprise, to shock, to annoyance.

"For someone who dumped me, you sure keep turning up a lot."

"I didn't dump you."

"Okay – disposed of me."

"That wasn't it either."

"Have you come here for some new nouns? Have you run out?"

"That's not a noun, it's a verb."

"Is 'get out' a verb?"

"I just want to talk."

"Pay a shrink."

"He told me to come here."

"You don't have a shrink." She hesitates. "Do you?"

"Would you care if I did?"

"I don't care what you do."

We lock stares. She does care. She's Lola – she can't just stop caring about people, about me. Well, that's what I'm counting on.

She crosses the room and shuts the door behind me. The scent of vanilla drifts under my nostrils.

"I should sack Tanya for letting you in here."

I show her my pass. "She thinks I'm Milton Friedman. So did you."

"I thought you were my one o'clock."

"I could be."

Lola folds her arms across her chest, and taps a pointed shoe on the carpet impatiently. I notice how healthy she looks. Her cheeks have filled out a little, and her hair is shiny, reflecting the light. She's luminous. I try to banish the thought that this is the effect of Josh, that he might be good for her. That I wasn't.

"Milton Friedman is that guy from *The Shawshank Redemption*, isn't he?"

"No. He's a right-wing economist. Although I suppose Morgan Freeman could be as well."

"What did they say to you at reception?"

"They said, 'Could you spell that for me?' and gave me directions to your office. Perhaps they prefer Keynes. It is kind of amusing."

"Maybe in your world, John."

"My world is sparsely populated."

She arches her eyebrows and sits on the edge of her desk, her arms folded in front of her.

"Go on then, talk. And make it short, I haven't got all day to waste on you."

It's at this point that I wish I had something of note to say.

"I just wanted to see how you are."

She narrows her eyes. "Kay told you about Josh," she says.

"No. Yeah."

She knows me too well.

"Which therefore explains why you're here." Shaking her head, she walks back round to her side of the desk, leaving me sitting in a cloud of vanilla. "You're so pathetic."

"I'm not here because of him," I say.

"He has a name."

"Yes, he does. But it's not about him. We were friends too, Lola. We can't just throw that away," I say.

"You're the one who did the throwing."

She's angry, showing a feisty side of herself I've never seen before. It's making me a little nervous. And, on a base level, the one at which I operate most of the time, it's turning me on.

"Lola-"

She holds a palm up. "Listen, John, I'm going to make this very clear, so I'm content in my own mind that there's no way you could've misunderstood me. I. Don't. Want. To.

See. You. Ever. Again. Like you said in such spectacular fashion, we're over, finished, done. I'm with somebody else now. I've moved on. I suggest you do the same and stop stalking me."

"I'm not stalking you. I just wanted to see you."

"That's what stalkers always say." She sighs. "What is it you want?"

I'm about to answer this with a yet as undecided explanation, when there's a neat rap on the door.

"Ignore it."

Lola keeps her eyes fixed on me. "Come in."

Asymmetrical Tanya pokes her dyed black head around the door. "Hiya. Is everything okay? I heard shouting." She glances at me and smiles coquettishly.

"Put your tongue away, Tanya. This is the bastard who broke my heart."

Tanya's mouth drops open. "This is 'John'?"

"Yes," snaps Lola. "This is 'John.'"

"I see. He's shorter than I imagined."

"He has bad posture," Lola says. "It's a side-effect of being spineless."

I almost laugh until I remember she's talking about me. I have become 'John'. This is bad.

This is my last chance – okay, one more time, with feeling.

"Lola, please. I never meant to hurt you. All I wanted-"

"Oh, here come the words – empty words. What did you want? You don't know, do you, John? But you knew what you didn't want. You told me to my face and a lot of other people's faces that you didn't want me. I'm fed up with trying to work out what goes on in your head, because the truth is that not a lot goes on in there. And you might even have done me a favour. Now, I'd like it if you'd stop showing up like this. Please, go. I've got things I need to do. Actually, I have a lot of things I need to do. Tanya will show you out."

To emphasise her point, she goes back to her computer and begins to type, even though I suspect she is simply hitting random keys and is typing things like 'fqafhqwkrhqr9350prna,dfwhrtlwi024rl.'

"Okay." I stand up. "Okay. It's fine. I'll see myself out."

Tanya doesn't hide her relief, as though being in close proximity to me might have poisoned her with something incurable.

"Bye, Lola."

Lola keeps typing, as though I was never there.

If things truly have to get worse before they get better, then I may as well open my arms and embrace the last bastion of horror – get it over with. After this is done, there will be nothing to fear, no further depths to plummet to.

So here I am, standing in the middle of my own nightmare, right outside The Parlour. I finish my cigarette, inhaling hard, like a man about to walk the steps to the electric chair which, in a way, I could be, although this is going to be much more uncomfortable.

It's nearly empty inside. There are a couple of people tucked in booths tapping away on their Macs, and there's a man by the window reading a paperback, and there's me. Oh yeah, and him. He has a name. Josh.

I pop some gum into my mouth, swallow it without thinking, and then immediately wish I had some more. One of my favourite songs – 'Cold Blooded Old Times' – is playing, a notch below comfortably loud. I'm struck by the thought that I'll never be able to listen to this song again without remembering this afternoon, and him. He's stolen a song from me as well.

He's sitting at the bar, his back to me, a newspaper spread out in front of him. Every now and then he rubs the back of his neck absently, the sleeves of his baggy sweater hanging down almost to his knuckles. Powered by the fuel of my own injustice, and also plain foolhardiness, I settle into the seat next to him.

Josh is oblivious, absorbed in his paper. I steel myself. This is when I'll see how accurate my first impressions are.

Basically, there are four types of men in the world. First, you have your James Bond Guy. This type holds down a regular to moderately prestigious job, but wishes he was brave/extraordinary enough to try for the SAS. He reads a lot of Chris Ryan novels and thinks they're real books, and drives his car way faster than he should do (even though nine times out of ten his car is crap). He wants a six-pack and pecs but does nothing about it. He lusts after women who are in a different orbit of attractiveness entirely, and his wife/girlfriend resembles Olive from 'On the Buses' on a bad day.

Then, number two, is the Sport Guy. Sport Guy covers a wide spectrum, from the tattooed, footie-obsessed bloke in the pub, to those who watch every kind of sport on television but rarely leave the sofa, to those who are always in the gym, pool, or squash court. A lot of Sport Guys are deluded, convinced that if only there'd been a scout present on the day they'd scored that wonder goal at the under tens five-a-side, they'd be playing for one of the big four by now. For this ilk of male, the best thing ever is being out with their mates. Consequently, their wives and girlfriends shout at them a lot.

Now, the third type, the Star Wars male, doesn't usually have a wife or girlfriend because no woman would voluntarily be with a man who keeps little plastic figures of Ewoks in his bedroom. These men haven't quite come to terms with the fact that their childhood is over, and hence their only recourse is to pretend it actually hasn't. They're mostly to be found on the internet, discussing how such-and-such film isn't as good as the comic, and ogling pictures of Jessica Alba.

I'm putting Josh in the fourth category: the *NME*/*Arena* guy. He's on the pulse, and trendily trendy. He knows his music, preferably the kind that no one else has heard before. He hates anything popular or commercial. He is too 'cool' for that. He dresses casually, but deceptively expensively. He cares about the world he lives in, about society, about his borough. He knows all the right places to go, to hang out in. And, in this case, he's taking my ex-girlfriend with him.

"Josh?"

"Yeah?" He peels his eyes away from his paper. He's looking at me. At his nemesis. "Yes?"

"I'm John."

There's a split-second, and then it registers.

"Ah. John."

A weird kind of stalemate descends.

"Hey, Toby…" The guy behind the bar – Toby – comes to attention. "Could you get us a beer, and..?"

"Beer's fine."

"Two beers, please Tobe. You okay with that?"

Toby nods a little uncertainly, and immediately reaches over in the direction of the spirits.

"Toby's my cousin," Josh explains in a low voice. "He's a little…slow. So."

"So."

"This is about Lola, right?" He says it calmly, as though he's been anticipating this turn of events for some time.

"What else?"

Josh nods and folds his paper – the *Guardian*, of course – and puts it to one side. Next to his iPhone.

Our beers are delivered surprisingly quickly, although Toby struggles to lever the bottle tops off.

"Hey, Tobe, like I showed you. Remember?"

Toby stares at him blankly for a second, and then it evidently drifts back to him. He puts our beers in front of us, and disappears round the corner.

"Cheers," Josh says.

Here's to not choking on it.

Josh wipes his mouth with the back of his hand. "Good?"

"Great." I feel ill.

We sit there for a while, both pretending the labels on our beers contain vital information we must absorb right away. Josh is the first to speak and that annoys me, as I wanted to be the one to break the silence, to take charge of the situation.

"You know, you look exactly as I imagined." He rolls up his sweater and rubs his arm. "Lola described you perfectly."

"Did she use the word 'bastard'?"

Josh smiles. "A couple of times. It's good you can laugh about it."

I'm not laughing. But I suppose he is. Touché.

"She said you write that column … what's it called?"

"'In the Black.'"

"That's the one. I'm sorry, man, I don't read it."

"Oh. Right."

"I don't understand any of that stuff. It's like a different language to me."

Despite the iPhone, I award him a point. This is evidently not going to be a competition. Why would it – he's already won.

"How is Lola?" It's brave of me to ask this, and it hurts that he knows the answer.

"She's good, yeah. She comes and meets me here most nights. I have to work a lot."

It kills me to say it, but he's very open. I can see why Lola went for him. When we first started seeing each other she told me how much she likes sincerity and authenticity. After nine barren years it must be a treat for her to be with someone who possesses the ability to be both.

"This place must take a lot of work," I say hopefully.

"It does, but luckily I have two partners so we split everything three ways. Unfortunately, that goes for the profits as well," Josh adds, a twinkle in his eye. I bet Lola likes that twinkle too. I, however, would like to surgically remove it. Or not even surgically – I could just poke it out, right now.

"Hey," he says, suddenly inspired. "Lola told me you know about money and stuff? Maybe you could give us some advice, go over our books and all that."

At this precise moment in time, I'd rather construct a scale model of the 'Mary Rose' using only pinheads and monkey semen.

"I think you need an accountant for that."

"Oh, we already have one of those. He takes more of our money than he saves."

"If you've figured that out on your own then I don't think you need my assistance."

Josh doesn't respond. He's watching me carefully.

"Lola was really in love with you. I can tell by the way she talks about you. I mean, what happened, man? You were with her for almost forever. What did she do?"

I take a swig of the enemy's beer, wondering if I can drink this skinny twenty-something into bankruptcy. Simon could probably manage it, but I can't hold as much alcohol in my bloodstream as him. I think fat absorbs more alcohol than muscle.

"She didn't do anything. I needed to be on my own for a while. We were together for nine years. It's a very long time to be exclusively with one person."

"Isn't that all the more reason to stay together?" he asks, offering the suggestion.

God, I hate him.

"Maybe. But sometimes people need space."

"So you got bored?"

"Is that what she thinks?"

"What is she supposed to think?" Josh says gently. He puts his bottle down on the bar. "Anyway, it doesn't matter now. She's with me. Do you understand?" He says this in the same pleasant tone he's used throughout our conversation. It's clear, calm, and non-threatening, and I understand exactly, to the nearest decimal point, what his drift is. It's a simple equation: I fucked up, he's with Lola now, and I'm not. So I merely nod my assent, to show that I appreciate the underlying subtext.

"You just make sure you look after her. Do you understand?"

Josh holds his hands up. "Hey, take it easy. I won't hurt her."

The subtext is clear there too.

Josh checks his phone. "She'll be here in a little while if you want to wait."

"No, I think it's better if I go," I say, standing up.

Josh leans on his elbow and gives me a long look. "Yeah, I think it is. Take care, man."

He picks up his phone and starts tapping out something on the screen. A message to Lola.

11

When you're the one who ends a relationship, it's not supposed to be you who cracks first. After all, it was your decision. The injured party can protest, cry, and plead all they want, but it's no use. You hold all the aces, if not the whole damn pack of cards. You should be the one in control.

Well, congratulations, Lola. With one deft move, a slick sleight of hand, you've turned this situation around. You're Commander in Chief. The balance of power has shifted, and I am now obsessed with you and your new boyfriend.

I've spent time – acres of time, too much bloody time – spinning it around in my mind. Josh and I are poles apart – he's the North Pole, and I'm the South Pole (which, I believe, is colder). He's my antithesis in every possible way. This has led me to three possible conclusions.

It could be that Lola has purposefully chosen to go out with someone who is nothing like me because she doesn't want to be reminded of me – perhaps she hates everything about me. Or maybe she doesn't want to make the same mistake twice, and would rather be with Josh and make a totally different, brand new mistake. Or, most terrifyingly of all, she's decided I was the wrong type of man for her all along – maybe Josh has converted her, and rendered me obsolete.

She's moved on. Really moved on. And the further she moves on, the more I want to hold her back. I can't eat, what the hell is sleep, and I can just about light a cigarette without my hands shaking too much. As for work, no chance. The features I toss onto Charlie's desk allow me to get by –

nothing more, nothing less. If I didn't have more pressing concerns I'd worry about Charlie noticing my column has suddenly become dull and contrived, that I'm plagiarising myself (hey, they don't call it an economic cycle for nothing). The only words I can concentrate on are the ones spoken by the enemy.

Josh said Lola and I were together for "almost forever." The more the quote reverberates and ferments inside my skull, the more clearly I see it. Our commitment to each other was never in doubt. We were never unfaithful to each other. In the entire nine years we were together, I never cheated on her – never wanted to. There was no one better than her. We talked about our future. We never shied away from it, never dodged the subject. We were comfortable making the assumption that we were going the distance. Only my distance turned out to be a lot shorter than Lola's.

Josh asked me what Lola did and the brutal truth is that she did nothing whatsoever. She's perfect. Okay, yes, certain aspects of her personality drove me a little nuts. Like the way she obsessively counts calories despite having less fat on her than a lettuce leaf, her lack of confidence in herself, and her compulsion to wake me up at ridiculous hours of the night by saying, "Are you awake, John?" Then there's the way she insists on buying fair-trade food, but refuses to accept that some of her clothes were made in sweatshops. And she'll chat through the programme I really want to watch, but demands the house is as silent as a coffin when *Eastenders* is on. And the way she can, and does, explain in intricate detail the history of Peggy, Bianca, Phil, Jack, Ian and Dot dating back to 1985, but can never remember the names of anyone in the Cabinet, no matter how many times I answer her "Who's that?" question when the news is on. But those idiosyncrasies aren't reasons to throw away almost forever. They're the reasons you love someone even more. And, truth is, being able to watch

Newsnight in complete silence is disconcerting. I end up flicking over to *Ellen* just for the company.

So now all there is to do is follow her lead. To move on. To tip my head back and let the air back into my lungs. To embrace the freedom I craved so badly, and was so happy to receive. I have my freedom now. In abundance.

I rake my fingers through my hair. My reflection, like the rest of me, is deceptive. The turmoil doesn't show on my face. I'll pass as a normal human being. Right, keys – where are my keys..? There's mess everywhere, and sadly since all of it is mine, the blame for this lies solely with me. I should start looking for my own place. There's nothing holding me back now. Is there?

My borrowed bedroom door opens, hinges squeaking, and a corpulent man eating a packet of Quavers enters the room. Unfortunately, I know him.

"Alright?"

"Did I hear you knock?"

"No," Simon says, licking his fingers. "I barged in. Is that a new shirt?"

I find my jacket behind the door and pick it up, hearing the reassuring jingle of keys in the pocket.

"Where are you going dressed like a pimp?" Simon asks, sitting on the bed and making himself presumptuously comfortable.

"Simon, how many pimps do you know?"

"Don't have to know any to know what they look like."

"Aren't you seeing Maxine tonight?"

He shakes his head and peers into the crisp bag. "Nah. She's having a girlie night tonight." He says this nonchalantly, apparently never having heard that there's no point lying to a liar.

"I've never quite understood what that means," I say, unearthing a shoe beneath my laptop bag. "Every night of their lives is a girlie night."

"Yeah, but they get all the props out, don't they? A girlie night is when they get all their mates round and watch *Dirty Dancing* and do each other's hair and wear face packs." His eyes light up. "Hey, do you think they snog each other and stuff?"

"I keep telling you, Simon. Those films you watch aren't real. Have you got any shoe polish?" Simon looks at me like I've just asked him to pluck my eyebrows for me. "Never mind."

"No, it's not that." He swallows his mouthful of crisps. "Penny texted me today. She's having a boy."

"A human one?"

"Yes, John."

"Ah, the wonders of modern science. And? How'd you feel?" I ask, because I think I'm supposed to.

He thinks about it for a second. "You know, not as bad as I thought I would. I think I'm-"

"Moving on?"

"Yes," he answers.

"That's good." My other shoe makes itself known to me, and I gratefully slide it on.

"You still haven't told me where you're going."

"I don't question you about what you do with Maxine."

"That's because I tell you everything," he says.

"No, because I hear everything. Beetfuckinghoven could probably hear what takes place in your room, and sometimes on the couch, when I'm in here trying to sleep. It's fucking disgusting."

"You've got Tourette's, haven't you?"

"Fuck off."

"Fine. Don't tell me then." Simon pouts and folds his arms. He goes over to the window and starts fiddling with the wallet I've spent the last thirty seconds looking for.

"Okay, okay," I sigh. "Remember Rebecca? The artist? That's where I'm going."

"A tortured artist! Is she foxy?"

I snatch my wallet from him. "Don't wait up."

So here's what I'm too ashamed to tell Simon, and what I can barely stand to admit to myself: I was lonely. I called Rebecca. Find a correlation between these two facts if you really must, but I prefer to keep them separate.

She'd picked up the phone after two rings. Yes, I was counting.

"Hello?"

"Hey. It's John," I added, as an afterthought.

"Oh." A beat. "Oh my God!"

"You haven't won a prize or anything."

"In a way, I have. You've phoned."

I scratched my chin. "It appears so."

"Well." I could hear something in the background – a microwave, a fan, or maybe a nuclear power generator – how would I know what she does in her spare time?. "So, what does this mean?"

"I think it means I wanted to speak to you."

"About..? Pardon?"

"I shrugged."

"Oh." Something beeped in the background. The microwave, perhaps, or the timer for the bomb she was setting. "I should invite you over."

"You probably should."

"We could try having that drink again."

"The same one?"

"The same, but different. Eight?"

"My favourite number."

"John?"

"Yes?"

"This isn't a rebound thing, is it? I won't be the rebound girl. I've been there before, and…"

"Of course not."

As I bring the car to a smooth stop in deepest and very darkest Clapham, I wonder who's fooling whom.

My finger hovers over the buzzer to her flat. This is it, the point of no return. There seem to have been so many of those lately.

I press the buzzer. This, Lola, is moving on.

"John?"

"The very one."

"Come up."

There's a click. I try not to think it sounds ominous. I block out the thoughts of what I'm leaving behind. If I looked back, there'd be nothing there.

Rebecca's flat is on the second floor of a building that people wouldn't pay money to live in anywhere other than London. The estate agents call it 'modern living'; I call it a slum. The lift appears to be broken, not that I'd have any intention of using it anyway, and the stairs have graffiti along the walls. This is Clapham though, so it's not just any old graffiti – it's probably 'art', and most likely can only be deciphered by an expert in hieroglyphics.

Thoughtfully, Rebecca's left the door ajar. I enter feeling awkward, clutching the obligatory bottle of red I bought from Oddbins to cultivate the impression I want to sit and drink Merlot with her, when really I've come here hoping for guilt-free but affectionate sex.

"Hello?"

"In here."

I go through to what the estate agents would call the 'reception room'. It's nice, all tie-dyed cushions and patchouli, but it's not much bigger than Simon's head.

"Hi." She stands up. She looks great – based on three viewings, she always looks great. But tonight, she looks extra great, all black skirt and slinky top. I take this as a sign she's hoping for guilt-free sex as well.

"Is that for me?"

I get back on clock just in time. She means the wine. "Yes. I hope you like red."

"Red wine, red roses, red sheets. All good. I'll get some glasses."

I note the mention of sheets. Ladbrokes have stopped taking bets on the likelihood of sex.

"You pour." Rebecca puts two rather large glasses on the table, and sits down beside me. I fill hers up right to the top, and allow myself a thimbleful. "I'm driving," I explain, when she gives my glass an amused frown.

I am driving, but I'm also hoping to have sex. The less I drink, the better I'll be, but the more she drinks, the less she'll remember, and hence the better I'll be.

"Mm, good. What year?"

"It's rude to ask a wine its age."

She consults the label. "Ninety-nine. Good year."

"I can barely remember."

She studies me in that intense way of hers. "I bet you can. You have a good memory."

"For figures and facts, not years, or important stuff."

She presses her lips together, that mischievous glint in her eyes. "Okay." She shifts herself towards me, and I almost flinch. Almost. She puts her hand over my eyes. "What colour are my shoes?"

"That's an old, and unfair, trick."

"What colour?"

"This is testing my powers of observation, not my memory."

"No matter, they're both important. Colour?"

"Blue."

Rebecca takes her hand away.

She's looking at me, I'm looking at her. She bites her bottom lip. I'm not entirely sure what I do with mine. She moves her body closer.

"You know what?" I stand up quickly, like the sofa's caught fire.

"Huh?"

"We should go out. I know a really great place."

"What?" Rebecca's cheeks are flushed. "Oh. Okay." There's a note of uncertainty in her voice, but she doesn't want to seem unadventurous so she says, "Sure. I'll get my jacket, shall I?"

"Great."

She goes into what I assume is her bedroom, giving me a quizzical frown. I just smile winningly, and jangle my car keys. Yeah, I'm moving on all right.

We pull up outside The Parlour about nine-thirty. I tug the key from the ignition a little too eagerly, and Rebecca's sitting quietly, as she has been for most of the drive across London, with a face like someone's just told her she's adopted.

"You okay?" I ask this, but I'm not sure I care too much about the answer. It's just a prompt to get her moving. I'm peering discreetly at the bar just beyond her shoulder, and it's busy. I need to get in there now, but Rebecca's a woman and no doubt there'll be a short delay while she takes it upon herself to answer this question as precisely as she can.

"Yeah, I think so." Here it comes. "It's just… I don't know what I'm doing here."

You and me both.

"What?"

"Nothing," I say.

"John…" She twists around. I note with growing impatience that she still has her seatbelt on. "Do you even like me?"

"Pardon?"

"I said I wouldn't be the rebound girl."

"And you're not."

"It feels like I am. You're acting strange."

"I always act like this. Ask anyone."

"Do you miss her?"

"Who?"

"Your ex."

"Who?"

Rebecca gives me a disapproving look. "That wasn't very convincing."

"It wasn't intended to be." I unclasp my seatbelt, so she'll get the general idea. "I'm here, aren't I?"

She gives me a long look. I wish she'd stop doing that. "I hope so. It kind of feels like you might be somewhere else."

I'm relieved when she stops staring at me and opens the car door. I check my reflection in the mirror. Well, I'm here in body at least.

We cross the street. She links her arm through mine and I hardly feel it. She says something to me, and I don't hear it. I'm no longer aware of how good she looks, of the possibility, of the chemistry she insists exists between us. It doesn't mean anything. The only thing that's remotely relevant and important to me now is The Parlour, and what might be lurking inside it.

The place is heaving. I just want to heave.

"Shall I get us a drink?" Rebecca shouts above the music, which has departed from jazz tonight: 'Embarrassment' by Madness. Quite.

"No, you're all right, I'll get them. What do you want?"

"Whatever you're having."

"Scotch."

She grimaces. "Get me a Martini and lemonade."

I grimace.

The barman – thankfully not Toby or I'd be here all night and most of tomorrow – pours the drinks I ask for, and my heart beats so loudly I almost apologise for it. I'm scared to glance around, to catch anyone's eye. Coming here was a mistake – one in an ever-increasing line of mistakes.

Rebecca's found a space for us to stand over by the cigarette machine. Good girl. Not only are we tucked away in the corner, but I'll be able to stock up on the inevitable four thousand cigarettes I'll need to smoke on the way home.

"Thanks. Ooh, a lime." She takes a sip. "I feel bad. It was my round."

"I brought you here."

"And what a place it is. I hardly ever venture north of the river." She looks around. I wish she wouldn't. "I'm impressed. Is this where you media types hang out?"

"I wouldn't know."

"You're not a regular here?"

"No. Yes. I was."

"Right." Rebecca takes another dainty sip of her Martini and looks away, and I feel a stab of regret at what might've been, what could be if I was that much of a bastard, and if I didn't like her.

"You're not going to make this easy for me, are you, John?"

"I don't make anything easy for anyone."

"Why are you so defensive?"

"Birth defect. Survival technique."

"She must've really hurt you."

"Who?"

"Stop saying that." She squints into the distance. "Hey, there's a guy over there waving at you."

My blood goes cold. I'm paralysed.

"I think he's coming over."

I turn around. Slowly. Excruciatingly. I don't make anything easy for myself, either.

Josh is winding his way carefully through his crowd of patrons, who are enjoying themselves and lining his pockets at the same time. A few of them nudge him and smile hello. All that's missing is a donkey for him to ride and people waving palms and shouting 'Hosanna'.

He lifts a hand in greeting, an easy smile on his face. His other hand, I note with growing nausea, is firmly welded to

Lola's. I find myself longing for something to separate them with. An axe, maybe.

A knot tightens in my stomach and then claws its way up towards my throat. By the time they reach me, I want the axe to decapitate myself with.

"Hey, John," he says, with what I suppose is authentic warmth.

"Josh," I nod, an action so strained I almost snap my neck.

"Good to see you here, man. Are you okay for drinks and stuff?"

I nod again, too busy staring at Lola to verbalise any kind of response. She tucks her hair behind her ear and looks pointedly at me.

On the journey over here, it occurred to me that Lola might be livid that I've dared to show up in what she probably regards as their place, and indeed, I am violating enemy territory. But if she's angry, she conceals it. All that shows is a blank kind of certainty, an air of resignation, one she's had cause to use many times. She's not surprised to see me here at all. She's disappointed. And then she notices Rebecca. Shit, I forgot about her.

One of the many thousand reasons why being a woman is fraught with difficulty is that you have to view every member of your sex as a threat. Remember, the sisterhood doesn't exist. So while Josh and I can stand next to each other in relative harmony (albeit mostly on his part), the second Lola and Rebecca lock eyes, they start sizing each other up: who's prettier, who's thinner, whose tits are bigger, who's wearing the best clothes, and who's got the better end of the deal.

"Hi, I'm Rebecca," she says when it's embarrassingly clear that I'm not going to.

"Lola. And this," Lola looks at me, "is Josh."

That was Lola letting me know she thinks she's got the better end of the deal.

"How are you, John?" Lola asks me neutrally.

"I'm good. You?"

"Good, yes." She glances up at Josh for reassurance. He squeezes her hand.

"We were just about to leave," he says. "But we can stay if you want some company..?" He looks from me to Rebecca, then back again.

"No, it's fine," I reply quickly. Too quickly. "We were just leaving too."

"We were?" Rebecca says.

She's trying to pretend otherwise, but I know Lola's smirking.

"Well, if you do decide to stay a bit longer," Josh says delicately, "drinks are on me. We don't want to be rude, but..."

The 'but' hangs in the air like the Sword of Damocles. Okay Josh, you've made your point, just say it. You're going home to have sex with Lola. Lola is going to have sex with you. Or – Jesus Christ – are you going to 'make love'? Don't do that. And don't tell me whether she likes it better with you. I don't want to know.

I'm gripped by the realisation that I'll never have sex with Lola again. He will, whenever he likes, in every position under the sun, but I won't. I suddenly feel ravaged by an overpowering need to drag Lola off to the nearest suitable space and relieve the increasing sexual tension that nobody seems to be experiencing except me. The ugly truth is that what I need more than anything else is to reclaim what is rightly mine, to mark my territory, put my scent back on her, to erase every last trace of Josh.

Lola tugs at his sleeve. It's a small gesture, but it demonstrates how close they've become in such a short time. What is it with young people these days? What's the rush – what happened to courting and no touching above the hemline until marriage?

Josh puts his arm around her, marking his territory. Nice, Josh, nice. Why don't you just piss on her and make it more obvious?

"We'd better make a move," he says. "Stop by sometime soon, we'll have a drink or something. I had fun the other night. Nice meeting you, Rebecca."

Lola's eyes fleetingly meet mine as Josh's hand steers her gently towards the exit. This time, I can't read her. I only know that the tightness in my chest has been replaced by a gaping hole, an opening that splits my sternum right down the middle. I watch them go through the door and out onto the street, and disappear from view. I can only torment myself with what they're going to do next.

Then, I remember Rebecca.

Her face is pinched into an angry expression, which I'm guessing I might be the cause of. Nine times out of ten, I am.

"That was her, wasn't it?"

"Who?"

"Don't make me throw this Martini in your face, John, because I will."

I weigh it up and can conclude that yes, she probably will. "Yes. That was her."

She's glaring at me now. This is why I usually prefer to lie. "You knew she'd be here, didn't you?"

She's still holding the Martini, so I choose my words carefully. "Not for sure, no."

"But she was."

"Yes."

Rebecca's face displays anger, and outrage. I eye the hand holding the Martini carefully, watching what she's going to do with it, but it's the other hand that proves to be the problem. That's the one she slaps me with.

"Bastard!"

I rub my face. She hit me surprisingly hard and it hurts, although not as much as my pride.

Rebecca downs her Martini, then snatches my Scotch and gulps that down too. She slams the empty glass onto the table behind her, and I wait for her to stop coughing. She's not finished with me yet.

"I'm not the rebound girl. And you, John Black, are a bastard."

She storms out of the bar, and people cheer. One guy even claps. Well if he, or Rebecca herself, thinks I'm going to follow her and protest, they're out of luck. She can paint a fucking picture of it, a big grey square called 'John the Bastard'. She could sell it to the Tate, and give interviews to the *Guardian* about it. Josh might even read it – how perfect would that be?

I put my hand in my pocket and pull out some change. I'm about to feed it into the machine when the guy who clapped comes over.

"It's empty, mate."

I know how it feels.

12

Sometimes, Simon's predictability can be comforting.

"She slapped you?" he huffs, his moon-face a spherical canvas of rage.

I do a quick glance over my shoulder, but the most attention our colleagues pay us is a few bemused glances, and a couple of irritated ones.

"She bloody slapped you!"

"Okay, Simon. I'm not sure people in Bangladesh want to hear about it."

He shakes his head. "You didn't deserve that. Well, you did a bit, but can you imagine if you'd slapped her back?"

"I'm not that much of a bastard."

"Exactly. But she had no concerns about slapping you, did she? It's wrong, so wrong. Too many double standards these days. Women thrive on them – exploit them. That's where they get their power." He swigs back his coffee. "They're all sluts, anyway."

I raise my eyebrows, my spider-senses tingling. "Something you've discussed with Maxine?"

Simon purses his lips. "Don't talk to me about Maxine."

"I see. So that's why all women have suddenly become sluts and I've had two nights of uninterrupted sleep."

Now Simon decides to lower his voice. "That girlie night she had? Well, it turns out she wasn't watching *Dirty Dancing* – she was bloody doing it! Her and mates went down the West End and she pulled some footballer."

"Footballer, eh? So we know for sure that she really doesn't go for brains."

"They all want footballers, John."

"Why? Surely there are easier ways to get genital warts."

"But they don't involve bottles of Cristal and a Bentley."

"And who wants a Bentley anyway?"

"Me," Simon says, proving once and for all that he has no taste in women, or cars. "Oh, she told me all about it, like it was no big deal. She said she didn't know we were having an 'exclusive' relationship. Can you believe that? I said absolutely no way, not having it. I said if that's what she's looking for, she can fuck off."

"What did you really say?"

"I told her I wanted to have an exclusive relationship."

"And what did she say?"

"She didn't really say anything. It was mostly laughter. She likes Bentleys too. And a man who earns more in a week than I do in a year. Bitch."

One of the secretaries peeks over her monitor and gives Simon a venomous scowl, exchanging glances with one of her colleagues. They both roll their eyes. Sensing Simon is about to become the catalyst for an office revolt, I lead him away from the vending machine and back to his desk.

Simon sighs and sits down. "And I've got all this to do." He gestures at a pile of lipsticks. "And I no longer have Penny to test them on. Huh, see, she was useful for something." I see the sudden flash of inspiration. It doesn't happen to Simon very often. "Hey, you could ask Valerie to be-"

"No way."

"But why?" Simon whines. "I need a woman."

"Yes, you do, but number one, I hate her, and number two, I'm against animal testing."

He clutches his fat head in his hands. "I'm starting to really hate this job."

"Starting? You've got a lot of catching up to do."

I leave Simon with his lipstick mountain and head back to my own desk, which is covered in the obligatory briefing papers and journals, all of which are obligatorily unread.

My computer seems to have accepted the fact that we're spending less and less time together, and is content to simply sit there and dare me to type something. I slump down in front of it, the steady blinking of the cursor mocking me. I run a hand over the stubble I didn't have the time or the inclination to shave, pull a subject out of my memory bank, also known as 'thin air', and begin to write.

Then, inevitably, about seven minutes later: "John?"

"Sarah?" I don't stop typing both because it's only Sarah, and for fear of losing the tenuous grip on my flow.

"There's someone here to see you."

"Tell them I died."

"John! Don't say that!" Sarah says, touching my arm. "She says it's urgent. Her name's Mrs Friedman, if that means anything to you."

Bollocks to flow. I spin around, my frail chair creaking. "Where is she?"

"Um, just out there." Sarah points through the glass doors that separate us from the civilised world. "I offered her coffee but she said she preferred tea, but we didn't have any, so – John!"

I'm on my feet, grabbing my jacket and pushing past Sarah, whose mouth opens and closes like a dummy with a mute ventriloquist. I dash past Simon's desk. He peers up from his lipstick empire, and frowns.

"John...?"

"Can't stop," I say. And I don't, not until I'm through those glass doors.

Lola's there, examining one of the tastelessly tasteful paintings hanging on the wall, her back to me. Her hair is tied in a ponytail; she's all business-like. She's beautiful.

"Hey. Mrs Friedman."

She turns around quickly. "You made me jump."

"Not intentionally."

"Nothing is with you." Lola runs her hands down the front of her skirt. "I figured it'd be okay to show up here unannounced and pretend to be a Friedman."

"Quid pro quo."

"'Rocking All Over the World' was my favourite."

"I prefer 'In the Army Now'. Poignant, and insightful."

Lola wrinkles her nose. "Anyway..." She takes a breath, tucking a strand of hair behind her ear. "We haven't sorted out what we're going to do about the house. And you haven't even moved any of your stuff out yet."

"There's no room at Simon's."

"No, you just can't be bothered."

"That too."

"Can you take lunch now?"

"Lola, it's just gone ten am."

"Oh. Is it?"

"Yes."

"It feels later than that." She fiddles with the St Jude around her neck, the patron saint of 'lost causes'. In a way, so is she.

"Do you think you could get out of here and come to the house with me? Just for a little while." Her brown eyes pin me to the spot. I peer in them, and it's to hell with everything else.

"Let's go."

And we almost get away with it. Lola smiles, sheepish, but relieved, and I guide her towards the lift. I don't know what this is about, but it feels good, like something might have shifted. Given that, I should've known something, someone, would come along and piss on my chips. And Valerie has such a great aim – she can probably even pee standing up.

"Lola! Where are you going with him?"

I swear under my breath as Lola disappears amid a tangle of Valerie's arms and mammoth hair. She seems to have a lot of both. Actually, Valerie Perkins would make a very good Medusa, if anyone's casting.

"Hi, Valerie," Lola says awkwardly. "I'm sorry, I just... We have things to sort out."

"Things?" The Medusa raises her eyebrows. "Oh no, you're not getting back with him. You have no 'things'. Your 'things' don't exist anymore. Not after what he's done."

"Don't be silly," Lola says, rather too quickly for my liking, "of course I'm not."

"And don't let him talk you into anything," Val snaps.

"Talk her into anything?" I say. "What am I, the Artful Dodger?"

Val folds her arms. It's like the O.K. Corral with laptops. "What you are," she elaborates, as I should've known she would, "is a-"

"Um," Lola looks at me, "we can't stop, Valerie."

"Oh yes, Val, we have 'things' to sort out, so you'll have to excuse us," I say, my hand on Lola's back, nudging her into the waiting lift.

"I'll excuse her, but not you. There is no excuse for you." Valerie grabs Lola's arm as we try to get away. "Call me, honey, we need to catch up."

"Right, yes. I'll do that," Lola says, in a tone that means she will do nothing of the sort. I'm such a bad influence.

I wink at Valerie as the lift doors close, mercifully blocking her from sight.

"'Honey'?"

Lola flicks her hair over her shoulder. "It's a term of endearment."

"I see." I press 'G', and the lift starts its descent. "Valerie thinks I'm going to talk you into something," I say.

Lola fixes her eyes on the lights flashing above us, counting down the levels. "You might. Well, you might try."

"I might."

"But please, don't try."

Neither of us speaks another word until we reach the ground floor. We walk out together, me with my hands stuffed into my pockets, her clutching her handbag tightly. Once we're in the open air, I manage to say it. It comes out suddenly, abruptly, truthfully.

"I'm sorry."

Lola looks at me, her eyes darker than I've ever seen them. "No trying, John. Please."

I was expecting the ride to our ex-house to be stilted, uncomfortable, but I'd forgotten that to Lola, every moment of silence is an opportunity to say something – blah mostly.

"...so then Mum said it would be better shorter."

"Your skirt?"

"No, John, my hair. What do you think?"

I exchange a brief glance with the taxi driver. Luckily, I can answer this one because for once I am actually listening. "I like your hair as it is."

"Do you really?" Lola runs a hand over the sleek mane of hair that, to me, is and always will be perfect.

"Yes." And then, because I can't help it, I ask, "What does he think?"

Lola glances confusedly at the taxi driver. "Him? Oh, you mean Josh."

"Yes."

"He has a name."

"Yes, he does."

Lola folds her arms. "And what about her?

"Pardon?"

"That girl. Rebecca." Lola, I'm pleased to note, laces her name with a tinge of disdain. "Who is she?"

"Just someone I met."

"What, met-met, or met?"

The cabbie shakes his head. I make a mental note to halve his tip. "I met her in a bar."

"Are you still meeting her?"

I scratch the back of my neck. "No. We've un-met."

"I see." Lola doesn't say anything else, and gazes out of the window for the rest of the drive. I can't tell if she's got nothing to say, or if she just doesn't want to say it.

If walking along my ex-street to my ex-house was weird, then following the same path with my ex-girlfriend by my side is completely bizarre. It's like we're in some hideous reality show, returning to the scene of the crime for the benefit of some unseen audience.

"Ooh look," Lola says. "Next door's still got that newspaper sticking out of her letterbox."

"'Her'? Have you uncovered documentary evidence that she's a woman?"

"John…"

"Sorry, sorry. I'm sure she's a perfectly nice 'woman' who just happens to look a little masculine. It's very common. If you ignore the facial hair and the sideburns, she's no stranger than your mother. But then, if you take into account the facial hair and the sideburns, she could almost be your mother."

"John!" But Lola's laughing. We're actually kind of having a good time, and we probably shouldn't be. She realises this at the same time as I do, and goes all serious again. "My mother wants to kill you, you know."

"Your mother has always wanted to kill me."

"But she really wants to kill you this time – slowly, and painfully. Stay out of Chelsea, for your sake." She fumbles around in her over-sized bag for the key.

"Can't you put in a good word for me?"

Lola slides the key into the lock. "And what good word would that be? The only words Mum would find good about you are 'he's' and 'dead.'"

She has a point.

The door creaks open, like something out of a horror film. The house feels desolate, as though no one has lived in it for years, a shrine to what once was. We're intruders, strangers in our own ex-home.

Out of habit, Lola goes to drape her coat over the banister, then snatches it back just in time. The habit is too familiar; it belongs in a different era.

"Right," she says. "Where do you want to start?"

I shrug. "Anywhere."

"Okay. How about upstairs? You need to pack the rest of your clothes, and your books and stuff."

"I don't want them." I sound like a spoiled child, and that's exactly what I am.

"John…"

"Okay, okay…"

"Come on."

She leads the way, as though I might've forgotten it. We pad upstairs quietly, as if we're trying not to disturb anything, and I notice Lola has dismantled shelves, uprooted frames from their hooks, fostered pot plants, and pulled up a few rugs. The discoloured squares on the walls where our memories once hung depress me. I did this. This is real.

I wonder if Josh has been round to help her, but cannot bring myself to ask.

The sight of the bedroom completes my sense of gloom.

"I see the bed is the sole survivor of the London furniture massacre," I say.

Apart from the bed, the clothes in my half of the built-in wardrobe, and a few bits of assorted crap – mostly mine – what used to be my favourite room in the house is practically barren.

"I thought we could sell it." I think she views this as a helpful suggestion.

"Okay."

"What? Don't you agree?"

"I said okay." I walk over to my side of the wardrobe.

"You don't agree, I can tell by your voice. John, I can't bring the bed over to Kay's. She doesn't have enough room as it is."

"Yeah, whatever."

I don't want to be confronted by the sight of my clothes. Not when hers are no longer hanging next to them. The first time I took stuff out of this wardrobe, I was jubilant, defiant. Now the sight of my few remaining jackets and shirts just makes me feel hollow. Where are all her things, her jamboree of stuff with their imaginative colours and textures. Fluffy pink robe? Vanished. The black dress that used to make me expire with lust? Missing in action. The yellow skirt she bought in the sales five years ago and insists she will wear one day? Disappeared.

I turn and face her.

"What?"

"Nothing," I say.

Lola sighs and flops down onto the bed, which is still groaning under the weight of all the pillows she liked to prop herself up with, one of the few remaining personal touches left in the house. She spreads herself out on the mattress like a starfish and I take advantage of the slight rise in the temperature and lie down next to her, so that our arms are almost touching. We keep our eyes on the ceiling.

"John, can I tell you a secret?"

"Sure."

She leans on her elbow, her head resting in her palm. "You promise you won't make fun of me?"

"When have I ever done that?"

"Do you want me to write a list?"

"That's okay. Go on, tell me the secret."

Lola draws a pillow up close to her chest, and hugs it. "Okay." She exhales. "A couple of times, after we … after you … since 'it' happened, I've stayed in this bed. At night, I mean. I slept in this bed by myself. I think," she continues, "it was because – I can't believe I'm telling you this."

"Go on." Even though I already know what she's going to say.

"It was because the sheets still smell of us. You know, not your smell, not mine, but both of us together?"

I nod, but I can't find the words – any words.

"John?"

"Yeah?"

"Do you remember how people used to tell us all the time that we wouldn't last?"

"Define last."

Lola brings her knees up closer to her chest. "Well, I guess they meant that eventually we'd fall out of love."

"Yes. I remember. They were wrong."

She swallows hard. "Then please tell me why we broke up because I still don't understand." There are tears in her eyes and I feel bad, and it's all so fucking unnecessary.

I put my feet up on the covers, scratching at my stubble as I try to come up with something. "I guess I needed a break."

"Oh, right. Cheers. That makes it a lot clearer. Why didn't you just have a Kit Kat like everyone else?"

"Are you being funny?" I ask, impressed.

"No, I'm really quite cross. A break from what, John? It's not like I was pressuring you to get married or anything."

"You bought *Cosmopolitan Bride*."

"Once, John, I bought it once. And I was premenstrual that day."

"Touché."

"Tell me the truth, John. Just for once, tell me the truth."

"When people ask for the truth, they usually don't like what they're told."

She folds her arms. "If you don't tell me, I'm going."

Okay, here it comes – the truth. I take a breath, and speak quickly.

"It's supply and demand. I'm the consumer, you're the supplier. So, we were together for nine years – that's a lot of supply, right? If you flood the market with something, over time the quantity demanded becomes less and less, because if there's too much of something, i.e. you, then I, the consumer, want less of it. It's simple economics."

Lola is staring at me as though I'm talking Urdu. "You're reducing our relationship to fucking economics? You're such a-"

"Before you use that word, hear me out." I sit up, warming to my theme. "In economics, there's something called the equilibrium, where demand meets supply. There's no excess, no shortage, everything's hunky-dory. The market naturally corrects itself, always settles in this equilibrium, so that supply and demand are equal again."

I'm rather pleased that I've finally found words for it, but Lola's face is like thunder. And that's being generous.

"Thanks, John. At last I have a sensible explanation to give to people when they ask me why we broke up. I think I'll stick to 'because he's a bastard.'" She throws a pillow at me – hard. "Are you physically incapable of giving someone a straight answer?"

"That is a straight answer. I needed space, Lola. There was too much supply, so I demanded less. I had to step outside of 'us' to want you again. I loved you, but I didn't know how to love you more. But I know now. The market is in equilibrium again – well, except now there's not enough supply. Of you. My demand has gone through the roof, and there's nothing to satisfy it."

She's just staring at me, her arms folded, her lips pinched together. I feel like a scientist waiting for a volcano to erupt so he can take some readings.

"I hate you," she eventually says.

"So you should," I reply.

"No, I really hate you."

"I know."

She runs a hand down the side of my face. "You haven't even shaved today."

"There's no point in shaving anymore."

"Are you going to grow a beard?" she says, still stroking my cheek.

"Would you like me better if I did?"

"No. My hatred for you is irredeemable and absolute."

"Right. I guess I may as well dust off the razor then."

Her face moves closer to mine. "I hope you slip and sever your jugular."

"I'll try my best."

"Yes, you do that."

I'm not prepared for how good it feels when she kisses me.

I think it might be the best cigarette I've ever smoked. I really feel like I've earned this one. Beside me, Lola watches the smoke drift towards the ceiling.

"I told my manager I was going home to bed," she says.

"You are in bed."

"I meant in the sense that I wasn't feeling well."

"I think you planned this whole thing."

Lola sits up, the sheet pressed against her chest. "You know I wouldn't."

"Why not? It's not unfeasible that you'd see fit to lure me here for sex," I say with a smile.

"Yes, it is. It's completely ridiculous. And don't make jokes about it."

"I'm not."

"You are. God, Valerie was right – you talked me into this."

That makes me chuckle. "Even I'm not that clever, Lola. How did I do it? Which words did I use?"

"Shut up! I've just cheated on my boyfriend. With my exboyfriend. You," she adds, in case I've lost track of who's who.

"So that's what he is now? He's been promoted to Premier League status, while I've just lost the play-offs."

"Please don't talk about football in the bedroom, John."

"Right. But you can talk about him. That's fine, glad we cleared that one up."

She lies down again, her hair splayed out on the pillow, tickling my cheek. I twist my head around as I exhale, so the smoke won't get in her face. She's not going to say it, so I'll have to ask.

"So, what happens now?"

She looks at me. "What do you mean?"

"With us."

She blinks a few times. "Why should anything happen?"

"I heard what you said."

"When?"

"A few minutes ago."

She sits up. "When?"

"Do you want me to give you exact co-ordinates?"

"I was about to have an orgasm, I didn't mean it," she says, plumping up one of the many pillows she's stuffed behind her head.

"Yes, you did." I flick the ash from my cigarette onto the carpet. I never liked it anyway.

"How do you know?"

"Because you were looking right into my fucking eyes, Lola. Even if I didn't hear you – which I did - I can lip-read."

Lola rubs her hand across her face and into her hair, sighing. "Just forget I said anything." She swings her legs out of bed, pulling the sheet with her, fumbling around on the floor for the clothes she was so keen to get out of an hour or so earlier.

"Sure, yeah. I'll do that, Lola. I'll be able to put it right out of my mind without any trouble at all." I stub out my cigarette on the nightstand that I never liked either and am finally able to vandalise.

Lola has her back to me, fastening her bra. "Maybe you could stay here and pack up your stuff when I'm gone."

"I don't want you to go."

She pulls her shirt across her shoulders. "It's a bit late for that."

I watch as she slides her skirt over her hips, then reaches for her jacket, flicking her hair out of the collar. It takes several seconds of scanning the room for her to find her bag and shoes, but it's still the quickest she's ever got dressed.

She stands in front of me. "I have to go."

"Of course you do. 'Josh' will be waiting."

"Yes," she fixes a steely gaze on me. "He probably will."

"Bye, John."

"Wait."

"What now?"

"How can you be sure I won't tell him about this?"

"Huh," she snorts. "He wouldn't believe I'd go anywhere near you."

"That makes me feel really good about myself."

"Tou-fucking-che."

She tosses her hair like a Charlie's Angel, whirls around and walks out of the room, and out of my life.

I'm lying there too stunned to move, too shocked to reply. I hear her going downstairs, and I hate myself for losing control. I have to have the last word, regain some dignity. So, despite the fact that I'm naked and the house is bloody freezing, I spring out of bed and dart onto the landing, where I see her opening the front door.

"What's wrong, Lola, did you get freaked out?" I yell. "Don't you tell Josh that you love him during sex?"

She glares up at me. "He already knows."

Lola slams the door, leaving me alone, astonished, and stark bollock naked.

13

Over the past couple of weeks, there have been several more of these 'episodes', as Lola insists on calling them. This morning's might have been my favourite one so far.

It started very badly, with me in my car, parked outside Kay's house waiting for Lola to be alone. Of course I wasn't stalking Lola – just because I'd been there for over an hour (who knew it took so long to get two brats ready for school and one brat ready for work), and was kind of crouched down low behind the steering wheel, doesn't make it stalking. My legs felt as though they'd been removed at the hip joint and folded into the sides of my torso, and who knew about my feet – my nerve endings dissolved around about the half an hour mark. But, on the bright side, my car is about the only enclosed space in the country in which I'm legally allowed to smoke, so smoke I bloody well did. I smoked so much I created a fog behind the windscreen, and almost missed Kay and Todd finally leaving the house.

Todd was first, briefcase (which appeared, at a glance, to be empty) in hand, tie knotted too tightly around his neck (although Kay might've done it, and that might've been the intent), a slightly baffled expression on his face, as though it was his first day. I have seen Todd on his way to work before, and can confirm he was wearing exactly the same expression, and possibly exactly the same tie.

Kay was next, her arms being yanked from their sockets by her two kids. Susie almost saw me. I thought I'd been clever and parked far enough down the street, but to my horror Kay and her entourage were on course to walk right past me. Kay doesn't know anything about cars except they have four wheels on the outside and one on the inside, and would never be able to pick out my car in a line-up, so she kept staring straight ahead and shouting at Jeremy, who was determined to walk and play on his PSP at the same time. But Susie – why the hell didn't someone buy her a PSP? – was on the passenger side of my car, and as the trio went past, she peered right in. Through the haze of Marlboro smoke, our eyes locked. Hers widened, mine narrowed, and I become 'Uncle Johnny' for the first time.

"Mum! That's Uncle Johnny! In that car!"

Kay didn't even blink. "Don't be ridiculous, Susie. Uncle Johnny is rotting in hell, where he belongs."

"Oh." Susie put her thumb in her mouth, and started skipping. "Hell! Hell! Hell! Uncle Johnny's in hell!"

I listened to Susie singing all the way down the street, the din fading as they turned the corner. Then I opened the car door, and promptly banged my elbow on it. Lola would later say that it served me right, that these episodes are all my fault – that I instigate them. I walked to Kay's front door – slowly, as it took a while for the blood the remember how to circulate through my legs – confident in the knowledge that I don't instigate anything. This is as much her as it is me.

I knew the coast was clear but I glanced over my shoulders anyway, feeling calm and breezy, a man very much in control of himself as I knocked once, twice, then simultaneously rang the bell and rattled the letterbox.

I could hear intermittent thuds and clanging noises coming from inside. The uninitiated could be forgiven for thinking that Kay and Todd were being burgled, but I was initiated nine years ago, and knew it was merely the sound of Lola getting ready for work. Recalling her chaotic morning routine was strangely soothing. She could never find anything. It was always, "John, where are my keys?" "John, have you seen my phone?" "John, where's my other glove?" The answer to all of these questions should've been, "How the fuck should I fucking know?" but somehow I did always know. "On top of the fridge." "On the mantelpiece." "Next to the cat food." And then she'd smile, and I'd feel like my presence on the earth had been validated.

She clanged and thudded, and possibly broke something, for a little longer, but eventually answered on my third ring and rattle cycle.

It wasn't an expression you'd hope to see from the other side of the doorstep.

"You."

"Hi," I said, probably as sheepishly as I looked. Her face didn't change. "Don't shut the door." Believe me, she was about to.

"I'm late."

"You're always late."

She rolled her eyes. "And what, you're now the speaking clock? Why are you here? I only came to the door because I thought you were the postman."

I opened my mouth to say it, but she cut me off.

"If you make a joke about having a package for me, I'll-"

I held my hands up. "It never crossed my mind. Can I come in?"

"Absolutely not." Lola had one shoe on, and no make-up on. The other shoe was in her hand, and I kept an eye on it – after Rebecca, I'm much more vigilant about what women do with their hands. "Why aren't you at work?"

"Phoned in sick."

She peered at me. "Are you sick?"

"In a manner of speaking."

She looked at me. I looked at her.

"Can I come in then?"

"No."

We ended up having sex in the hall.

I guess it's easier for her. She doesn't have these voids, these huge, cavernous spaces of time, like the one I'm floating in now. Here, gravity doesn't apply to me. It's an effort to move my arms and legs, and when I manage to, I never get anywhere, never touch anything – everything is too much of an effort to get to, out of my reach. I keep drifting along in this black vacuum with no direction, no speed, my eyes closed against the glare of the nothingness until I see her again. Only then does the light come.

She doesn't have these voids, because she has him. He fills her time, taking her mind off me – if she ever thinks about me. It could be the other way around. Maybe I take her mind off him.

"Are you ready yet?" Simon erupts into my room, an organic stink bomb of Brut, Lynx and Aquafresh. He surveys my motionless and clearly inanimate form, and his face falls. "Oh. You're not."

"I don't think I'll be very good company," I say, eyes still fixed on the ceiling, as though I'm admiring Highgate's version of the Sistine Chapel.

"It's the pub, John. You go there for beer, not company."

"Then you won't mind going on your own."

I don't have to look at Simon (always a bonus) to know he's put his hands on his hips, and is probably also pouting.

"Right, that's it," he says. "Stop sulking."

"I'm not sulking."

"Stop brooding then."

"I'm not brooding either."

"Then what, you're practising your audition for the most miserable man in Britain? Come on, you can't lie there engrossed in your own problems forever."

"I'm not engrossed in my own problems."

"Good," Simon says, picking my jacket up off the floor and chucking it at me. "Then you can come down the pub and listen to mine. I'll wait downstairs for you."

I remove my jacket from my face, where it unceremoniously landed, and Simon stomps out of the room, his legs as heavy on the stairs as if he'd had them amputated and replaced with wooden ones. He'll be in the lounge, in his favourite chair. He'll wait for me – as long as it takes. He's my best friend.

Annoying bastard.

With The Parlour annexed as lebensraum by the enemy, we're forced to go to our emergency pub. We hate it in here. It's smelly, in a pies and sweat way, and hasn't been refurbished since 1971, which coincidentally was apparently also the last time the landlady was sober. The pub is populated by people we don't like and have nothing in common with, namely fat men with receding hairlines playing darts and sitting around talking about the good old days. In other words, us in about fifteen years time. Yes, we hate this place, and spend at least three nights a week in here discussing precisely how it should be bulldozered and turned into luxury studio flats for key workers. Our discussions are so thorough that Simon's bar tab is larger than the national debt.

"Here you go." He plonks our beers onto the table, which wobbles on legs as unsteady as most of the customers. "That'll make you feel better."

"I don't want beer." I slide the bottle back over in his direction.

"Oh no," Simon says, pushing it back, his head so round it would give a Gala melon body dysmorphia. "You're not having Scotch. Not when you're depressed."

"I'm not depressed."

"Good. I fucking am."

I look at Simon, and realise I may well need this beer.

"What is it with women?" he whines. "What do they want from us?"

"Usually the opposite of what we're actually doing. Penny or Maxine?"

"Both. Penny wants a divorce, Maxine wants other men. Footballers. Apparently that's what the boob job was for. She won't see me exclusively."

"Did you ask her to?"

"Of course I did."

I sigh, and run a hand through my hair. "Simon, if you want a woman to go left, you tell her to go right." Simon's face tells me he might need a diagram for this one. "Okay…" I settle in to explain. "What you do is you tell Maxine that it's fine, she can see as many men as she likes – tell her she can sleep with an entire London borough if she wants, you're cool with it. You know what will happen?"

"Chlamydia?" Simon replies disturbingly brightly.

"Depends which borough she chooses. What'll happen is she'll come crawling back to you, implants in hand, saying she made a mistake and can you start again. Exclusively."

Simon's head deflates by a couple of cubic ounces. He glances at the dartboard, as though he expects to find the answer on it. Instead there are only two blokes with guts the size of an English county trying to add up their scores and running out of fingers.

"I don't get it," he says. "She'll think I don't care."

"Yes, she will. And then she'll wonder why you don't care. She'll ponder it for days, phoning up every female she knows to analyse it. The more she thinks about you not caring, the more she starts caring about you not caring, and then all of a sudden, she wants you back." I swig my beer, hoping Simon doesn't have the intelligence to ask me why I don't try it myself.

Luckily, he doesn't. "What about Penny?"

"Nothing about Penny. You want a divorce. Say yes as loudly as you can and sign any piece of paper she sends you. She's a separate case."

Simon thinks it through while I debate getting a bag or three of crisps. "So, I should've pretended I didn't care how many men Maxine slept with as well as me?"

"Precisely."

"I thought women hate it when we play games with them? All that 'not ringing for two days' crap."

"Three days, Simon. Three."

"See, this is what I'm talking about. I can't keep up."

"Don't feel bad. No man can."

"So why do we bother with them then?" He is suddenly so crestfallen I almost want to hug him. But he's too fat and ugly for hugs, and he has to learn.

"Because," I sigh, "we need them. We're crap without them. On our own we're just emotionally stunted, sad, pathetic human beings who can't do anything for ourselves except drink, and watch *Top Gear*."

Simon peers solemnly into his beer. "Is *Top Gear* on tonight?"

"Yeah, at nine. They're sailing across the channel in boats they made out of cars."

"Seen it."

"You've seen them all."

"So have you."

One of the fat men has bravely left the safety of the dartboard and is over at the jukebox. He's gone for one of the more modern choices – 'True' by Spandau Ballet. As it comes on, all the guys in here nod in a kind of "Ah" way. This indeed is the sound of our souls.

"So when does the game playing stop?" Simon asks.

"It doesn't. Ever. This is how it is."

"I hate playing games."

"Then join the priesthood. Or this lot." I stand up. "I'm getting a Scotch."

"Have you told Lola you want her back?"

"Not in so many words."

"What words then? Did you tell her you made a mistake? Oh, hold on, John Black is incapable of admitting he's wrong, isn't he?"

"Do you want another drink or a punch?"

"Beer. But we'd better be quick, *Top Gear's* on at nine."

I nod and go to the bar, taking my place with the other emotionally stunted, sad, pathetic men.

'True' is still on repeat play on my brain's iPod as Simon and I stroll home. I don't even like the song – I've never liked the song, but after over twenty years, I think I finally understand it.

It's drizzling lightly, muting the glow from the streetlamps. We pass the time by talking about work, football, and arguing about who's going to make the tea and bacon sandwiches when we get home. Then we argue about whether we actually have any bacon. In other words, we're avoiding the issues.

"My hair's wet," Simon moans, gazing longingly at a bus chugging past us.

"Be grateful. In five years time it'll be your bald spot getting wet in the rain."

"It's called a 'hair window' now, John. Why do you keep humming Spandau Ballet?"

"No idea."

"Hey, I just thought of a good name for a car wash – 'Spandau Valet.'"

I just look at him. Sometimes, there really are no words.

"What? It's funny, you know, 'valet.'"

We turn the corner into Simon's street.

"Simon, if you have to explain a joke, that means it isn't funny."

"Actually, I think you'll find-"

We both see her at the same time. Simon stops, putting an arm across me to block my path.

"John..."

"I know."

"I thought she hated you?"

"I might be bearable in small doses."

Simon gawps at me, and then at her. He gets it now. For a stupid person, he can be quite intelligent.

"This is not a good idea, John. What about her boyfriend?"

"Let's not spoil the mood, eh?"

Lola's seen us now. She's smiling, getting up off the step and coming towards us. I make a concerted effort not to wonder if she's come round for another 'episode'.

God, I hope she has. Every time I see her, and the more apparent it is that she doesn't want me back, the more I fancy her. Tonight, she's even more fanciable than ever. Why didn't she look like this when we were together? Oh, right, yeah. She did.

She's brought her practical pink umbrella. It's not doing much against this rain, which is falling at weird angles, as Simon's remaining hair will testify. She's wearing a thick padded jacket, the one that looks so good on her, the one that's my favourite. This is because it's mine. She's teamed it with an incongruous and inexplicable pair of flip-flops, the same shade as her umbrella. These, happily, are not mine.

"Hello," she says cheerily, as though her vigil at Simon's door is completely normal.

"Lola!" Simon booms in the most ridiculous voice I've ever heard him use. And I've heard a fair few over the years. "This is a… surprise."

Lola's face falls. She looks at me. "Is it?"

"Possibly," I say.

"I brought you this." Lola hands me a well-worn copy of an Andy McNab novel. "I found it with my stuff. I must've packed it by accident."

I cast my gaze from Lola, to the novel. "That's not mine."

"Oh. It's not?"

"No. I think Todd reads that kind of thing. Maybe it's his. That jacket's definitely mine though."

Lola glances down at it, as though she's just noticed it's there. "This one?"

"Does it keep you warm?"

"Oh yes," she says.

"Then it's mine."

The corners of her mouth twitch. I'd forgotten how Lola can flirt without uttering a single word. She got me completely with it once. It still works.

I know better than this, I really do, but when did that ever stop me?

"Simon, weren't you just saying you were thinking of visiting your mate?"

"What mate?" he replies. "Oh. Yeah. That mate. Yeah, I was just saying I'd like to visit, um, him, wasn't I? I know, I'll go now, shall I? Right now. When *Top Gear* is about to be on."

"You've seen it."

"Yeah, but I – oh. Yes… I have seen it." The words are audible, despite the gritted teeth.

"Great." I pat him on the back. "Take all the time you need. We won't wait up."

"No," Simon says, turning on his heel and heading back in the direction of the pub, "I bet you won't."

Lola giggles as Simon walks off, muttering to himself. "That was a bit mean."

"Ah well," I say, fishing a key from my pocket. "A bit of fresh air won't hurt him. But a few of the blokes in the pub might. Hopefully."

"You're twisted," Lola says.

Yeah, I am. But still you're here, you're laughing and, best of all, you're following me inside.

Lola sits opposite me, the flip-flops tossed to one side, her feet curled up on Simon's sofa. In an effort to create the impression I'm not thinking about potential episodes, I've made her a cup of tea, and I've been chatting to her, asking her questions and telling her stuff about nothing in particular in the way that women like. It was pleasant enough while it lasted, but now Lola's gone all wistful, which is never ideal.

"So, how've you been?" Lola warms her hands around Simon's 'Up the Arsenal' mug.

"Since this morning? Great, thanks."

"You know what I mean. Have you thought about me?"

Another riddle, one there's no correct answer to. "I've got a carpet burn on my elbow that won't let me forget you."

She hits me with a feeble slap as I sit down next to her. "Don't be crude."

"It's easy to say that after the event. It really hurts."

"Let me see."

I hold up my wounded elbow for her to inspect.

"Ouch," she agrees.

"If we're going to make a habit of it, you'd better tell your sister to get plusher carpet. Or I could buy elbow-pads."

Lola breaks my gaze, her eyes drifting over to the clock on the mantelpiece as it strikes nine.

"Shit. Excuse me a sec." I flop down in front of Simon's Blu-Ray recorder, which he's had for nearly four months and has no idea how to use.

"John…"

"Uh-huh…" I've turned the machine on. How hard can this be?

"That's what I came to talk to you about."

"Mmm?" Naturally, Simon's chucked away the manual. Not that I need the manual. Manuals are for vegans, and girls.

"John, I – what are you doing?"

"Recording *Top Gear*."

"No," Lola says, putting her cup down. "You're not."

At first I think she's saying this in a rhetorical way, like, "Oh no you're not recording *Top Gear*, you're damn well going to listen to me," but she sits down on the floor beside me, and it turns out what she means is that I'm not recording *Top Gear*, I'm breaking Simon's Blu-Ray recorder.

"Why don't you use the EPG?" she says.

I blink at her. "I have to wire it up to my heart?"

"No," she says, taking the remote from me. "The EPG – Electronic Programming Guide. Here, look."

She starts pressing buttons, okaying a few menus, biting her lip as she concentrates. "It's starting now, right? Okay…" She taps some numbers on the front of the machine. "You know you can do this via your mobile now – there's an app for it online."

"I have no idea what you just said. How do you know about this stuff? You can't even work the microwave."

"I can now. There you go." She gives me back the remote. "Josh had the exact same one before he upgraded. He showed me what to do – any idiot can set it. Oh, sorry. Not that you're an idiot."

"No." Even though recent events have shown otherwise.

Lola goes back to the couch, leaving me crushed like a clapped out Corsa.

"See," she says. "This is what I was trying to tell you. No more episodes, John. It's not right. We're hurting everyone."

I don't want her to elaborate on who 'everyone' might be. God, I hate him. He has everything, a Blu-Ray DVD recorder, a girlfriend – my ex-girlfriend! – who he's taught how to use it, like some kind of fembot. He's a fascist, that's what he is. He treats her like a slave, I bet.

"Plus," she continues, "there are other things." She hugs her knees. "It's not the sex that keeps me awake at night, John."

I postpone my immediate disappointment as she goes to elaborate.

"It's this, doing 'us' things."

"Recording *Top Gear*?"

She wrinkles her nose. "Ugh, I don't miss that silly programme. Josh never watches it."

And there we have it: conclusive proof that Josh is gay.

Lola sighs. "I don't know what it is about you. When I consider what a bastard you are, how abrasive, how cold, conceited, rude and selfish you can be, I'm amazed that

I still only feel like myself when I am with you. But you don't want me. Not properly."

"Well, I wouldn't put it quite like that, Lola."

"Oh? How would you put it?" she says expectantly, and I'm under pressure to come up with something profound. When in doubt, steal.

"It's like Robert De Niro said, sometimes you have to go away in order to come back."

But that just confuses her. "That wasn't in *Scarface*."

"Neither was Robert De Niro."

"Oh, that was the other one. Al Pacino."

"Yeah."

Another pause.

"So you're admitting you made a mistake?" Lola persists.

I consider lighting a cigarette just so I can stub it out on my eyeball - anything to take away what I'm feeling now, to avoid the inevitable.

"Yes, Lola." I enunciate the words slowly. "I made a mistake."

I wait for the yelp of triumph, the flash of lightning, the news headline that hell has reportedly just frozen over, air traffic controllers yelling that flying pigs are blocking the skies, but it doesn't happen. Lola leans back into the sofa, seemingly gathering her thoughts.

"How do I know you won't get bored of me again?"

"You don't. You have to trust me."

My heart's in my mouth while Lola thinks about it. I chew on it. Like everything else, it tastes like chicken.

"I can't."

"Right."

"Aren't you going to ask me why?"

"I never cared much for post-mortems."

"Can I tell you anyway?"

"If you feel you must."

"It might help you, John. In your next relationship."

I nearly laugh. "That sounds like the kind of thing I'd say."

Lola slides her flip-flops back on and rests her hands in her lap. "With Josh, I know I'm enough for him. He's not constantly looking over his shoulder for someone better. I feel secure. I can relax."

"Great. Why don't you go and relax with him now then?"

I regret it as soon as the words come out.

"I think I'd better." She stands up. To go.

I rub my temples. I can't let her. Not like this.

"Lola."

She takes her hand from the door, closing it shut. "Yes?"

I can't meet her eyes as I speak. "One last time?"

"You've got a cheek," she says, but her voice is soft. Oh God, she feels sorry for me. That's definitely pity in her eyes. Fuck it, I'll take pity – I'll take whatever I can get.

"But you stayed with me for nine years," I venture carefully.

"I'm not sure I know why I stayed that long, John."

I look at her, beseeching her with shameful honesty. "Stay."

Her lips part. "I can't."

"You can, if you want to."

She meets my eyes, leaving me in no doubt. "That's the thing, John. I don't want to."

She closes the door behind her. The click of the latch echoes through the empty house.

I stand behind the curtain so she won't see me watching her flip-flop down the path. I settle down on the ledge, lighting myself a comfort-smoke, and stay there until she becomes a Lola-shaped speck fading into the distance, making her way back to him, and his Blu-Ray recorder and EPG.

14

And so it seems, my career is all I've got. You wouldn't think so, from the way I've been treating it. I should be more grateful; I should keep in mind how long I spent slogging my way through journalism college, the crappy work experience placements in the provinces, and look back with a smile on my face at everything I've achieved. Or I should think about my father, who'd laughed when I told him that no, I'd rather not 'learn a trade', thanks all the same. "Well, you'll regret it son," he'd said. "Once you step into the rat race, you'll never get out again." Being me, I didn't care, because as far as I was concerned, I wanted to get into the rat race so badly that getting out again simply wasn't a concern. Well, guess what, it is now – the rat race is real. There is a rodent staring at me, sitting at my desk and beaming in wonder as though he's just seen Jesus Christ.

"Oh my God, you're John Black!" the rat says.

I open and close my eyes but the rat doesn't disappear back down the sewer he came from. Instead, he sits there, watching me with beady eyes. I can feel my colleagues' stares burning into the back of my neck. This little scene is interesting enough for them to down tool for a few seconds, to see what I'm going to do. I blink again. Surely any second now my alarm will go off, and I'll wake up.

"Would you excuse me?" I say.

I don't hang around for the rat to squeak a response.

I head straight for Charlie's office. He's surprised to see me again so soon after our 'discussion' over my 'experimental' feature, and I'm surprised I'm here too.

I'd planned to avoid him for the rest of the financial year.

He waves a large and hirsute hand for me to enter, which I'm doing anyway, without knocking or faking niceties.

"Johnny boy! What can I do for you?"

Charlie is being friendly. This is bad. This is unprecedented. I'm not going to like this.

"Why is there a teenage boy sitting at my desk?"

"Ah, you've met Percy. Lovely lad," Charlie says, as though no further explanation is necessary. "Percy's the son of a very good friend of mine. A very good friend of mine, Black. A very good friend of the paper's. I've agreed that he can do a placement here for a month before he goes to university."

I'm not sure whether to scream or vomit first. "Tell me you're kidding."

"It's only a month. I thought you could mentor him."

I glance around for the Candid Camera. "Charlie, I really don't think I'm the mentoring type." I think quickly. "But what about Valerie Perkins? She seems to have some spare capacity at the moment. And she's great with people." Cadaverous ones, mostly.

Charlie waves a hand to dismiss Valerie Perkins, which on an ordinary day would be fantastic. Not today. Today I'd pick up a pair of pom-poms and jump up and down singing, "Give me a 'V'!" if I had some to hand.

"Nope, it's down to you. For some ridiculous reason, you're his idol. He wants to be a journalist – because of you. You, Christ knows why, inspire him, apparently."

"Great. So what am I now, a bloody careers advisor?"

Charlie's brow furrows and the tip of his nose reddens. I had no idea he could multi-task. "You work for me, so you'll do whatever I bloody tell you. You will be nice to Percy. Being nice will be a change for you, a new skill for you to learn. Who knows, if you manage it, I might even mention it in your appraisal. The boy thinks the sun shines out of your saggy arse, so make sure you show him the ropes."

"We have ropes?"

"Yes, and I'll tie one around your neck if you fuck this up." He waggles his biro at me to emphasise his point. "Now get your arse out there," Charlie shoves his pen in front of him in case I've forgotten where 'there' is, "and give Percy a reason to have your sorry self on a pedestal."

We eyeball each other for a few seconds. There's no point leaving just yet because Charlie will have to have the last word. That's one of the reasons I despise him so much – everyone knows the last word is rightfully mine.

"And I hope you haven't been wasting your time writing any more of that candied cat shit. Remember what you're paid for."

"I've had it inscribed in blood on my desk."

"Your blood I hope," Charlie grunts.

I retreat to my desk with my head down, walking as briskly as I can without breaking into a sprint. The rat, apparently named Percy, is still sitting there, leafing through a report on something or other that I meant to read yesterday but never got round to. I clear my throat.

It jumps. The bloody thing jumps. I would've laughed, were I not so pissed off.

"Um, hello," it – Percy – babbles. "You have a lot of great stuff here. This inflation report hasn't even been published. Are these the final figures? Do they include mortgage repayments?"

I take one hand from my pocket and run it over my chin. Okay, I can do this. He's just a kid, and I'm the economics editor. I'm the top dog around here, and he – well, I haven't quite figured out what he is yet, and neither, from the look of him, has he.

"You're Percy?"

For a second, I think he might be about to stand up and salute. "Yes. Percy Van Childer."

"Dear God. How old are you?"

"Eighteen. I'm on my gap year. I'm going to be reading economics, of course at-"

"That's all very interesting, but you're sitting at my desk."

Percy gawps at me like a child who has just been told that no, he cannot have another scoop of ice cream. I take advantage of the lull in his enthusiasm to dislodge him from the chair that I am apparently now prepared to defend with my life. I sit down, rustling a few pieces of paper that contain doodles, a cartoon of Simon's face, and a list of things I need to furnish the new flat I was going to spend today searching online for. Of course, Percy thinks I'm handling my latest economic musings and watches me keenly, a sliver of tongue peeking out from the corner of his mouth.

Once I'm at my desk, the charade is easy. I take out a brand new biro from the pack, and begin to chew on it as though it were a sugar cane. I am in full 'In the Black' mode now, and I begin tapping out my thoughts on a piece of data I should've commented on a couple of days ago but haven't. It's "Please Miss, the dog ate my homework" all over again. But now I have Percy breathing down my neck to motivate me. The only thing is, it doesn't.

That's the way things are going for me: I wish consumers would stop buying stuff, I wish exchange rates were fixed, I wish public spending would grind to a halt, and I wish there wasn't an election around the corner so the government wouldn't keep deliberating over what to do with taxation rates and immigrants. I wish all these things – and many more – because I can't keep up. I look back at myself and wonder how I managed it before.

I've become one of those people who switch off when the business news comes on, and who put the financial section of the paper in the cat litter tray. In my line of work, this is not ideal. The FTSE has become a series of numbers as interesting and as relevant as small-print, and Dow Jones could be someone who I went to university with but never actually spoke to. I'd rather watch Sky One instead of CNBC. Actually, I'd rather watch anything than CNBC, even Jeremy Kyle. Instead of caring about the Retail Price Index, my brain is jumbled with other, more important, things. If had a cerebral car boot sale right now, I'd have a lot of junk to sell. So, yeah, this is a great time to have a Percy Van Childer to babysit.

I stop typing and lean back in my chair, wishing I could substitute my biro for a cigarette. I look round at him, and he smiles back at me – he even waves. This boy is so green, he's almost Kermit-coloured. It's evident in his freshly ironed – not by him, I'm guessing – shirt that resembles an Excel spreadsheet, his appalling loafers and slanted glasses.

"Can I write the piece on the mortgage approvals stats?" he gabbles, clutching the report that no one is supposed to see but me. "I have a whole spin for it already in my head."

Spin?

I snatch the report back from him. "First piece of advice – keep it in your head. I don't write up every single set of stats that comes out. Not until I've put them into context. I don't do news, I do analysis – there's a difference."

"Yes, but-"

"You see this?"

He's confused, but nods at the coffee dregs from one of the Styrofoam cups forming a wall around my desk that would make Hadrian proud. I pluck one from the stack and hold it out to him.

"This cup has been here longer than you. In the queue to write for the paper, this inanimate object is a good few paces ahead of you. Now, you're keen to learn, I can see that. And that's a good thing. So, over there is the vending machine, and the photocopier. Go and introduce yourself."

Percy watches me, his mouth agape, while I pick up a random stack of old notes from the floor beside my waste bin and shove them into his arms. "These need to be photocopied. Thanks, you're a great help."

I spin around and type 'Percy is a virgin' while he stands there becoming acclimatised to his designated rung on the ladder of journalism.

"With all due respect, John-"

"Mr. Black."

He is floundering – advantage JB.

"Mr. Black, I didn't come here to photocopy. I came here to learn to write like you. To be like you."

"Trust me, you don't want to be like me."

"Oh, but I do, Mr Black. I really do."

I need a cigarette.

"Okay." I take a piece of paper from the pile I have thrust upon him, holding it in front of his face. "You see this writing?"

"Yes."

"That's my writing. If you read it before you copy it, it's like studying. Read, and copy. Read, and copy. Everyone has to start somewhere, and this is quite possibly the best place. It's how all the greats started. Now, I really have to get back to this, but a coffee would be great, thanks."

I return to my screen, sensing that Percy is still standing there, wondering whether to start crying or phone Daddy.

"Mr Black?"

"Yeah?"

"How do you like your coffee?"

I allow myself a smile. "Black. Very black."

This might not be so bad after all, I think to myself when he finally leaves me in peace. I get my own little lab rat to experiment on, to torture and take the brunt of my silent rage with the world. Who knows, it might even give me reason to get up in the mornings again. I've been in the market for one for a while now.

I am just getting reacquainted with my keyboard, remembering where all the letters are and what's expected of me, when Simon decides to pay me a visit. I know he's coming because I can smell him approach.

"Perfume day?"

Simon nods. "Thirty tested and counting. I smell like Old Compton Street, don't I?"

"I was thinking more of a Dutch boudoir."

"How would you know what a Dutch boudoir smells like?"

"Same way you know what Old Compton Street smells like."

I scan the morning's efforts, whilst Simon assesses Percy.

"Did you show him how the photocopier works?" he asks, unable to avert his gaze from the car crash that is Percy's knack with technology.

"I figured the big green button marked 'start' might give it away."

"You might have to go and show him. He hasn't even worked out where to stick the bloody paper."

I look up and sure enough, Percy is standing there in complete bafflement, despite the photocopier having the most blatant paper feeder in the history of office equipment. It's actually quite comical. Less so for him, I'm guessing.

I shrug. "Well, he did say he was here to learn."

Simon pulls his ultra-serious face. It does happen from time to time. "I'm not sure you should be arsing about with the son of one of Charlie's mates, John. It's thin ice, even for you."

"It always holds my weight."

"Yeah, so far. Be nice to him."

"There's an old saying – 'When the student is ready, the teacher appears.' He's not ready, and I'm not a teacher. So he can bloody well photocopy and make coffee."

"You're bastard, John."

"You're not the first person to point that out."

"And I sure as bollock won't be the last." Simon pauses. "Any word from…?"

My muscles tense. "No."

He nods in sympathy. "How long has it been now?"

"Simon, you ask me this every bloody day."

"You're right. Three weeks?"

I pause. "And eight days."

"Four weeks then."

"Uh-huh."

"Are you going to call her?"

"No."

"Good," he says. "I wouldn't."

"Great, because you're my relationship role model."

"Get lost, John."

"I would, but this is my desk. Yours is over there."

Muttering something unintelligible, Simon glowers at me and skulks back over to his side of the room, presumably to douse himself in more perfume.

As he's allegedly my responsibility, I cast a cursory glance in Percy's direction. The photocopier is now obeying Percy's will – he's even got it to staple. At least he won't be able to say he didn't learn anything today.

It's not long though until boredom sets in. I manage to write something fairly comprehensible, although writing about the housing market is not easy when you're in the midst of selling your own house because you stupidly dumped your girlfriend, who has now found someone else, has no interest in you anymore and appears to have moved on amazingly quickly, making you feel utterly dispensable. But never let it be said that I'm not objective.

And I'm back where I started, feeling sorry for myself. I have to break the cycle. I have to do something radical – shock my system. I glance up from my desk and realise there is one option left.

Sarah is poring over a map, a big red marker clutched between her fingers.

"Hey."

She looks surprised to see me. That's fine – I'm surprised I'm here too.

"Hello." Only she could make such an anodyne word sound alarming.

"How are things?"

"Um, okay," she says, suspiciously. "How are you?"

"I'm great actually. What's that you're doing?"

"I'm not really sure. It seems a bit silly." She begins explaining the intricacies of the latest mind-numbing task Molly's given her, and I even listen to some of it.

I think Molly, who for the record I've never actually seen in person, is even more of a sadistic freak than I am. The tasks she gives Sarah to do are worthy of an Olympic gold for barbarism towards employees. Chores like counting the number of vowels in each English county, adding them together and multiplying the answer by the square root of the circumference of the tyres on a harrier jet are not beneath Molly.

Sarah never finishes explaining exactly what Molly is torturing her with this time as a careless swipe of her hand knocks her coffee flying.

"Oh no!" she yells, jumping up as the contents of the cup spill out slowly all over the table. "The Middle East is ruined!" she laments, trying to salvage the remains of the map she was colouring in.

I break one of my cardinal rules of office conduct and help her, blotting up the mess with a few of the paper towels I'm guessing she keeps on her desk for occasions such as these.

We contain the spillage, but the map is a write-off. She holds it up, surveying the blurred print with dismay.

"I'm supposed to be marking sites of recent suicide bombings! Now I can't even find the Gazza Strip!"

Christ. Maybe I misunderstood and it's simply that Molly cannot trust Sarah with anything approaching importance. Here it goes. I'm smashing the glass, pulling the emergency cord, and releasing my parachute. I say it before I choke on it.

"I could probably help you with that."

She gives me a grateful look, which quickly turns to one of distrust. As well it should. "Why would you do that?"

Yes, why would I do that?

"It seems ridiculous for you to be struggling when I could help you get that done in about half an hour."

She still isn't convinced. "Hmm. Well, I could use a hand, but if you help me it doesn't mean I'll help you with your column in return. Okay?"

I nod, only because the action keeps me from laughing. The only way I could envisage her helping me with my column was if I were drawing one instead of writing one.

"You know, Sarah, I've been thinking about what you said about mixing business with pleasure," I lie. She doesn't need to know I'm desperate.

She forgets about suicide bombings and looks at me quizzically, waiting for it.

"And, you're right," I continue, on a roll of untruth now. "I should make more of an effort. So, with that in mind, I was wondering if you'd like to have a drink with me sometime?"

Her mouth drops open, and it's an effort not to drop a paperclip in it. "Are you asking me out?"

"For a drink, yes." And God have mercy on my soul.

She folds her arms. "Are you on the rebound?"

I'm frequently amazed that women have this irrepressible compulsion to make things fifty times more complicated than they actually are.

"You've just spilt up with what's-her-face. You're using me to get over her," she says, the first and only point she's ever made.

This must be some kind of endurance test to see how sad and pathetic I've become. Damn my competitive streak.

"I'm not sure I understand the concept of 'rebound'," I say, crossing my fingers behind my back, "but if that's what you think then, okay, I probably am."

There, I've called her bluff. I know now that to deny a case of the rebounds is to admit your own guilt and risk a slap, and I'm not doing that again. I run a hand through my hair and make like I'm about to walk away. Which, as a matter of fact, I am.

"John, wait."

I turn back, exaggerating the movement.

"How about Friday?"

God, this is difficult. Friday is a serious day. If I agree to that she'll think my intentions towards her are serious.

"Friday is kind of awkward for me. How about Thursday?" I would've suggested Wednesday, were that not too soon.

She knows exactly what I'm up to. "Friday, or nothing."

I pretend to consider it. "Well, I really can't make Friday, so I guess we'll have to make it another night."

I slink back to my desk and check my watch. I'm timing her.

As soon as I'm seated, Percy scuttles over, carrying a bundle of freshly copied paper. He must've have come to terms with his chores as he seems brighter now, and even more enthusiastic. I see this vigour as something that must be quashed, a bug crawling on the skin of humanity.

"All done, Mr Black. Can I get you some more coffee?"

"That would be great, thanks. I think you're up to your next task now."

Percy's eyes gleam, and I can almost hear the imaginary Pulitzer Prize speech he's composing within the confines of his rodent skull.

"Right, you see that huge stack of books and reports over there?" I say to him, pointing out where we keep all our research documents and hard copies of back issues.

"Uh-huh," he answers, nodding furiously, his mouth almost watering.

"Okay, next to it is the shredder. Take the papers you've just copied, and put them through it. Thanks so much." I go back to my screen.

Percy's mouth flaps up and down a few times. "But … but I've only just copied them all!"

"Yeah, I know, and you did it so well, but it's a good way of getting you to read, and hence learn, which is what you told me you wanted to do. Read and copy."

"It's a terrible waste of paper."

"Very true, and we are very environmentally conscious around here, which is why you are going to take the shredded paper and put it into the recycling bin, which is just down there. Thanks Percy, you're doing a great job. There's no hurry for the coffee, whenever you're done."

It does occur to me that I might playing with fire a bit here, but then, that never stopped me before. I have the burns to prove it.

I check my watch again as she comes over. Seven minutes. Impressive resolve.

"Okay, John, I rang my friend and switched my thing to Friday night, so I can see you on Thursday after all," Sarah says, like it's no big deal.

"Great," I answer without looking up from my keyboard. "I'll meet you outside at six-thirty."

"Outside?" Sarah repeats, in case she misheard me. "Can't we leave here together?"

She'd love that, I think to myself. But I'm not prepared to surrender the enigmatic persona I've spent so long cultivating by publicising to the whole office that I've resorted to seeing Sarah in my free time.

"I'd really rather keep it quiet," I explain. "Valerie knows Lola, and I don't want her to know about it. It would be insensitive, you know?"

I came up with this off the top of my head and it's a fine excuse, although I'm so low on Valerie's list of considerations that I doubt whether she'd notice if I never turned up for work again. I'm more bothered about the humiliation of another human being knowing I'm desperate enough to go out with Sarah without a gun being pressed to my temple or my car being held hostage.

"Oh, I see," she says, giving me a suspicious glare. "Okay then, I'll see you outside on Thursday. You can decide where we go."

I nod. I'd already assumed I'd have to anyway, as women are so bloody indecisive and only ever say, "Oh, you choose," and then spend the rest of the night saying how they wish you'd taken them to so-and-so instead.

So I spend the rest of the afternoon surfing the Internet, trying to find somewhere that's expensive enough to show I have class, but that won't give Sarah the idea that I'm being extravagant to impress her. I also need somewhere not too far away, so I won't have to bear a long journey with her, but then it has to be far enough away to ensure I don't see anyone I know.

This search proves more difficult than I imagined, and Google keeps suggesting I go to The Parlour.

"Oi, John."

Simon was never one for conversational etiquette.

"Simon?"

"Is it true you just asked Sarah out?"

Sometimes there really is no justice in the world.

15

It started, as most dubious things in life do, with a drink. Then, as is usually the case when a drink starts something, a drink the following night makes it happen again. Then another drink the night after that turns it into a pattern; one more drink and it becomes a habit, then a routine. Then, before you know it, you're waking up in Sarah's bed. Or, more accurately, I'm waking up in Sarah's bed.

I spent ages debating where to take her – where to smuggle her might perhaps be a more correct summation of my thought process – for that fatal first drink. I decided the closer we stayed to the office, the less likely we were to be discovered. And it worked. Everyone else drifted off at six, seven o'clock, towards the West End. We left at seven-thirty for the pub just across the road. And it wasn't that bad. No really, it wasn't. Maybe my standards have slipped a little – a lot – or maybe I am now at the point where I hate myself enough to be able to tolerate Sarah's presence for long periods of time (where Sarah's concerned, anything over five minutes is a long time).

Sarah is, if you can keep her on one topic of conversation for more than thirty seconds, okay company. Sometimes she can even make me forget how badly I've messed everything up; sometimes she makes me more aware of it than ever. But what makes up for her lack of brain cells and self-awareness is that she's warm, affectionate, and her bed is always inviting. And, in my current state of mind, they are three very important qualities.

And dating (her word of choice, not mine – I still can't think of a suitable euphemism that won't upset her) Sarah does have its advantages. She's attractive in an easy-on-the-eye kind of way, and she gets more attention than the average woman, which means she usually gets served really quickly in pubs. Even her intellectual shortcomings have their benefits as it gives me licence to indoctrinate her with my political views, and my interpretation of world history and current affairs. We eat in the restaurants I want to eat in, and go to the places I want to visit. There's no discussion, no argument, she just assumes I know best – which I do. And she likes me all the more for it; calls me 'cultured', thinks I'm teaching her something. But *My Fair Lady* this is not.

Since that first drink, calling her and suggesting we go out later that evening has come to be something I do automatically. I've learned to endure how she has to link her arm through mine as we walk together, and I'm almost able to overlook her need to impart meaning into happenstance. For example, when I left my jacket at her place by accident, she thought it was her cue to ask for a drawer in the room I'm borrowing from Simon. She talks all time, and most of it is just air with sound. She constantly checks her phone for texts and then reads them to me, even though they are largely nonsensical and a frivolous waste of a good satellite. She thinks I'm actually listening when she insists on reading my horoscope aloud from about eight different magazines, and despite the fact I've made it plain that I don't care, she has to tell me in graphic detail about the dream she had last night. But, she's better than nothing. She's better than the silence ringing in my ears, and she's better than the space in the bed beside me.

When I spend the night with Sarah, I'm always aware of her presence, as she invariably has some part of her body draped across mine. Last night it was her arm across my waist, and I don't mind that manoeuvre too much. But she does this thing when I roll onto my stomach that drives me crazy – she half climbs on top of me, almost smothering me, and when I try to move, she rolls with me. It's like sleeping with one of the Red Arrows.

I'm smoking my breakfast when Sarah returns from the shower, dabbing at her dripping hair with a towel in an ineffectual manner.

"Do you have to smoke in bed?" she says with no real conviction.

"Do you want me to put it out?" I answer with even less conviction.

"No… I suppose the damage is done. You've started so you might as well finish."

I wonder if it's registered that manipulating her is a talent I think I was born with. It just comes naturally to me. Easy as pie, ABC – easy as ABC pie. I know that continuing to do something simply because you can get away with it is no justification, but… Actually, no, that is a justification. I'm fine with it.

Sarah sits down at her dresser and starts combing her hair from root to tip, stopping every so often to hike her robe up her shoulders. She is oddly quiet, and this has to be a bad sign, a portent of horrors to come.

"John?"

Here we go.

She puts down the comb and pivots herself round on the stool. "It's okay about… you know."

Women have renamed so many things 'you know'. 'You know' covers a variety of topics, issues, and nouns, and seems to be a substitute for words that they are afraid to say aloud. Sarah could mean anything – her vagina, the Holocaust, someone else's vagina, fiscal stimulus, tampons (no, wait, they're 'thingies'), vibrators, Immac… The list is endless.

I give her a blank look, and Sarah tilts her head skyward for a few moments, creating the illusion she's considering how to rephrase her statement. Maybe she is. I've given up trying to fathom what's going on in Sarah's head because, usually, there's more going on in an unoccupied dog kennel.

"I mean, the thing with, you know, is okay. I'm fine with it."

"Right. You might have to help me out a little here, Sarah."

She hesitates before eventually saying, "You know…"

I contemplate extinguishing my cigarette on my arm. It's either that, or I smother her with a pillow. I raise my eyebrows instead.

She makes face. "Sex!"

"Okay. What sex?"

She gives me a look of deep concern. "Oh, poor John…." She comes over to the bed and settles down opposite me. "It's not that I don't want to have sex with you, John – I do," she begins, "but if you're not ready yet, then I'm okay with it. I appreciate you must still be emotionally scarred after whatsit dumped you, so I'll wait until whenever you're ready. I'm very understanding. Just let me know when … you know."

"Right."

"It's such a shame your confidence is so low you've even gone off sex. It's terrible. Who's ever heard of a man who doesn't want to have sex! What's-her-face should be ashamed of herself."

I've discovered that if you persistently don't open up and reveal your feelings to a woman (and let's face it, who the hell wants to do that?), they'll invent a reality for you. It's not that I don't want to have sex with Sarah – she's pretty, has a good body, is probably quite dirty, and all the important stuff – it's just that I really can't be bothered. It's too complicated. If I 'you know' with Sarah it would move our relationship to the next level, and I'm in relationship stasis. Momentum has carried me along so far, but now I'm inert, suspended in motion. I only really want to 'you know' with the woman who only wants 'you know' with someone else, and nothing that interferes with my mental shrine to my ex-girlfriend interests me. I prefer to remain stuck where I am, and I just so happen to have dragged Sarah down with me. The problem is, she's such a willing participant.

So, naturally, Sarah has taken my sexual indifference and has spun it into an imaginative fairy tale that Alistair Campbell would stand back and admire. In her version of events, I am a fragile, wounded baby bird lost in the woods, needing someone to teach me how to fly all over again. It suits her better than the truth, which is that I am a cold, selfish bastard, and I might just be using her. She doesn't want to see it, so she doesn't ask. And if she doesn't ask, I won't tell. Actually, I won't tell even if she does ask.

I'm almost dressed now, refusing her offer of muesli, orange juice, and the use of her shower.

"Want me to drive you home?" is her next suggestion.

I try not to shudder. Sarah drives a Ford Ka. And when I say 'drives', I mean pushes the pedals at random until something bordering on motion is achieved.

"I'll walk. But thanks," I add, because she looks wounded and I'll be here all week if she goes off on one.

"It's probably very cold outside."

"I enjoy it. It's good for the environment too." I almost laugh. "And it really helps clear my lungs," I say, taking my cigarettes from the nightstand and slipping them in my pocket.

I kiss her on the cheek, promising to call her later. As soon as I am safely out of the flat and round the corner, I hail a cab, and go home for muesli and orange juice.

I had it all planned: get in, wake Simon up, disagree over whose turn it is to go out and get the papers, have a shower while Simon goes out to get the papers, eat breakfast, bit of Playstation, then down to the pub for a quick drink that'll see us through till closing time. Ah, perfect, unbridled domestic bliss. I keep telling myself this can last, that this can be our lives. Living like this, I can pretend I never met Lola, that she never existed. The outside world is simply something for us to comment on, something that happens around us. Simon and I can do it; we can block the world out.

But when I get inside, something's different. The air's heavier, sombre, still. The empty bottles of Bud have been moved from the hall and into the recycling bin, which used to be outside as we discovered it makes a great cooler. But someone's moved it.

"Si?"

The kitchen door opens. And it's not just the air that's heavier.

"Penny, hi. You look… well."

She stands there, Simon trailing sheepishly behind her, with her hands on her hips (well, in the general region of where her hips should be - who can tell where one part of her ends and another begins?). She's giving me the 'what are you doing here?' look which, coincidentally, I am also giving her.

She puts her hands around her bump, or an approximation of where her bump should be. Her body has housed all kinds of bumps for years. As far as I can see, pregnancy has thus far made very little difference, except to give one of her lumps a formal classification.

"You're still here then," Penny says, narrowing her eyes as I fling my jacket over the back of a nearby chair.

"So it seems."

"So Lola won't have you back then? I can't say I blame her," she says with a sneer.

Bump or no bump, I give her a shitty look, then I give Simon a shittier one. So much for muesli and orange juice – this is more like the breakfast time atmosphere at Auschwitz. After this, it's Simon's turn to go out and get the papers until 2019.

"And how's what's his name?" I ask, taking the one and only leaf out of Sarah's book. "Carl, was it?"

Penny scowls. I take some milk out of the fridge and drink it straight from the carton. I don't particularly like milk, or drinking it out of cartons, but I'm making a point here.

"Chris. He's waiting outside. We're not stopping."

For Simon's sake I managed not to say "good" just in time. I peer through the blinds and see a man in a Honda Civic, biting his nails. I'd bite my nails too if I had to sit in a Honda Civic, even more so if it were mine.

"How's his eye?" I ask in the innocent tone I save for special occasions such as these.

Simon lets out a snort of laughter.

"I don't know what you're laughing at," she spits at him.

"Shall I explain?" I offer.

Penny rises up to her full height, all five feet two of her. I'm not deceived though – beneath that short exterior she probably has more brake horsepower than a SSC Aero.

"You think you're so funny, don't you?" she says. "You think you're so-"

"Did you want something, Pen?" Simon finally speaks.

"Oh, that's it," Penny says, flinging her hands in the air, "take his side, why don't you. I don't know why you didn't marry him instead!"

"Well," Simon replies, puffing out his chest, "neither do I. He would've made a much better wife than you."

I'm not sure whether to be flattered or alarmed by this turn in conversation.

"Oh really?" Penny says. "Well, I wonder how your precious 'John' would feel about-"

I have to step in at this point because I really don't want to hear the rest of that sentence. Also, once they get going, their arguments degenerate into complete nonsense very quickly. They start off having a disagreement about something tangible and then they move onto other issues, such as why the sky is blue, which one of them breathes out the most carbon dioxide, and who sheds the most dead skin onto the sheets.

"Penny, you were saying – you're here because..?"

Penny turns her head and glares at me for a long moment. Then she grabs her bag from her shoulder and hunts around in it, making mumbling noises under her breath. I exchange glances with Simon. If she pulls out a knife, bump or no bump, I'm claiming it was self-defence.

"Here," she says, thrusting not a knife but a brown envelope at Simon. "Sign these. Then you'll be free to marry your precious John."

"Oh, don't worry," Simon says as she almost knocks him over in her rush to get to the front door, "I will."

We watch from the kitchen in horrified fascination as Penny waddles over to the Honda Civic. Again, pregnancy has had no impact here, either. Penny has always walked like that. I think she might have even waddled up the aisle on the day she married Simon.

Chris seems relieved to see her – or relieved to be going, one of the two, and the car sets off, the tyres screeching on the road.

"Simon?"

"John."

"I hope the 'I will' was for signing the papers and not the marrying me bit."

"Get lost. Who do you think I am – Elton John? But if I did marry you," he says, my blood chilling as he thinks about it, "it'd be better than my first marriage."

"Simon, the Ebola virus and cancer of the penis are better than your first marriage."

"Isn't Ebola that one where you bleed from every orifice and then explode?"

"Yes."

"Hmm. Yeah, you're right, less painful. Oh, this came for you this morning."

He hands me a letter. I glance at it, and feel that familiar sinking feeling.

"Aren't you going to open it?"

I take it from Simon and put it on the table beside me. "Later."

"Who's it from?"

"Manoli, Wilson, and Fitch These three faceless guys with cool sounding names."

"Lawyers?"

"Yeah. The house is almost sold."

"That's good news."

"Fantastic," I say. "You know, I should think about moving out."

"What? Because I said I'd marry you?"

"No, Simon. We can't carry on like this. We can't pretend we're nineteen and lounge around with no responsibilities. We're in our mid-thirties." I hold up the envelope. "We get letters from solicitors and documents from our estranged wives. Plus, you'll be moving from here at some point, won't you?"

Simon looks like he's about to open the cutlery drawer and find something to sever an artery with. "Will I?"

"Yes, you will."

"Oh. Yeah. I hadn't really thought about it."

"That's the thing – we haven't really been thinking about anything."

"I suppose… Where will you go?"

"I'll find somewhere," I say with a confidence that belies all the nightmares I've been having recently about ex-council studio flats in New Cross.

"And," Simon says, a slow smirk spreading across his moon face, "Sarah will help you."

I pick up my jacket. "I'll go and get the papers."

"Has she told you she loves you yet?" he calls after me. "Ooh, John – I loooooove yoooo!"

I slam the door behind me, trying not to think about my dear old (dead) mother reminding me that many a true word…

…is spoken in jest.

Up until now, the property market has been something hideous that I wrote about, but that happened to other people. We, and by this I mean me and the woman who's chosen some hip and trendy twenty-something over yours truly (a once hip and once mildly trendy thirty-something), bought our house years ago, before London became somewhere only the Sultan of Brunei could live in comfortably. Even with my share of the Tufnell Park house, my options are limited to south of the river – which in my eyes doesn't really count unless I'm planning to deal drugs or get stabbed, and I'm not as yet. The horrific dichotomy of rent in North London, or buy-to-die in South London, isn't really a choice at all.

And so I'm spending lunchtime in the pub with a copy of 'Loot' and Sarah who, as Simon correctly observed, is very eager to help.

"What about that one?" she says, her mouth full of the salt and vinegar crisps I bought in the hope of keeping her quiet. "Look, it's only one hundred and fifty a week."

"Sarah, that's in Elephant and Castle."

"Yeah, but it's on the Tube, isn't it? It could be okay."

"It's a flatshare."

She shovels more crisps into her mouth, proving my theory that you never truly know a woman until you've seen her eat a packet of Walkers.

"Yeah. And?"

"I'm sharing right now, with someone I know. Why would I want to move across the river to live with people I don't know, won't like, and who'll steal my milk."

Sarah thinks about it for a second. She can't think for longer than this without overheating like the radiator in

Simon's old Fiesta. "Ooh, I know – you could drink Soya milk. No one likes it, so no one will steal it."

I give her a look – 'the' look, one even she can understand – and go back to the paper.

The stab-or-be-stabbed dilemma of South London versus the relative civilisation of North London is reflected in the prices and availability. Supply and demand mocks me: every single possibility I circle and call up is either gone, going, never really existed, or just results in hysterical laughter from the other end of the line. I put my mobile back on the table, where it insolently informs me that the battery is low. Mine too.

"How about that one?" Sarah points at an advert I've read three times, and discounted three times.

"It sounds like a dump."

"Yeah," Sarah licks her fingers. "It probably is. They're all dumps. But you're desperate, right?"

Oh, if only she knew what irony means.

"Just phone up, JB. It's worth a shot."

Yeah, so is your forehead.

"I really don't think I can see myself living in Archway, Sarah."

"Don't be such a snob," she says. "Sometimes you have to be realistic. Anyway, I have to get back to the office for, um… I can't remember. You coming?"

"I think I'll finish my pint first."

Sarah glances at my empty glass, but thinks better of it. "Okay, I'll see you later, JB."

Just before she opens the pub door, she looks back and breaks into a huge smile when she sees I'm still watching her. She'll never understand that I'm still watching because I'm making sure she's really gone.

I sit there for a while, pondering what to do, trying not to think that in a parallel universe I have a lovely house in Tufnell Park, a ridiculously small mortgage, and am one of those people I now hate. I pick up my mobile. Yes, yes, battery low, I know.

"Is that Mr Ahmed? Yeah, I'm calling about the flat in Archway – is it still available?"

Sometimes you have to be realistic.

Simon offers to come with me, but I can't face the shame. It's like him offering to change my colostomy bag for me. Sarah would've happily accompanied me, which is why I didn't tell her I was going. She saw me putting my jacket on from across the office (she's like God and the government – she sees everything), and of course she emailed me instantly.

'JB – where r u going?'

Sarah thinks we need pet names for each other – quite why, she hasn't really explained. So she persists on calling me 'JB', and I call her 'Sarah'.

I replied, 'A meeting,' which, like all the best lies, was kind of true, depending on your interpretation of the word. Then I set off for deepest, darkest Archway.

As is the way with property adverts, it turns out that the flat isn't really in Archway, but Holloway.

"See," Mr Ahmed explains, "very close to Tube station."

I stare up at the flat. "Yes," I concede, "and also very close to a greasy spoon café." Or, to be precise, directly above it.

"Oh no, Mr Black," says Mr Ahmed, waving a podgy hand to dismiss my concerns. "No trouble from them at all. No noise, no problem."

"No," I sigh, following Mr Ahmed as he locates the key from a bunch so large it would seem that he is landlord to eighty-five percent of London. "No noise," I say. "Just smell."

We enter a communal hallway that looks like the set of *The Young Ones*, and probably hasn't been decorated since the programme first aired.

"This? Will be done soon," Mr Ahmed reassures me when he sees the expression of concern on my face. "No problem at all," he says, directing me up a flight of stairs so precarious, I insist he goes first.

"Very handy for Tube," he says once more as he opens what could be my front door, which means the inside must be even worse than the build-up.

It doesn't disappoint. I try to be objective, but all I can see is my old house in Tufnell Park. I see the wood flooring Lola made me put in when I was totally against the idea, the pictures she made me hang when I was trying to watch *Football Focus*, the paint she insisted I help her choose when I couldn't care less, the bathroom suite she told me we had to have when I'd have been happy with a bucket and a tin bath, and the kitchen cabinets she painstakingly designed and I painfully installed. I blink and Tufnell Park is gone, and there's only this: one-bedroomed Holloway Hell. It's vile beyond belief. It's brown and artexed, laminated and woodchipped. There's room for furniture only from a doll's house, and I don't even want to think about the previous occupants' diet, but judging from the toilet bowl, most of it was curried, and vegetarian.

It's horrible. It's expensive squalor. It's the face of my freedom, my bachelor pad; it's everything I've thrown away. It's what I deserve.

"You'll take it, yes, Mr Black?" Mr Ahmed is hopping from foot to foot in anticipation.

I slide my hands into my pockets and sigh. "No problem. No problem at all."

Mr Ahmed and I cut a deal. I get the keys in exchange for a cash deposit on the spot, and he agrees to knock twenty quid off the rent until he can provide me with some kind of official certification that the boiler doesn't present a choice between hot water and carbon monoxide poisoning. He's happy and I'm, well, I'm alive.

To celebrate both my new found independence and the worst day of my life, I decide to check out my new neighbours in the greasy spoon I'm going to be living above and, I'm guessing, Simon will pretty much be living in.

I order a full English from a man who is not even a bit English, and sit down hoping the citizenship test includes a section on how to make a decent fry-up. I check my phone – there's a message from Sarah that I delete immediately because she'll only repeat the whole thing to me later, verbatim: "John, did you get my message about blah blah blah…" And there's a message from Percy, which I also delete, because I told him to contact me only if the office, or his body, was on fire. I now realise I care about neither occurrence, so there's no need to listen to his reedy voice bleating on.

So, this is it then. The end of one era, and the beginning of another. I have my freedom, and Lola has Josh. Josh has Lola, and I have a flat in the constipated bowels of Hades. I now understand why we need the Samaritans, and why you can't buy more than two packets of Paracetamol at a time.

My breakfast is plonked down in front of me with unpatriotic disdain.

"Sauce there," the guy says (he couldn't really be described as a waiter with any real accuracy), pointing to a bottle of red stuff.

I shake my head at what's become of our great nation. "Do you have any brown sauce?"

"Brown?" he says, as though I've asked for a side order of Plutonium which, thinking about it, he's much more likely to have behind the counter.

"Never mind."

I'm tackling my bacon and sausages with gusto – they need gusto, they have the texture of a marinated flannel – when the bell above the door jingles in a 'oh my God, a customer!' manner. Instinctively, I turn my head. And then I wish I didn't have instincts.

It's Kay. With a child – Jeremy. And a guitar case.

I try to sink down into my seat, but of course, Kay is too quick. She's always been too quick for me. She spots me straight away, giving me a look that manages to combine surprise with disgust.

"Uncle Johnny!"

The boy rushes over and, bizarrely, hugs me. And I, bizarrely, am touched by this unexpected and frankly unwarranted show of affection.

"Mummy said you were in hell."

I glance up at Kay.

"Well," she hisses. "What did you expect me to tell them? And don't say the truth, because you don't know what that is."

She has me there.

"Can I offer you a seat? Or a sausage?"

"That's not a sausage," she says, sitting down.

"What is it then?" I ask, studying the portion I was about to put into my mouth.

"No idea. But it's not a sausage, let me tell you. Maybe you'll get CJD," Kay says somewhat hopefully.

I put the fork down. "You don't mean that."

"No," Kay sighs. "Sadly, I don't. Lola would only visit you in hospital and cry over your grave. Silly cow that she is. She'd turn you into St John the Martyr."

"I think there's already one of those."

"Is there? Jeremy, sit down."

"Nnnnoooooooooooo," Jeremy says as Kay forces him down into the chair. He swings his legs reproachfully.

"So," Kay says, "what brings you to these parts? This is slumming it a bit for you."

"Visiting a friend. And you?"

"Guitar lessons."

"I didn't know you played."

"Oh, ha ha. Him. He's learning. We take him to this bloke in Highbury. Victor, his name is."

I exchange glances with Jeremy. There's a moment of solidarity – a shared look. Were he not under eight, I'd sign him up to my cause.

"I hate Victor," Jeremy says.

"No you don't, darling."

"I doooo!" Jeremy insists.

"Stop being so ungrateful. You know your father wants you to learn to play."

My eyebrows lift of their own accord. "Todd?"

Kay rolls her eyes. "I told him it's a bloody crap idea."

"Ha! You said crap!" Jeremy says.

"Right, that's it." Kay straightens Jeremy's shoulders. "When we get home I'm telling Daddy you've been playing up."

This is like threatening Andy McNab with a pea shooter and a small badger, and Jeremy knows it. I wink at him. He starts grinning.

"Aren't you going to ask me about Lola?" Kay asks.

"No."

"Oh. Why?"

"Because I'm not a masochist. I know you want to sit there and tell me about how happy she is, but I already know."

Kay stares at me for a long time.

"What?" I ask.

"Nothing," she says, in the way women do when they mean 'something'.

I wait.

"It's just…"

Wait for it...

"It's just what?" I say, although I'm not sure I really want to know.

"Argh, I can't believe I'm saying this…" Kay puts her palms on the table, as though she's grounding herself. "But seeing you so randomly like this… Argh... John, I'm not sure she is happy. Although I'm at total loss as to why."

"And what am I supposed to do with that information?"

Kay shrugs. "Swallow and digest it – like your nonsausage. Or whatever you want. Just do something with it, because it nearly killed me to say it."

"You know what? I don't think I can. Really, I don't." I push my plate towards Jeremy. "Here, you finish it."

His eyes light up. "Cool!"

"I have to go."

"Do you want a lift?" Kay asks.

"No," I reply. "I'll walk. It's not far."

And then, the brand new, shiny and realistic me goes 'home' and, moments later, phones Sarah.

16

If I had the chance to be thirteen again, I'd revisit my discussions with the school careers advisor – perhaps my life would turn out differently.

"What would you like to do when you leave school, John?" the careers lady – I think her name was Mrs Grimstead – asked me.

Shrug. "Play football?"

"Okay…" I was probably the thirty-eighth wannabe foot-baller she'd had in front of her that morning, and I was probably the only one with the footballing skills of a one-legged ostrich. "But what about for a job, John? To earn money?"

"Play football," I said, without hesitation.

"Riiiiiiight. What about if you weren't able to do that – is there anything else?" Mrs Grimstead might've been the most patient person in North London.

"Dunno," replied the thirteen year old me, eyes focussed on one of the books behind her head.

Mrs Grimstead shifted positions, managing to keep the professional and kindly smile fixed on her face. "Well, what other subjects are you interested in?"

"P.E.?" I offered.

Her smile faltered a little. "What about academic subjects, John? Like science, or maths, or German?"

I shuddered.

"Okay, perhaps not German. Anything?" Mrs Grimstead was clearly groping around for straws to clutch, and at that early age I still cared about people's feelings, so I duly thought about it.

"English is okay I suppose."

"English?" Mrs Grimstead hardly dared hope for a breakthrough, and a sensible one at that.

"Yeah. I don't mind writing."

If only I'd known where those four words would lead me.

I link my fingers together, stretching them out in front of me, hearing the joints click. My desk is cluttered, my brain is cluttered, and I can't think of a useful word to write. I try to imagine Mrs Grimstead asking the thirty-five year old me what he'd like to do with his life. I think he'd shrug, then tell her he wanted to play football.

Of course, no one else in the office is having this problem. From the hive of activity in here, you'd think they'd all taken an inspiration pill with their probiotic yoghurts this morning. Even Valerie, who as a 'lifestyle expert' should be permanently unemployed, has hardly looked up from her keyboard. This, on a normal day, would be a good thing, but today the fact that she's writing and I'm not bothers me more than the sight of her gargoyle-like face.

The only thing I have to be cheerful about is that Percy is out at some conference or other with Charlie, the same some conference or other that I'm usually forced to go to with him. So it appears Percy does have a use after all. The conference bores me rigid, and I hate being seen out in public with Charlie, who usually makes comments about women's legs in a tone loud enough to be heard in Uganda, and he also picks his nose when he concentrates. So, I should be grateful for being Percy-less and Charlie-less and get down to work, shouldn't I?

"Hey JB!" Sarah peers over the top of my monitor, gurning at me like a camel chewing dinner. "Are you busy?"

"Extremely."

"Oh. It looked like you were just staring at that plant. What are you working on?"

She leans in to glance at the document I have open, which naturally contains only the cursor, and I can't even claim authorship for that. I minimise it.

"Actually, I'm writing a piece about the credit crisis." This would be true, if her question had contained the words "supposed", "to", and "be."

"Ugh. Is it important?"

I decide to treat myself and be cruel for a change. "It means all your credit cards might be cancelled."

Sarah, who thinks her credit limit is actually a target to be reached with the shortest possible time, pales and nearly faints. "What? Why? They can't!"

"They can. There's too much money floating around at the moment." Of course, that just confuses her. "You'll have to read it when I'm done."

"Oh, John, I will."

She has no idea that Halley's Comet will probably be visible before this feature is finished.

"So, what time are we going to lunch today?"

My stomach rumbles at the mention of lunch. "Actually, I've just eaten."

"What? Oh come on, you can have a coffee or something."

"Today's not the best day for me. Perhaps later in the week?" I think I have a window free on the thirty-second of never, at forty-two o'clock, if that works for you..?

She pinches her glossed lips into a pout and rests one hand on her tiny hips. I used to quite enjoy that pout, when I didn't have to see it all the time and it didn't come attached to all this "we" business – when are "we" going to lunch, what are "we" doing tonight, what time are "we" leaving work.

"That sounds very indefinite, John. I have something really important to tell you."

My appetite vanishes, and my 'fight or flight' reflexes kick in. Let me tell you, against a woman, I pick 'flight' every time. You'll never win an argument, but you can usually outrun them.

"Come on, John. I promise it's something you'll like."

Which only makes me even more certain it's something I won't like at all. Oh, and lo and behold, Valerie has taken a break from composing '101 Ways to De-junk Your Fridge' or some such bollocks, and is now giving me the evil eye, her eyebrows raised accusingly at the back of Sarah's head.

"Okay, but it'll have to be a short one. I'm pretty pushed for time right now. I'll meet you in the pub over the road, two o' clock," I say – anything to make her go away and stop Valerie glaring at me.

"Two o' clock? I'm hungry now! I'll never last that long!" she says incredulously and rather too loudly.

"Well, maybe you ought to consider eating something more substantial than a Slim-Fast for breakfast."

"I don't want to lose my figure," she says with a smile, doing a little twirl for my, and Valerie's, benefit, as though I'd forgotten what she looks like despite having only seen her naked a few hours ago. At least Lola maintained some kind of guarded privacy about her insecurities. Sarah, on the other hand, wears her stomach on her sleeve and, frankly, it's extremely boring. Listening to her droning n about her figure, her Body Mass Index, what size her skirt is, etc. is very dull, very draining, and makes me want to eat.

"I'll order you a salad. See you later."

She slinks off, some of her exuberance gone, but she got what she wanted. Valerie gives me an ominous scowl, picks up her cup, and goes off towards the tea-point. I'd like to go and talk to her, set the record straight, but there is no record – well, only that I'm a dickhead, and Valerie already knows that.

So I spend the rest of the afternoon constructing pie charts of the things I miss about Lola. It doesn't take me long to list more things than I have room for, so I concentrate on filling in the segments of the chart with as many different colours as Windows will allow me. Then I move onto patterns, and textures. And then, at two clock, having written nothing I can show Charlie, I hoist my jacket from the back of my decrepit chair, and pat my pocket subconsciously. Cigarettes? Check. Wallet? Check. Willpower? Negative

There are loads of attractive women in the pub, the kinds of women that, a few months ago, I thought I'd be hopping in and out of bed with, my life a flurry of dates, uncomplicated sex, and missed calls. Now the only thing I'm missing is what I gave up for this – a life of hopping in and out of bed with myself, to sleep.

Predictably, Sarah's arrived at the pub before me, and is waving at me from her favourite table. I have to walk past the attractive women to get to her, and I try smiling vaguely at one of them, the second most attractive one. I'm not sure it translates well as she glares at me as though I've openly farted in her direction.

"John!" Sarah calls, as though standing up and waving her arms like she's doing semaphore without flags wasn't enough.

The second most attractive of the attractive women glances at Sarah, and then at me, and pulls a knowing face at her friend, as though it explains everything. I want to grab her by her toned shoulders and say, "What does it explain?" And then maybe buy her a drink.

"Hi, John." Sarah kisses me on the cheek. "Mmm, you smell good. Issey Miyake?"

"Pardon?"

"Your cologne – is it Issey Miyake?"

"No. Cigarettes and Imperial Leather."

"Leather what?" Sarah sits down. "I got you a pint of Stella."

And indeed she has. This is good. But the expression on her face is bad. She's fidgeting, can't keep still – she's excited about something.

"How's your morning been?"

"Cluttered," I answer, because it doesn't really matter what I say here, she just wants me to ask, "And yours?"

I do, just to get it out of the way.

"Well," she takes a breath, "first of all, Molly had this…"

After that it just becomes white noise. I tune it out, like I do Radio One, and Madonna post-1989. I don't need to listen anyway. My role is simply to nod, say 'uh-huh' in key places, and try not to let my eyes glaze over too much. I've perfected the art of 'listening' to Sarah talk. She thinks she has my attention, when really I'm staring at something in the distance, on this occasion the attractive woman with the nice shoulders, who's looking at me. She smiles, and looks away. Wait, that means something – she's interested, right? Definitely interested. Oh, but Sarah. I tune back in. Oh God…

"Pardon?"

"I know, John. It's a shock for me too."

"Right." Okay, what is this? I know she's categorically not pregnant, so..?

Her eyes widen a little. "Aren't you going to say anything?"

I pull one of my best tricks. All I have to do is wait – if I hang on a bit longer, she'll repeat it. I pick up my pint, and pretend to be considering whatever the hell she's just said.

"I mean, I haven't felt like this since Steve," she says.

"Steve."

"Yes. I'm sorry to mention him, and please don't feel threatened, I'm not trying to make you jealous. Are you jealous? Wait, no, forget that – I'm only trying to explain how I feel."

Oh, yes, I remember now. Steve, her ex with the BMX. Wait a minute, how she feels? Okay, time for my masterpiece.

"So what are you saying, Sarah?"

"I'm saying," she says, staring at her hands at then at me, "that I think I'm falling for you."

Oh. God.

She gazes at me with those wide eyes – she really does have lovely eyes. The problem is they're attached to the rest of her. This is it though; this is the conundrum of balance. Sarah probably only likes me so much, or thinks she does, because I'm so distant with her, so detached. The more I pull away, the closer she tries to get. Poor Sarah. What has she got herself into? More importantly, what have I got myself into and, even more importantly, how do I get myself out of it?

"Sarah-"

"No." She holds her palm up. "You don't have to say anything. I know you're still wounded after whats-her-face dumped you – bitch – so I'm not putting you under any pressure. I just wanted to tell you how I feel, because it's important to be upfront about things, isn't it?"

"Oh yes, very."

"Good. I'm glad we had this little chat, JB." She lays her hand over mine, and squeezes.

And this, ladies and gentlemen, is the dilemma. Sarah, much like a cigarette, is good and bad for me at the same time. She's probably going to kill me one day, but I need her. She's comforting, she's easy – I don't have to think, I just reach for her, and she's there. I'm addicted. I can't believe I don't feel anything more substantial for her than that, but that's the harsh truth of it. I can't love her, I can't sleep with her, and I can't dump her, as that would mean cold turkey. Being alone.

Is that fair on her? No. Will that stop me?

"Sarah…"

"It's okay, John. I'm here for you. I'm not going anywhere."

I'm no longer in stasis. I'm in purgatory.

I can't get the fridge to work. Actually, I can't get anything in this flat to work. So far, I've moved in a bed, a sofa, a television, and a Sky Plus box, which one could argue is all a man really needs to feel at home, but really it's all this man can fit in his entire home.

I kick the fridge door almost closed – the door refuses to shut properly – and hand Simon a can of Coke.

"Thanks, mate. Feels a bit warm."

"That's because the fridge is a fridge in name only."

"Oh." Simon inspects the can. "This isn't diet."

"Neither are you. Did you try the greasy spoon downstairs?"

"Yeah. Smells better from up here."

"Wait until it gets into your hair and clothes. Then it's marvellous."

Simon gives me a solemn look, the one that indicates he's about to make an attempt at serious conversation. "Surely you can do better than this place, mate."

I go into the living room, which takes me all of four steps, and switch the television on. It's easier than telling him that maybe I don't want to do better than this.

Happily, thanks to the joy of repetitive digital channel programming, we've found *Top Gear* on some obscure channel, which is great as it means we don't have to talk to each other about anything more serious than the new Audi.

"Do you reckon," Simon says, "Clarkson would make a good drinking mate?"

"Jeremy Clarkson would never be seen in a pub with you. You're too ridiculous."

"Yeah, you're right. He's too intelligent anyway. I think I'll stick with you. What about Hammond or May?"

"Hammond might go drinking with you as you're shorter than him."

"I am not. Have you got any beer?"

I point in the direction of the fridge, i.e. a foot away.

"Which means it's warm."

"Like piss."

"Great." Simon starts biting his nails.

I give it a full minute. "What?"

"Nothing."

"Simon…"

"Penny phoned me yesterday. She had a fight with Chris."

"Over who gets to use the hair straighteners first?"

"I miss her."

I put my feet up on the table. This is what I call the upturned crate.

"No, you don't," I say. "You're just lonely. You're at the stage where anything is better than nothing."

Simon looks at me in amazement. "Wow. Is that one you made up earlier?"

"You were saying – Penny."

"I didn't come here to talk about Penny. I came here to cheer you up."

This means he's come here to talk about Penny.

"God, this flat is fucking vile," he says.

"Yeah, but it kind of fits where I am at the moment."

"Beirut? Kabul?"

I drain the last of my cold coffee. "Simon, do you ever feel as though your sense of self has become diluted?"

He thinks about it for a few moments. "You've lost me."

"I lost you at 'hello.'"

Simon scowls.

I light a cigarette and exhale the smoke high into the air, bolstering the graphic yellow already coating the ceiling. "I've lost sight of who I am. I hate my job, I hate the woman I hang out with on a regular basis…"

Simon scratches his melon-head. "Have you been reading this month's *She*?"

I shake my head. "What grade?"

"I'd say this is a five." He makes himself more comfortable on the threadbare sofa. As he does so, a spring twangs noisily. For once, this isn't a reflection of the quality of my furniture, but of the size of Simon's arse. "There's an article about women who feel guilty because they have great lives, but are still depressed. The guilt stems from having nothing to feel depressed about, when there are people starving and blah, blah."

"What's it called?"

"'Do you have the perfect life but want to end it?'"

"Wonderful, and a definite grade five, but I have plenty to be depressed about. Sarah told me she's falling for me."

"See, *She* is right. Sarah's a fit bird. Most of the blokes in the office fancy her. I do, sometimes, when I'm bored. You treat her like shit, she's falling for you, and you're still not happy." Simon narrows his eyes. "Have you slept with her yet?"

"Nope, not even in my dreams."

"What?" he says.

"Don't even want to. The only way I could get an erection anywhere near her is if I closed my eyes and pretended she's an Aston Martin."

"The DB9?"

"That's the one."

Simon nods gravely. "Point taken. What did you say to her when she dropped the bombshell?"

"I picked up the bombshell and said, 'I think you dropped this.'"

"Cold shit, even for you."

"True shit, Simon. It doesn't matter anyway. She thinks I'm 'fragile' because I'm still not over Lola."

"She's not as dense as everyone thinks then." Simon scratches his nose. "Have you spoken to Lola lately?"

"No." And then it just comes out. "I saw Kay. She told me that apparently Lola isn't happy with Josh."

"Do you believe her?"

"Even if I do, what am I supposed to do about it?"

"Just phone her. Tell you're sorry."

"I think she knows that. It doesn't make a difference."

He sighs. "What a pair of prats we are."

"Speak for yourself."

"Okay, I will. Penny's driving me round the bloody twist."

"What's new there? When you got married you walked her down the aisle via the bloody twist."

Simon regards me for a long time. "You are one harsh bastard," he concludes.

"It's what made me what I am today."

"Yeah, fucking miserable, mate."

After four episodes of 'Airport', Simon finally decides to call it a night. I sit on the sofa by myself for a while, drinking my ninety-seventh cup of coffee with an old episode of *Location, Location, Location* on in the background, mocking me. So it's just me, Kirstie, Phil, and the telephone. I look at it, and it looks at me.

I run a hand over my stubbled chin, checking my watch. She's most probably in bed and snoring, and won't be happy if I wake her up. But if I don't do it now, by tomorrow I'll be back to thinking it's a pointless and stupid idea.

It is a pointless and stupid idea.

Oh, fuck it.

I reach for the phone, scroll down, and hit 'call'. It rings once, twice, and I'm about to go, 'Oh, okay, at least I tried,' and chicken out, when she answers.

"Hello?" Yes, I've woken her up.

"Hey."

I hear something click. I'm guessing she's switched a lamp, or perhaps her brain, on. "John? What are you doing calling me at this time of night? Actually, what are you doing calling me at all?"

I shift in my seat, glancing at Kirstie and Phil for moral support. "I need Lola's new number."

"Absolutely not."

"Don't be like that, Val. It's an emergency."

"Are you dead?"

"No."

"Then I don't care. No way. Lola's my friend."

"Come on Valerie, I've never asked you to do anything for me."

"And why would you? I'd rather kill myself than help you."

I sit up straight. "Val…"

"No, John. That doesn't, hasn't, and will never work on me. Aside from the fact that my opinion of you plummeted even further than the rock bottom it was festering at before you started screwing Sarah Carter, and aside from the aside that I hate your guts, your entrails, your blood, and your skeleton, if Lola wanted you to have her new number, she would've given it to you herself."

"Maybe it slipped her mind."

"Goodnight, John…"

"Wait, Valerie don't hang up." I can almost hear the sound of her nails drumming on her coffin. "I want to make it up to Lola."

Valerie sighs. "She told me what you did. She won't have you back. Ever!" She sings the word, like she's onstage doing 'Madame Butterfly'.

"Then I've got nothing to lose."

There is a silence of epic proportions. My mind is racing. I'm fucked here – okay, what's Plan B? Right, Plan B: ask Kay, which is sure to be an even bigger waste of-

"All right, all right, but don't tell her you got it from me."

My relief tastes like vodka. "Of course not. I wouldn't dream of it."

"I have no interest in what you dream about," Valerie says. "Listen you hideous human being, I'm only doing this because Lola still loves you. I have no idea why – you're such a slimy, arrogant, insincere and overrated man, but unfortunately she doesn't share my perspective."

I let this slander slide as she spits out Lola's new telephone number like the venomous viper she is. I write it down on my arm.

"Don't upset her again or you'll have me to deal with."

"That, Val, is a terrifying thought."

"Drop dead."

"Ladies first."

Deciding to wait until I make myself some fresh coffee, and feeling somewhat bolstered by Valerie's surprisingly weak resolve (well, it is late, and I did have the element of surprise), I dial Lola's number. While it rings, I stumble around in my brain for something to say to her. I settle on simply coming right out and telling her that I'm sorry, I made a mistake, my life is meaningless without her, and I want her back.

"Hello?"

My throat goes dry. My perfect speech flies right out of my head. The room spins, and I see colours. I feel sick. Okay, get a grip. Let's dial again. Maybe that was the wrong number.

"Hello? Who is this?"

I cut the call off again. Nope, that's definitely a man's voice. A very specific man's voice. Oh, fuck…

No wonder Valerie caved in like a tunnel made of soggy toilet paper. Lola's new number is Josh's old number. She's moved in with him.

I sit there, staring blankly at the television, and then the lights flicker, and go off completely. I'm plunged into darkness. But somewhere, in Hoxton or fucking Shoreditch, the lights are on and shining brightly.

17

Now I've had time to think about it, to let the shock fade to an echo, it's hard to be surprised that Lola has moved in with Josh already. Where the big stuff's concerned, Lola makes her mind up pretty quickly. And I should know.

She moved in with me after only four weeks. Everyone I knew, my brother in particular, told me I didn't know her well enough, that I'd regret it, but I ignored all of them, my brother in particular, and Lola moved her cute little boxes of stuff into my flat.

It turned out that her cute little boxes contained ugly mountains of curios, not just clothes, books, and CDs like a normal person, but scarves and things called 'pashminas' that are actually expensive shawls; candles, cushions, and the fattest, rudest cat I've encountered, who preferred the floor to his litter tray. Soon there were potions and creams all over the bathroom shelves, and shoes strewn everywhere. She played her Shania Twain albums (and sang along) when I was trying to watch TV, she had baths filled with weird oils at bizarre times of the night, and she claimed to be cold in all weathers, even on the two days in June we call summer in this country, and she always, always stole the covers.

We moved into a house, with a garden, and she found new ways to drive me nuts. I thought having more space would be a good thing, but for Lola, the more space we had, the more she felt compelled to do something with it. She wanted to do gardening, she wanted to decorate – she wanted to renovate. She started watching *Property Ladder* and saying terrifying things like, "Ooh, that's an idea, John.

We could…" And when she said 'we', she meant 'you', and she always wanted me to do these pointless things when there were more pressing demands on my time, such as an FA Cup semi-final to watch, the business section of the *Independent* to read, toenails to clip, or, well, anything else. And despite all the hard labour I did in the garden, the cat still refused to set paw in it, and made a conscious decision never to shit or piss anywhere other than the kitchen floor (I was secretly elated when he died – Simon and I went for a pint to celebrate). And the more room we had, the more shoes Lola bought.

Oh, and she would always invite her girlfriends round for dinner when I was trying to work. I was not, of course, averse to her having friends over, but after a few glasses of wine they would invariably trickle into the study and proceed to quiz me like I was the Wizard of Oz.

AMY: Why are all men bastards?

It's the only way we can maintain any dignity.

SHELLEY: Why do men always say they'll call and never do?

We lie. It's just easier.

SAM: Why doesn't my boyfriend show me that he loves me?

What do you want, a strobe lighting display, fireworks – blood? What do you do to make him feel loved?

NATASHA: If I sleep with him on the first date, will he think I'm a slut?

No, he'll be thrilled. Your female friends will think you're a slut though.

KATE: I want a baby and my boyfriend doesn't – what shall I do?

Get a dog.

LOLA: Are we disturbing you, John?

Actually, yes.

But none of these things ever caused me to regret moving in with Lola. They were trivialities, and when

I consider it now, I was probably just as irritating. She hated 'big papers' as she called them, but did I ever stop leaving them lying around for her to pick up? No. Instead, I said why should I, when there were copies of *Heat*, *Instyle*, and something called *Closer* scattered everywhere. When she was scared at night because of a 'noise', did I go down to investigate? Sometimes, if I was awake enough. Did I cook? Occasionally, when the mood took me. How often did the mood take me? Not often. Did I do my share when she was busy at work? Yes, pretty much.

None of it matters now though, because she's with Josh, and I'm sure he is just swell at playing man about the house. I can imagine him, sitting there at the table reading the *Guardian*, all cool and Josh-like with his straight teeth and trendy sweaters. He and Lola probably sit together and flick through *Time Out*, deciding where to eat, who to see in concert, what film to watch, all of that. I bet she's even given up Sandra Bullock rom-coms in favour of movies with subtitles and women with cheekbones, and I bet she no longer yawns all the way through them. He probably takes her to all the galleries I took her to, although I bet she enjoys art with him. She doesn't make tutting noises, roll her eyes, and ask him if he can meet her outside Selfridges in three hours like she did with me. She probably even watches *Top Gear* with him – she records it for him on his Blu-Ray when he's out, using some kind of app. He's ruined my life, this fucking Josh.

I loosen my tie and exhale before I start to dwell on the sex again. There, I've thought it now. My fingers curl into fists. Lola and Josh are probably having fantastic sex. There, that wasn't so bad.

Well, apparently, you really can't kid a kidder, because the concept of her with another man makes my internal organs shrivel, not to mention the external ones. I remember Shelia from Starbucks and the cringe-making sex I had with her – and then there's Rebecca and Sarah, who I've failed to have any sex with at all. Why's it so easy for Lola? How does Lola know what to do with another man?

I'm opening up Google, hoping it may provide me with an answer, when Percy trots over to me. He doesn't even have good timing going for him.

"Mr Black, I think we need to have a discussion," the rat says, as though he's been practising.

I peel my chin from my palm and give him a look that conveys my indifference, fighting the urge to tell him to grate his eyeballs then pickle them. He's still wearing the fabric Excel spreadsheet, but his suit looks even more sharply pressed than usual. His mum must've been up all night doing that. He's squeezed the vast majority of his spots, except for the one on his neck, which I guess is hard to do without a life jacket and some safety goggles.

"Percy, I'm incredibly busy right now. You saw what the markets did yesterday."

His eyebrows creep up his forehead.

"You weren't paying attention? Well, there's your next task, get online and have a look."

I turn away from his grease-slicked face. I don't want to talk to Percy; I want to torture myself thinking about Lola's sex life versus my anti-sex life. Mine is like drilling for oil on a trampoline, whilst hers is one, huge phantasmagoria of explicit, abandoned, mind-blowing lust.

"I need to be challenged more."

Oh, Christ. I give Percy my best expression of unconcern to remind him where he ranks in the grand scheme of things I have to deal with on a daily basis.

"Perce, how long have you been here? Ten minutes?"

"Actually, it's-"

"And how long have I been in this game?" For the record, I never say things like 'in this game' but, evidently, I do to Percy. "And you're questioning my supervision?"

I watch him weigh it up, unsure how far he can push me. "No," he says carefully. "I just think I ought to be doing more. Getting some real experience."

"Percy, you can't make soufflé before you've learned how to turn the oven on."

"Huh?"

I'm not really sure what that means either, but I'm on a roll.

"Have you any idea how many kids would kill to get a placement in here?"

"Yes, but-"

"No buts, Percy." I reach down into a drawer and wave a pile of expense forms at him. "These are CVs from kids like you, all wanting to get a foot in the door. The difference between you and them is you're already in the door, and they're not. That state of affairs is easily remedied. Do you understand?"

Percy's mouth tightens. "I'm not a kid," he mutters, and shuffles over to an empty computer terminal and, as far as I can see, takes my advice. Stuffing the expense forms in an envelope to send to accounts (I've been looking for those for ages), I make a mental note to tell Charlie that I'm sure his prized Percy has done more than enough work experience for one gap year.

Having scored what I view as another notable victory over His Royal Rodentness, I have a discreet glance around. Valerie's not at her desk (woo hoo!), Simon's squinting at his screen and eating a baguette the size of Tower Bridge, and everyone else is wrapped up in their day jobs. Great. There's no one in earshot so I take a few deep breaths, then pick up the telephone so tenderly, you'd think the receiver was an Andrex puppy.

"Dobler and Larkin?"

"Hi. Can I speak to Lola Martinez?"

The person on the other end of the line is chewing gum. I can hear the air-filled munching, the saliva crackling, and the occasional bubble popping. Classy. "She's not here."

"Is she in a meeting?"

A pause – an ill-concealed, irritated one. “She might be.” Long silence.

“Well, could you find out, please?”

A definite ‘tut’. “Could you hold?”

It’s not really a request. The phone is clanked down, and I can hear muffled shouting and yelling, and the faint sound of music playing in the background – one of those terrible ‘emo’ bands who’ve appeared out of nowhere, like superbugs in hospitals and Dannii Minogue. I imagine the gum-chewer asking people where Lola is, and angularly coiffed heads shaking in response. I have no idea how she copes in that environment. I’d have killed myself or, more probably, everyone else, ages ago.

“Hello?” Wrigley’s Extra is back.

“Yes?”

“She’s on holiday,” she tells me with a frustrating lack of detail.

“Holiday? You mean as in ‘abroad’ holiday, or a ‘day off’ holiday?”

The line goes quiet for a brief moment. “I don’t know. It just says on the chart that she’s on holiday.”

“But do you think she might’ve gone away? I mean, has she been buying Euros and sun cream at lunchtimes? Looking up the temperature in Cyprus? Renewed her passport?”

A bubble pops. “Sorry, who did you say you were?”

I hang up.

I chew on a pen for the next fifteen minutes. I catch a glimpse of the pad in front of me, on which I ambitiously compiled a list of all the things I need to do before I leave work today. There are phone calls to make and return, research to do, figures to check. I look over at Percy, who’s studying something online that’s on my list of things to read. A voice somewhere inside me notes that Percy the Rat is stealing a march on John Black, but another voice, a much louder one, tells me that I don’t care.

I go back to pen chewing and then Sarah phones, telling me how boring the course is and how she wishes she was with me. I make appropriate "Oh right" noises without actually saying I miss her too, or admitting that I forgot she was on a course, or indeed even noticed she wasn't in the office. I cringe when she ends the conversation by telling me she can't stop thinking about me.

"Okay, bye." I make sure she can't say anything else by cutting off the call.

I still have the receiver tucked under my chin, so I dial before I have a chance to change my mind.

"Yeah …uh, hello?"

"Josh, it's John."

"Hey, John. How're you?" If he's surprised to hear from me, he hides it so well.

"I'm good. Is Lola there?"

"Yeah, she's out the back. Hold on, I'll give her a shout."

He puts the phone down, and calls out to her. It's weird hearing him say her name. It's like listening to someone sitting in my car and revving the engine.

My mind races. She never takes time off work, so what are they doing? What is the exact geographical location of 'out the back', and what is Lola doing there? As for the trillion questions I have about who's paying the rent (shit – mortgage?), whose idea it was to move in together, why the-

"John?" Now that was surprise.

"Yeah." I get my bearings. "Hi."

"Hi."

Neither of us says anything for a while.

"I know how you got this number," she says eventually.

"Are you furious?" She is silent. "Lola?"

"I shook my head. I'm cross with you for calling, not with Valerie for giving you the number. I know how you wear people down."

"That doesn't seem fair."

"Some things aren't. What do you want, John?"

I blurt it out. “I wondered if you’d like to have dinner with me?”

“Why did you wonder that?”

“Well…”

“I’m with Josh now.” She’s lowered her voice.

“I know.”

“And the ‘episode’ phase is over.”

“I know,” I say again, masking my disappointment. I knew that anyway, but I still had hope.

“So what’s the point of dinner?”

“The point,” I say, scrabbling around for one, “is that we were friends as well, weren’t we? I miss you. As a friend.”

She goes quiet. I’ve got her.

“Well… I suppose it can’t really do any harm…” She’s practically whispering now. “Tomorrow? Soho? That place on Old Compton Street?”

“Seven?”

“Fine. And, John?”

“Yup?”

“This is a secret. Strictly between you and me.”

“Naturally.”

I punch the air. One small step for John, one giant step for John Black. I roll my sleeves up, and start typing.

I sip my water, and wish I’d insisted on a different restaurant. I keep seeing us at every table, remembering moments from all the times we’ve eaten in here. Lola, because it appeals to her whimsical, creative side, loves Soho, and we’d come here to celebrate birthdays, anniversaries, the fact we were still alive – anything really. She’d always have still water and salad, and then eat most of my pasta.

I survey the other couples in here, and I can see us alongside them. Lola opposite me, her shiny hair and full smile, her brown eyes and elegant neck. We always had lots to say to each other. She’d talk, I’d listen. I’d make her laugh, she'd make me proud. I loved her. We were happy. We were. I know that now.

A quick and imperceptible glance at my watch tells me Lola is now officially seven minutes late. I begin to formulate a timescale of how long I'll leave it before I become formally alarmed. It's feasible that she might not come. She doesn't owe me anything. Well, except a slap around the face maybe, and she could achieve that nicely by standing me up. Just as I'm thinking that maybe I should leave, to prevent the humiliation, I see her at the window, and realise I've been silly. She's Lola. She doesn't have a spiteful cell in her body. And maybe that's where she went wrong.

Her face erupts into a huge smile as she spots me, a smile I'm not worthy of. But I block out my thoughts, just for a second, and pretend it's still my smile, the one reserved exclusively for John.

"I am so sorry I'm late. I couldn't find a Tube."

She takes off her jacket and rearranges her hair while I sit there with an amused smirk on my face. I can't help it; she has this effect on me.

"Did you try looking in a Tube station? I've heard they have a few in there."

She pulls a face. "You know what I mean. There were delays. And things. Oh, I'm so glad to be sitting down. Have you ordered?" she says, grabbing a menu from the middle of the table.

"I was waiting for you."

"Oh. Now I feel bad for being late."

"Didn't you feel bad before?"

"Not really. Well, maybe a little. God, I'm starving." She studies the impressive offering of food while I study her.

"You look great."

"Shut up." But her voice has a light tone to it.

"I mean it. You always look great, but…"

"Well, you look the same." She flicks her eyes over my features. "Except maybe a little more rugged."

"Rugged? Is that a euphemism for rough?"

"No, for terrible. Are you sleeping?"

"Like a vampire."

"In a coffin?"

"Now you're confusing me with Valerie."

"John, don't." Lola goes back to the menu. I keep staring.

Now I understand why women with boyfriends are the most alluring. It's true, they radiate an air of not caring whether you find them attractive or not, and it's sexy. And it's something else, something deeper – it's their capacity to love. I look across at Lola and I see that she's in love, or something like it, with Josh, and I want to be loved by her again. Totally, utterly, and completely.

The waiter comes over, brandishing a folded over serviette instead of a pad.

"Are you ready to order?" He asks in an Italian accent that's more Mill Hill than Milan.

Lola nods at me. I take my cue.

"I'll have the fiorentina, and she'll have the salad."

"No dressing, please." Lola insists. "Or tomatoes. Or onions – I don't like onions. And no dressing – did I say that already?"

"Yes, madam," he says, blatantly deciding to rinse Lola's rocket in his own spit. "Anything to drink?"

"A glass of house red for me, please. She'll have a mineral water. Still, i.e., no bubbles. And no ice – those are frozen cubes of water. Thanks."

Lola raises her eyebrows in playful disgust as the waiter throws one last sneer in our direction and then vanishes behind a set of doors, probably to defecate on my pasta.

"I might've wanted something different to drink," she says, resting her chin on her hand.

"Sure, like you might have wanted something different to eat."

"I like salad."

"Of course you do. How much are you willing to bet that you don't ask for a bite of my pasta?"

"Twenty pounds." She takes me on immediately, extending her hand towards.

"Done." We shake on it. "You're confident of your willpower."

"Yes, well. I've changed now. I'm no longer predictable."

"You were never predictable."

"I must have been." She tucks her hair behind her ear.

"How so? Oh, right, yeah."

She throws me a sarcastic smile, which just makes me fancy her more.

The waiter deposits our drinks in front us without uttering a word. He glares at me, as though he knows what I did to Lola. I hope he's aware that his tip depreciates further every time he looks at me like that. I wait until he's out of earshot before I confess something.

"You know, all things considered, I was pretty surprised when you agreed to meet me tonight. Those all things I considered being that you hate me."

"I don't hate you," she says. "I suppose … well, all that stuff I said when you first dumped me-"

"You have to keep using that word…"

"When you first *dumped* me," she continues, "I wanted to cut you out of my life completely, but it's not as easy as that. After being together for so long, it's hard to stay apart. I think about you sometimes…wonder what you're doing…I'm sure it's just a habit. I shouldn't be here."

She drops her gaze to her lap, and I don't say anything in response for fear she might talk herself out of this meeting and rush home back to *Time Out* boy.

"So," I decide to change the subject. "How's work?"

Some of the gleam vanishes from her eyes. "Oh well, you know … I didn't get that promotion I wanted."

"I'm sorry." She's forgotten that I don't know anything about a promotion. He knows, Josh, and I'm sure he provided a capable shoulder for her to cry on. I can picture her crumpling into his arms, him stroking her hair and whispering appropriate, comforting non-clichéd words that probably come so easily to him. He's there for her, and I'm not. It's his role now.

"I'm not too depressed about it," Lola says philosophically, a skill she must've picked up from him, "but I think I have nowhere to go at Dobler and Larkin anymore. My colleagues just seem to get younger, and they make me feel old and decrepit. I need a new environment, to prove to myself I can still cut it, you know?"

I nod.

"How about you? How's the paper?"

"Have you read my column lately?"

She gives me an apologetic smile. "No. I can't. Josh reads it though."

"That's nice of him."

"Don't be like that."

"Like what?"

Lola sips her water. "What's wrong with your column?"

"It's a pile of shit. I've lost the magic, whatever that was."

"No, you haven't," she says.

"Trust me, I have. I'm treading water."

She regards me for a few moments. "So what are you going to do?" She is genuinely concerned, and I draw foolish hope from this.

"No idea. I showed Charlie some of my other stuff."

"And? What did he say?"

"He practically threw me out of the office. Looks like I'm stuck with the balance of payments and sterling against the dollar. He's just not interested in anything else I want to write."

She puts her glass down on the table. "You should jack it in and write a book. You could be like that song – what's it called?" She clicks her fingers as it comes to her. "'Paperback Writer.'"

It hits me like a bucket of icy water. "The Beatles."

She nods, grinning. "Yes, them."

"Since when did you start listening to the Beatles?"

"Since now."

"But you hate the Beatles, Lola."

It's true. I tried for nine years to get her to acknowledge the greatness of the Fab Four. Tried and failed. She told me 'Yellow Submarine' is "stupid", 'Yesterday' is a "cover version", 'All You Need Is Love' is "idealistic" and 'Hey Jude' is "too long and boring." Those were the results of the Martinez jury.

"The Beatles are actually very good," she says, as though she's the first person to have discovered them.

"Congratulations. But my point is you've always detested them. You gave my 'Revolver' album to fucking Oxfam for God's sake."

"I know, but Josh played me-"

She stops, realising she's struck me where it really hurts. And she has. Josh has converted her to the fucking Beatles. How could he succeed where I failed? Anyone else, he can have – Smog, the Beta Band, the Jam, Dylan, but the Beatles – no way. The fucking Beatles … the fucking Beatles!

"John, stop calling them the fucking Beatles. They are not the 'fucking' Beatles."

"I'm sorry, Lola. I'm in shock."

"What's the big deal? The song just came into my head. It was relevant."

"All right, so is 'We Can Work It Out.'"

She shuts up, and glares at me. Even her glare is sexy now.

The waiter hovers beside us, throwing our plates down. Pepper and Parmesan cheese are used to season our food without our consent. We're both too engrossed in our own musings to protest. The waiter arches his thick eyebrows questioningly, and I'm so desperate for him to leave us alone that I almost wrestle the pepper-mill from him and club him around the head with it.

"Valerie told me you've been seeing that Sarah," Lola says when he disappears behind the swing doors. "I'm pleased for you."

I start to laugh. "Great. Thanks for your blessing."

"I mean it. I'm glad you have someone. I just didn't think she was your type."

"And what's my type?"

"I don't know, John. Your type was me for nine years."

God, she's getting good at this. And God, it's sexy.

"Sarah's a nice girl." I manage to keep a straight face as I say this.

"Nice – ha! That means she's boring."

"She's not boring," I say, untruthfully.

"Valerie says she's thick."

"And Val would know. When's the last time she had a boyfriend? I think it was 1987. Oh wait, I forgot about the guy she went out with who looked like Vladimir Putin – do you remember him?"

Lola frowns. "No. So? Is it serious?"

I twirl some pasta around my fork. "Yes." In many ways…

Lola spears her lettuce. It remains speared on the fork for the rest of the evening. "You haven't been seeing her that long," she says. "How can you know?"

I give a non-committal shrug. "Sometimes you just know. I mean, look at you and Josh. You've moved in together."

"That's different."

"How?"

"It just is."

"So you have moved in together."

"Yes."

I push my plate away. "You've known him for five minutes and you're already shacked up together in Hoxton."

"Shoreditch, actually."

"Oh, well, that's just marvellous."

There then follows a good, solid chunk of quiet. I chew some pasta and wonder where the night is going. Lola's simply sitting there stirring her green stuff around her plate, occasionally stopping to sip her drink. I wait for her to speak first, because I don't trust myself not to say something I'll regret.

"This was a mistake, wasn't it, John?"

I run my hand across my chin. "Probably."

"Does this mean we can't be friends?"

I wish she wouldn't look at me like that. "Probably."

Lola's eyes are glistening. Mine might be too.

"Oh, God..." She puts her head in her hands. "But I can't not see you. I can't not speak to you."

"I know," I say. "We just have to work harder at it. And you'll just have to not talk about him."

"Josh."

"Him."

"And you can't talk about Sarah."

"Fine."

"Fine."

She picks up my fork. "Can I try some pasta?"

"It'll cost you."

She reaches for her purse and sighs. "It already has."

After that, we do a good job of papering over the cracks. She's almost the old Lola – funny, warm, engaging, and indecently beautiful, and I'm the old John, although I've realised I don't like him very much. He makes bad choices – stupid ones, ones that make no sense.

It's almost like old times, except for the agonising bit where she goes home not with me, but to another man, and I go home to my appalling flat, to dwell on how I let her go. I practically handed her to Josh gift-wrapped and on a diamond-encrusted platter. And now he's playing her the fucking Beatles.

I go over to the stereo and put 'Help' on repeat until one of the greasy-spooners from downstairs starts banging on the wall.

18

It's only half-past stupid in the morning, but Sarah's phone is ringing already. It's on the windowsill that doubles as a nightstand, which of course is right next to my ear, the Nokia tune blaring into it with deafening precision. If I shut my eyes, it might stop.

It does.

And then starts again.

Sarah moans. "Johhhhnn…"

I stretch out an arm – fuck, it's cold – and hand the thing to her.

"Thank you, baby." Sarah kisses my shoulder, then checks the display. "Oh my God - it's Theresa. Hello..? Oh my God!"

I tug the duvet over my head. Sarah's phone is always ringing, and it's always one of her drama queen girlfriends, and the rule is that "Oh my God" will be said by one of them within the opening seven seconds of the conversation.

I lie on my back, listening to them (it's impossible not to). It's like lying in the middle of a runway and while a 747 takes off above my head.

"You didn't! In front of Marcus? Oh my God, Theresa, noooo!"

Okay, I give in. I sit up, rubbing my eyes, entertaining the notion of getting up and going into work early – making a start on the things I meant to do yesterday but didn't because I couldn't be bothered. But, annoyingly, I'm now mildly curious about what this Theresa did in front of so-called Marcus.

Sarah's up now, pacing around the bed, stopping every so often to examine the polish on the ends of her nails as she listens and dispenses pearls of wisdom, all of which are phrases she's absorbed from American talk shows. I watch her, and wonder how I got here.

Actually, I know exactly how I got here. I can hear the Sat Nav telling me: "Turn left past the Lola, right after the Rebecca, and pull over here next to the vacuous girl you just can't seem to extricate yourself from."

"I'm so sorry, John," Sarah says, tossing her mobile into her bag. "That was Theresa." It doesn't matter to Sarah that I have no clue who Theresa is – it may as well be Mother Theresa for all I know.

"Theresa went out with Marcus last night." Again, the fact that I don't know Marcus is not a deterrent to Sarah. "She dropped her bag on the platform at High Barnet. Quelle nightmare!"

I blink at her. "Why? Should she have saved it for East Finchley?"

"What? No, John," Sarah replies, as though I am the one talking nonsense. "Her stuff went everywhere." She extends the syllables to compliment her hand movements. "Eh-veree-where. Marcus had to pick up her hairbrush and her...you know."

"Incontinence pads?"

"John! This is serious!"

The thing is, to Sarah, this is serious. Never mind tsunamis and earthquakes and high school shootings. For Sarah and her drama queen friends, this is a matter of life and death on an epic scale. They'll be expecting CNN to do a live feed from outside the station, interviewing shocked eyewitnesses.

I reach over and turn off the alarm.

"I've got to get to the office," I say.

"What, now? Shall I make you some breakfast before we leave?" Sarah sits on the bed beside me, gazing down at me like I'm a baby lamb or something. 'We'? I said I had to be in the office.

"Sure. Pass my cigarettes. They're over there." I point at the pile on the floor where, in lieu of actual storage, I keep everything.

Sarah sighs, and watches me as I light up, almost spoiling it for me but not quite. I deliberately make a show of how good the smoke feels in my lungs, my eyes closed in ecstasy as it no doubt forms the beginnings of a cancerous growth. I exhale high into the air, adding more layers of yellow to the ceiling.

Sarah frowns at me. I'm tempted to tell her she'll get lines if she doesn't stop doing it.

"Every cigarette you smoke takes twelve minutes off your life." Sarah folds her arms.

"Is that all? Maybe I should smoke two at a time."

"Don't say that!" she says. "I thought you said you were going to stop smoking in bed, anyway."

"I did. In your bed. This is my flat."

"This flat is icky," she says.

This is vintage Sarah. In her dictionary there are words like 'icky', and 'oogy', 'thingymidoodaa', and 'yukorama', which is my personal favourite. She wrote them in there herself, and only she is entirely sure what they mean.

I lean back into the pillow and consider her for a few seconds. "Sarah, do you like the Beatles?"

"They're okay," she replies. "For old people."

"Right. Do you mean for old people to listen to, or 'for old people' meaning that the Beatles themselves are old?"

She chews the inside of her cheek and considers my question. "Gosh, I don't know." She ruminates on it for few seconds. "Aren't most of the Beatles dead?"

"Fifty percent of them, yes."

Sarah shakes her head. "No, you see, I can't listen to music by dead people," she says in the most decisive tone I've heard her use to date.

I'm afraid to ask but, I have to. "Why?"

"Because it's scary. I'm frightened that if I play their music it'll make them rise from the grave or something. Like doing an Ouija board." She lowers her voice and leans in towards me. "I worry they'll haunt me."

I consider the immense talent of John Lennon, and give a nod to Sarah's ego. Only she would believe that a genius like him, a fucking icon, would waste his time haunting her when there are so many other things he could be doing, like laughing at Paul McCartney's love life.

"John? You've gone all quiet."

I'm trying not to scream.

"Are you okay?" She cups my hand. "What are you thinking?"

One of my least favourite questions. I know she wants me to respond with, "Darling, I was just thinking how beautiful you look in this light and how much I love you, want to marry you, and whether our children will have your nose or mine." However, usually the answer to this question is I'm thinking about whether I'm hungry, if there's enough petrol in my car, or breasts – not necessarily hers.

But if I said, "I'm thinking about how I like Lola's tits better than yours", I'd get a slap. And likewise, if I say, "I wasn't thinking about anything," I'll get the "No, come on, tell me" conversation, which can go on for hours until one of us ends up getting exasperated and leaving the room (usually me). I can't be bothered with this rigmarole, so I tell Sarah the truth.

"Actually, I was thinking that I'm going to be late."

Her face falls. She was hoping for something more exciting. "Oh. Okay. Oh, I'm tired." Sarah yawns, stretching up her arms and flashing her breasts gratuitously, clarifying for me that yes, I do indeed prefer Lola's.

But, you know what I've realised lately – I could do a lot worse than Sarah. She's annoying, yes, but most women are in some form or another. It's how their annoyingness fits into the grand scheme of things that matters.

Some women are annoying in major ways (Sarah), some in more tolerable, manageable, even endearing ways (Lola). Lola is untidy, and picks at her food, but Sarah doesn't even eat food. She is inherently irritating. She can't help it; it's embedded in the very fabric of her personality. But then even that's relative when juxtaposed to how aggravating Valerie is, or God forbid even Penny, who makes a mosquito bite you can't scratch seem perfectly anodyne by comparison. And let's not forget, 'I'm divorced, let's have sex' Sheila, who probably has a man buried under her patio by now or, equally likely, building her a patio that she'll bury him under later. As for Rebecca – well, Rebecca was pretty much normal, but she couldn't deal with me, she had too much dignity. Sarah can. Sarah is a 'yes' girl. She'll do anything I want, when I want, she thinks all my ideas are fantastic, that I'm clever – even though she can't spell IQ – and is happy for me to treat her poorly. What more do I want? I could marry her, settle down, get it over with. I could have a quiet(ish) life with a woman who thinks I shit Swarovski crystals, and not have to worry about it anymore. But I don't want that, do I? So what do I want?

"Oh well," Sarah says. "If you're sure you don't want anything for breakfast, I'll go and jump in the shower." She kisses me on the forehead, enveloping me in a cushion of soft, fleshy breast. "See you in a bit." She gives me a sultry smile and what I think was intended to be a sexy wave as she walks the four paces into what Mr Ahmed optimistically calls the 'shower room'.

Yes, I could do a lot worse that Sarah. And she likes me – she's 'falling' for me.

"Sarah?"

"Yuh?" She puts her head around the door, her – wait, my – toothbrush in her mouth. I decide to ignore that.

"C'mere."

She pads over to me, that sultry smile etched nicely on her face. She puts her Colgate-tinged mouth on mine and, for the first time, when I close my eyes I don't think about the Aston Martin DB9.

Of course, the instant it's over, the weight of the mistake is as heavy as Apollos one to thirteen landing on my torso simultaneously.

"Oh, John…"

Sarah lies beside me, panting for breath. I feel this isn't a deserving reaction to my performance, and neither were the other three 'Oh Johns' she's sighed in the two minutes of otherwise silence since we had the sex (which is still possibly longer than the actual duration of the sex).

"Mmm…" She cuddles in towards me, resting her head on my chest.

I, naturally, lit up as soon as I came, and would've done so before I came to ensure my cigarette was ready, but it all happened so quickly. Or, really, I happened so quickly. Now I'm tempted to use her head as an ashtray.

"John…"

Don't say it, Sarah. Don't spoil perfectly bad sex by saying it. Please God, don't…

"Yeah?" I hear the fear in my own voice.

"I think I lo-"

"I'll get in the shower," I say, flinging back the duvet.

"Okay," Sarah says, sighing and fluffing a pillow. "It'll keep."

Yeah, I think, turning the 'shower' on to it's one and only setting of 'scalding'. That's my new problem.

Despite my best efforts to suddenly remember I have an interview to do in some remote part of London, i.e. anywhere south of Pimlico, Sarah insists we go to the office together. "After all," she tells me, "everyone knows we're a couple, so what's the point in hiding it?"

Yeah, everyone knows because you fucking told them. And now, I think sadly as we step onto a crowded Tube, she'll probably send round a group email with the subject header, 'John and I had sex', and a jpeg of my penis.

I know now that my body, and the DB9, were protecting me. Now I've succumbed and had sex (if it lasted long enough to be technically called that) with her, Sarah thinks this it. She thinks I like her, that there's a future to our relationship (again, if it can technically be called this), and that me giving her one (or maybe half of one) means I feel something. The truth, which I should probably keep from her, is that the only thing I felt was a bit sorry for her, and really sorry for myself, which therefore rendered sex a good idea. But now, with her clinging to my arm and gazing at me as though I'm made of chocolate, I know beyond a doubt that it wasn't.

There has never been a sorrier man on the Piccadilly line.

She doesn't prise her grip from my arm until we get outside the office, when she sees a gaggle of third-floor Sarahs, extracting herself from me to rush over to them. I have to skulk in the lobby while she yabbers at them, probably telling them all about the sex we had an hour or so ago. The silver lining is that Sarah cannot tell a story without embellishing it, and hence I might come out of it sounding like a competent lover. If a miracle occurs and she tells the story how it actually happened, I'm resigning.

"John," she says when she returns, a pink flush on her cheeks that she didn't have during the actual doing of the sex, only the telling.

"Mmm?" I press the button for the lift.

"I've done something bad…" She glances at her shoes.

My spirits lift a little – I hope she's cheated on me. "What?"

"Well," she says, tucking a strand of hair behind her ear. "Mia and Angie asked me to lunch, and…"

It takes me a few seconds to realise Mia and Angie are the other Sarahs. "Oh, right."

"Which means we won't be able to have lunch today. Are you angry?"

Of you leaving my sight for two hours to tell a bunch of girls I'm great in bed when I was actually terrible? I'm furious!

"No, you go ahead."

"Are you sure?" Sarah sidles closer to me. "I could always cancel?"

The lift pings. Valerie walks out of it and gives me a look that says 'please die in a horrible accident where they can only identify you by the powdered remains of your upper molars'.

"No, Sarah. Please don't cancel."

"Ah," she says as we get in the lift, which doesn't smell as though Valerie's farted in it, although I wouldn't put it past her, especially if she saw me in time to force one out. "You're so understanding. We can't have lunch, but we can spend tonight together, so it's all okay."

That's the same as a doctor telling me, "We were able to save your legs, but you'll be paralysed from the neck down."

It gets worse once we get to the office.

Despite the fact that I'm sitting only a few hundred yards away from her, Sarah insists on sending me emails with subjects such as 'Hey Handsome', 'You're so cute!' and 'Can't wait for 2nite!' 2nite? That's assuming I haven't committed suicide by then. Between her emails and Percy smirking at me all morning, as though he knows what I did, I am rapidly losing the will to live. If this is survival of the fittest then I'm seriously out of shape.

It's at that weak and vulnerable moment that Lola decides to call.

Lola and I have spoken on the telephone a few times since that night in the restaurant. She told me about how she's thinking of setting up her own PR firm, but surprise, surprise, she's too scared. I told her about how I'm thinking about going freelance, but surprise, surprise I can't be bothered. She said she was worried about me, remarking that my newfound career ambivalence doesn't seem like me at all. I debated asking her if she was concerned enough to nurture me back to the 'real me', but thought better of it. The 'real me' is the reason she's with someone else.

"John?"

"Hey."

"It's Lola."

"I know."

"Oh. Well. Hello."

"Hello."

"How are you?"

I have no idea how to put it, so I settle for, "Okay. You?"

"Oh, you know…" I don't. I never did. "I can't talk for long," she says. "Kay's having a dinner party next Saturday night, and I wondered if you wanted to come."

"Excuse me?"

"You heard."

"I know, I was hoping you'd repeat it."

"I said," she sighs, "would you like to come?"

"What about Josh?"

"It's not a date, John."

"I know, but shouldn't you be going with him? He's your significant other."

Lola sighs again, with more feeling. "I know, but Todd's having some kind of 'issue' with Josh, and he'd rather you came instead."

Way to go Todd! I'd never have put Todd down for such a blatant and unashamed show of solidarity, but it just goes to show that you find support from the most unlikely suspects.

"What you mean is, Todd thinks Josh is a prick."

"John!"

"Sorry. Couldn't help it."

"Please try."

I think it through for a second. "What about you? Do you want me to come?"

"I wouldn't have asked otherwise, would I?"

I don't know – would she? I guess not.

Then, I regain some pride. Lola's got a cheek. What does she think I am, some kind of trophy ex? Just because her incumbent paramour isn't as intellectually stimulating as me, she thinks she can use me as her dinner party reserve. I got out of being her plus one, and I'm not about to resume that unhappy role just because I'm a sparkling raconteur and Josh isn't. Fuck that. I am not a performing monkey, or a dancing bear.

"All right, I'll come."

"Great! See you Saturday, John."

"Bye."

I spend the next few minutes feeling rather pleased with myself, even though answering the telephone and agreeing to go to a dinner party is hardly an achievement. But it is though, isn't it – Lola invited me, which has surely invoked her sister's wrath (which I know from first-hand experience is pretty terrifying), and yet she did it anyway. This thought lifts my spirits so considerably that I even open up the feature I meant to finish (well, actually, start) yesterday, and it seems like normal service might almost be resumed, until Simon catches my eye from across the office.

He's either drunk, or he's giving me the secret signal. He's raising an eyebrow and holding his Arsenal mug in one hand, his other thumb held at a horizontal angle like Emperor Commodus, who now seems straight in comparison to my so-called best friend.

I stand up, and nod at him over my computer. I pick up the mug with a map of the underground on it, and pretend I am going to the kitchen, even though I have only been there once in the past six months, and that was to vomit after a heavy one the night before.

These are our emergency procedures – we only do this when something serious has come up, although the last time Simon signalled me like this was when his broadband connection went down at home after he spent five solid hours on the Victoria's Secret website. I argued that was hardly an emergency, but he saw it differently.

I drum my fingers on the pristine sink – no one uses this kitchen except to vomit the morning after – and Simon bursts through the swing doors.

"Fuck, bollocks, fuck and more fuck with little sugary coloured things on," he says.

"They're called hundreds and thousands."

"Fuck them too." Simon stuffs one hand into his pocket and jangles his change, as though he's thinking of putting in an offer for the unused scourer on the draining board.

"Mate, I don't suppose I could move in with you for a few days?"

"If you can stand the constant smell of black pudding and you don't mind sleeping in the wardrobe, sure. What's happened?"

"Well," he says, glancing over his shoulders to check there's no one listening, even though the kitchen is empty save for a bottle of Fairy Liquid. "I was on the Tube this morning, and it hit me."

"What, the train?"

Simon gives me an irritated look. "Be serious for once, will you?"

"Sorry. Go on."

"Okay, I'm on the Tube, and I suddenly realised – you were right not to get married."

"Right." I scratch my cheek and glance at the virginal microwave, wondering if I should bring in a frozen lasagne tomorrow and pop its cherry. "Because...?"

"Okay," Simon is babbling now, "you've broken up with Lola, yeah?"

"Mmm."

"And I've broken up with Penny..."

"Yes..."

"Except Penny and I are grown-ups, so I don't get dumped, I get divorced. I'm thirty-four, and about to become a divorcee. Not cool. How am I supposed to live with that?"

"Easy. The same way you live with your big head and your fat arse."

He glares at me. At least, I think that's what he's trying to do. "Do you not know how to empathise?"

"No. Not if it means I have to stand in this kitchen agreeing with you that your life's shit. It isn't. You're free now – ding dong the witch is dead and pregnant with some poor duffer's kid. Hooray. Now you get to sit around in your pants eating chips and watching Spongebob all day. And you can watch the match in peace without getting dragged to Tesco, or Lakewater, to pick her up. You can do what you want, when you want, and if you're lucky you might even get to do it with someone else every now and then. Enjoy it, mate. You're free."

This all comes out of my mouth so quickly, so seamlessly, that I don't have time for a quality control. It sounds great, polished, like I really believe it. It's my mission statement. But it's utter, utter, bollocks. I suddenly understand what it must be like to be an MP.

But Simon's gazing at me in awe, as though I've told him the new speed limit on the motorway is five thousand miles per hour.

"Wow, John – you're living the dream, aren't you? We'll have a great time, won't we?" He nudges me and winks, something I hope he never does in my presence ever again. "Time to find out what I've been missing out on all these years, eh? Cheers, John."

He walks out of the kitchen, pushing the swing doors and whistling something by Bananarama, which is the only thing he can whistle without looking like he's performing fellatio on a squirrel.

I peer into my empty cup, knowing that even I, the guy with no idea what empathy is, do not have the heart to tell Simon that all he's been missing out on is an existence based around convenience food and repeats of old programmes on Bravo. Still, a few days of living with me, and he'll discover that for himself.

The thought makes me so depressed I contemplate using my head to pop the microwave's cherry. And yet, that discussion with Simon turns out to be the highpoint of my day.

I'm deliberately ignoring my in-box, because Sarah keeps sending me emails with stupid subject headings about how bored she is, and forwarding pointless messages containing pictures of roses and kittens informing me that it's 'national friendship week'. Much harder to ignore, sadly, is Percy.

At the moment – mercifully – he's on the telephone, gesticulating wildly and occasionally massaging his temple, as though he's under extreme pressure to make a decision. It's probably his Mum asking him what he'd like for tea. Since this morning, he's been giving me these looks – chilling, portentous, sideward glances, like the kid at the end of *The Omen*. Simon and I should grab him late one night and hunt for the '666' on his scalp.

He smirks at me, as though he's seen the exact moment the world will end and my death is particularly gory and painful.

"Alright, John?" he says, putting down the phone.

'John'? Since when did he think he could call me that, although admittedly it is my name.

"Busy?" he asks, shuffling a pile of papers I suspect are comprised of back issues of the *Dandy*. "Oh, hello, Mr Cannon."

Mr Cannon? Oh, shit.

"Hello, Percy," Charlie replies, so fondly that for a moment I think he's about to ruffle the rat's fur. His back arches, making it appear as though he's offering us his corpulent stomach as a pillow. "Great interview, by the way. I'll get back to you on it this afternoon."

I have to clench every muscle in my jaw to keep my mouth from dropping open. 'Interview'?

"Ah, John," Charlie says, though he's only just noticed I'm sitting right under his bulbous nose. "I take it you haven't read my email?"

There's never an easy way to answer that question.

"I was just about to," I say. Out of the corner of my eye, I think I see glee on Percy's face.

"Well, don't bother. I asked you to come to my office at three o'clock. You're late."

Charlie folds his arms, which is an impressive feat for a man with a stomach the size of Bulgaria.

"Apologies," I say, as I always do when I'm either crawling, or not really sorry – in this case, both. "I've been a little caught up today."

Percy, I note, is practically biting his knuckles. I decide I'm going to have to beat him up in the toilets later.

"But I'm free now," I offer.

Charlie grunts. "Yes. You are."

Sighing wearily to demonstrate what a huge inconvenience this is for me, I gather myself from behind my desk and follow Charlie on the meandering walk to his office, not forgetting to give Percy a look that should provide him with an inkling of how much I'm going to hurt him later. He must've snitched on me for being a bastard to him, the spineless little prick. I assumed he had the balls of a castrated monk, but it seems that was an over generous estimate. Charlie's really going to enjoy administering this scolding. He hates me as much as he loves Percy.

"Sit down, John," Charlie says in his gravel-like tone, even though I'm seated already. "Right, there's no easy way to say this …"

I hate you, Percy, I think to myself as Charlie launches into it. I can just imagine you at your public school, sucking up to all the teachers, hanging around in the library by yourself whilst all the other kids ran around being normal. Well, you can't hide behind Charlie forever. As soon as we're alone I'm going to-

"Excuse me?" I blink at Charlie.

"I'm sorry, John, but that's what has to happen," he says, launching little crusty flakes onto his shoulders as he shakes his head.

"I don't..."

"Try not to take it personally, Johnny, but the decision has been made."

"By whom?"

"Me, the powers that be, and the powers that control them. Don't worry though, we'll see you right for a bit of compo – something to keep you going for a month or so."

"Oh, well, that's fine then."

Charlie regards me carefully. "I know this is tough for you, but surely you didn't think you were indispensable?"

My resultant silence informs Charlie that I did indeed think I was indispensable. Charlie scratches his cheek, peering at me over his crescent glasses before easing himself out of his chair.

"Come on, son," he says, pacing around his office, "you must be aware that over the past few months your writing has been, well, absolute bollocks."

The only good thing about this sentence is that it's spoken quietly.

I clear my throat. "There's a perfectly good reason for that," I say, but he waves away my attempts at an explanation before I even have time to make one up.

"I understand completely," he says.

"I tend to doubt that."

"No, Johnny, I do." He stops pacing, which I'm glad of, as the constant motion was about to send me over the edge. "Your heart isn't in it anymore. You want to write that namby-pamby stuff – you've been inspired. I understand.

Actually I don't, because it's fucking sautéed shit, but it's obvious to me and the rest of the civilised world that you don't want to write about economics, and you don't want to write for this paper."

"I wouldn't put it quite like that," I say, back-pedalling, unable to believe I'm being sacked by someone who uses the phrase 'namby-pamby'.

"Bollocks. You're a professional – you know how competitive this business is. There are a lot of kids out there who'd give their parents' pensions for your job." He reaches for a stack of dog-eared papers from his in-tray and waves them in front of me. "Do you know what these are?"

I feel sick.

"These are begging letters from kids out there," again Charlie gestures out of the window to remind me where the outside world is, "who are desperate to write for this paper. Kids like Percy, who are young and have promise."

"Jesus Christ, Percy? What the fuck has he ever written apart from a letter to Santa every Christmas asking for pubic hair?"

"For your information," Charlie replies tersely, "Percy can write very well for someone of his age, and he has a very good voice."

"That hasn't yet broken."

Charlie ignores me. "His father is very pleased with him."

"That's what this is really about, isn't it? Friends in high places."

"Yes," Charlie concedes. "Maybe. The point is that you have no friends in any places, not anymore. Percy is young, and fresh."

"Of course he's young and fresh. He's twelve."

"No, son," Charlie sighs, "it's more than that. He cares about his subject – you don't. You're full of contempt. You think you're too smart for this paper – for everything. Your mistake, Black, was not knowing when to leave. You should always bail out of something before it gets old and stale, otherwise it always comes to this – it always gets ugly. At the end of the day, we can sit here until the Queen dyes her hair blonde and changes her name to Judy, but you're still yesterday's news. So to speak," he adds, when he realises his unintentional witticism.

For the first time in my life, I think I might faint.

"So, Johnny, here's what's going to happen. You will write one final 'In The Black', and then Percy will take over."

I scramble to my feet. "I'm sorry, Charlie. I can't listen to anymore of this lunacy."

"Get your arse back into your seat, John. We need to discuss content. I was thinking of some kind of retrospective – 'The Black Years.'" He peers into the distance, seeing the by-line in his mind. "What do you think?"

"I think you're about to give my job to a virgin who still lets his Mum dress him."

"His appearance is irrelevant. He's in, you're out. Of course, we'll have to call it something else and everything, but we'll work on that. Now, what do you reckon? Black – the finale. Any thoughts before I tell you what to write?"

I stare at Charlie, not quite able to compute what has happened. I'd like to smack him one in the face, then take a dump on his desk. Then I'd go over and beat Percy around the head with a hole-punch, then I'd like to lock Valerie in the stationery cupboard, light a match, and burn down the building. In the end though, I do none of these things. I delve into my pocket for a cigarette, put it into my mouth, and say, "My final subject, Charlie, will be a piece entitled, 'Fuck. You.'"

I say the words slowly, with a grin on my face, and then I walk out of Charlie's office, slamming the door hard, hearing the glass crack.

Then I stroll leisurely past my former colleagues, who are either staring at me open-mouthed, or avoiding my eyes. I leave my desk exactly how it is, slinging my jacket over my arm and giving Simon the thumbs-up and a gobsmacked Sarah a cheeky wink as I stride out.

I get outside, feeling like I'm suddenly able to breathe after years without air. Then, after a few seconds of that, I go straight into the nearest pub, and have a drink. And another drink. Okay, I have quite a few drinks. And then, I pass out.

19

The next morning, I'm woken by a headache so intense it can only mean my brain is being dragged out of my skull through my nostrils. My limbs are lead weights, my hair smells of vomit, possibly not all my own, and my eyelids have been stuck down with Bostik. Someone is doing work inside my skull with a drill used to construct the Channel Tunnel, and yet Simon, who must know my condition is delicate, stomps around in the kitchen using some utensil I was unaware I owned. I can hear a kind of 'rrrrrrr' noise, although that could perhaps be the sound of the blood desperately trying to circulate amongst all the alcohol in my system. Urgh.

I lie still for a few minutes, wishing I was still drunk or, even better, in a coma, a nice vegetative, unfeeling state. I wish for both, crossing my fingers, but all that happens is that Simon starts singing. Well, when I say singing, I mean he's warbling, "Ai yi yi yi ya ya", which I think is supposed to be Haircut 100, or then again, he might be performing surgery on his own backside. This yodelling adds to the cacophonous racket created by whatever- the-fuck appliance he's using, and convinces me that I have to get up and kill him. Outside, someone revs the engine on their Ford Focus and yells at their kid to put their coat on for school.

School? Shit. This means it's not even afternoon yet. My plan was to sleep until at least one o' clock, effectively killing off the day. The evening could be rendered null and void by going to bed early, but instead I'm awake and will have to face the gaping expanse of nothingness that is now my existence.

I give up. The kid from outside would evidently rather run up and down the street yelling instead of finding his coat and going to school. I'm on the verge of volunteering to make him a new coat out of his own skin and some industrial staples, when Simon moves onto Erasure – all I can hear is 'rrrrrrr' and "Oooooooooh, sometimes…" I ease the duvet from my body, and crawl out of bed to the kitchen (for once I'm glad it's only the length of three badgers away), clutching the walls I now realise are far too bright for this degree of hangover.

"Morning!" Simon beams. "How are you on this gorgeous sunny day?"

"Dying." My legs and brain have just about enough of a connection left to facilitate sitting down.

"You also smell really, really bad," he says, holding his nose. "Like a battery farm."

I go to tell him what he smells like, and do a double take at the glass in his hand. "Simon, what the fuck is that?"

"It's a Slim-Fast." He says this as though it's a satisfactory answer, taking a long swig of the brown liquid nestling in the pint glass. "It's pretty good, actually. It says," he reads the can, "that if I have one of these instead of food, I'll lose weight."

I rub a hand over the bristles on my chin. "They'll be putting men on the moon next."

"Well, it was in your cupboard, mate."

"It's Sarah's," I say, as it dawns on me.

"Sarah? But she's built like a bloody ironing board."

"And now you know why. I need a drink."

I grip the sides of the table, hauling myself to my feet.

"Er, don't bother mate," Simon says, fiddling with the tap. "You're out of coffee, it doesn't appear you ever had any tea, and the milk smells worse than you. But," he adds cheerfully, "there is another can of Slim-Fast."

"I'm not drinking Slim-Fast."

"Suit yourself," Simon says, shrugging.

My tongue is stuck to the roof of my mouth. I can taste each of the three thousand cigarettes I smoked last night, and someone's mistaken my frontal lobe for a snare drum.

"Give it here," I say, stretching for the other can.

Simon grins. I ignore him. Later, when I'm feeling better, I will kill him.

He leans back against the worktop. Beside him is a food blender with a dollop of brown sludge at the bottom of the jug..

"Si, what's that?"

"A blender."

"What's inside it, apart from your head in one minute's time."

"Oh. Banana smoothie. I made it earlier. Tasted like crap."

"Where did you find it?"

"The banana was at the back of the cupboard. The blender was next to it." He gives it a loving pat. "Handy little bugger, it is."

"It's Lola's."

Simon looks like he's just wet himself in the carpet department in Harrods.

"Oh, mate, I didn't realise it was special or anything. It was just sitting there with the banana and the other plate."

"I bought it for her," I say, remembering. "For some reason, she really wanted it. Now, I guess, she doesn't."

Which is a shame – she might need it when she tires of Josh and wants to dispose of the body. Although she could just call me instead, I'd be glad to help. I'd even supply the chainsaw.

I sit back down at the table, wondering where I put the Paracetamol and whether the only way to cure my headache is to ingest the entire packet. Simon settles himself down opposite me, bringing his Slim-Fast with him.

"Are you seriously going to drink that?"

He raises his two-thirds of a pint, puts it to his mouth and glugs it down, returning the glass back to the table with only a few dregs left in it. "Nice, really nice. I don't know why women are always moaning about losing weight. It's a piece of piss."

"Can I quote you on that?"

"I'll give you an exclusive. Seriously, if all you have to do to drop the pounds is drink a couple of glasses of this stuff, you're laughing."

I return to the sight of the remaining brown sludge. Nothing about it makes me want to laugh.

I reach behind me and pluck my cigarettes from the worktop. Lighting one, I marvel at how well it compliments my hangover. Who am I kidding, it compliments everything.

"John?"

"Just ask."

"What actually happened with Charlie? Everyone was talking about it all afternoon – speculation was as rife as anything I've ever heard in there. Do you want to know what they were saying?"

"Actually, I really couldn't care less."

"They were saying it was a travesty. No one likes Charlie and they think he fucked up. They all want you to come back."

"Just what I need," I say. "They've granted me posthumous adulation."

"It's true, mate. Straight up." He puts his hand over his heart – on the wrong side of his chest, but the sentiment is there. "They're saying the paper won't be the same without you."

"They'll be fine once they've found a new focus for their combined dislike."

Simon shakes his melon-head. "It's not hating you they'll miss, it's your talent. I mean, what the fuck does Percy know about writing?"

"How to hold a pen."

"Exactly. You know, you should appeal." He gets more insistent as I start to smile. "Seriously. You know loads of lawyers - hire one. Take Charlie to a tribunal. It's all the rage in the City."

"Thanks for the support, but first, everyone already hated Charlie before he fired me. Second, I refuse to be the poster boy for a revolution against him. Third, I don't care, and finally – most finally – I'm not going back."

Simon gives me the kind of 'Are you stupid?' look I give other people. "Now you're being silly."

"I'm not. I'm glad he kicked me off the paper."

"It's not a good time to have an attack of false pride, John. You might be the economist, but even I know people need jobs otherwise they starve to death and get eaten by pigeons. What are you going to do, sit around watching *Homes Under the Hammer* for the rest of your life?"

"I didn't come out of the womb with a copy of the *FT* under my arm, Simon. I am capable of doing other things."

"Oh yeah, like what?" He glances around my flat. "Can't really see you as a painter-decorator or interior designer. You can't fix cars – you can barely drive them properly. You're crap with people, and animals. As far as I can see, you've got no skills whatsoever apart from writing."

I pick up my Slim-Fast and stand up, hiding the discomfort the movement triggers.

"So, then, I'll write."

I go back in the bedroom to do precisely that, but end up under the duvet again, pulling it over my thumping head.

Long after Simon has left for work and I've made the transition from bed to sofa, I'm still pondering. The alcohol I poured down my throat last night diluted the shock of being sacked and now, well, I'm just kind of frozen. I was miserable in that job. I'd reached the point where I was turning up every day through habit rather than choice. But I don't have the luxury of being in a job I hate anymore, and I have to find something else to define me. And Simon's right – all I have to offer the world is my writing. So I should just write.

Right?

The clock on the video informs me that it's ten minutes past two or, as I now think of it, five minutes to *Homes Under the Hammer*. I drum my fingers on the arm of the chair. It's sort of liberating how long the day is without any structure. I had breakfast an hour ago, which means I can have my lunch at dinnertime, and so on for however long I decide to stay awake. I can play on the Playstation until the small hours of the morning with no consequences – hell, 'morning' means nothing to me now. I can do anything, go anywhere: read for pleasure, wank myself into a semen-less stupor – no word count, no deadlines, no news bulletins to care about, no papers to worry about. The planet is my oyster. The trouble is, all I really want to do is read a paper.

I stumble into the bathroom and face my reflection in the mirror. I look like a human landfill site. Jesus Christ. I wonder which euphemism Lola would use to describe my appearance now? 'Tired', 'stressed', 'crestfallen'? Or maybe she'd just be straight and say, "You look like shit, John." Jesus, I look bad. In fact, if I put this to Jesus directly he'd probably reply, "Yes, John, you do. You look worse than I did when I was dying on the cross to save mankind. Now piss off and write something."

I need a shave, but any attempt at doing this is likely to result only in me severing my jugular, and probably really only a full facelift will make any difference to my appearance. So, I make do with a quick splash of (boiling) water on the worst affected areas, and return to the bedroom to retrieve last night's clothes from the floor.

The newsagents, fortunately, is conveniently situated just at the bottom of the street. In the short time I've been in Holloway, I've got to know only the people able to sell me a pizza, a kebab, milk, or cigarettes. There are a few non-retail people I know by sight, like the blonde with the over-plucked eyebrows who wears a pink velour tracksuit that's way too small, and the man who passes me now carrying a child who always, without fail, seems to be sucking a lolly. He's seen me too, but being Londoners we completely ignore each other, reminding me why I wouldn't live in any other city.

I'm a fraud, walking along the path in what used to be my work suit, pretending to be something I once was. I need clothes more in keeping with my new employment status (a velour tracksuit?). It's a chilly afternoon, and I wedge my hands further into my pockets, although I'm glad I haven't gone the whole hog and put my suit jacket on as well. That would be too mendacious.

As it is the lady in the newsagents, who introduced herself to me on my second day in the neighbourhood as Mrs Frears, is surprised enough to see me at this time of day.

"Off work today, love?"

I tuck a jar of coffee under my arm and go over to the piles of newspapers. "Yeah." This is true.

"Having a rest, eh?"

"Uh-huh." This is also true.

Mrs Frears nods, as if this makes perfect sense to her. "You need it. You youngsters, you're always running around." I'd take this as a compliment, but considering she's old enough to remember the battle of Agincourt, I probably do seem young to her. "It's rare to find a man like you these days, Joel. Most men your age are so work shy. My nephew, Howard – have I told you about him? Well, he's …"

She's told me about Howard approximately fourteen thousand times, so I concentrate on deciding which paper I want to read. They each beckon me, lying there flaunting their headlines, daring me to choose. The tabloids are trying to entice me with some soap star caught in a phone box (are there any of those left?) with a teenage 'temptress'. The broadsheets are appealing to my intellectual side, all running various speculative accounts of the impending Cabinet reshuffle. I shift my weight from one foot to the other as I weigh up my choice. Fuck it – I'll buy them all.

"… But Howard, he'll never listen, I – ooh, I say, you're planning to do an awful lot of reading today."

"Yeah." I hand her the crisp ten-pound note I found in my trouser pocket before I came out. I have no memory of how it got there, which means I'd better spend it.

"Well, I don't blame you," Mrs Frears continues, beginning the epic task of putting the literature through the till, which appears to have been manufactured pre-decimalisation, and before anyone could count higher than four. "If you have time off, you might as well make the most of it. Of course, I'm stuck here most days, but I don't mind so much. It gives me a chance to catch up on what's going on around here, do you know what I mean?"

I do know what she means. She means she's a nosy old bag.

"Not that there's much to-"

"Actually, I'm kind of in a rush, so if you could ring those up as quickly as you can, I'd be grateful."

She flinches at my brusque tone, but Jesus, I haven't got all day. A few moments later I feel a little guilty when I remember that I have indeed got all day. And all night, if need be. And I'm pretty sure I have a window the day after that, and – oh, fuck.

She scans the barcodes in silence, a silence that lasts an entire four seconds.

"Here, you won't be wanting this one," she says, causing the till to make questionable buzzing noises as she tries to void the transaction.

"I want everything in that pile." I feel my patience ebbing away.

"But don't you work for this paper, Joel?"

She holds it up in front of me, and I experience an unexpected sense of loss. I did more than work for that paper actually, Mrs Frears – it was part of my identity. My name was synonymous with a particular page, my picture emblazoned on it every day. I've been consigned to the relics of journalistic history, and even I'm not arrogant enough to believe such a thing exists. People might notice today, they might still comment upon it tomorrow, but after that, 'In The Black' will be forgotten, replaced in the public conscious by … no, I can't begin to contemplate it. It's too horrific.

"I used to work for that paper. I don't anymore."

"Oh." Mrs Frears is dejected when I tell her this. She's worried I might end up like Howard the Fuck. "How come, luvvie?"

"Career development," I say, giving her the ten quid I now remember I won in a bet with a Norwegian guy called Harald in the pub last night. I don't wait for Harald's change. He can afford it.

I begin the short walk home, telling myself I won't look at page six as I know reading Percy's 'column' will only make me feel sick. On the other hand, I could be magnanimous and work on my karma at the same time by reading it and sending him a telegram to congratulate him. I could attach t to a wreath. Or a loaded gun, with instructions on how to best position it in his mouth.

I turn the corner, smiling at the thought of Percy killing himself, and see Sarah standing on my doorstep, looking up at my window. That, folks, is karma for you.

I consider my options. I could hide behind a nearby tree, but this is Holloway not Kew Gardens, and hence the only one in sight is about a foot high and almost dead. I could throw myself under a passing bus, or I could just turn and walk back the other way. Yeah, I'll do that.

But my karma doesn't hold out.

"John!"

I remember my cargo and wish I were carrying something less embarrassing, like a pile of women's underwear, a large marrow, and some lubricant.

She walks towards me, her face etched with concern. "How are you?" She lays a hand on my arm. Christ, it's like I've lost a job but gained bowel cancer.

"Good, fine. You?"

"Oh, I've been so worried about you! I took a half-day to come and see you."

"Lucky me."

She nods – not because she agrees that I'm lucky, but because sometimes her head just moves of its own accord when she doesn't know what to say. She stands there giving me a look of, yes, sympathy. Just when I felt confident my life couldn't get any worse, Sarah, who has a smaller brain than a lobster and regards MTV as a proper channel showing actual programmes, now feels sorry for me. She sees the newspapers in my grip, and her eyes widen.

"Oh, John – I don't think reading all those is going to help. There's no point wallowing in it."

"I can't go the rest of my life without reading a newspaper, Sarah." Unlike you, I long to add.

"Maybe you should, for now. There's not much going on in the world at the moment, anyway. Oh! But Kimberley from Girls Aloud has-"

"It's fine, really."

"Well, you know best," she says, clearly convinced I'm about to totally lose it and disappear off in the direction of insanity.

"Yes, I do."

We spend an awkward moment simply dawdling on the pavement, with her giving me that concerned look, and me reading the telephone number on the side of a van that's stopped at the lights, wondering what 'Islington Bathrooms' could do with mine.

"John, I need to talk to you."

"I'm kind of busy right now."

"Please. Don't shut me out."

Oh, here we go. This is one of Sarah's favourites. It never occurs to her that I if I want to share something with her, I will. She prefers to think that I deliberately keep things from her merely so she can enjoy the triumph of coaxing it out of me. And half of the time – as in this case – there is nothing to be 'shut out' from. Sometimes I'm monosyllabic because I'm reading, watching TV, or just enjoying the quiet, but I get the "Don't shut me out" routine nearly every fucking time, when what she really means is, "Don't shut me up."

"I need to talk to you, John. In private. It's really important."

"Like I said, I'm pretty busy. Why don't you just tell me now?"

Her mind ticks over. I can hear the ancient machinery above the traffic. If she were smarter, she'd ask me what I was 'busy' with. Then I'd struggle.

"In the street?" she asks, glancing over her shoulder at the man peeing in the entrance to the library, and the old lady shuffling along so slowly that her bread will be mouldy when she gets home.

"It will save you walking all the way back to the flat." All fifty yards.

"Well … if that's what you want."

I sneak a quick glance at my watch to emphasise the fact that I am very busy, and note with annoyance that it's stopped.

Sarah wrings her hands for a few moments, and I want to grab hold of her, stick my hands down her throat, and pull out the words myself.

She takes a breath. "I don't think we should see each other anymore."

"Pardon me?"

"It's not working."

"What? It was working yesterday morning." She can't look at me. "Oh, right, I get it. You mean, 'You're not working anymore.'"

Sarah looks shocked, as people often do when you've articulated something they were trying to hide. "What? Nooooo! It's just... It's me. I'm not over Steve."

"Who's Steve?"

"My ex. With the bike..?"

"Oh, him. It's not about him."

"It is! Well… The thing is, John, it's just, when we started going out, you had a column in a national newspaper. And now … well, everyone knows we're going out, everyone at work – what am I supposed to tell them? It could damage my career."

"What career?"

"The one I have. At work."

I rub my forehead. "So you're dumping me because you're ashamed of me?"

"No, that's not it. What are you smiling at?"

"Irony. It gets me every time."

Sarah bites her lip. "Are you cross?"

"No. I'm happy."

"For me and Steve?"

"For myself."

I push past her, and fumble in my pocket for my key, trying not to ruin my exit by dropping the papers. She's behind me; her hands still clasped together, her eyes dewy. Mrs Frears must think the Royal Shakespeare Company has come to the neighbourhood.

"I'm sorry, John" she calls out. "I did have real feelings for you, you know. I thought you might be the One." Her voice is cracking and everything. It's impressive.

I open the door. "Don't be sorry, Sarah. We'll always have the DB9."

"What? Who's that?"

Her face is completely blank, like the rest of her. I wink at her, and shut the door. Let's face it, my karma cannot possibly get any worse.

Percy's page is terrible, really fucking first-rate awful. I should know, I've read it seven times in the past half an hour.

The theory is all there; I can't fault his knowledge of basic economics (underline basic), but there are no original ideas.

It's as though he's read *Economics for Dummies* (and I know he has) and simply regurgitated the easy bits. All Percy's column tells the nation is that high inflation is bad, and low inflation is good. There's even a diagram to illustrate this – the British public are stupid, but they're not ignorant.

I assumed an above average level of intelligence for your regular paper-reading Joe Schmo, and made it my place to give the column some teeth – no, fangs. I saw it as my responsibility to come up with as much creative conjecture as my grey matter would churn out. I wanted to have something fresh to say – anyone can regurgitate an old theory, but I wanted to make the piece a talking point. It was my aim for people to get to my page and think, "What has John Black got to say for himself today?" or for them to watch the news and think, "I wonder what John Black will make of that?" and actually look forward to reading my thoughts on a particular theme.

But then, one day, I realised that no one cares, and it all went to shit. So, who knows, maybe Percy will succeed where I stopped trying. Or maybe no one will notice the change in columnist. Perhaps, as usual, I'm flattering myself.

I'm sure Percy's piece on the declining rate in consumer saving as a percentage of real disposable income would get him an 'A' if this were an exam, but what does that mean to someone in a council flat in Tooting?

Charlie may be a fat, supercilious, chauvinistic, archaic, egotist, but he's not dumb. He'll read Percy's piece, and know he's in serious trouble. I pull the ashtray closer to me and flick my cigarette in its general direction, most of the ash landing on Percy. Good. I could call Charlie and tell him I've read it. He might offer me my job back, and I could put this right – apologise to the country and give them journalism that'll mean something to them.

But then, I don't want to go back. I can't go back. What with being dumped by Sarah – which is almost funny –

here's an opportunity to make a completely clean break. No more paper, no more Sarah, no more anything. This is what I really wanted. I've got my second chance. I truly am answerable to no one now. I will never be more powerful than this.

I look at the clock. Five o'clock. I wonder where Simon is. Great, I'm turning into Penny. It's only been twenty-four hours of unemployment and I'm already going half crazy. I need to do something to occupy my mind. I need to write, to remind myself what I'm capable of.

I pull the laptop onto the sofa, and open it up. It makes appreciative whirring noises that sounds to me like, "John! Where've you been? I've missed you." I wait for Windows to do its thing, cracking my knuckles because now I'm free and there's no one around to go, "Yuck, John!" I rest the machine on my knees, flexing my fingers. No excuses now.

An hour and twenty-eight minutes passes, and I'm on my sixteenth game of Solitaire, and my fourth cup of coffee. I've achieved nothing except the making and consumption of a mayonnaise sandwich, a few visits to the toilet, and a peruse of the TV guide (there's an old episode of *The Professionals* on in twenty minutes but I'm far too busy to watch it – oh, I suppose I could have it on in the background). Just as I'm reaching for the remote, the intercom perforates the air. I freeze. It sounds again.

I'm not answering it; it'll disrupt my creative flow. Simon is the only person I'm prepared to tolerate at the moment, and he has a key.

I flick on the TV – lovely, the theme music is just starting, and fish my cigarette from the ashtray and shift positions. Yep, this is really going to help my writing. God, Lewis Collins was such a cool fucker. When the intercom goes again, I turn up the television. I settle back as Gordon Jackson starts shouting at everyone, and marvel at how they truly don't make 'em like this anymore.

About fifteen minutes later, there is a knock on the flat door. Whoever it is they're determined, I'll give them that much. The knocking continues without a pause – they're not leaving without an answer. I give Bodie a regretful glance, and haul my protesting body over to the door, vowing that if I open it to find Simon standing there contritely telling me he's forgotten his key, I will no longer be John Black but John Rambo.

I open the door.

"Hi."

Now I'm wishing it was Simon.

"I heard about …" Lola presses her lips together and changes tack. "One of those German blokes from downstairs let me in. I'm really sorry, John."

"They're not German. They're Polish."

"Really?" Lola flicks her fringe out of her eyes. When did she get a fringe? "Does it matter?"

My gut reaction is that yes, it damn well does, but probably not to her.

Lola cranes her neck, peering over my shoulder and into the gloom of the flat. "Is thingy here?"

"No. Thingy's not here. She'll never be here again. She dumped me."

If I were Lola, I'd laugh at me right now. But she's Lola, thankfully, and she just cocks her head to the side and looks sad on my behalf.

"I'm sorry about that, too."

"Don't be. I'm not."

I think she might be about to say something, but changes her mind at the last second. "How are you?"

"Fine."

"Good." A beat. "You look terrible."

"Thanks."

We stand there awkwardly for a while, until she says: "I can't stay, I just thought I'd pop round and see how you were. I won't stop or anything."

"Do you want to come in?"

"Yes, please."

I open the door wider in what I hope is a welcoming manner, and Lola steps inside. As she passes I get a waft of that vanilla fragrance, and my immediate thought is that I don't want her to wear it anymore. She wore that scent all the time when she was with me – surely she should get a new perfume for him. It doesn't seem right for her to be wearing the very same fragrance that scented almost every single thing we did together.

Lola busies herself with exploring the flat, which takes her all of twenty-five seconds. I watch her, tall and elegant in her favourite shoes and her black skirt. God, she's so… So Lola.

"I like what you've done with the place," she says, stepping into the kitchen, where I'm making yet more coffee.

"Which is precisely nothing."

"I know. You should though. It's awful. What's going on with that wallpaper?"

"The apocalypse, perhaps. No tea I'm afraid, just coffee."

Lola takes the cup, even though she doesn't much like coffee. "Thanks. Valerie told me what happened."

"Great, I bet she's still in the throes of orgasm over it."

"Don't be like that, John. She was shocked. She said everyone is. It's not right that Charlie gave you the elbow so he could score points with his mate. It's so underhand."

"Alternatively, maybe I just fucked up. I seem to be doing a lot of that lately."

Lola doesn't – won't – take the bait. "No way. Your column was so popular. Surely he can't afford to get rid of you just like that? It doesn't make sense."

"He wanted me to write one final column."

"See, I knew. He says one final column, but it could lead to-"

"I told him to fuck himself and walked out."

"Oh John, you didn't…" I look at her. "You did, didn't you?" She sighs. "It's not like you to burn your bridges." She bites her lip, and then gives an adamant shake of the head. "Actually, it is. You burn everything – the bridge and the river."

I almost open my mouth to question this latest Lola-ism, but change my mind. I've missed the way she talks. "What are you going to do now?"

"I have no idea."

"Well, you shouldn't just sit back and take it. You should appeal."

I put my cup on the floor. "I really can't be bothered."

"John!" Lola says in an indignant tone she should've saved for someone less indifferent.

"What? I can't. It's saved me the hassle of quitting."

"But what about your career?"

"I'll think of something. I always do." I break her gaze by sipping my coffee, before I say something I might regret. "I like your hair."

"Really?" She combs her fingers through it.

"It's nice."

She cut it for him. Isn't that what women do when they want to get over a guy? They change their hair. I'm sure Simon and I read about it in *Cosmopolitan* once. I imagine Lola with her stylist:

"And what are we having done today, Madam?"

"Cut it all off," Lola probably answered.

"Ended a relationship?" Hairstylist X said sympathetically.

"Yes. He was such a prick. I'm much better off without him. In fact, I've met someone a million times better. And he's called Josh."

"Josh? What a lovely name!"

"I know! How lucky I am!"

"Let's give you a style so fabulous that Josh will be positively purring when he sees you."

Hairstylist X starts cutting, and I feel every snip of the scissors.

"How're things?" I ask Lola, not wanting to know but having to know.

"You mean Josh?"

"No, I said 'things'. That's a generic term, covering every aspect of your life, up to and excluding him."

"Okay John, things are okay. Work is tough, the new place is really nice, and everything else is fine."

"Great. Now I'm asking about Josh."

"He's okay. We're okay. It's good, you know?"

I nod. I do know. I know exactly.

We're silent, and the noise from the television fills the room where we no longer can. Martyn Lewis pushes someone onto a car bonnet.

"Oh, you're watching Bodie and Doily."

"Bodie and Doyle."

She waves a hand. "Yes, that's what I meant. What?"

"Nothing."

The atmosphere changes. I'm looking at her, her piano fingers, her elegant neck. I see what he sees – Josh. I see her properly, the same way I did at that party in Archway.

Lola pretends to laugh at Gordon Jackson's put-down and drains her mug.

"I'd better go. I hope you manage to sort things out one way or the other," she says evenly.

I'm still just staring at her.

"I'd like to come round again sometime, if that's okay. I want to help you. You should be writing, John. Writing is you."

I can't speak.

"Well then," she winds her scarf around that beautiful neck. "I'll be going."

I grab the sleeve of her coat.

"John? What …"

I pull her towards me. I inhale that vanilla smell as I hold her tightly, my face in her hair. She's unsure at first, but after a few seconds, I feel her body sag in resignation. She winds her arms around my neck, massaging it with her fingers. I release my last fragment of self-control, my lips millimetres from the soft skin behind her ear. She stiffens.

"John, I have to go."

"Stay."

"I can't."

"Can't, or won't?"

"Shouldn't."

I tilt her chin, and her eyes meet mine. "Lola, please. I want you to stay."

I see her battle with the lump in her throat, making me feel less self-conscious of my own. She cups my cheek with her palm. Her hand moves slowly down my arm, until our fingers connect and entwine.

We lie on the bed, and we talk – not about work, or us, or Josh, or any of those things. We talk about the most important thing in my life. We talk about her.

She stretches out on my springy mattress and tells me things I've forgotten, things I didn't ask about – things I should already know.

Beside me, she comes undone.

She's insecure, she says. She feels fat but knows she's thin. She thinks she's not clever enough, not pretty enough, that her parents prefer her sister. She thinks she's a failure – that she should've achieved more – she feels invalid. She feels jealous of other women, younger women, who have it all still to come, their futures waiting shiny and unblemished in front of them. She says she's made mistakes, and she regrets them – they keep her awake at night, sometimes. I feel brave then, so I ask the question: am I one of those mistakes? She curls her fingers around mine and squeezes. No, she tells me, and I'm grateful, so bloody grateful.

"You never talk about yourself," she says. "I could count the things I know about you."

And, yeah, she could. And that's the way I like it. I'm John Black, the enigma, the man who plays his cards so close to his chest, you'd think the game was for real. Keep it all in, don't let show. That's what I've always believed. But now I see that it's not all about me – it should never have been all about me. Next to her, I come undone too.

So I talk. And I can't stop. I tell her the whole story – my mother, my brother, and the silhouette of my father. I tell her who I was, and she nods like she understands who I am now, who I became. I leave nothing out, the things I've done, the things I've said and can't take back, the mistakes I've made on purpose and walked away from, my conscience clear. And when I finish she's still there, lying next to me. Her face hasn't changed, her eyes are the same. All she says is, "I'm so sorry, John." She holds me. She holds me together.

I trace her features, her cheekbones, and the straight slope of her nose. I watch as her eyelids get heavier, and start to close. She fidgets, tangling her feet in my duvet. She gives in to sleep and her eyes shut tight, and then her lips form a word, one final syllable before she drifts off where I can't reach her.

"John…"

It feels like my greatest accomplishment. It means everything.

I ease myself off the bed, gently so I don't wake her, and go over to the desk. Pulling the chair out carefully and soundlessly, I open my laptop and begin to type.

20

I’m still writing when Simon knocks on my bedroom door the next morning.

“Come in.”

He pokes his spherical head into the room. “Is she gone?”

“It would appear so.”

Confident the coast is clear, Simon takes the liberty of barging in, and I allow this because he’s brought coffee with him. He leans on my desk, watching me save the file.

“Phew, she was here a long time?”

“Why was that phrased as a question?”

“Dunno.” Simon slurps his drink. “Must’ve gone well then?”

“Why are you talking like an Australian?”

“Me?”

“Who else?”

“Oh,” he says, apparently surprised. “Am I?”

I slip the memory stick from the port and put it into my pocket. “What time is it?”

“Just gone seven, mate”

I worked right through the night. I can’t remember the last time I felt inspired enough to do that.

I stretch my arms above my head. I’m almost useful again. I have a purpose. It’s a nice feeling.

Simon’s standing beside me, fidgeting. “So…”

I swivel my chair to give him my full attention. “Simon, give it a rest.”

“What? Okay, so, I heard you calling her a cab at three am.”

"You can tell the time now – excellent." I turn back to the laptop.

"Oh, just tell me what fucking happened."

Because he'll only keep whining if I don't, I tell him the story. Well, the story minus certain parts. I tell him how Lola turned up unexpectedly, and I admit to him, under heavy questioning, that yes, I was pleased to see her. I tell him how she concerned she was about me, and I let him speculate a little bit about what this might mean. But I end the story there. I don't tell him how magnificent it felt when she held me, how good her skin smelt, and how light I felt when I opened up to her. And I definitely don't tell him how sad she looked when she left.

"Is that it?" Simon looks like I've just told him the FA Cup is made of polystyrene.

"Yes. Like you said, I called her a cab around three, she went, and here I am. And, sadly, here you are."

"Oh. So you didn't..?"

You can't choose your family, but you can choose your friends. And I chose this one.

"Simon, must you?"

"What? It's a reasonable question." He puffs out his chest. "And I have a right to know."

"So my sex life is subject to the Freedom of Information Act now? No, Simon, we didn't."

"You didn't have sex?"

I pat my pocket for my cigarettes, and then remember I'm all out. "No, we didn't have sex."

"Oh, okay. You mean in a Bill Clinton not-having-sex-way, right?"

"I mean we did not have sex. In any kind of way."

"I see." Simon nods, as though he does see. "So, why did she come round then?"

"I told you, to offer her condolences."

"Oh yeah, yeah. Your ex-girlfriend coming round to commiserate about your ex-job. Nice." He gazes at the carpet and sips his drink.

"Is that Slim-Fast again?"

Simon looks at his glass as if to check, swishing the brown liquid around. "Sorry mate, I've finished it off."

"That's quite all right."

I close the laptop, contemplating whether I should try and get some sleep now. If do, it's the first step on the road to living the vampiric life of the unemployed, a step I'm not willing to take just yet. I'll do something more worthwhile instead. I'll go out, get some cigs, then lie on the sofa and watch television and smoke until I can see the hole in the ozone layer. Sounds like a plan.

"So, you're writing again," Simon says, nodding at the desk. "That's great. What is it? Who's it for?"

"It's a new string to my bow. And it's for me." And you know what – it really is.

"Can I read it?"

I shake my head. "It's not ready yet."

"I don't mind…"

"I do."

"Oh, okay then." Simon nods, as though he understands, but he can't possibly, because by the time he's finished a feature half the world and their dogs have read it.

"Hey, do you want to know what I did last night?"

"Does it involve a blow-up doll?"

"Only in passing." Simon pauses for effect. "I went up the West End with Bernie."

I raise an eyebrow. "Bernie Finch?"

"The very same." He grins, as if this is a Good Thing.

"You hate Bernie Finch."

"No, I don't," he says. "You hate him. Bernie likes you though – he was asking after you."

"I hope you told him I'm dead."

"If I did, he'll have forgotten by now. He was so drunk he puked over one of the lap dancers."

"That sounds like an amazing evening."

"Oh, mate, it was! We're going out again next Thursday if you fancy coming."

"I'll certainly give it some thought."

"Good." The clock on the nightstand catches his eye. "Bollocks, I better get moving. I'll see you tonight. Oh, and John – don't let her mess with your head. There are an awful lot of women out there. Trust me, I know." He winks at me, and leaves me in peace.

I wonder what he knows – if he knows more than me, and if I should make him stay and tell me everything. But then I remember that Simon knows nothing. Nobody does – not even me. Especially not me.

I open the laptop again, and power it up.

And that, pretty much, has been my life for the past few days. I write, I smoke, and then I write more. I can't stop, my fingers darting all over the keyboard, gobbling up the letters. I've hardly left the flat – my world consists only of my computer, the odd Pot Noodle, cigarette-flavoured everything, and frenzied updates from Simon about what's going on in civilisation. And – the strangest thing – I'm actually enjoying myself. If I'd known writing could be this fulfilling, I'd have got fired from the paper years ago.

Percy's doing a good job of killing my column – or 'Economics with Percy Van Childer' as it's now called. From what I've read, it seems like he's chosen to give it a slow and painful death. Simon says Percy's hardly ever in the office – Charlie's forever sending him to do 'interviews' and 'research'. I suspect Charlie's making Percy camp out in Costa Coffee with the *Beano* so he doesn't have to stare at his mistake all day long.

I, on the other hand, am rather pleased with Charlie's mistake.

I'm on the sofa, enjoying a break and a cigarette – not necessarily in that order – when Simon bursts into the flat, his face and hair splashed with rain. He smells of sausages, which isn't unusual. Since he's been staying with me he's eaten all his meals in the greasy spoon downstairs.

"Mate..." Simon has a flush on his cheeks, not all of which is due to the joys of a fried breakfast. He dumps his jacket on the floor. "You have to see what they've done now."

"Are you going to pick that up?"

"What? Oh, later. Later. Look, my friend, at this. And marvel."

He flings a newspaper – my old paper – onto the sofa. It lands next to me, that familiar font and masthead staring mournfully at me. I know what the punch-line is going to be. It'll be the fifth one in as many days. I sigh as I pick the paper up, as though I'm so over this but, secretly, I'm tingling.

Simon bounds over, like a cocker spaniel that hasn't yet been house-trained, and squashes up beside me.

"Page five," he prompts. "Man, this is classic. Can you imagine Charlie's face? This takes the biscuit, the biscuit tin, and the shelf the tin was sitting on. It's genius."

I flick through the pages and even I, the seasoned cynic, the guy who was last impressed in 1995 when I saw James Bond jump off a dam in *Goldeneye*, have to suck in a breath.

"It's the dogs proverbial, isn't it?" Simon says, folding his arms across his spacious chest. "Imagine running that ad in our own bloody newspaper! I mean, the ones in the other papers, fair enough, but this is fan-fucking-tastic!"

I have to agree with Simon, the brashness, the audacity, of it, is nothing short of astonishing. I read the ad again.

BRING BACK BLACK!

Join the campaign for the return of the country's premier economics journalist.

Like the others, it takes up the whole page, and carries no other information – no links, no email address, nothing.

The only difference between this one and the ones in the other papers is that it carries a fuzzy picture of me that I don't recall having posed for.

"Mad, isn't it?" Simon says, beaming. "I told you, mate, you have support. Whoever's been doing this has gone to a hell of a lot of trouble."

He's right. And who would? Someone who doesn't know me – or someone who maybe knows me too well.

Simon screws his face into a quizzical expression. "Do you think it's an inside job? Valerie, maybe?"

"Yeah, right. If it's her, she's either gone so mad her face has imploded, or the ink is poisoned and we'll be both dead in seconds."

I drag the paper closer, inspecting the photograph of me that some mysterious person has felt the need to inflict on the nation. It appears to have been taken by the world's most incompetent photographer.

"Come on, John. You must know who's doing this. Hey…" Simon's had the flash of inspiration that comes less often than a leap year. "Maybe it's Charlie. Maybe he's doing it to get you back without losing face."

"It's not Charlie." I scoop up the paper and toss it on the floor, on top of Simon's jacket.

"Oi, where are you going?" For a second I think he might be about to add "at this time of night" or "come here when I'm talking to you".

"To get ready."

"For what?"

"Did I read my birth certificate wrong, or are you my mother?"

"But I thought we were going to watch the match together."

I freeze. "Match?"

"D'uh, yeah? It's the big one today, Arsenal vs. Spurs? Please, John, don't tell me you've forgotten."

"Of course not," I say. I had forgotten - completely. "I didn't say I'd watch the match."

Simon snorts. "You didn't have to say you were watching the match. Do I say, "John, I'm just going to breathe now, I'll be back later." What the fuck?"

"Simon, football's not like breathing at all. And if you say it's more important than that, I will fold your face in half so compactly you'll be able to lubricate your eyeballs with your tongue."

"Oh, come on! I've invited some of the lads round. Bernie's coming."

"Is that a pro or a con?"

Simon folds his arms and pouts. "Seriously… What's so important that you have to miss the game? Are you having a kidney transplant?"

I put my hands in my pockets. "Heart." I pick up my car keys. "But you and Bernie have a great time."

"Oh yeah," Simon says in a sarcastic tone, one he doesn't carry off very well because he sounds like he's about to start crying, "we will. And I'm not taping the highlights for you."

"Fine."

"Fine!"

And although I feel sick about turning my back on the game, it is fine, because this is more important. She's more important.

Hooray for something, at last: I'm carrying the wine again. I leave the flat with the bottle in my hand, tempted to tap the kids loitering by the post box on the shoulder to say, "Look at me! I'm rejoining society!" but opt not to. They'd only steal it from me.

So I lay the wine gently down on the passenger seat, as though it's a virgin I'm about to make tender love to. I'm proud of it. It's symbolic. Not only is it the first bottle of red I've spent over twenty pounds on, it's also my ticket back into the warm and fuzzy world of middle class suburbia I was so desperate to escape.

I grind the gears into reverse (car, if you fail me now I promise I'll trade you in for a Nissan Micra), and drive to the end of the street just in time to see Bernie Finch walking up the path carrying a load so large, I can only assume the off licence across the road is now completely empty. I shudder, and say a mental prayer asking for him not to puke on my carpet. But then, the carpet looks like vomit anyway, so I might not even notice – Mr Ahmed definitely won't, considering he can't even acknowledge the flat is smaller than a hamster cage.

The traffic is light, and I try to pretend that this is not because all the sensible North Londoners are at home in front of their Sony Bravias, watching the match. I fiddle with the radio and then quickly switch it off as it tunes itself into '606' and I'm told by the over-excited presenter that this is shaping up to be the match of the season. You know what, I don't even care about the match. It will probably be a nil-nil draw anyway. Probably.

I brake and clutch as the lights turn red, drumming my fingers on the steering wheel. If I turned around now, I'd easily make it home in time for the start of the first half, and maybe even before Bernie starts puking.

The lights switch to amber.

All I have to do is a quick spin around the roundabout, and it's straight back down the road.

The lights turn green.

I lift my foot off the clutch, and move forwards.

Kay greets me at the door.

"This wasn't my idea," she says, hand on her hip. "I wanted Josh instead. But, as you're on the dole, I might officially feel a bit sorry for you."

"You're too kind, Kay."

"I know, it's my one and only weakness. That, and Cadbury's." She snatches the bottle from me. "Well, the dole's obviously gone up a lot."

"Yeah, they even pay it in pounds now, not shillings." I kiss her on the cheek and step inside.

"God, affection – have you had a bang on the head, John?"

"No, but there's still time."

A small smile flickers on her mouth. "Todd's in there," her voice rises several octaves, "watching the football!"

There's a murmur from the direction of the lounge, and the sound of the TV being flicked off.

Kay gives me a serene look. "I hate it when we have guests and he watches television. It's the epitome of bad manners, don't you think?"

"Absolutely. It's not like the match is important or anything," I say, following her into the kitchen.

"I know, and it is only a game. God knows there'll be another one on next week," Kay says. "I've tried cancelling the sports channels, but apparently it's part of a package and you can't do it without losing all the good channels like Living. Can you believe that?"

Of course I can. It's a rule invented by men for men. We need rules like that to survive.

Kay puts the bottle on the side and goes to stir one of the enormous pans she has bubbling on the hob. I wonder where Lola is, and try to have a discreet peek around without Kay noticing.

"Lola's not here yet, and God knows when she'll get here. Her car broke down on the A40. She's waiting for the AA."

I try not to laugh at the fact that Lola's hateful car has finally done what I warned it her it would. "Can't the Boy Wonder rescue her?"

"Unfortunately not. He's at some meeting all day."

I seize this perfect, God-given opportunity.

"Where exactly is she? I could go and get her." I do a good job of sounding breezy, even though it's quite possibly the first time Kay's heard me volunteer to do something nice for another human being.

Kay blinks at me first in surprise, then in suspicion. She's a smart woman.

"I don't think the A40 is a good place for a woman on her own," I continue, thinking on my feet. Top corner from thirty yards out with that one. "Plus, you know her – she probably hasn't even brought a jacket and it's pretty cold out there." Oh, brilliant, John – the icing on the already sugary-sweet cake.

"That's unusually selfless of you. Very unusually." She weighs it up. With Todd and her kids, she's become adept at making quick decisions. "Oh, you might as well. God knows what time we'll get to eat otherwise. I did ask Todd if he'd fetch her, but he's more interested in bloody football!" Again, this last bit is shouted, and again, Todd's furtive attempt to check the score is thwarted.

"It's not problem at all." I'm inwardly high-fiving myself.

"Okay. There you go." Kay tosses me a grubby pad of paper stained with various stages of preparation of whatever she's cooking, and Lola's precise location. Kingsland Road – not good for Lola, but hilarious for her stupid car. I retrieve my keys from my jacket pocket.

"I'll be as quick as I can."

"As quick as you can means a fine – there are speed cameras all down there, John. Just be careful."

I nod. I always am. Sometimes.

I start the car up as though it was a Bugatti Veyron instead of a – hey, where's this joker going? Twat.

This, even though I say so myself, is a stroke of genius on my part. Not only do I get to be the hero by rescuing Lola while Lover Boy is mincing around somewhere – earning me a few begrudging brownie points from Kay, I also get to spend some time with her alone, in the most sacred of territories, my car. And, as a bonus, her car is dead. It's a win-win-win.

The journey doesn't take me very long, partly because I'm still pretending I'm in a Veyron, and mostly because the majority of the residents of North London are ensconced in a stadium, pub, or their own front rooms. I consider turning the radio on, but I'd rather not know. And this magnificent turn of events is much, much better than anything that's happening at the Emirates Stadium.

Kay's directions are pretty good, for a woman, and Lola's defunct Beetle (ha, ha!) is exactly where she said it'd be. I promise myself I won't tell her I told you so, but I did tell her so. I warned her that the chassis was weak, but since the Beetle was pink (pink!) and Lola doesn't know, or care, what a chassis is, my opinion counted for nothing. She bought the car so she could drive (and I use the term loosely) around in it looking like Penelope Pitstop, and now she's broken down in it, looking like Penelope Pitstop.

I pull up behind Ms Pitstop and her useless Beetle, resisting the urge to ram into the rear bumper in triumph. I see her check herself in the mirror as I stop my car. She starts applying lipstick. I find the gesture oddly encouraging.

I crouch down and tap on the window. Before turning to me, she fluffs her hair a little, so that it falls silkily onto her bare shoulders. She gives me a resigned look, one I know well, and the window winds down.

"Don't say it."

"I told you this car is a piece of shit."

"I said don't say it, John."

"What did I tell you? I bet you want to hear about the chassis now – what did you say in the showroom? 'Oh, the chassis isn't important, John.' It's important now, right?"

"Are you giving me a lift, or a boring car lecture?"

"Both, if you like."

"Then I think I'll stay here."

"Okay," I say. I love it when we duel like this. "You stay here and wait for the knights on yellow automotive horses to save you. You know they're all huddled around a TV set watching the match, don't you?"

"What match?"

"And they'll just laugh at your pink girl-mobile."

"Oh, shut up, John." Lola says, pushing open the door. I turn around and give the Beetle the finger. "I saw that."

She folds her arms across her chest as we head back to my car, although I know she will never admit that she's cold.

"What'll happen to my car?

"Well, no one's going to steal a car you'd only get forty-nine pence for, so don't worry about that. I'll get it sold for scrap."

"John! I need it!" she says in a tone of horror unworthy of a pink VW Beetle.

"Unfortunately, I'm just kidding. I'll sort it – it'll be fine. Come on, get in. Don't forget your sister is at home waiting to poison us."

"Kay's cooking is very nice, John."

"You have to say that, you're related to her. I'm totally impartial."

"You're totally…"

"What?"

She tucks her hair behind her ear. "Nothing."

The indicator ticks. Lola glances at me, then at the speedometer.

"You look nice," she says. "But you're driving too fast."

"I'm only doing forty, Lola. And 'nice' makes a refreshing change from 'rough.'"

"I said that once, John. And you did look rough." A pause. "I haven't seen that shirt before."

"This? It's old," I lie. "Just because your dress is new, don't tar me with the same superficial brush."

"This is an old dress. I normally only wear it on special occasions but everything else is at the dry-cleaners."

"Oh, of course."

We rejoin the throng heading north and I settle into my seat, relaxing my grip on the wheel.

"So," she begins. "How're things?"

"Great, actually." She gives me one of her 'Yeah, right' looks. "I'm fine, Lola. Really. Unemployment agrees with me."

"Are you sure? You're not a sit-around-the-house kind of guy. Well, not completely."

"Which is exactly why I've been writing again."

"Writing what?" she asks, immediately intrigued, instantly interested, and I feel an errant rush of affection for her.

"Just something I've had in my head for a while but never had the time to put to paper."

"Well, you've got plenty of time now," she says. "Pots of it. I must admit, I thought you'd well be back in your old job by now."

"Really? And why did you think that?" I ask with a smile.

She flicks a bit of fluff from her dress. "Oh, that Percy's column is so terrible, you know?"

"Well, Charlie loves him, and maybe the public like him. You know how stupid they are. Although," I add, as though I've only just thought of it, "there is a 'campaign' to get me reinstated – have you seen the ads?"

"What ads?"

"Someone is apparently crazy enough to take out full-page ads in the main papers demanding to 'Bring Back Black'. You must have seen them."

"No, I haven't heard about that. How very odd. But nice for you – you have fans."

"Oh yeah and, so Simon says, a Facebook page."

"Facebook?" She looks impressed. "And you can't even use Facebook. Wow."

"Yeah, that's what I thought. Whoever it is, they've thought of everything. And you know what, today they even took out an ad in the very paper I was ousted from. It's insane."

"Very. Who'd care about you that much?"

"My sentiments exactly." I adjust the mirror to get a better view of the wayward Vauxhall Tigra behind me. "It worked though."

She sits up. "What do you mean?"

"Charlie called me at six this morning and offered me my job back."

Lola twists round in her seat. "That's fantastic! What did you say to him?"

"I provided him with the coordinates of a suitable location to stick his job."

"Oh John… Tell me you didn't."

"You want me to lie?"

"John! I can't believe you did that! Except I can, as you are the proudest man I know," she sighs.

"I'm better off this way. I can write about things that interest me. I am now artistically liberated."

"Skint and unemployed is what you are."

"Hey, don't start on me – you're the one with a broken down Beetle."

"What's that got to do with it?"

"Nothing, I just like reminding myself." She scowls at me.

"Hey," I say softly, noting how disheartened she is. "I'll be okay. I appreciate the effort anyway."

Her head snaps up. "What effort?"

I give her a wry smile. "The 'campaign'. Very creative."

She adjusts her seatbelt, trying to distract me. "Okay, you're talking crap."

"Lola, you used one of our holiday photos in the last ad."

Her mouth opens and closes and she turns away, fixing her gaze on the windscreen and scowling. "It was the only photo I had to hand."

"I'm stunned you had any to hand. I thought you'd have burned them all by now."

"That one escaped."

I can sense she is embarrassed so I let it drop, and neither of us says anything for a while. This is good, as I don't quite know what to say.

"That night…" she begins. "I'm sorry about getting myself into such a state." A lock of her hair trails down her shoulder, and the urge to plant a kiss on her skin is so strong I nearly swerve the car into the next lane.

"Hey, don't be silly."

"But I was being silly." She laughs. "I mean, what was I waffling on about?"

I give her my one and only sincere look. "It wasn't waffle."

She stares at my profile. "When did you get like this?"

"Like what?"

"All…sensitive and caring. You're like New Labour." She starts to giggle. "New John!"

"Does that mean there's no difference between me and the Conservative party?"

"Yes, and I wouldn't vote for them either. Anyway, I wanted to do something for you in return for listening," Lola continues, "something to pay you back."

"You don't have to pay me back," I say, briefly taking my eyes from the road so I can look at her. "It was a privilege to listen."

Lola has slipped her shoes off, and she has one lean limb curled up underneath her. She tilts her head towards me. "That stuff you told me – I was the first, wasn't I?"

I say everything by saying nothing.

"That stuff I told you," Lola says. "I've never told anyone either. We're even. Okay?"

"Okay."

New John is silent, but duly honoured.

If I were enough of an optimist, I'd say that Lola might be flirting with me. We've been seated next to each other, closer than our hosts intended as Lola has pushed our chairs together. By the time Kay deposits what can only be described as a cauldron full of pasta into the centre of the table, Lola's hand seems to be brushing my arm on an almost regular basis.

She laughs at my jokes, even – especially – the ones that make Kay roll her eyes and bite her lip to stop herself from saying, "Did I mention how much I like Josh, Lola?" Lola maintains eye contact for much longer than necessary, and I cannot, will not, break her gaze. She flicks her hair, plays with the stem of her glass – all of those things. All she needs is a Cadbury's Flake to bite into. But why is she doing all this? From the expression on Kay's face, she's clearly asking herself the same thing.

Lola starts giggling at my latest harsh, but fair, remark, and Kay goes to exchange a glance with Todd, but he's much more interested in scooping up the last remaining dregs of sauce from his plate with the last remaining hunk of bread. Lola finally stops laughing, and lays her hand over mine. I can't help but think there might be a red glow on my skin when she takes it away.

"Oh God, John, you can be so evil! What did he do when you told him that?"

"Well, I don't think I'm on his Christmas card list anymore, which is a terrible shame, as I do so love Christmas cards."

Kay's hurls a fork onto her plate with unnecessary force, but Lola doesn't even notice.

"Anyway, John, how are you coping?" Todd says, not to tactfully change the subject, but because he may have only just realised there are other people in his house.

"With what, exactly?"

Kay takes my empty bowl and places it with a clatter on top of her growing pile of crockery.

"Unemployment," he whispers it like it's a dirty word. "How are you?" he says, as though I'm recovering from piles, or genital warts.

Lola stifles another giggle. She shouldn't laugh – it'll only encourage me. Kay knows this, which is why she's lingering over one of the bread knives and staring at the back of Todd's head.

"It's great. I get to watch repeats of 'Whose Line is it Anyway?' and wear nothing but underwear all day. How about you – you're doing pretty well now, from what I hear."

"Yes, John. I have to say, things have really picked up since I got the website set up. Thanks for recommending that guy – I owe you one."

Kay is still holding the knife and hovering malevolently behind her husband.

"Toddy, anything for you." I take a sip of my wine, and Todd beams gratefully at me. He scrapes his chair closer to the table.

"You know, if things get tough, there's always a job for you at our place, John."

I force a smile. I don't have the heart to tell him how 'tough' things would have to be for me to take up this offer, but it involves selling myself to fat Belgians outside King's Cross, or joining the Civil Service. "Selling replacement windows?"

Lola emits a snort that doesn't quite become a giggle.

"Yes." He nods once – this is enough to underline his point. "I think you'd be great at sales."

Unable to control herself any longer, Kay throws a serving spoon into a bowl. "Oh yes, he would. John would excel at any career that requires him to be insincere and disingenuous. That's why he was such a great journalist. Right, John?"

Todd shrinks into his chair. "The offer's always there," he says in a low tone.

"I appreciate it, Todd. Really," I lie. "It's a great offer, but I have a couple of things in the pipeline, and I'd rather wait and see how those turn out."

"You have a pipeline?" Lola asks, running her fingers up and down her neck.

"You know me, Lols, I never leave anything to chance."

She arches an eyebrow. "I do know you, and you have left a few things to chance."

"Like what?"

She plays with the ends of her hair. "Oh, well, I remember when-"

"Okay," Kay says, "before you two take a leisurely amble down memory lane, I need some help in the kitchen." She turns to me. "John, bring those plates in." She motions to the pile she's constructed in front of her.

"Oh right, sure." It's not a suggestion, so I'd better obey.

I get out of my seat, reluctant to break the mood between Lola and I, but Kay is all too happy to, and she wants me for more sinister purposes than loading the dishwasher. I follow her, giving Lola an apologetic smile as I saddle myself with dirty plates and cutlery. Todd, almost unable to believe he's been let off the hook, seizes the opportunity to creep into the lounge and have a sly glance at the football score.

Whenever I set foot in this kitchen, I'm reminded how empty my life is. The fridge is plastered with paintings, crayoned sketches, and letters of the alphabet spelling out words like 'poo', and 'bum', all of which could only have been created by someone under the age of ten (or, perhaps, Todd). Plastic plates, mugs and tumblers with various cartoon characters and super heroes I haven't got a hope of recognising line the worktop, and the pile of clothes by the washing machine reveals two sets of P.E. kits.

In my flat, I only have things intrinsic to my life. Everything inside it is evidence that my existence is solitary. In this house however, it's impossible to see where one person begins and another ends – they're all so tightly interconnected. I guess that's what family really means, an implicit binding of personalities. I never had it, so I wouldn't know. It's what I crave most, and fear most.

Kay grabs the dishes from me and shoves them on the counter. She stands to face me, her hands gripping her ample hips. Suddenly, the frequency of Todd's acquiescence makes perfect sense.

"Okay, what's going on between you and my sister?"

"Absolutely nothing."

Kay exhales, lifting her curly fringe. "I know when you're lying, John. Your lips move and you're breathing."

"It's not lying. I prefer to call it 'impression management.'"

"That's because you're deluded as well. Why are you flirting with each other? What will it achieve?"

"I wouldn't call it flirting."

"I might be married, but I still know what flirting is when I see it." She pauses, cocking her head to one side. "Did you hear that?"

"Hear what?"

She steps towards the door, straining to hear something. "Do not move."

I fish around in my pocket for a cigarette, while Kay goes out into the hall and bellows up the stairs. "Jeremy! Go to sleep, or I will send your father up there!"

Yeah, that'll scare him. He'll be awake all night laughing at the very notion.

Kay comes back into the kitchen, more irritated than before. "That boy is such a nuisance. Honestly, I considered putting Nytol in his dinner tonight, just to get him to go to bloody sleep." I put the cigarette in my mouth. "Where was I? Oh, yes. Did you know that Lola and Josh are having problems?"

"No. I didn't know. But she doesn't really talk to me about those things."

"That's because you're the enemy." She snatches the cigarette from my lips and drops it into a nearby mug. I try not to cry. "It's all your fault, you know."

I fold my arms. "And how is that?"

"She's still in love with you. She can't let go. You're like a verrucae she can't get rid of."

"How flattering. But what do you want me to do about it? She's the one that keeps phoning me and coming round to my flat. Do you want me to tell her to stay away? Are you warning me off?"

"Don't be silly, she's a grown woman. She makes her own messed up choices." I watch as she stoops down to remove something from the oven that looks bad, but smells good. She lets the door snap shut. "I've met him, you know – Josh."

"Lovely."

"Yes, he is. Really sweet. So good for her. Perfect, even. He's everything you're not, everything you'll never be." Kay prods a knife into what I think is an apple pie, no doubt wishing it was my head. "But I want her to be happy. And she doesn't look at him like she's been looking at you tonight," she says in an offhand tone. "Trouble is, John, you hurt her so badly, and she can't trust you. If only you could find a way to make it right…"

Kay reaches towards a cupboard for the dessert bowls. They're stacked up high, so I help her.

"Sometimes I can't make you out, Kay."

She folds her arms. "Well, that's something I must've have picked up from you."

In spite, and because, of Kay's words, I find myself analysing everything that passes between Lola and I. I notice how she uses my name a lot as we talk, the lingering looks she gives me as she spoons some of her dessert into her mouth, and pushes the rest of it around her plate. She's funny, effervescent – maybe just a little drunk, and she's lovely. On a good day, like this one, we're the complete couple. She's soft where I'm harsh; I'm slick and cool where she's earnest and open. Our anecdotes are flawlessly synchronised, and we listen to each other as though we're hearing every story for the very first time. We can, on a night like this, sit at a table opposite anyone, and we're great company. I am John Black, Lola's plus one. It's a label I'm wearing with pride.

I put down my spoon as I finish what really was an apple pie. "That was a lovely meal, Kay," I say, maybe even meaning it.

"You're welcome," Kay replies, definitely not meaning it. She casts a gaze at Todd, who's tapping his fingers on the tablecloth, probably wishing he were still eating so he wouldn't feel obliged to think of something to say. "Todd? Shall we make a start on the clearing up?"

"Huh?" Todd's face is blank. "Why can't we leave it until morning?"

"Because we can't," she answers.

"Why?"

"Because!"

Lola and I instinctively swap smiles. This is what married people call a 'disagreement', or what I call 'a reason never to get married'.

"We usually do." Todd insists, for possibly the first time in his life. There then follows the sound of shoe hitting flesh as Kay kicks him on the calf.

"Ow!"

"Come on then," she says, gathering up our bowls. "Let's make a start."

Grumbling under his breath, Todd complies and the two of them disappear into the kitchen, the table now barren except for our glasses, the candles, and a solitary bottle of wine.

I rub my chin. "Do you think we've been left alone on purpose?"

Lola nods. "Oh, absolutely." She takes a sip from her glass.

"This wine is good. It's not like you to bring decent wine."

"No? What is like me, then?"

Lola licks the wine from her lips. "Did you know," she says, "that they now think you don't have one soul mate in life, but six. Then after number six you meet your seventh, your goal mate."

"They think? And who would 'they' be exactly? *Marie Claire*? *Elle*? *Heat*?"

She rolls her eyes. "God, you don't still read them all, do you? That's so sad, John."

"Knowledge is power, Lola," I say with a smile.

"Do you still grade them?"

"This could be a nine." I settle back into my seat. "Come on, hit me with it."

"Well, they said that-"

"Hold on, who wrote it?"

"I knew you'd ask this…It was in *Glamour*, and someone called Felicity Burrows wrote it."

"Ah, *Glamour*, yes. Go on."

"Okay, it said," she says, gesticulating more than is necessary, which she always does when she's warming to her theme, "that as you go through life, you also go through your soul mates. There's the one you learn from sexually, the one who mentors you, the one you shop with-"

"Hold on – shop with?"

"Ye-es?"

"I never shop with anyone. I can barely stand shopping with myself."

"John, please let me finish before you annihilate what I'm about to say."

"Of course. I always get finishing and annihilation round the wrong way. Sorry."

"Right, so, there's the one you shop with, then there's your intellectual soul mate, and so on until you find the one you're meant to be with – your goal mate." She puts her hands back into her lap, pleased with herself. "I was trying to work out which one you are."

I let my hand brush her shoulder. "And? Which one am I?"

She stares at her fingers, then at me. "I couldn't think, at first. Then I realised you're all seven rolled into one."

"And what does this realisation mean?"

"It means …" she falters. "I don't know what it means, John. Maybe it means nothing now."

Kay bursts into the room, cradling a small bundle in her arms that's either a child, or a pile of smelly washing she's extremely fond of.

"Guys, I'm afraid Susannah's been sick." Kay holds up a section of the kid's soiled nightdress, in case we needed verification of this occurrence. "Would it be okay if we called it a night?"

Lola stands up straightaway, and I'm glad. The instant liquid is ejected from a child's orifice, I'm heading for the nearest exit. "Sure, no problem. It's late anyway." She strokes Susannah on the cheek. "Are you okay, baby?"

Susannah gives Lola that wide-eyed 'I'm ill' look which I myself have given her a few times over the years. And you know what – she was just as kind to me too, although I was clearly close to death on several of those occasions.

Susannah sobs at Lola, and then buries her head back onto Kay's shoulder. "I'm really sorry," Kay says, "but this is what happens when you have kids."

Great. I'm going for a vasectomy first thing tomorrow morning.

"Don't worry," Lola says. "I'll call a cab."

I take my cue. "No need, I'll drive you home."

"Are you sure?" Lola asks, stepping into her shoes.

"Absolutely," I say, jangling my keys in my hand.

God bless that chassis.

Naturally, as soon as we get in the car, Lola starts moaning about being cold, so I've given her my jacket. It swamps her tiny frame, the tips of her fingers peeking out from the edges of the sleeves. Now, of course, I won't be able to wear that jacket again, as it'll remind me too much of her, and how much better it looks when she's inside it.

She's still shivering slightly, so I turn up the heater in the car so that hot air is blasting right in my face. I'll probably expire from third degree burns in about five minutes, but Lola merely pulls my jacket more tightly around her thin body.

"Ugh! Why don't I move somewhere warmer?" she turns and asks me.

"Because you don't like venturing any further than Milton Keynes."

"Where's that?"

"Exactly."

Lola frowns. "I miss my car."

"You car is dead – get over it."

"Well," Lola says, "then you'll see it in hell. Don't laugh, John..."

"That's a good one."

"Well how would you like it if I said that about your car, your precious-"

"Don't you dare."

Lola allows herself a smile. She's made her point, and how I hate it when she does that. She slips off her shoes and stretches her legs out so that her feet are resting by the glove compartment, her painted toes wriggling contentedly, enjoying their freedom. "Put some music on."

"But we're having such a good time," I say. "Why spoil it by having the fight that inevitably results whenever we try and listen to music together?"

She throws me a playful look. "I've changed."

"Right."

"I have!" she insists. "Try me. I can cope with your boring music now. Scarf-wearing dead people don't bother me so much anymore."

"Bob Dylan is not dead."

"Well, he's about the only person you listen to that isn't."

I think for a second. "Debbie Harry isn't dead," I say.

"She doesn't count. She's a woman."

"Right. And women can't be dead?"

"No, John," she replies, almost in despair. "Women are not morose."

I decide not to go with my initial response. "Of course not. You're absolutely right."

"Come on," she fidgets in her seat, "I want to hear something other than the air conditioner thingy."

"That's the heater."

"Oh, is it on?"

Ladies and gentlemen, this is my ex-girlfriend's circulatory system. Eat lettuce all the time and you too could have the body temperature of a fossilised pterodactyl.

"The CDs are in there," I say, nodding at the glove box. "You choose one, or else I'll crash into the back of this Mazda RX8."

"I don't need to know what every car is called, John," Lola says, reaching forward to open the latch. "Okay, what about this?" she says, holding up a disc. "There's no label."

"I don't like labels. Put it on."

Of course, it takes her about ten minutes to work out where the CD player is, and another three to figure out that the illuminated red button with the triangle on it, with the additional clue of saying 'play' underneath it, means 'play'. The volume, I take care of myself as otherwise I'll need a calendar to time how long it's taken her to put the music on.

"Todd Rundgren?" She says this somewhat incredulously.

"Very good. Have you been studying?" And then, too late, I realise he's been teaching her. I skip forward a few tracks. She watches me.

"What are you doing?"

"Listen to this."

"What is it called?"

"Just listen."

We wait, behind the Mazda RX8, for Todd Rundgren to start singing.

"'Can We Still Be Friends?' Tacky."

"But a good choice."

She shrugs in resignation. "A good question."

It starts to rain as we come into Shoreditch, which is perfect because it means I can't see it very well. It reminds me of the night we 'broke up'. We're in the same car, under the same weather, but sitting in a different silence. Lola gazes out of the window until the song ends.

We pull up outside chez Nobface, and I keep the engine running so I don't forget I'm only the designated driver. She slips her feet into her shoes, and disentangles her limbs from my jacket.

"Keep it on if you want. Put it over your head to keep your hair dry," I suggest nonchalantly, although truthfully I am as far from nonchalant as I've ever been.

"It's okay. I only live up there." She points up to one of those fashionable converted warehouses, the ones I hope now all burn down. "Top floor." She hands me back the jacket. I want to fling the useless garment out onto the road and reverse over it.

"Right."

She hooks her bag over her shoulder. "Thanks for the lift. And for coming. And for rescuing me. For everything."

"You're welcome."

"See you soon?" She unclasps her seatbelt. "I could call you? If you want."

"Sure."

"Okay then."

I don't know how it happened, but we're just sitting here in the hideous, clumsy silence, too afraid to look at each other. We're fumbling in the dark, wading through honey, pushing at a locked door.

"The stuff in the papers … how did you do it?"

Lola smiles and taps the side of her nose. "It's my job."

"Well, you're great at it."

"I hope so. I'm thinking about branching out on my own soon. I might use it in my portfolio. I'll pretend it worked."

"It did work – he offered me my job back. You'll be fantastic, Lola. You are fantastic."

She puts her hands to her temples and keeps her eyes on the windscreen, at the falling rain. "Why can't I get over you, John? Why's it so hard?"

"Maybe you're not meant to."

"What? What is that supposed to mean?"

"It means… Maybe we weren't supposed to break up. Maybe I just really fucked up."

She twists around her seat, undoing the seatbelt. "Yes. You did. We did. And truly, there really is nothing left to say."

"And what does that mean?"

Lola opens the car door. "It means, goodbye, John."

The words are trapped in my throat, a tiny, pathetic squeak, as Lola gets out of the car, making a dash across the spattered streets. She fumbles in her bag for her keys as she runs, and I kid myself that the light that flicks on in the window is not Josh. He's not waiting up for her, and he's not delighted to see she's home. He won't wrap her in a towel and tenderly dry her off. He won't cover her face and body with kisses, and he won't lie down and make love to her. Afterwards he won't hold her and press his body into her curves and smooth skin, drifting into the best sleep of his life.

I sit in the car, frozen despite the heat, my hands gripping the wheel, the squeak in my throat now a scream. And when I look up, into the mirror, she's still standing there on the street, the rain soaking her, watching me. But it makes no difference. She belongs here now. With him.

21

I'd like to reveal my secret, maybe write a book serialised in the *Times*, explaining exactly how I did it, how I set myself free. Unfortunately, for once I can't lie and say it was easy; tell the world how good life is now. It isn't. And, in the end, it turned out that my liberation wasn't really about me at all.

Three months after the final goodbye, the one she meant and the one I had to accept, she's the one who's truly free. She's happy. She's ensconced in Shoreditch in the converted warehouse, and from what I hear (okay, what I hear from my frequent Google searches and word-of-Valerie), she's setting up her business – she's making her dreams come true. So, who'd have thought it – John Black finally does something helpful for someone else, albeit with selfish intent. She's lost me, her arrogant, rude, yes, moody, and all the other adjectives she liked to use, boyfriend, and she's gained him, Josh, the one who'll do anything for her, who puts her first, who cooks, cleans, and probably puts the rubbish outside without her having to nag for twenty continuous minutes.

Now that she's gone, that it's real – neither of us are going back, or even meeting in the middle (or in bed) – the world looks different, it feels different – sounds different. When I say 'the world', of course I mean other women.

They're out there, just as I knew they would be. I can meet any of them: blonde, brunette, slim, curvy, fat, whatever, they're all there, as promised. And it's easy, a real fucking doddle, to reel them in. It's so much simpler than I ever dared dream about during those afternoons when Lola made me wander round John Lewis looking at things we didn't need and that I'd have to assemble later. All this time we men have happily gone along with the notion that women are these complex, incomprehensible creatures, whilst men are nothing more than a group of clumsy, beer-swilling oafs – give us a football match and a burger and we'll be happy. Well, it turns out that we're not the simple ones. They are.

And here it is, what they don't want you know: they really don't want nice, decent men who'll love them, and worship the ground they can hardly walk on in their impractical shoes. They want bastards. Like me.

I prop up bars and I mooch around galleries – whatever the setting, it makes no difference. They find me; they seek me out. They have a nose for men who'll treat them badly and trample over their hearts with their size elevens and run off with their underwear as a souvenir. This is why Simon can never maintain a relationship – he's too nice. Beneath that fat and stupid exterior, he just wants to love and be loved in return, to care for someone. He wants to nurture, to share life, to share himself. I only want to take everything for myself, to give nothing away, and for this I'm rewarded with phone numbers, offers of coffee, dinner, and tickets to shows and films I don't particularly want to see. Guys like Simon are left watching, scratching their heads, while arseholes like me shrug and say, "Sorry, I lost your number."

So now, I'm doing it. I don't call when I say I will – if I bother to say it at all. I don't return texts; I'm clearly only after one thing, and I tell them straight that I'll only make them as miserable as I've made myself. And where does it get me? It gets me everywhere, and a second date if I want one. Which I never do.

I'm attractive to women because I'm 'bad', and because I'm unavailable. It's obvious when you think about it, and I'm surprised we men haven't cottoned onto it before. Women are obsessed with things they can't have – designer shoes, cellulite-free thighs, that scruffy bloke from *Twilight*, clothes that will never fit them in an entire decade of Sundays. Even I, long ago, came to terms with the fact that, barring some error on the part of my bank, I'll probably never own a DB9. But if I were a woman, I'd be picking out the floor mats and imagining what the engine is going to sound like.

I'm not playing hard to get – I'm not playing at all. I'm not interested; my heart and my mind are elsewhere. And, even after three months of trying to get them back into the present, they'll probably always be stuck in the past.

So that leaves me in this weird and permanent limbo, in the privileged position of being able to conduct research to inform and empower the rest of my gender and, just maybe, to stop some other poor schmuck from making the same mistake as I did.

Just last week, I was talking to a girl named Lucy (or was it Louise?) in a pub in Covent Garden. As tends to be the norm, within about five minutes Louise had told me about her childhood, her university course, and how All Men Are Shit. I didn't disagree with her, and I just about refrained from asking her what makes women qualified to make such a sweeping judgement. Instead, I listened and nodded my head when required to, which is all you really need to do to get your foot in the door, and let her tell me the whole story.

We were sat there for the next three hours.

Louise droned on and on about her ex-boyfriend and how he never said he loved her, and never took her anywhere exciting. When I suggested that perhaps he didn't say he loved her because, actually, he didn't love her, she couldn't absorb the words. It didn't – wouldn't – compute. And this is just it – women hear what they want to hear, even if we're not actually saying anything. It gets them into all kinds of trouble. It's how they end up with guys like me.

So now, I'm putting everything I've learned to good use. Fuck the housing market, the multiplier, and the economic slowdown – no one really wants to know about the important stuff. If I want people to listen and care about what I say, then I need to talk about something they're actually bothered about, to go out on my own, away from the safety of a popular newspaper. I've gone behind enemy lines, penetrated from within, and I will win. I'll strike a blow for my fellow men, and maybe one day we will, all of us, outsmart them. One fine, sweet, sunny day.

I exit the building that will soon be my new home from nine to five, smiling my best, and only, breezy smile at the blonde on reception who, to my mind, should rethink the Day-Glow eyeshadow. To celebrate this victory over the old enemy, I decide to go for a stroll along Sloane Street to laugh at all the rich people deliberating over Gucci tablecloths and Prada toilet roll covers.

I explore for a little while, peering into shop windows at things I wouldn't buy even if they were reduced to thirty-six pence, and remember why I hardly ever venture into this part of town. It's populated, on the whole, by people I don't like, people with vast amounts of money and very little dress sense; people who drive cars I want, badly. People like Lola's mother.

Cynthia lays eyes on me at the exact second I spot her, so there's no time to blank her, or to throw myself gracefully into the path of the first black taxi to rumble past. She's sitting outside a restaurant she would probably use a ridiculous phrase like 'chi-chi' to describe, a huge pair of sunglasses on top of her head, nestling in her silver hair. She looks at me distastefully, the only way she's ever looked at me, and it's clear that she expects me to say something.

"Well, this is a surprise," is the nearest I can get to a positive greeting. I don't know why I went to the trouble.

She fires back with, "Yes. Indeed it is. What brings you to Chelsea?" This roughly translates as "fuck off back to Holloway – you're making us affluent types feel bad about ourselves."

"Work," I reply, as usual feeling like I have to justify myself. "New job."

"Oh, yes. I heard you were fired from the paper." She picks up her glass and sips her water, which despite containing enough ice to sustain the polar bear population until Armageddon, is probably still not as cold as she is.

I'm about to point out that technically I wasn't in fact 'fired', but then remember that it doesn't matter what she thinks anymore. The record can be straight, or bent, or hanging slightly to the left – it's no longer relevant.

"Please," Cynthia says. "Won't you sit down?"

I almost glance behind to check it's me she's talking to. "I'd love to, but I can't. I have to get back. My friend's leaving town today."

"Which friend?" she says, as though she doesn't believe it's possible for me to have friends.

"Simon. He's been offered a job in-"

"Just for a second. Sit." Cynthia holds my gaze.

I shrug, and pull out the chair opposite her. I sit down, and instantly feel out of place. My clothes are wrong, my hair's wrong, my entire life is wrong for Cynthia and her crowd, and has been since the day I was born. I fiddle with the edge of a menu and am unable to stop my left leg from jigging up and down, making me look apprehensive and impatient, both of which I very much am.

"So, John – how are you?"

"Since when did you care?"

She recoils a little. "John, don't be like that. I only asked how you were."

"Yeah, but are you asking me how I am, or how I'm not? No, I'm still not in a better job – whatever that might be – and no, I'm still not living round here. And I still don't drive a Jaguar XKR."

Cynthia smiles – well, I think that's what she meant it to be. Her skin's so tight it could be made out of cling film. "Actually, I have a Vantage now."

Total and utter bitch.

"Are you seeing anyone, John?"

"I'm presuming you're not asking because you and Al are having problems."

"Don't be so utterly preposterous. I take it that means no?"

"I take it you've heard of the concept of minding your own business, or at least know of people who've done it?"

She sits back in her chair, doing the nearest she can to an amused expression. "John Black – always so testy, so touchy. Why is that?"

"Only with you, Cynthia."

She stares at me for a long time, and I realise I've flattered her. She signals to a passing waiter.

"You never became part of the family, did you, John? Even after nine years you still couldn't manage it."

"After nine years I realised I didn't want to."

"Oh, you did. And you still do. Ah, yes." The waiter appears, pad eagerly in hand. I want to kick him in the shins for being so subservient. "I'll have the sea bass, grilled. John, what about you?"

"I'm already being grilled."

"Sir?" The waiter looks at me. "The seared rabbit is particularly excellent."

"No, thanks," I tell him. "I'll only choke on it."

"John, please. Thank you, Peter." Cynthia thrusts our menus at Peter, who obligingly tucks them under his arm, and appears to do something akin to a little bow. It's like 'The Worm That Turned'. Well, if the worm's going to turn anywhere, it's in Chelsea.

"The food here is nothing short of superb," Cynthia says.

"Yeah? I prefer McDonald's."

"I can quite believe that. Much more your league." Cynthia puts her elbows on the table and props her chin up on her knuckles. "You know they're thinking of getting engaged. She told me last week. Al's delighted. Josh is perfect for her. He's almost good enough. It'll be a wonderful marriage."

I swallow hard, then go to say something. But I'm not quick enough. She sees the look that crosses my face.

"Don't worry, John. You won't be invited."

"I wouldn't have been invited if it were me marrying Lola."

"I would never have let you marry Lola." Cynthia pats her hair as a grey-haired man walks past and gives her a second glance. "You're-"

"Not good enough. I know."

"It's finally sunk in then. Forget my daughter, John. Forget everything about her. For your own good."

I stand up, my chair scraping on the pavement. "I can't do that, Cynthia."

"Well, how about this – she's forgotten you. Nine years, gone," she clicks her fingers. "Just like that. She's going to marry Josh. She always wanted a big white wedding."

"No she didn't."

"Maybe not to you." Cynthia's really enjoying this. "She'll be so happy."

"No, Cynthia, she won't. Because you'll still be her mother."

I put a cigarette in my mouth, and I turn my back on Cynthia. Just like that. If I had it in me, I'd key her Vantage on the way back up Sloane Street. But I don't. I'm not good enough, but I'm not quite bad enough either.

Due to signal failure at good old Caledonian Road, it takes me an hour and a half to get home. Due to signal failure in my brain, my time-passing options are limited. I'm unable to read any of the what seems like thousands of free newspapers scattered around the carriage, listen to my MP3 player, or even play 'Snake' on my phone like one of those saddos with no friends and puppy fat. All I can think about is Lola, Josh, and her 'big white wedding'.

She really didn't want a wedding – of any colour. Occasionally – usually when she had PMT, or shortly after one of her friends flashed their new diamond solitaire under her nose – she claimed to want a small ceremony in her local church. But don't all women? Lola and I came to a compromise pretty early on in our relationship: I wouldn't propose, and she wouldn't expect me to. If it ain't broke, I managed to persuade her, then why make all your mates wear suits and spend loads of money you haven't got fixing it? Well, something's certainly changed, because she wants to fix it now. She wants to fix it with him, with Josh. And that's fine – for her. As for me, well, like the song goes, there will always be something there to remind me. Maybe I should do a Simon. Maybe I should just leave.

Just as I'm giving the idea some serious head space, the train grinds to a slow and inevitable halt in the tunnel, and the driver starts muttering something incomprehensible that might be about signal failure, or he might simply be relaying the night's football scores. I lean my head against the rail. The things that remind me of her are the reasons I could never leave.

My best friend though, knows when it's time to quit. He can't wait to leave everything behind. But it's easier for him – he's the innocent party. He has a genuine right to his grief. Me? Well, it's only fair that I should stay and wallow in mine.

When I get home (no quote marks anymore – this is definitely home), I find that Simon has turned my pitiful lounge into a luggage carousel. He stands in the centre of the organised chaos, his hands on his fat hips. He looks so camp, I could hit him, but I suppose I won't be seeing that pose for quite some time.

"All right?" he says when he finally notices me.

"Yeah. What's all this – has British Airways delivered all the cases they've lost since air travel began?"

"No, it's my luggage."

"Right. And what makes you think Qantas is happy for you to use up the baggage allowance of every other passenger on the plane?"

He bites his lip. "Do you think they'll make me pay excess?"

"Yes. They'll charge you excess just for your spare tyre. And it'll cost you the same as a semi-detached in Putney."

I throw my keys onto the coffee table (I have one now), and step over three holdalls, one of which, I note, is mine, and flop down on the sofa. I flick the TV on.

"What time's your cab coming?"

Simon checks his watch. "Fifteen minutes ago."

I nod, and change channel.

Simon squeezes past a Louis Vuitton case (which used to be Penny's and, interestingly, has the same leathery texture as her face), easing himself down next to me, making various old man noises as he does so. I'm still channel hopping with one hand, and reaching for my cigarettes with the other.

"You nearly missed me," he says.

"Yeah, the Tube delay wasn't quite long enough. Cigarette?"

"Don't smoke."

"You don't go to Australia either, but you're still doing it."

Simon thinks about this, and then takes one from the packet. I throw him my lighter.

He looks at it, making up his mind. "How was Amanda Martin?"

"She was surprisingly fine."

"She liked the feature?"

"She's running it next month. I'm in."

Simon's face erupts into a grin. "Oh, mate, that's fantastic. Send me a copy?"

"Sure."

We both look at the screen rather than each other. I switch channels again, away from Jeff Randall and the news according to Sky.

"Lola's getting married."

"Marri- oh."

"Yeah. Oh."

"John…"

"Don't. It's fine. It's okay. I'll get drunk after you've gone. It'll be fine."

"I don't know what to say, mate."

"Anything except 'I do.'"

We keep our eyes on the television, and the ascending channels.

"Hey, stop!" Simon yells.

I go back a channel, and there it is – the comforting theme tune, the silhouettes of the presenters. We sit in silence, just watching. I run a hand over my chin. We're both thinking it.

"John, I-"

"If you dare say you're going to miss me, I'll make sure you're never allowed back in the country, okay? Because you will be coming back to this country."

"Oh, yeah," Simon says, grinning. "For sure. In a year or so."

"Best year of your life."

"After the one I've just had, let's hope so, mate."

Jeremy Clarkson appears, like the final member of our gang, and there's a beep of a horn from down on Holloway Road which, for once, may serve a purpose.

"That's your cab."

"Oh…. Right. Well, I suppose I've seen this one, so…" Simon gets up and wipes his palms down the front of his jeans, glancing nervously at his cases. "This is a lot of stuff. Oh well…" He bends down and picks up one at random, which of course is my holdall. Then he picks up the Louis Vuitton, for good measure. "I guess this'll have to do me. I'll either have a lot of pants and socks, or twenty pairs of trousers and some Marmite."

I get up too, rubbing the back of my neck.

"Well, John, I could never have done this without you. If you hadn't jacked your job in-"

"I was fired."

"As I was saying, if you hadn't jacked your job in, I'd never have had the courage to go for this."

"And you got it."

"Yeah." Simon beams. "I did, didn't I?" He hands me his unsmoked cigarette. "Here, you have it."

"No, you might need it. Save it for the plane. There might be a baby in your aisle."

"What? I can't smoke a fag in front of a baby."

"It's for the baby to smoke."

The horn sounds again.

"Sure you won't come to the airport?" Simon says.

"I'm sure. Public goodbyes aren't my thing."

"How could I forget?" He shuffles towards the door. "Well, see you in a couple of months, John. Don't forget, we'll have a whole new continent of women to win over."

"Yeah, because you won over so many in this country."

"John, you're a bastard. And I wouldn't change you. See you in Oz."

"See you."

I watch from the window as he squeezes his bags, and himself, into the cab with no help from the driver, who's more interested in the fingertip he's just removed from his nostril. I hover behind the curtain, and hope Simon doesn't look up.

He does. His melon-head tilts towards me, his face alight with a degree of animation that Cynthia Martinez could only fantasise about. He gives me a thumbs up, and I wave back.

The cab zooms off towards Heathrow, towards Simon's new life.

The flat feels emptier than ever. On television, James May is being eloquently rude about a Citroen. I watch for a few minutes, but it feels like something's missing, so I turn it off. And then I remember it's always harder for the one that's left behind, so I keep my promise – I go and get drunk, but not quite drunk enough to forget how much has changed.

22

I've been wandering around the supermarket for the best part of half an hour with good intentions, but so far I've picked up only a few cans of Coke, some Pot Noodle, nearly everything from the confectionery aisle, and a bag of spinach (I need something to put in my fridge to justify owning one). So what, ladies of North London, do the contents of my shopping my basket say about me? No, you know what, save it. It's probably better that I don't know.

I traipse half-heartedly up and down the aisles, blending in with the other nobodies, and trying not to faint when I learn how much a four-pack of canned tuna goes for these days. I stalk the tomato soup and the baked beans, unable to resist those little sausages with spaghetti hoops, but snubbing the fancy olive oils and exotic pasta shapes. There's no place in my life for food like that now.

Actually, there's no place in my life for most of the things in this supermarket (or do I have no place in a supermarket?), other than newspapers and cigarettes, so I head for the former first. I think I'll and buy *Auto Trader* or something to cheer me up, and I'll get a paper to see how Percy's replacement is getting on, and to find out what's on tonight after *Watchdog*.

I'm within sight of the magazines – *Grazia* is beckoning me with an irresistible cover story promising '50 Ways to Bag That Man' ('bag'? What, after you've killed him and cut him up into little pieces?), when a trolley hits me full force in the shin.

"Hey! Will you fuc… Kay?"

"John?" She's not disappointed to see me, she's disappointed she didn't know it was me. She'd have rammed the trolley harder if she did. "Well," she smoothes down her curls, not to make herself more presentable, but to prepare for battle. It's her equivalent of taking the safety catch off. "Fancy seeing you here. In a supermarket."

"And you." As for me, I'm kind of glad to see her – glad in the same way I'd be if Hitler was coming round for dinner and Mussolini turned up instead.

"Actually, I go to the supermarket more often than I go to the toilet. And here's cheaper than Waitrose. What's your excuse?"

"It's not Tesco."

"Oh, okay," Kay rolls her eyes. "You're one of those. I should've known." She peers into my basket, which I now wish I could put on the floor and pretend I've never seen before. I should've put in that wild rocket and ricotta cheese instead of the jumbo mint Aero. "Is that your food for the week?"

"Maybe just for tonight. Tomorrow I'll be eating organic gooseberries and shallots."

"Yeah, right. My kids eat those crisps." She points at the coloured packet on top of my spinach. "They make them hyperactive."

"I know. They're cheaper than ecstasy and speed. Just. You on your own?"

"Todd's around somewhere with the kids. He's buying a lottery ticket."

I nod – of course he is. Hope, for Todd, springs as eternal as the hair growing out of his ears. And no, I'm not disparaging his optimism. I envy it.

"So…" Kay pushes her trolley backwards and forwards, as though there was a baby in it instead of the entire Kellogg's range and enough Evian to fill an Olympic swimming pool.

"So."

"There's an elephant in the room, isn't there?"

"Maybe you could give it one of your ethically-sourced bananas."

Kay makes a face – the face, the one she never knew she could pull until she met me. "Why don't you just ask?"

"It's been five months, Kay. The asking zone is a dot in the rear-view mirror. The window of enquiry has closed."

"Right, fine. Lola's-"

"Engaged, I know."

Kay's eyes expand to the size of the Wagon Wheels in my basket. "Is she? Where did you hear that? Did she tell you?"

"No. Your mother did."

"Ah," she says, as though that explains it all. Actually, it does. "Of course she isn't engaged." Her eyes wander to the cover of *Prima* on the shelf behind us. "And if Mum told you that, why on earth didn't you phone me and find out more?"

"One, because I'm not a woman, two, see my earlier point about the asking zone, and number three, that'd be like self-harming. I'd rather cut the insides of my arms with a Bic razor whilst listening to My Chemical Romance."

"Who?"

"Too much MTV."

"Okay, whatever." Kay snatches the *Prima* and throws it into her trolley. "If you really want to know – and I know you damn well do so don't insult me by pretending otherwise – Josh dumped her."

I scratch the side of my neck. "Dumped is harsh word."

"How else would you describe it?" Kay says. "He ended their relationship. He broke it off. Snapped it."

"I see." I was indeed about to pretend otherwise, but with Kay, there really would be no point, so I go ahead and ask. "Why?"

"Why?" She looks at me as though I am the most ridiculous man on earth. "Why does anyone need a reason – did you?"

"Well…"

"Oh," she waves a hand, "Lola told me all that rubbish about supply and demand. Crap. Unlike you, Josh did have a reason. And, to be honest, I'm amazed he lasted this long."

"What was his reason?"

"Huh, you know the reason. Poor Josh. He never stood a chance against you."

Even after he's dumped her, he gets to be 'poor Josh'. The Vatican will probably canonise him within the next few hours.

"When did it happen?"

"Two months ago."

And it all falls into place. "I saw your mother two months ago. She's either got a great imagination, or she doesn't know what dumped means."

"What do you expect? She hates you, John. She'll kill me if she finds out I've told you the truth. Oh God, what's that idiot husband of mine doing now?"

Todd is walking towards us, two excited children in tow that I hope are his, carrying a box that appears to contain the world's largest, and only, dinosaur-shaped paddling pool.

"What," Kay asks, purely rhetorically, "are we supposed to do with that?"

"It's a paddling pool," Todd explains with pride, the kids beaming at him. "We fill it with water and-"

"I know what to do with it, Todd. I want to know what *we're* supposed to do with it."

"You could use it to drown your mother," I add.

"Dad, can we? Can we?" Jeremy asks, tugging Todd's sleeve.

"Todd, darling, go and put it back where you found it."

"But, Muuuuuum…"

"Susie, no. See what you've done?" she hisses at Todd. "Honestly." She shakes her head as a dejected Todd and two equally disappointed children slope off to return the paddling pool from whence it came. "Sometimes I really doubt whether my husband has any working brain cells."

"Maybe he sold them all on Ebay."

"Todd doesn't know what Ebay is. Anyway," she turns her attention back to me. "What about you? What are you going to do?"

I look at her. "Now? Now I'm going to buy some cigarettes, and maybe that copy of *Grazia* to laugh at, pay for my hyperactive food, then go home and get high."

"And after that?"

"After that…" I glance at the magazines on the shelf. "After that, nothing." I pick up *Grazia*, and the magazine sitting next to it in the rack, and toss it into my basket, where it rests ominously, dangerously, hopefully. "See you, Kay."

I dump the contents of my shopping on the backseat. The spinach appears to be wilting already, and I almost feel sorry enough to eat it and put it out of its misery. The car grumbles as I push the start button, probably because I've parked it in between two Toyotas, and I have to threaten it with a service before it agrees to come to life.

I'm in third, but my brain's in neutral, and just when I'm thinking that maybe I'll be able to keep it there, a song comes on the radio. Not 'the' song, but one of many songs, the first in a long list of things I can't avoid, no matter how hard I try, or how tight I've fastened my blinkers. I crash into these things everywhere, mostly when I'm not expecting to which, somehow, I always am.

I stop at the lights, letting the song play on. I could put my foot down and just drive. I could just go. But there'd be songs there too, wherever I went. Wherever I go, she'll be with me. I wonder if she sees it the same way – if she hears the same things.

When I get home, carrying my bags of junk food, there's a postcard waiting for me, a bright sunny vista of an impossibly green ocean, and a perhaps even more impossibly toned man surfing on it. I flip the card over, and ask myself why Simon thinks he can use this postcard to subliminally suggest that he might've miraculously lost all his puppy fat since arriving in Australia. As for the surfing – well, Stephen Hawking will be found on a surfboard riding the waves before Simon Murphy will.

I settle down in the chair and can't concentrate on *Watchdog*, or *Eastenders*. I pick the postcard up several times, re-reading the few words Simon's scribbled on the back in case there's something I've missed. Halfway through *Shameless*, I realise there is: I can go. I can leave. I don't have to go far and, the best thing is, I can take her with me.

When I broke the news to Mr Ahmed, he appeared to take it as badly if I'd told him I were burning the flat down rather than moving out of it.

"But you have only been in it a short time!" he said, his voice rising in pitch.

"I know. It's a personal thing," I told him, unsure why I was having to explain myself.

"Flat is very good, no? Flat is very good!"

I held the phone away from my ear, as I'd planned on still being able to hear out of it after the conversation was over.

"The flat's great," I lied. "It's just time for me to move on."

Time to move on in a purely geographical sense, naturally.

So, I'm packing again, and you'd think I'd be pretty good at it by now. But, the thing is, packing and unpacking all my stuff just continually confronts me with an unwanted stock take of what I amount to. Clothes I've never worn, clothes I don't like, clothes that fitted me ten years ago, books I bought with good intentions but haven't read yet, CDs in cracked cases, an MP3 player I feel stupid using, car magazines I can't bear to throw away, and Lola's blender. That's it, the sum total of me. I'm tempted to leave it all behind and start again – construct a different me. I mean to start boxing up things, really I do, but somehow it's much more rewarding to sit here and pop the bubble wrap.

For twenty minutes.

Until the intercom goes.

Shit – that'll be Mr Ahmed. "No problem at all," he'd said when the penny finally dropped that I was indeed moving out and there was indeed bugger all he could do about it. "When will you be leaving, Mr John? I shall come round and be collecting keys. No problem."

No problem for him, but a big one for me, since all I've managed to pack is a fruit bowl, and I'm not sure that counts because I'd never unpacked it in the first place.

I press the button down. "Listen, hey, I'm not quite done yet. Just a couple more things to pack."

"Pack?"

Shit.

"John?"

"I'm here."

"Can I come up?"

"Sure."

I am once again grateful for my uncanny ability to sound much more confident than I feel.

I throw the bubble wrap over the nearest box, not really creating the illusion that I'm in control of the mess I've made – actually, not creating any kind of illusion at all. It looks exactly what it is – the final desperate measure of a desperate man.

She knocks on the door. I run my sweaty palms through my hair and straighten the collar of my shirt, something I'd never consider doing for Mr Ahmed.

"Hi."

"Hey."

We stand there for a few seconds, looking at each other. I haven't forgotten my manners, just temporarily mislaid them.

"Can I come in?"

"Yeah, sorry."

Lola steps over the books and DVDs I'd started to organise into a pile that got rather too precise (packing things in alphabetical order, or genre, just took up too much time so I gave up).

"You said 'pack'. Either that, or you're having a jumble sale." She scans the reams of junk littered everywhere. "Is that my blender?"

"Yes. Yes, it is. I think you left it behind, and I packed it by mistake."

"Oh. I see. So now you're packing it again."

"By mistake. Again." I notice she has the magazine clutched tightly to her chest. My stomach lurches but I'm too proud, and too scared, to ask her about it.

"I'm moving."

"How come?"

"This place, me – we weren't really compatible from the start."

She closes the door behind her. "Where are you going?"

"Tufnell Park."

"Oh, nice. Back where you started."

"Not quite."

Lola presses her lips together. "When are you going?"

"Today." Lola opens her mouth. "I know, I know. I'm a little behind schedule. I meant to start earlier, but…"

"But what?"

"I couldn't be arsed."

Lola rolls her eyes. "You're hopeless. Hey, who's the postcard from?" she says, pointing to Simon's slick surfer dude.

"Simon. He's living in Australia now."

"What?" Lola says. "Been he's never been further than zone six."

"Well, he's in zone ten thousand and six now. Go ahead, have a look."

She takes the card from the table and frowns at Simon's scribble, which is fair enough, as his handwriting hasn't changed since he was five. While Lola reads, I study her, trying to take in every last detail. She's changed since I saw her last. Her hair's been highlighted with a few copper strands that frame her face and she looks fresh, unblemished by the world – by me. She's shiny and new, and as I look at her I feel reborn, as though I'm getting another shot at something I thought I'd lost forever.

"John, what does S.Y.L.J.Y.C.B. mean?"

"I'd rather not say."

"Come on, we're way past all that. Is it rude?"

"Define rude."

"John…"

"You asked, okay?"

She nods. She loves it when she thinks she's finding out something she's not supposed to know, even though it almost always results in her saying, "Oh John…" and pulling her 'I am disappointed in you' expression for the next hour.

Lola grimaces when I tell her. "Oh, that's charming. Why are you two always so rude to each other? I'd never say that to Valerie."

"I would."

There it is – the 'Oh John…' look. "What's he doing out there, anyway?"

"He's got a secondment to *Aussie Girl* for a year."

"Wow. That's so good for him. And it sounds like he's really enjoying himself."

"Yeah, he is. And, amazingly, they haven't deported him yet for making people on Bondi Beach feel sick. I'm going out there in a few weeks to see the new Antipodean Simon Murphy for myself."

"Who are you going with?"

"I'm going on my own."

"Oh. Excellent. Well, that'll be nice. Don't forget to take sun block with you. At least factor thirty, just to be safe." She puts a hand to her mouth. "I'm sorry, I don't know why I said that. It was stupid. You don't need me to nag you about what to take with you. Forget I said it."

"I will."

"No, you won't, because now I've turned it into a thing, and made a big deal of it. I'm making a fool of myself, aren't I?"

I just about manage not to smile. "As it happens, I hadn't thought about sun block as yet."

She flops onto the couch, the magazine flopping with her, nestling in her lap. "Josh dumped me."

"I know."

"You know."

I sit down next to her. "I saw Kay in Sainsbury's. She told me."

"You were in Sainsbury's?"

"Hey, even bastards are allowed Nectar cards."

Wisely, she ignores that. "When did you see her?"

"A couple of weeks ago."

Lola prods the hem of her skirt. "And you didn't call me?"

"And what would you have done if I had?"

"Called you a bastard and hung up."

"Exactly." Phoning Lola after Josh dumped her would've been like picking road kill off a dual carriageway and calling it Sunday lunch. But I don't tell her that.

"I'm sorry, Lola." I don't have to make my voice sound sincere as, for once, I actually do mean what I'm saying.

"It's okay. I'm pretty used to being dumped by now."

"I'm sorry again. Really."

She lets out a long breath. "Don't be, it's not your fault." She pauses for a second. "Actually, it's completely your fault, but don't feel bad about it. Want to know why he dumped me?"

"If you think it's necessary to tell me."

"Necessary isn't the right word, but I don't know what is." She sighs. "He said he couldn't bear to be second best anymore."

I try not to high-five myself. "I see," I say solemnly, as though this news is terrible instead of cause for a global day of celebration.

Lola fingers the corner of the magazine. "I read the article."

She opens the glossy cover and it falls opens on the right page. There's a clear fold mark down the spine, as though it's been opened at this page frequently. I hope it has.

My heart feels as though it really is in my mouth, along with cotton wool, both of my feet, and a small armadillo.

"I had no idea if you'd even see it."

"I nearly didn't, I've given up with women's magazines. But Valerie has a subscription. She showed it to me."

Good old Valerie – I've always admired and respected that woman. Val, consider the hatchet well and truly six feet under.

"Don't smile, John. She's cancelled her subscription now."

"Of course." I'm still smiling.

Lola shifts her body round so that she's fully facing me. "Is it true? Is it really how you feel – it's not bullshit? I knew it was about us because of the title. Those words have been stuck in my head since they came out of your mouth."

I fill my lungs with air, hoping it will expel the butterflies from my stomach and iron out my goose bumps. "I meant it. Every single word."

She closes her eyes for a few seconds, and lets out a deep breath. She opens them again. "Everyone's talking about it, you know. Kay bought it, just for your feature."

Hearing this, from the one person that matters to me, makes my chest swell. "They're making my column permanent."

"Oh John, that's fantastic!" She runs her fingers over the page. "'The View From the Black'. It's perfect. If anyone should be writing for a women's magazine, it's you. Although," she adds, tipping her head to one side, "I don't think Valerie will be very pleased."

"Maybe I'll write a piece for her."

"What, 'People I Hate'?"

"No, I like her now. She's a national heroine. I am, sickeningly, somewhat in her debt."

Lola closes the magazine. "John?"

"Yeah?"

"I was hoping you'd be able to tell me what we do now."

"Now?"

"Yes. Right now." She twists her body towards mine, her knees together. "This means something, this whole thing. We've been through so much, most of it your fault, but look at us. We always end up coming back to each other. We always return. Like pigeons. We return home. When I read your article I felt happy, so happy, but so sad because we're not together. And we should be. And yes, I know that you can be abrasive, and cruel, and you get moody," she holds her palm up as I open my mouth. "Yes, John, you are moody. You are. And you're sarcastic and full of your own self-importance, but when I think of you, John, I just know. Do you understand?"

I nod. I do. Utterly.

"When I try asking myself why I'm so sure about you, I can't come up with an answer. I just know. And when I think of where I want to be in ten years, in my head and my heart you're always there beside me. I know about you, John."

She blinks at me, her dark eyes drawing me in, daring me. For the first time in my life, I am equal to the intensity of her stare. I can meet the implicit demands hidden in them, the tricks, the tests, the riddles and obstacles. I can take on her baggage and carry it easily and without complaint. I can be everything to her; I can be the one she comes to for protection, comfort, joy, and all of life's other idiosyncrasies. I'm ready to accept that my fate inexorably lies with her and her alone. And I want her – alone.

"I know about you too." I wipe the tear slipping down her cheek. "I'm not going anywhere, Lola."

She's thrown the dice. But this time, I know I'm making the closest thing there is to a safe bet. She can trust me now.

Lola inhales deeply and wipes her face. She tosses the magazine into a nearby box, where it lands with a resigned thud.

"I think you should keep that," she says. "To remember."

I tuck a strand of hair behind her ear. "I don't think I'll need to remember. I'll never forget it."

She presses her palms to my face, stroking my cheek, bristles and all. Then, she gets to her feet slowly. Lola offers her hand to me.

This is the final challenge. To take her hand is to accept everything that she is, that she will be, to entwine her life with mine, forsaking all others and staying on course whatever, forever, however long the distance might be, and whoever else comes along. I let go of her hand once, and I understand now what that means.

It's a no-brainer.

Without reservation, I slide my fingers into hers.

THE VIEW FROM THE BLACK

THE MYTH OF SUPPLY AND DEMAND BY JOHN BLACK

It's said that an economist will try to explain everything using the laws of supply and demand. Until recently, this economist was no exception. And why not? The theory is brilliant, and can be applied to anything – tea, crisps, cars, breasts, and – especially – relationships. So, when I ended my relationship with my girlfriend and she, quite understandably, wanted to know why, I told her. I explained it to her the best way I knew how, admittedly the only way I knew how. I told her to blame supply and demand, and not me.

There was, I said, too much of her around, too much supply. She was there when I needed her, when I expected her to be, and this was a bad thing. There was no surprise, no thrill, and I'd begun to wonder what I was missing out on – my demand for her had declined. After nine years, monogamy and security had lost its appeal, and I wanted to plunge head first into the big, shiny world of singledom. My girlfriend was furious. I was elated. I was free.

So there I was, unattached, a bachelor again after nine years. I could do whatever I wanted, at any time I wanted, with whomever I wanted. And after quite a few 'whomevers', the novelty, I'm afraid, wore off after about, oh, twenty-five seconds. Not that I was counting, you understand. I had my freedom, but it was a pyrrhic freedom. Every woman I met, I compared to her, and they all came up short. They weren't as clever, beautiful, successful, eloquent, understanding – oh, the list goes on. The conversation was hollow, the laughter false, and the sex I'd promised myself as a reward for being faithful for so long was unsatisfying, the absence of emotion jarring.

I imagined I'd be spending my time flicking through my not so little black book, meeting women in sleek bars and trendy clubs, in which I wouldn't look like a thirty-five year old having an identity crisis, but a hip and happening thirty-something, unaware of the clock counting down. I thought that each step I took out the front door would turn into an erotic adventure, that every female I met would arouse and intrigue me, that I'd throw my head back, gaze skyward, and wonder why I'd spent so much time in the shackles of a long-term relationship.

Instead, I learned the truth behind the clichés.

The grass is not greener – it looks that way but, trust me – it's mostly weeds and moss. There are plenty of fish in the sea, but also the odd floating turd and bits of toilet paper. The only proverb that makes any sense is that a bird in the hand is worth two in the bush. I know this because the two I had in the bush weren't a patch on the bird I had in my hand, but let go.

But wasn't I expressing my masculinity? Wasn't I doing what men are designed to do? To chase and pursue, to have sex, to watch sports and re-runs of *Top Gear*, to seek out and consume the last remaining foods with E numbers in them, and to fart at will? Well then yes, I was. I did all of those things, some more than others, and discovered they are all vastly overrated. Let me tell you, men need women much more than they need us, and not because they possess the chromosomes that enable them to successfully iron a shirt.

I sacrificed the one thing that was so precious that even I, the economist, couldn't see its true value, in order to seek out my destiny as a male, to sow the oats that, as it turned out, I didn't actually have. In trying to embrace my masculinity all I succeeded in doing was magnifying my faults. She soon found her life without me was fuller, richer, that she'd been putting up with second best for too many years. She found a hip and happening twenty-something who wasn't rude, arrogant, selfish and, okay, could possibly sometimes be a little moody. She discovered she could manage very well without me, thank you very much, but I discovered I need her more than oxygen or, even more essential, my car.

I'd become complacent. I'd failed to notice that the way she held my head when I came in complaining of a headache actually did make me feel better. I took for granted the times she called me during the day just to say 'Hi', and I hadn't worked out that even though she talked crap most of the time, I still liked hearing it. Her familiarity, the way her smell made me feel safe, and loved, had gone unnoticed. Instead of being in awe of the bond we enjoyed, I looked back on every minute we spent together as though I were forgoing some other more appealing alternative. I resented it. I thought she was holding me back. But, actually, the reverse was true.

One thing I've discovered since I've been without her is that the alternative is anything but appealing. It is, in fact, an excruciating pit of perpetual longing, where there is always the notion that there's something missing, but without being able to place exactly what that 'something' is, and knowing you'll never get it back. It's like owning an Aston Martin and then waking up to find that from now on you'll only ever be able to drive a Hyundai Amica for the rest of your life.

It all boils down to this: I used to believe that commitment is a choice between stability and excitement – that they cannot coexist. Now, I have to disagree with myself and yeah, here it comes, admit that I was wrong. The last time I did that was probably about 1983. So here's my new theory: commitment opens more doors than it closes. Now, I love that she knew me inside out, and I'm honoured she let me get so close to her. She could've spent those nine years with anyone, but she chose me, and I didn't deserve her. I was blessed to be important to her. If she changed her mind about me – and why would she, but let's just go with this happy ' if' for a while; if she changed her mind and wanted to spend another nine years with me, I'd do everything differently. Familiarity, in my mind, is something to be earned, something to cherish rather than run screaming in the opposite direction from as though my hair's on fire. There is nothing to fear from a comfortable, well-worn love. I know now. I know how to love her.

So now, it's time to face it: she won't change her mind, and my demand for her will continue, despite this lack of supply. And what does that mean for the future of economics? It's not for me to say – I've taken my hat out of the ring before someone stands on it. But let me state here, for this very record, that John Black wants the world, and her, to know that he no longer believes in economics.

Black Will Be Back

Email John: JFYBlack@gmail.com

Lightning Source UK Ltd.
Milton Keynes UK
24 August 2010

158914UK00001B/86/P

9 781907 652585